"This collection is written by a squad of fine writers--some of whom are current or retired real-life cops. Gritty, hard-hitting, authentic, and edgy--and guaranteed to keep you turning the pages."

- **Raymond Benson**, author of the James Bond anthologies **The Union Trilogy** and **Choice of Weapons**

"Nobody writes about these guys. These are the cops we keep locked in the deepest, darkest precinct basements. Now they're out. And the reader is in for a rare treat in these wild, wonderful, and all too real, stories. It's about time."

- **Lt. Ed Dee, NYPD (ret.),** author of **The Con Man's Daughter**

"Bad Cop, No Donut *is a fast paced journey through the darker side of law enforcement. Not only are the stories written by seasoned cops, but they are road-tested writers, as well. It is a page-turner in the classic sense - you really will be asking yourself 'what could possibly go sideways next?' With this anthology you will make the trip in law enforcement from bad to worse, with an occasional side trip to redemption - well, almost."*

*-**Lt. Raymond E. Foster, LAPD (ret.), author of** Leadership: Texas Hold 'em Style*

PADWOLF PUBLISHING BOOKS BY JOHN L. FRENCH

PAST SINS: The Matthew Grace Casebook

BAD COP... NO DONUT edited by John L. French

BAD COP, NO DONUT

Stories of Police Behaving Badly

Edited by
John L. French

PADWOLF
PUBLISHING

PADWOLF PUBLISHING

WWW.PADWOLF.COM

Padwolf Publishing & logo are registered trademarks of Padwolf Publishing Inc.

BAD COP NO DONUT

edited by John L. French

Cover Art by Ver Curtis

ISBN: 10 digit 1-890096-45-8   / 13 digit 978-1-890096-45-8

Printed in the USA

First Printing

Every hour of every day, thousands of brave men and women put their lives on the line in the name of duty. They are state troopers, city officers, county sheriffs and federal agents. They are patrol officers and detectives. They deal with the worst humanity has to offer so that we don't have to. They sacrifice their nights and weekends, their holidays and their family time. And sometimes they sacrifice their lives – all to keep us safe.

It is to these brave men and women that this book is dedicated.

Let's be clear about one thing. The vast majority of cops are honest, hard working men and women who would never think about behaving badly. Okay, they might think about it, but they'd never do it. The ones who make the news, the ones you see on TV, the ones whose wrongdoings fill the headlines – they are the exception, not the rule.

But it's no fun to read about people who follow the straight and narrow, who never break the rules or step out of line. No, the real fun is reading about the bad guys, the lawbreakers, the ones to whom the rule of law is simply an obstacle in the road to what they want. And it's even more fun to read about them when they are the very ones who are supposed to be upholding the law.

At least we hope so.

And with that in mind, we hope you will enjoy reading our tales as much as we did writing them.

THE LINE UP

Cover by Ver Curtis

No one ever tells the truth about murder, but to close this case it would take…

HENKIN'S LAST LIES
James Chambers

It wasn't the first time Detective Gary Henkin had to give someone bad news about a case, but it was the first time he'd ever had to lie doing it. He'd expected it to be easier. Maybe the kids playing on the nearby jungle gym and the chatter of people walking through the park were screwing up his mood, but the lie felt more acutely wrong than any he'd told in recent memory.

Still, he kept his voice steady when he met Brancusi's eyes and said, "I'm sorry, Dennis, but there isn't anything more to go on. We got plenty of rumors and hunches, but we got nothing definite that tells us Abe Bruno did it. Nobody knows anything for sure. It's been two years. The file's gone cold."

Brancusi's face looked the way it always did: like a steam boiler running high and held together by spit and chewing gum.

Henkin understood.

The writer had lost his parents and his pregnant sister nearly two years ago when a bomb meant for him blew their Volvo station wagon to charred pieces. Brancusi had become a target because he had a big mouth. He was a writer with a knack for digging up dirt on racketeers and crooked cops, and after half a dozen major newspaper articles and two books, the people Brancusi wrote about had gotten their fill. Henkin remembered the first thing Brancusi said to him when they met: "Thank God I never got married or had kids."

They'd gotten together a couple of times a month since then so Henkin could give Brancusi updates on the case. Brancusi kept an office in Mineola near the Nassau County courts and police headquarters, and in good weather, he and Henkin held their meetings over sandwiches at a neighborhood park. It was a busy place; there was a hospital and a train station nearby. Brancusi liked to meet that way because he wanted to show that he hadn't been scared into hiding. He wanted to be seen with the police, and he often wrote about the case and what Henkin told him on his blog. At first Henkin had thought that the murders had cracked Brancusi. The man had to be nuts to flaunt himself in the open, knowing people wanted him dead. After he got to know him, though, Henkin realized Brancusi was doing it to poke a finger in the eye of his enemies

He was an intellectual pit bull. Once his jaws clamped shut, they simply wouldn't unlock even if his head was cut off.

"Bruno did it. You and I know Bruno did it," he said.

"We know he *probably* did it." Henkin pulled the paper wrapping away from his sandwich, took a bite and began to chew. "That's not the same."

"I blew his racket over at the Coliseum, so he finally went after me. He did it. You going to tell me he didn't?"

Henkin swallowed. "No. I'm not."

"So then we know. You and me. He did it."

"That won't move the D.A. or convince a jury."

"Give me the file. Let me work it. I can get you a lead."

"Forget it. The captain has threatened the pension of anybody who so much as leaks a name. They've clamped down tight on this case."

"They're covering up. The evidence is there. It has to be. I got friends you don't know about telling me it is."

Henkin only shrugged, as if to say, *It is what it is.*

"I'll get a lawyer and get the file."

"You got the right. I wish you luck."

Henkin chewed on another bite of his sandwich. Brancusi left his unopened on his lap.

The cop watched the writer's hands to see if they were shaking. They weren't. That unnerved Henkin. Brancusi never got rattled, and for as tightly wound as he was, he always looked like he was in absolute control of himself. Sometimes Henkin envied Brancusi's self-assuredness.

The detective's life had fallen apart over the past few years. Laura had finally left him eighteen months ago, and he couldn't shake the feeling that things would've been different if they'd been able to have children together. Then his father had died a few weeks back. Now he felt alone and adrift, and he'd begun to see clearly the rotten core upon which he'd built his existence. The taint he'd always been able to rationalize away in the past hung heavy on his conscience these days. He'd been thinking about his old mentor Roddy Boyd a lot, especially the last chance Boyd had tried to give him. Brancusi reminded him of Boyd.

"But why would I want to waste time with a lawyer?" said Brancusi.

"Search me."

"There are faster ways."

"You know a judge?"

"Sure. I know lots of judges, even some honest ones. Or maybe I could bribe someone to copy the file for me. You're not the only homicide cop whose home number I got on my cell."

"Good for you. You got options."

"Do I? I turned fifty last month. I haven't had a girlfriend who lasted more than a month in eight years, and all the family I had in the world got turned to cinders because I like to write true things about bad people. After I lost them I only had two things going for me. One was the chance you might actually close this case. The other is that people like my books, so I got plenty of money, and money makes all things possible."

Brancusi's voice chilled Henkin.

Throughout the investigation he'd seen the writer angry, thoughtful, sad, even desperate, but he'd never heard the man sound so cold and determined. It was as if a weight he'd been bearing for far too long had suddenly turned to vapor and blown away.

"Truth is, Gary, I've always known this day would come, that you and all the people working with you, and the full force of the police and courts wouldn't bring us where we needed to go on this one. Still, I held out hope. I'm hardheaded like that. I figured if you could pin this on Bruno and bring me a little justice, then maybe all the work I've done that led to this horror show was somehow in some little way justified. But it's not. I wrote what I did because I thought people should know when they're being victimized. I thought that once they knew, they could make a difference. Except all I wound up doing was tearing a hole in the curtain and exposing just enough to make everyone feel uncomfortable."

Brancusi stood and looked around the park.

"You can't change things the way I tried to change them. Not honestly. But there are other ways to make changes."

"Tell me you're not thinking about doing something you'll regret."

"I don't do things I'll regret."

"Everyone does stuff they regret."

Henkin crumpled up the remains of his lunch. He tossed his garbage into a trash bin beside the bench and then stood and straightened his jacket.

"I know cops, lawyers, judges, sure," said Brancusi. "I know plenty of guys on the other side, too, and they're not all fans of Abe Bruno.

And, you know what, if a grade-school reject like Bruno can get away with murder, then, hell, anyone must be able to do it. He used a goddamn bomb, and nobody could trace it back to him. How hard can it be?"

"Shit, man, don't say stuff like that, not to me."

Brancusi caught Henkin's stare and held it. The cop felt himself being measured and judged, and he realized the writer was making up his mind to trust him. Brancusi thought he and Henkin were on the same page. It saddened Henkin; he wanted to grab Brancusi by the collar, shake him, and order him to shut up for his own damn good.

"I'd think you'd be as eager as anyone to see Bruno gone. How hard could it be? An untraceable weapon, a little inside information, and the world becomes a better place to live in."

"You positively should not be saying this shit to me. Words have consequences. You know that. You may not like what comes of what you're saying."

"You going to take me in?"

"If I have to."

"No, you won't. I'm only a writer. I'm thinking of giving fiction a try. That's only a plot I'm mulling over. I'll probably drop it. Too mundane. People like over-the-top, world-at-risk sort of stuff. They don't much care for one man's anguish." Brancusi shook Henkin's hand and turned to walk away. "Don't sweat the small stuff, Gary. And thanks for everything."

Henkin watched the writer walk down the path.

He wanted to let him go, to let things end in this park, but he had a job to do. He'd known the things Brancusi had said had been knocking around the man's head for months. He'd seen the signs and heard the clues in the writer's words. He'd hoped it wouldn't come to this, because the people Henkin lied for saw Brancusi's rage as an opportunity. Henkin, though, had come to think of Brancusi as a friend, and he wanted him to simply accept defeat and go on with his life, pick something safe to write about, and maybe, down the road, even find a little happiness. Because if Brancusi could do that then maybe Henkin could hope for the same someday. But the writer really had lost everything in the explosion. There was no ground left for him to stand on except never giving up.

This, Henkin thought, *is turning out to be the mother of all depressing, sunny afternoons.*

He started down the path.

"Dennis, wait."

Brancusi stopped and turned back.

"I really wish you hadn't said those things."

"You arresting me?"

Henkin took out his notepad. He jotted something down, tore out the sheet, and handed it to Brancusi.

"No. I'm doing something too stupid to speak aloud."

"What's this?"

"You get serious about Bruno, you look up that address, and then you call me."

Henkin didn't wait for a reply. He hurried past Brancusi and walked to the parking lot. He got in his car and sped out of the park onto a side street without looking back. *The worst part wasn't the lie*, he thought, *it was how easily everything fell into place because of it.*

"I ever tell you how Roddy Boyd died?" said Henkin.

Sitting next to him in the car was Detective Joe Valenzuela, who was texting on his iPhone. The cops were parked down the street from a two-story colonial in Baldwin, waiting for a tip to pay off.

Eight days ago a woman was found dead in her car in the woods along the Southern State Parkway. It hadn't taken long for a neighbor to finger her husband, who except for his shaky alibi was doing a great job convincing the police he was utterly distraught and totally innocent. The neighbor, a retired widow, said she saw him going out in the middle of the night a few times a week, and that there was often a blue Honda Accord parked in the driveway when the wife wasn't home. She thought he was having an affair. She'd even written down the Honda's tag numbers. Henkin had run them. The owner lived one town over. She was a single woman and a former coworker of the husband.

Thank God for nosy old people, Henkin had thought.

Then he'd set out with Valenzuela to watch the place for a few nights. It was 2 a.m. on night three, and if the husband turned up, they would take him in on the spot and let him try to explain himself.

"Who the hell is Roddy Boyd?" said Valenzuela.

"A senior detective when I made homicide. Guy knew how to work a murder like nobody's business. Had the best record of anyone on the squad then."

"So? What has he done lately?"

"Other than decompose, not a whole lot. I said he was dead. You paying attention? Who the hell are you texting?"

Valenzuela smiled. "You know the girl works the counter overnight at the Jericho?"

"The brunette?"

"Yeah."

"No way. What the hell could she possibly want with someone as ugly as you?"

"You know exactly what she wants. You only wish she wanted it from you."

"You ever think about anything other than food and girls?"

"I think about money, and sometimes I think about catching killers. What else is there?"

Henkin ignored the smartass grin on Valenzuela's face. He didn't think much of the detective. He tended to be short on investigative work and long on working people in the interrogation room. When another cop couldn't get someone to talk, they brought in Valenzuela. The guy rarely got physical, but he had a way about him of suggesting horrible violence through a gesture that scared the life out of most people. Henkin figured Valenzuela served a purpose, but he also thought the guy was a half step away from committing some psychotic police brutality.

"This is important shit I'm telling you. Boyd taught me most of what it means to be a homicide cop. You'd have done well to have known someone like him."

"What he'd teach you that's more important than the brunette at the Jericho?"

"Everything's more important than the brunette at the Jericho. She's as smart as a box of rocks."

"That's how I like them." Valenzuela sent the message he'd been typing then slipped his phone inside his jacket. "Seriously, man, tell me this guy's story. I want to know."

Henkin had lost the mood to talk, but the street was dead quiet and there was no sign of the husband, so he figured at least it would pass the time.

"First time I went out with Boyd, we caught a drug-killing. Piece of shit case, except we had a witness, a woman, high as a kite, locked herself in the bathroom because she's terrified of being busted for possession. Wouldn't come out, said she'd kill herself if we went in. The uniforms were talking to her through the door, getting nowhere. So we show up and Boyd goes up to the door, knocks, introduces himself, and says, 'Ma'am, I'm a homicide cop. I solve murders. Now I got a dead man out here, and I want to find out who killed him, and I don't give a rat's ass what you've got on your person, in your person, or what you might put on or in your person tomorrow, because that's narcotics and those guys are a bunch of tight-assed pricks who screwed up my crime scene at the last drug-related killing I worked. So, let's you and me make a deal. You come out of there, close the door behind you, and talk to me, and I promise no one here will open that door or look inside until after you've left.'"

"What happened?"

"She came out. Closed the door behind her. Gave us three names. We picked them up before midnight, and two confessed. The case went down in less than a week. And no one opened that bathroom door until after the woman left."

"Why didn't she just flush the stuff while she was in there?"

"Toilet was busted. It was overflowing. There was an inch of water on the floor when someone finally went in there."

"That's rank."

"Shit, yeah."

Valenzuela laughed.

"Boyd showed me two things that day," said Henkin. "One, stay focused. You got a crime to solve, you solve *that* crime. Two, you got to know how to talk to people to get results. If you want someone to believe what you're saying, you have to believe it, even if you don't."

"That how you got Brancusi on the hook?"

"Part of it."

"He made the call, right? He's going after Bruno. And Bruno will be waiting. All you got to do is feed the dummy a gun and a date, and then he digs his own grave when Abe shoots a trespasser."

"That's the plan."

A car passed by, rolled to the end of the block, and then turned into the driveway at the colonial, where the garage door was opening. The driver pulled inside, and the door closed after him.

"That was our guy's car," said Henkin.

"Oh, Romeo, wherefore art thou," Valenzuela said.

"Busted, that's where."

Henkin picked up the radio and called for backup. Valenzuela started the car and crept down the block with the lights off.

"Hey, you never told me how Boyd died."

"No, I didn't," Henkin said, and then he said nothing more about it.

***

Henkin tailed Brancusi from his office to the brick cape in Uniondale where Rudy the armorer lived. Given enough time Rudy could lay hands on almost anything that fired a projectile, up to and including a surface-to-air missile Henkin had once seen in Rudy's garage. Nearly a third of the illegal guns in Nassau County had passed through Rudy's hands at some point. He paid healthy kickbacks for the privilege of doing business, and he owed Henkin more than a few favors.

Henkin parked in the driveway of an abandoned service station at the corner and watched Rudy's house. Brancusi circled the block twice before parking across the street. The writer waited fifteen minutes and then got out of his car, walked to the front door of the cape, and rang the bell. One of Rudy's men answered and ushered Brancusi inside.

Henkin stared at the house.

There was no way he could see inside, but it didn't take much imagination to picture the scene. Half a dozen handguns would be laid out on a flannel cloth on the coffee table. Some of Rudy's guys would be hanging around as insurance against trouble, and Rudy would be extolling the virtues of each weapon, grinding his sales pitch as slick as a two-term senator. If he did his job right, there was only one possible choice Brancusi would make.

A .45 caliber Smith and Wesson, retailing for just under $800, but for which Rudy would charge $1,500, guaranteed untraceable.

Henkin knew the gun well.

He'd given it to Rudy that morning.

He'd chosen it himself.

Twenty minutes after he entered, Brancusi left the house, no sign of the gun, which he probably had tucked under his shirt. Henkin watched him get into his car.

His cell phone rang. It was Rudy.

"Yeah?" Henkin said.

"He paid cash. I threw in ammo and an extra clip. Easiest sale I ever made. So, tell me, why'd it have to be that gun?"

"You're kidding? Right gun for the right job. I thought that was your motto."

"Damn straight. And that's all I need to know. Stay safe, pig."

Rudy clicked off.

Henkin pulled out and followed Brancusi along the side streets toward Hempstead Turnpike. From there the writer started back toward his office, stopping once at a coffee shop to pick up lunch. Henkin stuck with him. He was sitting in his car down the street from Brancusi's building when the writer called his cell phone.

"Henkin."

"It's Dennis. Thanks for the info. Rudy checked out."

"Good. He won't be in business much longer. He got a reprieve because he's informing on a case," Henkin said. It was another lie, but not one that troubled him. "He'll be locked up before the end of summer, but he can still be useful until then. You look up the address?"

"Yeah. Drove out there a few times."

"And?"

"He's there in the evenings. There's no one around. The place is dark as a grave. Apparently Mr. Bruno likes his privacy when he's relaxing. Most nights his guys leave by nine. But he's got girls out there two or three times a week. Different nights."

"Girls?"

Henkin hadn't known that. Brancusi was being more careful and thorough than he'd expected.

"Let me rephrase: high-priced whores. Two or three at a time sometimes, but I guess he's got the money for it, because he sure as hell doesn't have the looks or the charm."

Henkin laughed. "No shit."

"So what else is there to this?"

"You need me to tell you that, you better forget the whole thing."

"You said you'd have more helpful information."

"Yeah, I will. A safe date."

"When he'll be there?"

"Yeah, and I'll confirm he'll be alone. So sit tight. Do nothing. I'll call you back."

"Why are you doing this, Gary?"

"Because Bruno's a bad guy. And you and I know he did it."

"If that's all, you could just give me the case file. What's the real reason you're helping me?"

"You fucking writers always wanting to know the *why* behind things. Let's say you're not the only one whose life didn't turn out the way he wanted. Sometimes the only way to make things right is the hard way. Leave it at that."

Henkin hung up, started his car, and drove away. He headed to police headquarters to pick up Joe Valenzuela. It was time for them to make a run out to Bruno's.

***

Abe Bruno's beach cottage was off the beaten path. It faced the Long Island Sound, and it was isolated even by the standards of a neighborhood where property lots came no smaller than half an acre. Dense woods covered most of the grounds, and though the cottage itself was modest, the view and the scenery made the location spectacular.

Henkin parked on the sandy patch at the end of the gravel driveway. He reached into the back seat and pulled out a fat manila envelope then followed Valenzuela out of the car. A salty breeze brushed over them, and the crashing of low waves against the beach murmured behind the house. To the west the sunset painted the sky. They were earlier than usual, but Henkin didn't think Bruno would mind. They were bringing good news.

He knocked on the front door.

Moments later, Bruno opened it and directed them inside. Two of his guys sat on recliners in the small living room. Two more were outside on the back deck, visible through open French doors.

"You're early," Bruno said. "Told you it's better you come out here after dark. People don't need to see us together."

"What people, Mr. Bruno?" said Valenzuela. "You worried about dolphins and seagulls?"

"Don't be a wiseass, Joey."

Bruno popped open the envelope and eyeballed the packets of cash stuffed inside. He removed a small one and handed the envelope to one of his men, then he pulled out a few bills from the packet and handed some to Henkin and Valenzuela.

"You got good news for me, I'll give you the rest."

"I got good news," said Henkin.

"He take the date?"

"Yeah, you're all set. He's coming the night after our next drop off, week from tomorrow. Work for you?"

Bruno nodded. "Day after payday? That works. Next week's going to be a good week."

He handed the rest of the cash to Henkin, who gave half to Valenzuela.

"I already got a gun picked out. Got it at Wal-Mart." Bruno pointed to a Mossberg, double-barrel shotgun resting in a rack above a small fireplace. "It'll make a nice addition to the evidence locker, don't you think? That sonofabitch snitch dodged me once, but he won't walk away this time."

Valenzuela mimed holding a shotgun at his waist and gave two low growls like gun blasts. Then he laughed. Bruno laughed too and slapped Valenzuela on the shoulder.

"You got it, Joey. You may be a wiseass, but you're no dummy. That's why I keep you around." Bruno gestured toward the deck. "Go on out and have a drink, enjoy the sunset, then get yourself the fuck out of here, cause I got some ladies coming over later, and all of you mooks are going to make yourselves scarce. Nothing like a little party on payday."

Henkin walked out onto the deck and took a seat. He grabbed a bottle of beer from a bucket on the patio table, cracked it open, and drank. Valenzuela followed suit.

"You ever nail that brunette?" Henkin asked.

"Oh, momma, you bet your sweet ass, I did."

"What brunette?" asked one of Bruno's guys.

"Over at the Jericho. Works the counter at night," said Valenzuela.

"The dumb one? No shit."

"Yeah, man. She was sweet."

Valenzuela launched into the details, but Henkin tuned him out. He was staring at the water of the Sound, thinking how he would never in his life ever come close to living this way even though his soul was no less black and rotten than Abe Bruno's. Even if his wife hadn't left him and his father hadn't died, Henkin knew he'd still be a lonely man. He'd always be lonely.

As alone as Dennis Brancusi, he thought.

He wondered about how he'd fallen in so deep that he was arranging for men like Bruno to get away with murder. He wasn't a mindless fist like Valenzuela, and though he liked the money, it had never been a compulsion for him. He'd simply never expected things to go this far when he first went on the take.

When Henkin was fresh on homicide, it had taken Boyd only three weeks to figure out he'd been crooked since he was a street cop and that he still was. But Boyd hadn't turned him over. Henkin thought that was because he'd proven to be a good homicide cop and Boyd thought he could turn him around. Working murders, the opportunities for graft were limited.

Even so, Henkin hadn't kept his nose clean. There were always favors to be sold, strings to be pulled, and people to be handled. Boyd tried to wean him off it. It didn't seem possible, but still Boyd had tried a long time.

Two years after Henkin had started homicide, Boyd was getting ready to hand him to Internal Affairs. He'd given Henkin a last warning. It was one Henkin took seriously. He respected Boyd, and deep down he wanted to be a good cop, but he wasn't sure how to break the habit. He was positive Boyd was going to turn him over, that his career was about to end, and there was a certain amount of relief in the knowledge. But then came Boyd's last case, and it had all simply gone away, and life had gone back to the way it always had been.

***

"Fuck. We're so late," said Valenzuela. "Bruno's going to be pissed."

"Two envelopes this week. That'll take the edge off his mood. Besides, he told us to come after dark." Henkin turned off the main road onto the beach road to Bruno's neighborhood. It was close to midnight, and there were no other cars in sight.

"We should've been there and gone a couple of hours ago."

"Don't sweat it. Bruno's not going to give us a hard time. He's got too much riding on us right now. Besides, can I help it if I caught a murder at the end of my shift?"

"You could've dumped it on Chinaski."

"You kidding me? Guy's got the biggest caseload on the squad right now."

"So? Never stopped you before. He'd have taken it."

"Got to do my job sometimes."

"Whatever. I'm just saying."

"Okay, you said it. Change the subject."

"Fine. You ever going to tell me how Roddy Boyd died?"

Henkin laughed. "You really want to know?"

"I'll reserve judgment. Let's hear it."

"Sure. Why not? Roddy got on a hot streak, and caught one murder after another that he was putting down within a couple of days or weeks at most. Some he got lucky breaks. Mostly he worked hard and fast and made his own luck. I worked on maybe half of them. Sherlock Holmes, Mike Hammer, and Jim Rockford put together couldn't have worked cases any better than Boyd did while his streak was running. He was driven. He was trying to make a point."

"Which was?"

"Shut up. Let me tell the story."

"Okay, fine. So, tell it."

"He gets his last call. It's a high school kid. A good kid. A girl, sophomore, honor student, top athlete, all that, and she took a bullet in the head when someone at her neighbor's house started shooting. Me and Roddy happened to be in the neighborhood, so we get there fast. Not even the ambulance is there yet when we pull up. The family is screaming and crying, and the situation is explosive. And Roddy, he's convinced the shooter is still around, hanging out in the crowd that's gathering on the neighbors' lawns. So he says, let's work the crowd before it goes cold, and that's what we do.

"We split up. We ask questions. We're pressing people, and we're looking for suspects, witnesses, anybody, and we're getting lie after lie after lie once we get past people's names. But there's this one guy – young, clean-cut looking, and I can't shake that there's something not right about him. He knows something. I can feel it, but I can't say why. It's dark because it's overcast and it's getting late, and I can't see him perfectly clear, but I feel it in my gut. Something's off about this guy. So I finger him for Roddy, and he takes one look, squints and flashes his light in the guy's face, and says, 'Gary, my son, you are a damn good police.'

"Then Roddy, who's easily 6'4" and built like a brick wall, walks up to the guy, and says right to his face, 'You killed a little girl today. Maybe you didn't mean to do it, but if you lie to me about it, then your life is going to become a worse hell then you can ever imagine.'"

Henkin stared at the road, a gray strip of pavement hedged by overgrown beach scrubs and scraggly pines.

That was how it happened, wasn't it? he thought. *It was. I picked the guy.*

"Yeah, and?"

"So the guy drops to his knees, and then Roddy is on him, cuffing him as he helps him up, and the guy is blubbering that he never meant for anyone to get hurt, it wasn't even his gun, and on and on, and he goes to jail, and the case goes down that night.

"Roddy comes up to me after the shooter is locked away in a cruiser and asks what tipped me. And I tell him I don't know. It wasn't any one thing. Maybe it was that the guy's hands were trembling or maybe it was that his eyes were bloodshot, and the first thing I thought was he'd been crying. Believe me, I've tried to pin it down, but I can't. The best I could ever say is like I told Roddy: there was something off. So Roddy slaps me on the back and says, 'Whatever. You got good instincts. You got a good police inside you.' And that's the point he was trying to make that whole time on his streak. He was showing me what a good police could do. Only I was too fucking dumb to see it. But I see it now. I understand. You know, Boyd knew everything about me. There was no hiding it from him. He was getting ready to hand me to IA, but he was throwing me a lifeline first, trying to win me over to the right side."

"Shit. Exactly how did this supercop die?"

"After we collared the girl's killer, he went into the car to write down his notes. Had a massive coronary, died in seconds, and it was half an hour before I got back to the car and found him. Doctor said it was brought on by extreme stress. Had to be because he was getting ready to blow me to IA and because he was pushing himself so hard, trying to turn me around. He died doing it. Died and took the problem right off the table."

"Lucky break for you."

"That's what I thought then." Henkin turned down the gravel drive to Bruno's cottage. "Anyway, that's how Roddy Boyd died."

Halfway along the path, Valenzuela twisted around in his seat to look out the window.

"Stop the car," he said.

Henkin braked. Valenzuela rolled down his window and turned his flashlight on the deep brush. A small, dark car was parked there, stuck half into the shrubs.

"Whose ride is that?"

Henkin shrugged. "Bruno's probably got some girls out here. It's payday."

"What girls you know park in the bushes fifty yards from the house in the dark?"

Henkin didn't answer.

He drove up to the cottage and stopped. Lights were on inside the house. Henkin and Valenzuela knocked on the door. Nobody answered. Henkin tried the door, and it pushed open. He stepped inside and listened.

Creaking sounds and low voices came from the second floor.

"Upstairs," said Valenzuela. "Hello? Abe?"

Henkin glanced at his watch. It was a little past midnight.

Someone screamed. Then a gun fired.

"Holy shit!" shouted Valenzuela.

Footsteps stamped along the upstairs hallway. Valenzuela drew his gun. Henkin grabbed the Mossberg from over the fireplace.

A half-naked woman came charging down the stairs so fast that Valenzuela jumped in surprise and fired two shots into her. The woman slammed into the banister and then tumbled down the last few steps and crashed to the floor.

"Fuck!" he said. "You think Brancusi's up there? I thought you told him *tomorrow*."

"I lied," said Henkin.

"What the hell does that mean?"

"I've never liked you, Joe."

Henkin leveled the shotgun and blasted Valenzuela with both barrels. He crossed the room, stepped over the dead woman, and started up the stairs. His heart slammed inside his chest, and he felt nauseous. He had hoped this would be easier, but as he inched his way toward the open door at the end of the hall, he felt like he was breaking apart from reality, becoming a spectator in a sequence of events that he'd set in motion and couldn't control. He slipped inside the room. Brancusi stood across from him in the opening that led out to the deck. The writer raised his gun and fired. Henkin threw himself sideways, hit the ground, and discharged the shotgun, cutting a swath of holes in the ceiling. As he fell he glimpsed Bruno lying back on the bed with a mess of blood pouring from his chest. He clutched a .38 in his hand.

"Henkin?" said Brancusi. "That you?"

"It's me. Don't fucking shoot!"

Henkin crept back to his feet, holding the shotgun upright. Brancusi kept his gun leveled on him.

"Wasn't sure you'd come," said Henkin.

"I almost didn't. I almost waited till tomorrow night, figuring you'd set me up. Maybe you did. He was supposed to be alone. So were you."

"Plans change. I figured the woman would be gone by now."

"We got to clean this up fast."

"No. Leave it. Give me that gun and get the fuck out of here. I'll give you five minutes before I call this in."

"What are you talking about?"

"Give me the gun."

"Why?"

"Because it's mine."

Brancusi looked at the weapon. "I don't get it."

"I set you up, only not how you think. I was supposed to get you here tomorrow night, when Bruno would be ready to kill you after you broke in. This way, you got him. You got what you wanted. Now hand me the gun and run. When the cops show up, I'll tell them my partner and I got here late making a payoff to Bruno. We surprised him, and he fired at us, killing my partner, who shot his whore. Then I'll tell them I shot Bruno before he could kill me, and because that's my gun and it's registered to me, they'll believe me. And because I have two envelopes stuffed with cash in my car, they'll believe the rest of it. Your name will never come up."

Henkin stepped forward and held out his hand for the gun. The anger and rage so often clear in Brancusi's face was erased by shock.

"Rudy sold me *your* gun?"

"I was baiting you in the park that day, and I prayed you wouldn't swallow the hook, because I didn't want to do what I was supposed to do. I've been struggling to live with myself for a long time. You're the closest thing I have to a friend, and if I let you die for Abe Bruno's sake, then it would've killed the last part of my soul."

"Shit," said Brancusi. "I knew you were less than clean, but this is blowing my fucking mind."

"We don't have a lot of time here. I owe people. I owe you. And this is the only way I can pay that debt. A lot of people are going to fall over this, but you'll be safe. Maybe if I'd had the balls to do what I should've done a long time ago, your family never would've been killed."

"Gary, man, this…"

"Why did you trust me?"

"Because you only lied to me when there really was no more you could do."

"Guess we're both too smart for our own good. Listen, with what I'm doing, I'll be lucky to be alive this time next year, so do me a favor, okay? Write about me someday. Maybe I can be in that novel, because I don't know who the hell would believe this shit really happened. Now give me the gun and get out of here. Fast."

Brancusi handed over the gun.

He backed out onto the deck into the dark, waved once, and then he was gone.

Henkin waited until he heard a car motor start and then fade away. When it was gone, he began his count. Five minutes later he picked up the phone and dialed 911. He gave his name and badge number, reported an officer down and requested backup, and then started studying the crime scene.

Bruno's .38 would have to go.

The Mossberg would have to be placed in his hands.

There were other adjustments Henkin would have to make to cover the details. He had to get the lies straight in his head so none of this came back to Brancusi. He'd been able to give the writer a measure of justice, even if he did it the wrong way. He wanted him to enjoy it.

Henkin didn't think this made him a good police, but he hoped at least that Roddy Boyd, who'd never hesitated to bend the rules, would've cut him some slack.

Wally wasn't a good cop who went bad, he was a bad cop who got worse...

BENT COP
Gary Lovisi

The neighborhood…it was all his now. They gave it to him and he wasn't giving it back!

Most cops hate to walk a beat; can think of nothing worse than being back out on the streets they hate. Among the skells. Away from their warm, comfy prowl cars. Not this cop. Not Wally. He loved it. He loved the action. Loved the perks.

Wally was six foot, four inches, 240 pounds of muscle ready to bust your face. He was good with a billy club – lotta practice cracking heads – but better with a gun, when it was necessary.

Today was Wednesday. Shakedown day. When the honest store owners on 13th Avenue paid their bills, when the mob guys running the drug stores, whorehouses and gambling dens paid to be ignored. Wally always looked away, as long as his price was paid. He loved walking a beat.

Today he wasn't On The Job. It was his day off. But he was still in the 'hood. Walking. Always walking, looking. Looking for goodies. What did he want now? It was all his, just for the asking. Or the taking. As long as he did it right. And Wally knew how to do it right. How to get the restaurant owners to give him free meals – he ate only the best these days, steak and lobster with imported wine. Or free clothes at Ralph's Men's Shop, free shoes at the Florsheim, free haircuts and shaves at Vinny's Salon, free poon at that new Chinese house up the block. Add to that a big tab at the gambling den over the pizza joint and it didn't get much better. But he was smart and did it right so no one would talk, or not talk for long, anyways …

There was this new place over on 5th and Wally decided to pay them a visit. See what they had. He walked in and looked over the merch. Good, high-quality stuff. He was wearing civvies, just another happy citizen shopping on his own time and enjoying his day off.

Guy comes over. Short, fat, but dressed like a pimp. Smiling greasy. Smelling a big sale.

"Can I help you, sir?"

"Sure can," Wally says. He's holding a pile of shirts, ties, a nice leather jacket, other things he felt he'd like or might be needing. "I'll take all these."

The store owner smiles, thinks he's made a big sale. He can almost smell the cash.

"Fine, sir, if you'll just follow me to the register …"

Wally smiles back, "Why?"

The store owner's smile drops to the floor, a little nervous now, but standing his ground in his own store. "Why, to pay for the items, sir."

Wally smiles, "What I said was I'm taking this stuff. I didn't say I'm *paying* for it."

Now the store man fumes, stammers, uncertain what to do. He tries to knock some of the merch out of Wally's hands before he can walk out the door. Finally, and Wally doesn't know how he does it, the store man pulls Wally back and knocks all his fine new stuff to the floor.

"Now get out of my store!" The owner shouts to Wally.

Wally looks around, sees there's no one else in the store. Smiles, says, "Okay, new guys gotta learn sometimes. Might as well learn you right the first time."

The store man realizes they're alone now and grows scared.

"Get out or I'll call the cops!"

Wally laughs, draws his badge stabbing it into the man's face.

"I *am* the cops, moron!"

The store man doesn't say anything, but doesn't look that surprised, he knows the score, stands there fuming, working it over in his mind. Figuring the loss. Wally looks at the guy hard, he's mildly pissed, decides that this new guy needs some education before he does something foolish.

"You got a problem with that?"

Wally grabs the guy by his throat, lifting him off the ground, bangs his head a couple of times on the counter, "Just to get your attention," he tells the guy. There was a little blood on the man's forehead but not too much.

He's moaning, scared, shaking.

"Now pick up my stuff. I'm in a hurry!"

Guys like Wally usually don't like to shop. They just don't have the patience. But when you're a cop in this town and the price is right, they figure, hey, it's worth the time and effort when you get a *really good deal.*

***

Wally was out in Chinese poon heaven. The new place called Chopsticks. Strictly illegal, as in illegal aliens and sexual slavery, but fat old Uncle Woo paid very well. In cash, in drugs, and in free samples of the latest hot dish on the menu.

Wally was just polishing off his favorite dish when he got the call. The guy at the other end was a slimeball loan shark named Ernie. Ernie made a lot of bread, which meant Wally made a lot of bread. Which meant Ernie and Wally had a kind of relationship.

Wally kept the losers off Ernie's back, stopped them from complaining when they got their faces busted by Ernie's goons. But lately there was this hardhead named Greco who'd lost it all – house, wife, kids. That kind of loss all at one time can really shake a man, make him do stupid things.

Ernie told Wally that the guy was threatening all over the place, saying how he was gonna blab about all the corruption in the neighborhood, at the precinct, with the cop on the beat. That last meant Wally himself. Wally naturally didn't appreciate that. So Wally called his boss, told him what Greco was planning.

"Pay that boy a visit, Wally. You know what to do."

"Sure thing, Captain," Wally said, putting on his pants, zipping his fly, leaving Uncle Woo's and walking over to the Upton Building.

Greco sold insurance. Kind of ironic, Wally thought, since *he* was the one in serious need of it *now*. Greco had a nice office on the top floor. At least until the end of the month when he'd end up being evicted for being too far behind on the rent. Money that Ernie and Wally felt they were putting to better use now anyway.

Greco was gonna talk. He'd called some newspaper guys and told them to come down to his office tomorrow morning. Told them he had some interesting stuff to tell.

Wally decided to pay Greco a visit *today*.

On the way over Wally stopped at Han's Grocery to pick up some fruit.

When Wally reached Greco's building he went upstairs carrying a bag in his hand. Said hello. Said he wanted to talk to Greco. Greco was alone in his office.

Greco saw him come in and said, "I got nothing to talk about to you!"

Wally just opened up the bag.

Greco got nervous. He didn't know what Wally had there. Maybe he had a sap or a gun? A bomb?

Not quite.

Wally pulled out a large light green Honeydew melon. It was big and ripe and smelled real sweet.

"You didn't come over here to offer me a slice of that, did you, Wally?" Greco said, relieved it *wasn't* a gun or bomb, trying to joke his way out of this and screwing it up badly.

"No, Greco, it's for demonstration purposes."

The look on Greco's face showed deep concern edging toward panic.

"Calm down, Greco," Wally laughed good-naturedly – and if you knew Wally that was the time to be the most scared of him. He shrugged, held the melon, showed it to Greco, said, "I'm not going to hurt you with this. It's just a damn Honeydew melon. I couldn't kill anyone with a melon even if I tried."

Greco knew Wally, so he wasn't so sure about that. He returned a sickly smile.

"I just wanna show you something," Wally added.

"Yeah?" Greco said suspiciously.

"Yeah," Wally answered matter-of-factly.

Greco wasn't buying, but there wasn't anything he could do about it either. Wally wasn't leaving. And Greco couldn't *make* him leave until he'd had his say. If Greco made a stab for the phone, or tried to run, Wally would break his face for sure. And Greco knew it. He knew Wally too well. Greco and Wally went back a ways.

"W-what you want, Wally?" Greco stammered.

"Come here," Wally said, as he practically sauntered over to the window, opening it wide. The noise and dirt of the city streamed into Greco's office, but neither man noticed any of that now.

Wally picked up the big Honeydew melon, hefting it in his hand, feeling the measure of its weight. Greco's eyes shot from the melon to Wally's eyes, back to the melon again. There was the frantic look of a cornered rat in his expression.

"Come here, Greco. Closer. By the window. I wanna show you something."

Greco didn't move one inch. He was scared now and Wally was glad to see the reaction. Savoring it, in fact.

"Man, what a big pussy you are! Get the hell over here or I'll *really* get mad, and then you'll really have something to wet your pants about!"

Greco knew all too well how Wally was when he got mad. He slowly walked forward, trying to keep himself out of arms reach of the big cop. Trying to keep Wally between him and the open window. Making sure he stood on the right side of Wally, because Wally was holding the big melon in his right hand, and he figured that while Wally held the melon he couldn't draw his gun. Or throw him out the window. At least Greco *hoped* Wally couldn't draw his gun or throw him out the window from that angle.

"Look at this." Wally motioned Greco closer to the open window, nearer and nearer until both men's bodies hung out over the sill, looking down below. It was only seven floors down but it might as well have been a mile. Greco was shaking badly, Wally holding him steady while he moved his arm out with the melon.

"I wanna show you something, Greco. They say one picture's worth a thousand words."

Then Wally let go of the melon.

Both men watched entranced as it fell downward. So fast. Greco's eyes glued to it like a man possessed, silent, shaking, eyes bulging. It was all so unreal. Almost like slo-mo. The melon finally hit the sidewalk with a silent plop exploding into a spray of soggy green mush.

"Now that," Wally said meaningfully, "coulda been your head, Greco." Then he pushed the terrified man away from the window and he walked toward the door. On the way out Wally added, "A word to the wise, Greco. Keep your mouth shut. You keep quiet and you'll keep your head. Remember that melon. That kinda damage can never be repaired."

Greco fainted.

The first thing he did when he came to was call the newspaper guys and tell them to forget all about what he had said.

"So they got to you too, Greco?"

"You're damn right!" Greco barked, slamming down the receiver.

***

Wally celebrated at Ernie's place over the pizza parlor. A whore in one arm, a bottle of Daniels in the other. A pile of chips in front of him that Ernie gave him on the house, payoff for taking care of that 'little problem' with Greco.

Wally liked cards, gambling. He played hard and reckless, lost the pile fast, got another pile from Ernie and lost that too. Finally he said the hell with gambling, took the whore upstairs in Ernie's backroom, did her, then passed out. Drunk and sexed-out tired.

When Wally woke up the next morning he saw Ernie in front of him with a newspaper.

The front cover showed a photo of Greco. There was a story next to the photo about a failed insurance man, newly separated from his wife of 17 years, who'd just committed suicide.

Ernie said, "The guy landed pretty hard, Wally. I really did appreciate your work yesterday, but I wanted to make sure Greco didn't change his mind."

"He wasn't going to change his mind," Wally said knowingly.

"Well, I just like to make sure about these things," Ernie replied. "I sent Joey."

Wally shrugged, "That's okay with me, Ernie. Never much liked Greco anyway."

Ernie smiled, "You know, Wally, I like you. I never really liked any cop before, but I *like* you."

"I like you too, Ernie," Wally said, making a face like he was about to vomit. "That mean we're going steady now?

Ernie laughed. "There's a pile of chips waiting for you any time you come here. All the young putas you want, too."

"Now, that's *real* nice of you, Ernie," Wally said.

"Nothing's too good for my cop buddy."

***

Of course Wally knew Ernie was low-life scum that had to go down. He was trying to smooze Wally with cash and whores so he'd let him slide, not report his action to his boss at the precinct, play like he didn't see all the goodies Ernie was busy keeping hidden and stashing away.

Though Wally was corrupt, he wasn't stupid. He wouldn't double-deal his own boss. Just those under him. Ernie had gotten above himself, made a move that wasn't his to make. He expected too much, which meant he had gained himself a place on 'the list' and was moving up. The higher up you got on "the list", the more *they* felt they had to do something about you. Not an enviable position to be in. Ernie was moving up fast, and Wally was grabbing all he could get while the getting was good.

***

There was a time when Wally didn't accept bribes, shakedown storeowners for merch, beat the hell out of citizens, ball-bust troublemakers that had too-big mouths. But those days were long gone. He remembered how it had all begun though. That nice old lady in the wheel chair. She'd withdrawn $5,000 in cash, all in twenties in 10 five-hundred dollar bundles from the bank to pay for her daughter's operation.

She'd seen Wally, a young cop on the corner walking his beat, and had asked him to escort her home. He was about to tell the old bat just where she could go when she said she didn't want to get mugged by no punks on account of all the cash she was carrying. Then she took out huge wads of bank-wrapped bills to show him just why she needed his help.

Well, Wally became *real* helpful after seeing that. He walked the old lady home to her rat-trap apartment, thinking all the time about the right way to ask for a tip, somehow knowing she wouldn't go for that. Then he thought, "Why take some when I could have it all?" So when she wasn't looking he pushed the old lady and her wheel chair down the steps. Then he took the elevator down to the first floor, took her money and took a walk to Ryan's Bar on the corner.

He needed a drink. Murder and robbery was a big first step.

It was an hour later when a black and white pulled up from a 911 call put in by the building super who'd just found the body. Wally paid for his drinks, then took a walk over to the crime scene to lend assistance. He pulled in a young black kid along the way that was loitering in an alley across the street, knocked him unconscious, planted some dope and five twenties – $100 still in the bank wrapper in the kid's pocket. Brought him over to the Sarge, had another cop frisk him. They found the drugs, figured that's how the kid had spent the rest of the money. Anyway, he was a convenient collar. It was almost too obvious but no one worried about it that much.

"Kinda incriminating, ain't it, Sarge?" Wally said, as he held the kid.

Sarge nodded seriously, "Lousy bastard, why he wanna hurt a nice old lady like that for?"

Wally smiled, mentally spending the cash as the kid was taken away.

The kid crying, wondering what it was all about.

Wally sighed remembering. Yeah, those were the good old days.

Wally had spent that $5,000 like it was water. After that, Wally got the appetite real bad. He wanted more, needed more, made damn-well sure he got more. He figured he deserved it. He'd taken an oath, "To

Serve and Protect," but to Wally all that meant was "Serve myself, protect what's mine. Take what you want, while you can."

Well, those had been the good *old* days, but these were the good *new* days, and Wally liked these days even better.

***

Slick Ernie sat at his desk counting the week's take. Business was good, getting better. The worse the economy got, the more people seemed to need Ernie's services. Drugs. Gambling. Girls. And the loans to pay for it all. With a vig high enough to make damn sure even the most determined borrower would never be able to get out from under.

Wally decided to pay Ernie a visit, was ushered into his private office, saw the piles of bills. Twenties. Fifties. Hundreds. A drop of drool involuntarily slipping from between his lips, dripping onto the clean pressed blue of his police uniform.

Ernie was surprised to see Wally. He didn't like the boys letting anyone in the office when he was counting the week's take, but Ernie got up, said, "Hey, Wally? How ya doing?"

Wally shook Ernie's hand. Then in a quick move twisted the loan shark's arm behind him, almost breaking it as he pushed his face into the wall. Once. Twice. Again.

"I had it handled, Ernie," Wally said as he relived Ernie of his piece. "Greco wouldn't have talked. And we could have used him, used his business. He writes the policies, we stage the accidents, we get the insurance. You cost us, Ernie. You cost me. So now I want the money, all of it!" Wally demanded in a cold voice, so matter-of-factly Ernie thought better of coming out and saying what he normally would have said to anyone else under similar circumstances. See, Ernie knew Wally, or thought he did. He was scared with good reason. To have Wally on his ass now, to be helpless against him, meant he had to think fast and smart.

"That's an entire week's take, Wally!"

Wally expended increased pressure upon Ernie's arm, but said nothing as he did so. His eyes glassy, staring at all the money.

Ernie grunted, said, "But it's okay, Wally. It's okay with me. See? Go ahead and take it. Take it all!"

Wally smiled, said, "Thanks, Ernie. I'm so grateful. But I'm thinking I can't trust you anymore. So I think I'll send you on a little trip – twenty stories down!"

Before Ernie could scream, beg, or fight, he was thrown face-first through the plate glass window of his office. Flying through the air, he was still trying to get that first scream out of his throat when he hit the ground face down with an ugly little splattering on the sidewalk.

Wally opened the door to the outer office. Stuck his head in the hall. Got the attention of the hood on guard duty at the foot of the stairs.

"Clem, you come up here a minute? Ernie wants to ask you something."

The huge hoodlum came into the room, didn't see Ernie, looked around, didn't find him – but found two slugs in the brain from Ernie's .380 held in Wally's gloved hand.

Clem and Ernie's gun hit the ground at the same time in opposite ends of the room, as Wally began to fill up a suitcase with the cash. He left the gun where it would be found sooner or later.

A fallout between two hoods and Wally home free.

***

Wally was off-duty; at home in the dive he had near his beat, the one not even his boss knew about. He was counting the take. He had all the bills out on his bed in neat piles of hundred, fifty, twenty, ten and five-dollar bills. It was like money-heaven to Wally. This much bread could hold him for a while. Maybe as long as a few weeks, if he kept himself under control. He just laughed at that. An impossibility for shit-sure.

Wally packed the cash into nice neat bundles. Made a few phone calls. The guys at the other end of the line were anxious for the cash Wally seemed so ready and willing to spread around.

Wally thought he'd invest the money in drugs. For the average person, citizen or low-life, not normally a good idea, but Wally wasn't average. Not even most bent cops would do such a thing. But those who knew Wally would never doubt for a minute he'd do that and a whole lot of other stuff. Wally was capable of anything. A lot of bad. A lot of just plain stupid. But he didn't care, there was always more money. Besides, you couldn't snort cash the way you could that pretty white powder.

Wally called up the job, took some sick time. Coked himself up to get into the mood. Got an airline ticket for Vegas.

On the way to the airport he picked up the late edition of the *Star* and saw where a gang hood named Slick Ernie had been killed by one of his own henchman in a bizarre power play for control of neighborhood gambling interests. The henchman, some guy by the name of Clem something-or-other had been blown away with Ernie's .380. Ernie himself had been flung out the window as they fought. All cut and dried, nice and neat, the way the cops downtown liked things. You see, downtown liked easily closed cases. And no one likes loose ends or complicated questions. Especially cops. Especially the cops in this town.

Wally made a nice score on some drugs in Vegas, reselling them on his return to an up-and-coming dealer from the Islands. He took a substantial amount of the cash and decided to take another trip out West. Another big-time week in Sin City and he found himself high and dry and flat busted, back home and back on his beat.

And now his head hurt like a hammer was slamming it. His eyes were red, puffy and watering; seeing double when they could look straight at all. He felt like shit but he'd be better soon. He shrugged; maybe he'd take a walk to Nino's Pizza Shack for some free eats. Then go to the Hot Spot Bar for a shot of hard stuff to clear the tonsils. Then he'd trot over to Maggie's place to do one of the new girls. He was back on the beat. Just the way he liked it.

Back in the neighborhood…

The neighborhood that was all his.

Wally loved it, and no one was going to take it away from him…

…*And he was never going to give it back!*

A swordsman, a ninja, a cop who thinks he's Doc Holliday...

LUNATICS
O'Neil De Noux

My partner, Paul Snowood, is not crazy. He just thinks he's Doc Holliday.

He wears western clothes – cavalry shirts with two rows of buttons, rope ties, denim pants, cowboy boots and of course, a ten-gallon Stetson. And he talks with a cowboy accent, until he gets excited and sounds like he's from New Orleans like the rest of us.

Thinking you're Doc Holliday isn't that bad, I guess, except he keeps calling me *Wyatt*, as in Earp. It started after I shot a killer last year, rare for a homicide detective. We usually write people to death, you know, "the pen is mightier than the sword." With a pen you can send someone to death row without having to stand in front of a pain-in-the-ass Grand Jury and justify why you used deadly force.

Wyatt. Besides being a lawman, the only thing I have in common with Wyatt Earp is my moustache. Hell, he was a white boy. I'm Sicilian-American with an olive complexion and a nice Italian name – Dino LaStanza. I'm short too, five-six.

Sitting at my gray metal, government-issue desk, which abuts my partner's desk, I look at Snowood and try not to laugh. Tonight he wears a scarlet shirt with silver buttons and fringe dangling from the pockets, sand-colored denim pants and a wide brown belt with a silver buffalo head belt buckle. His feet are up on his desk, showing off his snakeskin boots. His brown Stetson lies in pristine magnificence on his desk, just out of my reach. Lord help anyone who touches his hat.

Snowood thumbs through the newspaper sports section and mumbles something about the damn Saints. I guess he figures I'll ask for clarification. I don't.

I look over at the glass wall of the homicide squad room. The green film, which is supposed to shield us from the sun and snipers, has peeled from most of the windows, giving the glass the look of leprosy. A gust of wind outside makes the film flap like batwings.

"So," Snowood drawls. "You comin' or not, Wyatt?"

"Fuck no. And quit calling me Wyatt."

"You start calling me Doc and I'll stop. Aw, Come on. It's just 'round the corner."

"You go. I've got paperwork to finish."

He puts the paper down and looks at the sheets I've scattered on my desk. "You're sandbagging me, pardner. You done finished yer paperwork. You just want to stay here and do nothin' all night."

We already had this argument. I'm not going over it again. He knows full well this is the last night before my vacation, before my wedding Saturday and my honeymoon. He's dying to get me into shit that'll mess up my plans. I can see it in his devious eyes.

"It's Thursday. Nothin' happens on a Thursday night." He grins devilishly.

Yeah. Right! In New Orleans, every night is bad. We've already had thirty-two murders this month and November's not over yet. We're about to make 1981 the bloodiest year since Bienville founded the city back in 1718.

Standing, I stretch and move across the room to the raggedy windows. A full moon, bright and huge, hovers over the city. I can see its craters clearly, even through the leperous glass.

"Come on, now." Snowood whines behind me. "Pa – leez."

I hate it when a grown man whines. Staring at the moon I know better than to go out tonight. The full moon brings out more than werewolves, it brings out the muggle-heads and the space-zombies and the loony-tunes. I swear one full moon night, when I was a patrolman, we chased Yosemite Sam (red hair and beard and shooting up the town with a pair of six-shooters) along Felicity Street up to Claiborne Avenue all the way to the Superdome where he escaped in a hot rod driven by an Elmer Fudd look-a-like. I swear.

"Pa – leez! I gotta fetch that statement from that witness afore we go to trial. Pa – leez."

I remind him we're not supposed to go to the Monte Carlo, not after what happened the last time. "Your witness can just drop off the statement."

"Yeah, like he'll do that."

"Last time we went there we wound up where?"

He doesn't answer.

"I.A.D. and for no good goddamn reason."

"But I.A.D. likes you. You get away with everything and they serve good donuts. Pa – leez. Pa – leez. Pa – leez. Pa – leez!"

I wheel around and tell him to shut up. I'll go. Just shut up.

"Oh, goody!" He actually says that as he starts packing his briefcase. I move back to my desk and pack my own briefcase. Our shift's half over so I don't plan to come back. Snowood keeps rattling on, as if I'm listening to him explain how it's just around the corner, how it'll be a snap, I'll just go along for the ride. We're not up for the next murder anyway. Tonight I'm an assisting fool, just assisting.

I've heard that one before. I brush my index finger and thumb down over my moustache. I do that when I'm nervous. Sucking in a deep breath, I tell myself there's nothing to worry about.

Yeah. Right! I'm going into the night with that tall drink of water himself – *Defective* Paul Snowood. Maybe, just maybe, I'm the one who's crazy. Crazy enough to be bored enough to go out tonight. I tell myself I need some fresh air. I'm tired of the smell of stale coffee.

I straighten my gray tie and pull on my black suit coat, readjusting my stainless steel, .357 Magnum, which rests in its holster on my right hip. As we cross the squad room, I look out at the moon again and feel a twitch in my belly. That's not a good sign.

On the way to the garage, Snowood asks again about the wedding. He's been needling me ever since I told him how my future in-laws changed our wedding ceremony after watching Prince Charles and Princess Diana get married in July. Set in St. Louis Cathedral, it's no longer a wedding. It's a coronation with twenty bridesmaids.

"That's what ya' get fer marrying a rich girl," Snowood repeats, for the hundredth time. "Even if she is a handsome filly."

***

The Monte Carlo Apartments is at the corner of Tulane Avenue and South Rocheblave Street. Once a motel, the single story, brick building is a crumbling shadow of better days (if there ever were better days on Tulane Avenue). Its wrought iron balcony, supported by two-by-fours, looks as rickety as the gate that hangs by a lone hinge from the low brick wall that surrounds the place. The parking lot is littered with junk cars and pick-ups.

Snowood parks our unmarked LTD on the sidewalk in front, just outside the low wall. Inside the wall lies a swimming pool. As I step out of the car I see the moonlight reflecting off the pool's scummy water. The night smells of garbage and urine. So much for fresh air.

I reach back in and grab my portable police radio, which we call an LFR (little fuckin' radio, as opposed to a BFR, better known as a boom box). Snowood, poky as ever, follows me through the gate. As we round the pool, a sudden movement in the shadows on my left catches my attention. A shirtless man, swinging a sword overhead, lunges at me.

All I can do is raise my left hand to block the blow. The sword slashes down, shattering my LFR.

"Aaaaa!" The shirtless man screams.

Behind me Snowood yells, "Whoa! Whoa! Whoa!"

Falling back, I pull out my Magnum and cock it in one movement. Just as I raise it, Shirtless swings the sword at me again. I fire before I can aim and the man spins, the sword flying through the air and into the pool. Shirtless looks at his hands. There's no blood.

He bolts away from me, racing around the pool toward the building.

I follow without thinking – running a police description of Shirtless in my mind – white male, five-ten, skinny, long dark hair.

Behind me Snowood yells, "Whoa! Whoa! Whoa!"

Shirtless hits the stairs, and takes them two at a time. I'm right behind as he reaches the balcony. He slows by an open door and I hit him broadside, slamming him into the door frame.

He goes, "Ooof!"

I grab his stringy hair with my left hand and yank him backwards, shoving the muzzle of my Magnum against his right cheek.

"Freeze!"

His wild eyes ogle me as his hands go limp and he starts to whimper. Breathing heavy, I smell his body odor and an even stronger scent through the open door. Marijuana.

Snowood arrives with his Glock in hand. No six-shooter for this Doc Holliday. Snowood carries a twenty-shot Glock, a plastic-steel NATO gun. So much for the Wild, Wild West.

"Jesus Fuckin' Christ! What is all this?" The country accent is gone.

"Just cover him and I'll cuff the fucker."

I tug on the hair again and snarl at Shirtless. "Don't fuckin' move!"

Holstering my Magnum, I slip the cuffs out of my belt and cuff the man's hands behind his back. I pat him down, then press him against the wall.

Snowood, bouncing on his toes, his shirt fringe flailing around, slaps me on the shoulder. "Jesus Wyatt! Shot the sword right outta his fuckin' hand!"

"I was aiming at his head."

Shirtless lets out a whimper. I tell him to shut up and ask Snowood to call headquarters.

"Anything you say, Wyatt." He steps back and tries to use his LFR to call for a marked unit. Static only, so he moves down the balcony to the top of the stairs and tries again.

Another breath of marijuana-laced air washes over me so I step into the open doorway and peer into the dark apartment. It takes a second for my eyes to adjust.

Something moves quickly toward me and I step back just as a nunchaku strikes the door frame at eye-level. Another shirtless man with curly hair jumps into the doorway and swings the nunchaku in a criss-cross in front of him. Taller than the first shirtless man, this Nunchakuer is uglier, with a pock-marked face straight out of the House of Shock. Like Shirtless, he looks to be in his late twenties.

I step back and pull out my Magnum again. Cocking it as I raise it into a standard two-handed police stance, I aim my weapon at the man's sunken chest.

"Hiyaaa!" Nunchakuer screams and takes a step toward me.

Snowood starts yelling "Whoa" again, as if it'll fuckin' help.

I step back again, my left leg brushing against the balcony railing. I fix my sights on Nunchakuer's sternum.

"Police!" I tell him. "Drop it."

The nunchaku clicks as he swings it, wood on metal chain. I have a vision of going to my wedding with a nunchakued face.

"I'll kill you!" Nunchakuer says as he leaps toward me, swinging the nunchaku in front of him.

I squeeze off one round. The man whirls around as the shot echoes and the nunchaku flies out of his hands and down into the pool.

Nunchakuer turns and runs straight into Snowood.

The air smells of cordite now as I turn and shove Shirtless back against the wall. "Don't fuckin' move, asshole!"

I turn to help Snowood just as the Stetson flies off his head. By the time I reach him, he has Nunchakuer face down on the balcony. He hands me his cuffs and tells me to cuff the ass-hole. He hurries down the stairs to retrieve his fuckin' cowboy hat.

I cuff Nunchakuer behind his back. He smells worse than Shirtless, his skin reeking of onion-flavored B.O. As I stand him up, sirens echo down Tulane Avenue. I see blue lights heading our way. The cavalry's coming.

Snowood returns, brushing off his hat.

"It didn't get dirty, did it?" I ask as seriously as I can, as if I mean it.

Without looking up, Snowood says he doesn't think so.

"Good." I wheel Nunchakuer around and into Snowood, which almost causes him to drop his hat.

"Whoa!" Snowood backs up a step.

"Just take the fucker," I tell him as I head back to Shirtless. He's looking inside the apartment until he sees me then looks away. I'm not the least interested in what's in there. It's probably as drug laced as these two ass-holes. I have two damn shooting forms to fill out now, thanks to these two. I have to justify why I fired my weapon. Damn Snowood!

Shirtless leers at me over his shoulder.

I look at his wild eyes and almost ask him if he's fuckin' nuts. Only … I know the answer. I pull my ID folder and fish out the laminated Miranda Warning card inside. I read Shirtless his rights and he nods in response.

A marked unit slides to a stop behind our unmarked unit and I wave down to the patrolmen who step out. For a moment I look up at the moon. It's as bright as a silver jack-o-lantern; and I swear, the man in the moon is grinning at me.

Shirtless starts crying. I pull him away from the wall.

"He did it," Shirtless says. "He killed him. I swear."

My stomach bottoms out for a second. We stop and I look at his eyes again.

"He killed Jimmie. He did it."

Slowly, I step around Shirtless and reach into the apartment and flip on the light. It takes a moment for the scene to register – a floor littered with half-empty pizza take-out cartons and dozens of white trapezoid-shaped Chinese food cartons – walls painted purple and pink – a bright green sofa with the body of a heavy-set white male.

Shirtless lets out a little cry behind me.

I feel vibrations on the balcony and Snowood's high-pitched voice echoes. He's telling the patrolman about Wyatt. I lean out and tell the first patrolman to hold on to Shirtless.

Tiptoeing, I move in and check the body, my instructor's voice from the police academy echoing in my memory. "Your first duty is to render aid to the injured."

He looks to be in his late twenties with long, greasy hair. Draped across the sofa, he wears a yellow tee-shirt and cut off jeans. No shoes. A thin ligature is twisted around his neck. A blue tongue protrudes from his mouth. I touch his throat and it's cold. No pulse. His wide face is flaccid and waxen with the unmistakable dull look of death.

Stepping back on the balcony I see everyone heading down the stairs.

"Snowood! Who's up for the next murder?"

"You got me, pardner." Snowood shoots me a shit-eating grin for a second then lets it fall away. "Why you askin'?"

"Get Mason on the LFR. And get your Country Ass back up here."

Snowood leaves Shirtless and Nunchakuer with the two patrolmen. He bounds up the stairs, removes his Stetson and wipes his brow with his free hand.

"Come on, Wyatt. Ain't no time to fuck around."

I step out of the doorway as he arrives and point over my shoulder at the scene. His jaw drops. It actually drops. And he looks at me as if I did it.

I grab the fringe on his shirt and pull his hillbilly face down to my level. "It's Thursday. Nothing happens on a fuckin' Thursday!"

He looks back at the body, then back at me and pulls the fringe out of my hand. Straightening the fringe, he shrugs. "Well, Wyatt. Sometimes ya' just get bushwhacked."

Jesus!

A half hour later, our sergeant arrives. Rob Mason, in his freshly cut flat-top, his black tie disheveled, his lean face as weary looking as his faded khaki pants, steps up to us as we stand next to the pool.

Snowood pulls Shirtless and Nunchakuer around in front of me, takes off his hat and tells Mason, "Well, sheriff. It was like this. We were a moseying around that there pool when this desperado (he points the Stetson at Shirtless) bushwhacks ole Wyatt with a goddamn sword. Wyatt shoots the fuckin' sword out of the desperado's hand and into the pool. Then this other desperado (the Stetson points at Nunchakuer) waylays ole Wyatt with one a those nunchaku things. *And Wyatt shoots it outta his hand too!*"

Snowood puts a hand on Mason's shoulder.

"Sheriff, as God is my witness. It was the finest exhibition of gunplay since the O.K. Corral."

Snowood waves his hat in the faces of the two prisoners and sneers at them. "Boys, this'll learn ya'. Never, ever fuck with Wyatt Earp."

Mason narrows his tiny eyes at me and slowly pulls the ever-present cigarette from his mouth.

"What the fuck is this idiot babbling about?"

I tell him straight and he doesn't blink until I finish two minutes later. He takes a deep drag on his cigarette, then flips it into the pool. He looks up at the balcony at the patrolman standing outside the apartment door. A motley collection of civilians is assembled at the far end of the balcony.

Mason looks back at me. "Where's the sword?"

I point to the pool.

"We're gonna need it." He starts for the balcony and the crime scene.

I turn Shirtless around and uncuff him.

"What ya' doin'?" Snowood asks me.

Tucking my cuffs back into my belt, I lead Shirtless to the pool and shove him in. When he comes up for air, I tell him don't come out without the sword.

"Hey," I call to the patrolmen assembled at the foot of the balcony stairs (crimes scenes draw as many curious cops as civilians), "y'all shine your flashlights into the pool so this asshole can find his sword."

Several of the cops chuckle as they step over to shine their lights into the scummy water. And we all stand there, lights bathing the green water as Shirtless dives for his sword. The motley crew at the far end of the balcony leans forward to get a better look.

It takes Shirtless four dives before he comes up coughing, sword in hand. He dog-paddles with it to my side of the pool and hands me the sword, handle first. I take it.

Shirtless tries to climb out and I step on his head and tell him to go get the nunchaku too. It takes him four more dives. He tosses the nunchaku out and climbs out, still coughing.

"I probably caught some disease," he whines.

Snowood steps up and waves an index finger in front of the man's nose. "That's what ya' git' fer fuckin' with Wyatt Earp."

Shirtless stands and I see it coming. He snatches the Stetson and tosses it in the pool. Snowood reaches for it and almost falls in himself. The Stetson plops into the scum and slowly sinks.

Shirtless walks away from Snowood, to the cheers of the motley crew in the background. He gets two steps away before Snowood wheels and catches him by the neck. And for a moment, I watch a Loony Tunes Cartoon. Wiley Coyote has the Road Runner by the neck, jerking him up and down, up and down. Shirtless bounces, his arm flailing. Snowood growls like a rabid canine.

I step over and grab my partner's arm.

"All right, Doc. That's enough."

Snowood lifts Shirtless as high as he can and drops the man. Shirtless bounces once and lies prostrate at my feet. Snowood turns and looks back at the pool, his face red, his breath coming out in short rasps.

Two newly arrived patrolmen rush up and grab Shirtless. I ask one to cuff him and put him in their car.

It takes Snowood a minute to catch his breath. He steps over to the pool's edge and looks into the water.

"Need some light?" a patrolman asks, which causes everyone, cops and civilians, to roar with laughter.

Snowood turns to me with a hangdog look.

"That was my favorite hat."

"I know." I pat him on the back. "I know."

I look up at the moon and the man is sticking his tongue out at me. I smile wearily and tell the man in the moon, "I know. I know."

Snowood looks up at the moon and says, "That's a coyote moon."

I shake my head, figuring I'm about to hear another story about Whispering Gulch or Dead Man's Hollow.

"The night weren't a total loss," Snowood adds. "You finally called me Doc, didn't you, Wyatt?"

Jesus, help me.

***

The sword lies on Snowood's desk, next to the nunchaku. I have the first of the shooting forms in my beat up Smith-Corona and I know I'm going to be here all damn night.

It's hard concentrating as Snowood goes through his monkey-shines, describing in minuscule detail how ole Wyatt shot the sword out of one desperado's hand and then shot nunchucks out of a second desperado's hand. We're surrounded by the entire Detective Bureau evening watch. The place reeks of burnt coffee and cigarette smoke.

"The first desperado went 'Hiyaaa!' and we all know that's the war cry of the Northern Cheyenne . . ."

I pick up my phone and call Lizette. She answers after the second ring.

"You're still at the office?"

"Paperwork," I tell her.

"I thought you were coming by." Her voice sounds harried. I close my eyes and envision her face – those gold-brown eyes, her long dark hair, and those full, imminently-kissable lips.

"You want to hear the latest my mother's pulled?"

Oh no, here it comes.

"Sure." Why not. This is the night for loonies.

"We're riding from the Cathedral to Gallier Hall in horse and buggies."

Jesus!

"And not just you and me. Each bridesmaid has her own buggy."

I start laughing. I can't help it.

"It's not funny."

The laughter comes out harder. I cover the mouthpiece.

"Dino! It's not funny."

I can't catch my breath.

"Dino!" She huffs on the other end of the line. "*Dino!*"

I suck in a breath but can't stop laughing. Everyone in the squad room laughs at Snowood who is showing them nunchaku moves now.

"*Dino!* Is everybody laughing at us?"

"No," I manage to say. "Snowood!"

"Oh." Her voice drops an octave. I hear her breathing as she waits for me to quit laughing.

I manage, until I hear myself ask, "You mean we're going to be in a parade?"

"Exactly. Twenty-one horse and buggies right through the French Quarter."

I lose it again and almost drop the receiver. My side aches as I laugh until I cough. Lizette is still on the line when I recover.

"It's not that funny," she says but her voice has lost its anger.

"Do we get to throw beads and doubloons?"

She almost laughs.

"So how was your night?"

I hesitate. Why upset her? Being a cop's wife is not going to be easy. And there's enough lunacy at her house.

"Fine," I tell her. "No problem. Just paperwork . . ."

Area D.C. cop Eugene Kingsley is an ace homicide detective.
Will his expertise allow him to get away with murder?

THE KINGSLEY AFFAIR
Quintin Peterson

I'd known for about six months that my wife Delilah was having an affair with my former partner and so-called friend Lyle Cummings, but it was just a week ago that I decided to kill them … though the idea had been forming in my mind for some time.

I don't know how long they'd been betraying me before I found out. I learned of their affair quite by accident. I came out of the shower one night and found that my wife wasn't waiting naked for me in our bedroom. When I didn't find her on the first floor, I sought her out in the basement. Before I could make my presence known, I overheard her in our rec room, whispering lovingly to someone on her cell phone, telling him how much she would rather be with him than me, how she hated the sight of me, hated my very touch; how making love to me was an ordeal she had to endure.

I stayed out of sight in the stairwell and continued eavesdropping until she hung up. Then I slipped back upstairs, undetected. Soon after, she came to our bedroom, disrobed, and climbed into bed. There she acted as though I was the love of her life. Her performance was flawless. I played along, of course, despite the fact that she now revolted me. Love and hate are two sides of the same coin – heads love, tails hate. Her infidelity had tossed the coin and it had come up tails. From that day on, I stopped making love to her. Instead, I screwed her with anger and treated her like the dirty whore she was. Apparently, she never knew the difference.

Later that night when she was sound asleep, I checked the call log on her cell phone to get the number of who she'd been talking with while she was downstairs. My intention was to track down the identity of her lover via phone records, a simple task for a police officer such as myself. Imagine my surprise when I recognized my buddy Lyle's cell phone number.

Some would argue that a man of my age, disposition, and supposed wisdom should have known better than to marry a younger woman, period, let alone a beautiful, young, self-serving sexpot from the wrong side of the tracks like Delilah Evans. My first wife even went so far as to describe her as a home wrecker not a homemaker. Evidently, merely becoming involved with her on a purely physical level was shameful, but marriage was a travesty. I was old enough to be her father; in fact she was one year younger than my own daughter. One former girlfriend had the nerve to ask me if I had molested her daughter Mia when we were seeing each other, Mia being the same age as Delilah. I pointed out that the notion was absurd because Mia was only ten years old when we were involved. "I am *not* a child molester!" I protested. Another ex told me that I had turned to a little girl because I couldn't handle a grown woman. According to all who bothered to express their opinion, I deserved whatever bad things happened to me because of my foolishness. But the heart wants what it wants.

Of course, the fact that she was an up and comer who, with my help, had made a name for herself as a successful realtor at her tender young age, wheeling and dealing million-dollar properties and pulling down substantial commissions, did nothing to "legitimize" my relationship with Delilah in the eyes of my family and friends. They were not impressed that she was apparently mature beyond her years or that she was cordial and well versed in politics, literature, film, art, and fine dining. (Though they had no idea that she herself couldn't boil water.) The consensus was that she was a gold-digger and that I was just a cradle-robbing Sugar Daddy; that she didn't love me and never would and that I had mistaken lust for love.

They were wrong, I argued. I told them that there was far more to our relationship than mere physical attraction on my part and much more to Delilah than her looks; that she was a decent, caring, bright young lady who appreciated me for qualities she couldn't find in men her own age: intelligence, kindness, trustworthiness, loyalty, dignity, generosity, and wisdom. She once told me that I had gravitas, and I was as touched that she thought that of me as I was impressed that she knew the word. It means substance, weightiness, a dignified demeanor. Delilah considered me to be a dignified man of substance. She'd told me so and I'd believed her. I'd already made her wealthy, so why would she flatter me needlessly? What did she have to gain by lying to me when I'd already seen to it that she had everything?

Then we got married. Brother! One would have thought that I

was the village idiot. As things turned out, perhaps everyone was right.

I have been a detective for most of my police career, starting with four years in vice, which is where I met Lyle when he was a rookie investigator. I trained him and later partnered with him for seven years in Homicide until he transferred to the Special Victims Unit. There were four years with the hotel burglary unit and almost eight years now with Homicide, where my high closure rate has made me the envy of my peers. So investigating Delilah and Lyle and keeping tabs on their tawdry love affair was a breeze.

They met frequently at the Hilton during the initial stage of my investigation, and only sometimes at his house or mine, depending on my or his wife Melissa's work schedule. Love in the afternoon. But soon, they began to have their trysts almost exclusively at our homes, with the occasional quickie in their automobiles, in properties Delilah was showing, or in parks and other public places. I guess that was for the added excitement generated by the possibility of being caught in the act. Nothing fuels lust like danger.

When Delilah was out-of-town for a week "visiting her aunt" in Syracuse, which coincidentally was the same time Lyle was away in New York City attending a Fraternal Order of Police Convention, I installed wireless miniature digital camcorders and microphones all over my house, all hooked to a control center hidden in the attic that I could access via the Internet using my laptop or any computer. I could watch them "live" and also record their torrid, sweaty sex sessions with more positions than showcased in the Kama Sutra, which I could play back whenever I wanted. To my chagrin, their triple-X encounters revealed to me that my lovemaking paled by comparison. It was the difference between a child's leisurely pony ride at a petting zoo and the front-running jockey's home stretch at the Kentucky Derby. Seeing her in action with Lyle, her facial expressions and her moans of ecstasy and the vigor with which she participated, I realized that I'd never seen the real Delilah, and knew with certainty that I had never satisfied her sexually. Never, not even when I screwed her with anger. It had all been an act, great performances worthy of Golden Globes, Emmys, and Oscars. And despite the fact that it tore me apart, I watched the sordid recordings over and over and wallowed in all of the emotions generated by their shameless betrayal: jealousy, envy, despair, rage, and hatred. Above all, hatred.

The pivotal recording revealed Delilah's desire to get rid of me

… and Lyle's professed complicity … although I'm still not entirely certain that he actually meant what he told her. He could have been just humoring her to keep the sex coming.

Sweat drenched and spent, caressing each other in my bed, Delilah the femme fatale whispered … no, *cooed* into Lyle's ear, "… Gene's pathetic, he can't satisfy me at all, baby, but you make my toes curl …" and "… God sure blessed you. I'm so sore …" ending with "… all we've got to do is make it look like an accident. Shove the old fool down the stairs or something, say he fell. He's heavily insured. *Heavily*. We've even got insurance that pays off the mortgage in the event of a spouse's death. You can divorce Melissa and we can travel, see the world. You can get rid of Gene, baby. You're a homicide detective, so you know how to get away with murder."

Funny thing was Delilah was already worth as much as me, maybe more. Sure, I'd helped her acquire her first apartment building, but she took to acquiring investment properties like a duck to water. When she was plotting my demise with Lyle, she already owned four apartment buildings, just like me. Nothing fancy, just small places with four apartment units, two one-bedrooms and two two-bedrooms, with laundry rooms in the basements. But these modest buildings provided excellent cash flow. One third of the rent she collected from tenants took care of the mortgages, escrow accounts, property taxes, and property management fees, leaving the other two-thirds of the monies as profit. And, like me, she owned the washers and dryers in the laundry rooms, unbeknownst to the renters, under the business name of Premium Coin-Op (I called mine Supreme Coin-Op), which provided hassle-free extra revenue from the properties. Not to mention her real estate commissions. That's how we were able to get our fabulous home, that and her insiders' information on properties before they hit the market.

So you see money as her motive for killing me was outrageous. A divorce would have yielded her half of everything, but half wasn't good enough. She wanted it all.

I would never have imagined that Delilah was just plain greedy. Oh, I knew from the start that she was ambitious and materialistic, but I would never have believed that she was greedy. But what do we really know about people anyway? Aside from what inadvertently may be revealed to us over time, we only know what we choose to believe about them and what they choose to show us.

Not even the day before I made my decision, that day when I

discovered that they were plotting to kill me and run off together, did I decide to kill them. Sure, I'd thought about it, but I still planned to use the evidence of the affair I had compiled to get an uncontested divorce as well as bring charges against them for conspiracy to commit murder. No, it was something simple and innocuous that occurred at a cookout that brought murder to the forefront of my mind.

We were at the Hendersons' Fourth of July cookout when it came to me. I was watching Delilah and Lyle playing volleyball, on opposing teams composed of tanned and fit beautiful people. Delilah was teamed up with Dorothy Henderson, Dot's teenage daughter Ruthie and Lyle's wife Melissa, and Lyle with Jeff Henderson and his grown sons Bobby and Danny.

Delilah was eighteen years my junior and so were Lyle, Melissa, and Dot. Jeff and I were the two dinosaurs, but at least Jeff, who is three years younger than me, is athletic and enjoys physical activities, while I'm resigned to being over-the-hill and content with drinking beer, smoking cigarettes, and watching. Watching is my favorite pastime, in fact. And I especially liked to watch Delilah.

Dot, Melissa, and Ruthie are lookers too, but Delilah was really something special. She was perfect ... well, she *looked* perfect. Everywhere we went people just couldn't keep their eyes off her. She was young, gorgeous and sexy, just this side of slutty, in fact. Whenever the weather permitted, and sometimes not, she always crammed her luscious body into clothes that showed off her shapely long legs and ample bosom; clinging, too-short skirts or shorts without a telltale panty line – she wore thongs or nothing at all – and skimpy tops that were tight and low-cut, made out of no more material than that of a handkerchief.

Bronze and glisteningly with a light due of perspiration under the afternoon sun, she giggled like a school girl as she attacked the game with vigor, occasionally brushing away from her lovely face any errant strands from her magnificent head of shoulder-length auburn hair. Braless, her ample, firm breasts bounced, jiggled, and strained against the threadbare top button of her formfitting blouse, her erect nipples prominent beneath the shear fabric. It seemed the loosely attached button was about to pop at any moment, a thought I'm sure was also foremost in the minds of Jeff and his sons, as well as good ol' Lyle. *"Pop,"* I'm sure they were all thinking. *"Please, pop!"*

When the game ended – I can't say which team won – the teams gave each other congratulatory hugs. Lyle's back was toward me when he hugged Delilah. He whispered into her ear and just then the scene seemed to unfold in slow motion. She looked directly at me over his shoulder as she listened to Lyle and her full sensuous lips framed her perfect smile…and then she laughed. And I *knew* that Lyle had made a crack about me and that she was laughing at me, that *they* were laughing *at me*, like I was some kind of goddamn clown. *That's* when I made up my mind that they had to go.

Cheat on me, betray me, plot to murder me, sure, but nobody laughs at me. Nobody!

As I watched the shameless adulterers cavorting at the cookout, Delilah's words resounded in my mind: *"You're a homicide detective, so you know how to get away with murder."*

For several days, I was consumed with plotting their deaths, how best to murder them. Informed by experience, ever mindful of the mistakes made by common murderers with a similar motive; I concocted and dismissed several scenarios. So-called untraceable poisons and staged accidents would not work for two, a staged street-robbery-gone-bad was far too clumsy and risky, and murder-for-hire was out of the question because of the loose end of the hired killer. Although I could eliminate the killer after the job was done to ensure his silence, that scenario was still too complicated, chancy, and messy. Like the other ones, it just wouldn't do. No, the best way to dispose of Delilah and Lyle was to make their deaths look like a murder/suicide. That way, the case would be closed almost on the spot – the lead detective would have his murderer and as I'd naturally be the number one suspect as her spouse, I need not worry about being a suspect for very long, even though I planned to have a good alibi that no one would bother to check up on anyway. What better way to get away with murder?

Where to commit the murders was my only concern. My house was definitely out of the question because of all of the video surveillance equipment I'd installed. But all I had to do was wait for an opportunity to present itself. Opportunity knocked soon enough.

The lovebirds gave me what I needed during their last sex session at my house. Lyle told Delilah that his wife Melissa was going to be out-of-town visiting her mother in Albany over the weekend and that they would have the house all to themselves. They arranged to meet several times that week, making sure that she could get away for their rendezvous without raising my suspicions. I had their entire schedule … and was able to choose the best time to execute my plan. Sweet.

Melissa caught her plane to New York Friday afternoon. Lyle and Delilah planned to meet at his house at 7:00 o'clock that evening.

Delilah told me a couple of days before that she had to go to closing on a property Friday evening so she'd be home later than usual. I told her that I didn't mind because I was working the 1500-2300 tour of duty that Friday and Saturday, filling in for Lt. Menzer.

Imagine her surprise when she arrived at the Cummings' home and I answered the door instead of Lyle.

My service pistol in hand, I smiled and said, "Come in, honey."

"G-G-Gene," she stuttered, before stepping into the foyer. "I-I thought you were working. W-what are you doing here, dear?"

"I *am* working, baby," I replied. "Everybody at work knows that I'm on the job right this minute. I'm having lunch, and then interviewing a witness in the Temple murder case." I let that sink in, the fact that I had an alibi, and smiled. Then I asked her, "What am *I* doing here? What are *you* doing here? *That's* the question."

"Oh, I stopped by to see Melissa ..."

I cut her off. "Melissa's out of town. You know that. Besides, you told me you were going to be closing on a house at seven." I glanced at my watch. "It's seven now."

"Uh, Gene, well, the closing was postponed," she lied. She paused and then added, "You still haven't told me why you're here, hon."

"Neither have you ... hon," I said. "But you don't have to. Lyle's who you're here to see." I motioned with my gun and said, "Come on, he's over here."

Delilah stood there trembling. I pointed my gun directly at her.

"Over here, Delilah. Go on ahead of me."

She complied, moving ahead of me on shaky legs.

"T-t-take it easy, G-G-Gene ..."

"Oh, I am, sweetie," I said, "I *am* taking it easy. Keep walking."

She almost collapsed when she saw the corpse of her lover seated in his *La Z Boy*. His brains had been blown out of his left temple, his left shoulder and the right side of the reading lampshade next to him covered with gore.

"Oh, God!" she cried, her body trembling uncontrollably as she stared at her dead lover.

Shortly before Delilah's arrival, Lyle had also been surprised to see me when he'd opened the front door to find me standing on his porch instead of Delilah. He'd tried to play it off, but he was visibly shaken, knowing that my wife would arrive at any moment. I asked if he was going to let me in and he struggled to come up with a plausible excuse not to. I saved him the trouble. I pointed my Glock at him and said, "Back up."

I walked in and closed the door behind me, forced him to take me to where he stored his service handgun and took possession of it. Afterward, I marched him back to the living room, ordered him take a seat in his recliner, and then stood behind him. I told him in detail about my knowledge of his affair with my wife and their plot to murder me. He denied my accusations. Then he begged for his life.

He started to stand, but I commanded him to stay seated and to keep looking straight ahead.

"Laugh at me now," I told him.

"What?" he asked.

"Laugh," I said. "Let me hear you laugh."

I pressed his service handgun to his right temple, pulled the trigger, and made the mess the treacherous bitch was whimpering about.

"Shut up," I yelled at Delilah. "You'll be together again soon."

I moved quickly around the sofa to position myself in front of her and behind Lyle.

"You wanted to break off the affair," I told her, "but he couldn't live without you. So, he killed you, and then turned the gun on himself."

"No, G-Gene, no," she begged.

"Laugh at me now," I said.

Delilah looked puzzled.

I shot her once in the chest, right through the heart. She folded like a lawn chair.

I put Lyle's gun in his right hand, extended his arm as far away from him as possible, and raised the gun, pointing the muzzle at the ceiling. I put his dead finger on the trigger and then fired once into the ceiling, the idea being that just before he'd shot her, he first fired a warning shot to stop her in her tracks when she was attempting to leave, and then ordered her to turn and face him before he shot her in the chest. But the primary goal of doing this was to make sure that he had gunpowder residue on his hand.

After the ceiling shot, I placed the muzzle of the gun to his temple, right up against the entry wound, and then let the gun fall from his hand to the floor near the right side of his easy chair.

I walked over, looked down into her dead green eyes, and whispered,

"You won't laugh at me anymore, you ungrateful whore." I then quickly left the house, took off the rubber footies and latex gloves I wore to prevent crime scene contamination, shoved them into a pocket of my suit jacket, and then made my way back to my cruiser, which I had parked a few blocks away. I then drove to a witness's house not very far from Lyle's place, a Mrs. Lorraine Haskell, stopping briefly on the way to toss the gloves and footies into the Potomac.

I interviewed Mrs. Haskell for about a half-hour regarding the Temple murder case. Afterward, I drove back to Homicide HQ. I made certain to be seen by as many detectives as I could, talking with them and subtly establishing the times of my contacts with them. Hell, with one of them, I even used the old "my watch has stopped" ploy, and asked for the correct time so that I could set my watch. Ham-handed but effective.

I had made sure not to bring attention to the exact time I was at Luigi's Italian Restaurant where I had dinner just before I went to Lyle's house, and paid in cash so there would not be a credit card receipt to pinpoint the exact time I'd paid my check. I just made certain that employees could place me there sometime that evening. It didn't take much. I just complimented the help on their service and said things like, "This Pasta Primavera is excellent! Give my compliments to the chef." You know, that kind of thing. After all, it was busy, as usual, so no one would really remember exactly when I was there that evening only that I *was* there.

Around ten o'clock that night, like a concerned spouse, I started calling Delilah's cell phone and leaving her messages: "Where are you, baby? Give me a call." Etcetera. Just before midnight, I started calling Delilah's family members, co-workers and friends, first apologizing for bothering them at such a late hour, adding that I had gotten their phone numbers from Delilah's personal address book, and then asking if they had seen her. She'd told me that she was going to be closing a deal on a property that evening, but I hadn't heard from her since early that day. She wasn't answering her cell phone and no one else had heard from her. I was worried about her. And when I was through, they were all worried too.

The following morning, people were calling me, asking if I'd heard from her, and then conveying their sympathy. How was I holding up? And my answer was that I was a complete wreck. Yes, I'd reported her missing, but so far police had turned up nothing. "Sweet Jesus," I moaned, "Please, God, let her be alright."

I had practiced and my performance was convincing.

I'd also practiced considerably for my performance when the police informed me of Delilah's death. "God," I moaned to myself in the mirror, checking out my facial expressions. "Dear God, no!" But that was over the top.

"No," I whispered. "No."

Perfect.

I was practicing in the mirror when you came to my house this afternoon, well ahead of the timeframe I'd predicted as the earliest the bodies would be discovered. I believed that Melissa would discover them when she returned home from her trip to New York. When I opened the door and saw you, it was a struggle to conceal my glee. *Here we go*, I thought. *The death notification. Okay, get into character…*

Imagine my surprise when you showed me the arrest warrant and told me that I was under arrest for the murders of Delilah Kingsley and Lyle Cummings.

I still thought that I had a chance to beat this rap, right up until you played the video footage of me killing Lyle and Delilah. There's no way I can win, not when a jury actually sees me pulling the trigger. A trial would be a waste of time and money.

***

Homicide Detective Raymond Larkin nodded. He turned to Detective J.A. Jones, the videocam operator recording Eugene Kingsley's confession, and ordered him to stop taping by way of a simple slashing motion with his right hand across his own throat. He then directed Detective Jones to leave the interrogation room by pointing at the door. He wanted a moment alone with the man who had taught him everything that he knew about murder investigations.

When Jones exited the room, Larkin turned back to Kingsley, picked up a pack of cigarettes off the table, and offered Kingsley one.

Gene Kingsley took one from the pack and Detective Larkin lit it with his Zippo, and then lit his own.

"Thanks," said Kingsley. He drew in deeply and then exhaled before continuing. "Who'd have thought that Lyle's wife would have hired a private investigator to get the goods on Lyle … and have surveillance cameras and microphones set up all over her house …"

"Just like you," Detective Larkin interjected.

Kingsley smiled and nodded. "Yeah, just like me. I sure didn't figure it. I underestimated Melissa; I thought she was oblivious to the whole affair. And who would have figured that there was an honest P.I. out there who would actually report the murders and turn over evidence to the police instead of blackmailing me? Wonders never cease."

Kingsley shook his head. He took another drag and then blew smoke rings into the stale air. He chuckled and then looked Detective Larkin in the eye.

"You gotta admit, Ray, if Melissa hadn't hired that P.I., I would have been home free. Without that video, no one would have been the wiser. I would have gotten away with it. My murders were perfect."

Larkin exhaled blue smoke and nodded in agreement. "Yeah, Gene. Perfect."

Only PI Jack Hagee could set out to propose and find the air filled with bullets instead of love.

A FINE OFFICER
A Jack Hagee Story
C.J. Henderson

Sally and I had just gotten done ordering. We were in the Spumoni Gardens restaurant, my favorite neighborhood place. My name's Jack Hagee. I'm a private detective. I cover the city, but I live in Brooklyn. Sally is Sally Brenner, a local news anchor with more than a foot in the network doors. We weren't celebrating anything special, just the beginning of that feeling – if you're old enough, you know what I'm talking about – that stirring above the loins, that finally, maybe, possibly...

We'd both been married before, her for fifteen months, me for seven. Both of them a long time ago. We were long past our pain, though, closing in on getting past our suspicions as well. To make a long story short, to me a partnership was beginning to look like a good idea.

Dinner was supposed to start with the minestrone, followed by us splitting the cold seafood antipasto, orders of fried calamari, shrimp Scampi, and the veal in mushrooms and onions, all to be divided with a great deal of romantic nonsense. On the side we were supposed to have linguine, hers with white clam, mine with red sauce.

The Gardens bakes its own bread – it's really good. They also give you a free order of baked clams whenever you have dinner there. They used to do it for everyone, I hear, back in the day. Now, it's only if you're a good customer. Really good, they might even throw in dessert, a.k.a. their world-class spumoni. It's a nice touch, I hear.

We never saw it that night, though. We never saw any of it. No, wait – we did get to see the soup. We never tasted it – but we did see it. I remember...

I remember we were smiling, staring at each other through the light from the candle in the cheaply blown red glass holder at the table's center. We'd only known each other nine months – not real long, but – long enough. It must have been. Being with her, it made everything, what could I call it ... better.

It made the candle in its 99-cent store cup seem like a vague shimmer surrounded by cut crystal. The white, hard-creased cotton tablecloth hung like French linen, dazzling with the flash and shine of the Arctic snows at noon. The warming smell of the fresh bread was a passport out of Bensonhurst to some back street in Napoli, where the air outside wouldn't have been the second most polluted on the continent, where the language in the streets would have been one of love, and where the waiter approaching the table wouldn't have been bringing a message along with the minestrone.

"Excuse me, Mr. Hagee, you have a phone call at the door station."

I gave Sally an honest I-could-skip-this-in-a-heartbeat looks, to which she responded, "No, go on. It could be important."

Striking a Latin-lover, matinee idol pose, I whispered with a French accent, "Nothing is more important than our passion, my sweet." She flashed me an oh-gawd look, then burst out laughing, telling me;

"Don't worry, I'll be right here. I won't even touch my soup until you get back." Then she took my hand and squeezed it, "Go on, you big goof."

I smiled – my eyes darting her a look that promised adventure – then turned and walked the eight steps to the phone. On reflection, I should've never taken so long.

"Yes?"

"Why do you not carry your cell phone?"

I grimaced. It was Maurice, a freelance operative who works for an information specialist named Hubert.

"I didn't want to be bothered."

"Such a charming person." Something in the voice on the other end of the phone kept me listening, despite the banality of the conversation up to that point.

"Say 'hello,' big white person."

Circumstance has pulled the three of us together on a few jobs. What he could want I had no idea. When I asked him to get on with it, he posed a question of his own, his lisping voice filled with mischief. "What do you think of my peoples, the black peoples of this world?"

"Is there a point to this?"

"Oh, yes, I would think so."

"Christ, there better be," I growled. "What's going on?"

"Sincerely, big Jack, I must beg you to listen – please, like a good boy. I am considering a matter most delicate. My life will be in the balance if it is learned I have passed on the information I have for you, so – I must wonder – is it worth it to me to relay it to you? Believe me now when I tell you that time is short and just respond to the question. What do you think of black people?"

"Brother. You picked a fine time for this." I almost hung up, but something in the back of his voice told me to give him his answer. "I think the same thing of black people that I think of all people – that we ought to kill off all the stupid ones in the hopes that if we get rid of all the stupid people everywhere we might have a better world. I know that wouldn't leave very many blacks, but then again, it wouldn't leave very many whites, either. Now what's the goddamned point here, huh?"

There was a long pause, one that almost snapped my patience, until finally, Maurice's voice came through the phone again.

"Ultimately, a good answer. I am forced to admit that if Mr. Hubert trusts you, well then, so must I. Listen to me, darling. Have you ever heard of the Domino Boys?"

Who hadn't? The most ruthless of New York's black gangs, their colors were worn in the shape of dominos – white paint on black jackets. They got a dot for every white person they killed. At least, that was the rumor. Maurice informed me that the rumors were true.

"That is not all. There are two double sixes now, Raymond Green and Martin Albert, or as they are known in the street, Mailbox and Picnic."

Swell, I thought, two of the city's prize murderers – men that killed grandmothers and babies just to run up the tally of white people they've killed – men the courts wouldn't put away because of the pressure groups frightening off their judges and juries – now had something to do with me.

But what? I wondered. Maurice continued to answer that question for me in his own fashion.

"Both of these charming lads are now wanting to claim gang leadership. The Domino Boys move a great deal of `merchandise' in our humble hamlet – making kingship of their gang a not unattractive position. Neither will willingly give up the throne. They are both popular...and popular boys always have many followers..." His voice hit a whisper.

"A physical dispute within their little social club would be very unattractive – police and politicians and reporters getting involved – this is not what they want."

I tried not to let what was running through my brain show on my face. From the look on Sally's face, it wasn't working. Maurice, not able to see either of our faces, continued.

"So, to avoid a civil war, the gang's chief wizard has come up with a way for them to settle their dispute. They have picked a well-known, but supposedly not-easy-to-kill white target. Whoever kills this target is the new leader. Very practical...yes?" He paused for a breath. I didn't bother. I'd forgotten how. He started again.

"This information was sold to Mr. Hubert's organization early this afternoon. But, alas, he was not here – he is not even in the state. I processed it approximately one half hour ago. It has taken me this long to find you. Mr. Hubert would have moved heaven and earth to do so, I am certain. But ... I do not love you as much as he does. Do you understand what I am telling you?"

I did. Pushing the nerves out of my voice, I asked, "Are they are on their way now – here?"

"You are not that hard a man to find...obviously," he paused for his effect. "I am surprised you are still on the phone."

I hung up. I was back to the table in three paces, throwing money at the red glassed candle, grabbing Sally's arm, apologizing to the waiter, dragging the woman I loved up out of her chair like I would a wino I wanted off my stoop. As she began to protest I spun her around. Grabbing her with both hands I growled;

"Shut up. We're leaving. Now – move!"

I propelled her through the door and ran for the parking lot, digging my keys out of my pocket. I give her credit – she understood that something was wrong. By the time she reached the parking lot, I had the trunk open and was digging into my road survival kit – three-pound coffee cans filled with automotive, bad-weather, or accidental-disaster gear on top, other kinds of disaster gear on the bottom. I pulled the .45 free and tossed it to Sally. She caught it with a look that told me she had a feeling I was expecting her to use it. She was right.

Dragging my shotgun up from the bottom without clearing everything out of its way first, I caught it under one of the cans. With a tug I sent the can flying out into the parking lot – flashlight, batteries, candles, wax-coated matches, disposable light, red bandanna – other things – who cared? The stuff slammed a car behind me – glass cracked. By that time I had clips for both weapons stuffed in my jacket pockets.

Trunk lid down – around the side of the car, have to get the right key ready, fingers shift, shift dammit! Key ready, passenger door open – inside – fast. Sally follows. I ram the ignition key in – turn over you beast, turn/turn/turnnnn...got it. We leave. I hand her a clip as soon as I can drive with one hand. She sends it home. I wasn't worried – I know what she can handle. The `klik' makes us both feel better. Once we were out of the lot and headed off into the darkness, she sensed it was safe to talk. She pretty much knows what I can handle.

"Jack," she said, sounding a kind of surprised I didn't think she could be. "You're sweating."

I told you she was a good reporter. She doesn't miss a thing. Keeping my eye on the road, I answered, "Yeah, big hairy bucketfuls."

"Do you plan on telling me why?"

"Yeah, I do." Drifting through a red light, not daring to stop the car completely, I told her, "Now you listen to me – that call – someone just gave me word I'm on the Domino Boys' hit list."

"What? Why? What for?"

"They pulled my name out of a hat. Two hot wires named Picnic and Mailbox need a bull's-eyed white boy to prove a point and I got elected. That tell you what you needed to know?"

She sat back against her seat, letting frustration slam her neck against the headrest. "Things like this wouldn't happen if we didn't live in this crummy city."

I made a sharp turn around a hard left, agreeing that there was no doubt she was right. As we cruised down Eighty-sixth Street in the dark, shying away from the streetlights, I suddenly pulled over to the curb next to a row of public phone stalls. Seeing them reminded me that it might be a good idea in the future to carry my cell phone turned off on important nights. Leaving the engine running, I turned to Sally, telling her;

"Stay here. Keep your eyes open. I'll be right back."

I had to get some kind of official help. Once a gang ruling is handed down, it's law. I couldn't hide for the night and expect things to blow over. The hunt was on, and it wouldn't stop until either I dropped both Picnic and Mailbox or they killed me. Of course, I could hide out for a month or three, wait for my reputation to dry up and blow away, then I wouldn't be worth hunting anymore. Yeah, I liked that option all right.

Slipping around the car, I edged into the first phone shelter only to find the mouthpiece broken off. I moved on to the second and lifted the receiver to my ear only to find it silent – dead. Grabbing down the receiver to the third, my heart skipped a beat on hearing a dial tone. I rammed in a quarter and punched in the number I wanted. The machine spit my change down and ordered;

"Forty-five cents for the first one minute, please."

I jammed the coins in as fast as I could, fighting the panic scratching at me, trying not to drop the receiver. The phone asked again;

"Forty-five cents for the first one minute, please."

"I gave you the..."

Then I caught myself, stopped yelling at a machine, got my coins back – I dialed again, fed change in again – the phone didn't care.

"Forty-five cents for the first one..."

I hung up, stepping back from the phones, balling and unballing my fists, reining in my anger. There was one phone left. I tried again. It rang. I shuddered as the grateful joy of hope needled through my body. A desk officer from the precinct I live in picked up on the eighth ring. I demanded to talk with Captain Fisher. He put me through.

"Yes?"

"Captain Fisher – Jack Hagee."

"Hagee?" He said my name with exaggerated surprise. "Aren't you dead yet?"

"No. And I'd like to stay that way."

"Well...good luck. I heard about the shit comin' your way. Toooo bad." He laughed in a sick, green kind of way. "I can't wait to see the morning papers."

I gripped my temper, the strain filling my face with blood flush, roped anger throbbing my head with pain.

"Captain. Through no fault of my own, I'm in one bad place all of a sudden. I would really appreciate some police protection."

"Oh, you want some protection, do you?" he sneered – his voice filled with payback. "Hire a detective, wise guy."

Fisher. The bastard and I go back a long way. None of it friendly. Fate has forced me to dog my way out of a number of situations at his expense. I knew two things. One, that every cop in the city would know about my problem right now, and that, two, Fisher was the only one I could call that might give me anything that resembled the truth. I don't care what you're willing to believe about the police. I knew at that moment that half the cops in the city would have sold me out in a New York minute if they'd known where I was.

The only actual friendlies I have on the force are in Manhattan. My one chance in Brooklyn was Fisher. Elsewise, I was on my own. I'll never know if I would have tried any harder to get his help if I only had to worry about myself – but I wasn't by myself. If I couldn't get him to do his job I was a long, far way from anything else that could get Sally clear. I did what I had to. It wasn't enough.

"I'm not askin' – I'm flat crawlin' and humble as you want me. I'll cut any deal you'll take. Name it. Just get me and my girl friend out of here."

"Forget it, tough guy."

"Just her, then – just send a car to get her clear. Do it – what's it going to cost you?!"

His voice sneered. I knew what was coming, but craven hope kept me glued to the phone. "I'm gonna do you a favor and save you embarrassin' yerself further. I'm gonna let you know right now that I ain't gonna do nuthin' for you. Die, you fuck scumbag, you bastard shit fuck – die!

"Big fuckin' deal, hot shot Jack Hagee. Me help you? I hope they take your woman and do things to her that'll fill the front page for three months. I hope they fuckin' tear your balls out and shove them down the throat of her severed head and leave the whole fuckin' thing on a pike somewhere on a roof in Bed-Sty where it rots for twenty years before anyone finds it.

"Tell me where you are, you fuck – I'll tell `em myself!

"Tell me!!"

"I'll tell you where I am," I growled, seething hate through the damn wires at him, "I'm out in the street...coming for you." I gave him a beat to let it sink in, then I told him, "You tell anyone you want to. It doesn't matter. You're dead, Fisher."

I hung up and headed back for the car, not having the time to waste on threats. Moving away from the curb, I said;

"Okay. The police are not going to help us."

"What else is new?"

"Not much. And that makes it big question time."

She stared at me, damned if she'd say anything and give me an opening. I breathed out – hard – through my nose, then pushed my teeth apart, and asked;

"We've got to make up our minds fast what we're going to do. Do you want me to dump you somewhere? Is there any place I can get you where you'll be safe?" I looked her in the eye and told her the truth.

"Nowhere's safe for me. No one with me is safe until I get clear of this. And that's not going to be easy." She swallowed, dry-throated, gravel filtering through her velvet voice.

"Tell me one thing, Jack." I flashed her a look that said "go ahead." She continued. "What's going to be easier? I think we both know I'm going to be a target in this, too. Let's face it, there's no way they don't know about me. Do you think the Domino Boys are above taking hostages? Do you think there's anything they're above?"

I let silence hang as an answer. She understood.

"That's what I think, too. So, tell me...are you better off with me or without me?"

"Goddamnit, Sally, that's not the point!" I turned onto Highlawn Avenue–highly white neighborhood – easier to spot the enemy. "Things are going to get fuckin' deep around here – and soon!"

"Then make up your mind," she spat back at me. "Yes, I'm afraid. I'm afraid to stay with you and I'm afraid to be by myself." She shuddered in a way that made her neck seem brittle and alien. "If my opinion counts for anything, I want to stay. I'd feel safer with you. Shit – who am I kidding – in this city? I'll just plain be safer with you. Period. My only fear is that worrying about me might slow you down and get us both killed."

"I'll be honest, sweetheart," I told her. "I'm going to be worried about you wherever you are."

"Then I want to stay."

I spun the wheel, turning down Kings Highway toward Ceasar's Bay. Things were moving too fast for me – all of them things I hadn't planned on having in my evening. All I'd wanted to do was take out my girl friend and make her my fiancée. That's all I'd wanted. Now the two of us were running for our lives from the death tag hung on me by a gang of murdering thugs. The only guy I could count on in any real way was out of town – anyone else I could pull in would only get killed along with me. The closest police wanted me dead worse than the gang. Only in Brooklyn. God – I hate this city.

My best option was to get Sally in front of the cameras. Grouse about gang violence and the police's inability to protect citizens. At least get her safe and off limits. Some people might worry about what that would do to their image...some people think there's nothing wrong with using the rent money to buy drugs when their family needs food...some people beat their children for telling the truth. The world's full of people – most of them stupid.

My next move was to ask Sally if she knew of any helipads open that late at night – a quick chopper to Manhattan and she'd be safe – I never got to ask. As I flicked my vision toward her my eyes ran over the rear-view mirror, spotting the car tailing us. I told her;

"Well, I thought I had a great plan, and I did – but it's a little too late."
She turned, seeing what I meant.

"Are you sure it's them? And are they sure it's us?"

"Pretty sure – both counts. Which means this party starts the second they're as sure as we are." Turning down one of the darker side streets, I checked to see that my shotgun was still balanced where I'd left it. "Better get ready."

Sally cocked her .45. I listened to the slick crack of the metal, remembering the last time I heard it in her hand, felt her remembering it as well. She reached over and took my hand, squeezing it lightly.

"Jack...?"

"Yeah, sweetheart?" She paused for a long beat, the silence scaring me more than the violence rolling up behind us. Finally, she whispered;

"Kill as many of them as you can."

I looked over at her, squeezing her hand in return. Why not? Raindrops splattered down out of nowhere. It was a light sprinkle, but also a complete surprise. Knowing I'd get no better chance, I hit the gas a sudden blast. The Skylark rolled up to a rapid sixty, tearing down toward the end of the block with me laying on the horn the whole way.

The car behind sprang to life a touch too slowly, but tried to make up for it with violence. Automatic weapon fire blew out my back window, splashing glass against both of us. Sally hit the floor. I hit the gas.

I made the right at the corner, stop sign ignored, oncoming cars ignored – almost too closely. The car behind spun out at the corner, barely avoiding the already skittish traffic I'd stirred up, its back bumper burning sparks across the left side of a fast black Caddie. It made it across the lanes of traffic, though, gunning to catch us.

Roaring down Twentieth, I stayed on the horn, dodging across whichever lanes were open, using the sidewalk only once. Eighty-sixth Street produced a red light and an unbreakable wall of cars pouring along under the elevated train. I turned sharp to the right, tearing into the thin lane between the traffic and the parkers, skinning my way between cars both stationary and moving, and the massive steel-and-concrete pillars holding up the railway. The car behind followed for a moment but lost it, piling into an oncoming truck. Traffic from the other direction jumped around us – cursing, hating.

Hanging a U-turn no more dangerous than any of the other shenanigans I'd been pulling, I screeched back to the accident scene. Leaving the motor running, I hopped out with my shotgun. People on the sidewalks moved back toward the walls of the buildings – few of them leaving the area – waiting to see what would happen next. Using the butt of the shotgun I knocked out the driver's window and then pulled him head first out where I could see him. He was black, wearing Domino Boy colors – enough to make him guilty in my book.

Leaving him hanging out of the window at the waist, I slapped him awake, then stuck the shotgun in his face. "Where are Mailbox and Picnic," I asked. He didn't answer. Not out of courage; he was just too groggy. Slapping him again, I spit wet spray in his face then yelled;

"Picnic! Mailbox! Where are they?!"

A bullet flashed past my head. I brought the shotgun up to window level and blasted the inside of the car, nailing the shooter, showering the crowd on the sidewalk beyond with bloody bits of glass. Shrieks rang out from the crowd. I didn't have time to worry about them. Turning back to the driver, I slapped him again, looking for the same information. He moaned, trying to answer.

"Picnic...Picnic...he, ooaughhaagggghhh–da pain, da pain–I'm dyin', man. I'm dying."

I grabbed him and shook him. "Tell me where Picnic and Mailbox are, or..."

"You kilt Picnic, man. Dat's hims in da back. AaaaahhhHHHH–hahaaaa, oh God, man. Hep, hep me, pleasssse – I'm dyin'. Hep me."

"Yeah, I'll help you. Give me a quarter, I'll call your parole officer." I slammed his head with the shotgun. He lost a tooth. I nudged him again. "Where's Mailbox?"

"I don't know," he answered, drinking blood. "He and his boys, dey went down Coney. Agggghhhhh–ahh ahhh ah ah ahhh ..."

More blood started gushing from his mouth, propelled from something breaking deep inside him. I headed back to the car, knowing I'd get nothing more out of him. Jumping in, I gunned the motor and headed up Eighty-sixth in the opposite direction. I wasn't worried about witnesses. Half would say I was black. The rest would say there were ten of me.

Looking over at me from her side of the car, Sally asked, "What do we do now?"

"I've got an idea."

"Is it a good one?"

"Will be if it works." Figuring she deserved at least a scrap of good news, I told her, "One of the delinquents in the car was Picnic. That's one down."

"Why don't you sound happier about that?"

"Because I can't just ditch the Mailbox and walk away. That would just be a challenge to the whole gang. I've got to finesse this thing, and I don't have a whole lot of time to do it."

"And," she asked, with all the right in the world, "what exactly is it you think you're going to do?"

"I told you," I answered with an insincere grin, "I've got an idea."

"If it's as bad as that fake smile you're wearing, let me off at the next bus stop."

"That's my girl," I laughed. She punched me in the arm, a good, solid shot just like I'd taught her. Hurt like hell. As I made a right off Eighty-sixth and headed for the Belt, she asked;

"Are you at least going to propose before we both get killed?"

I spared one eye to glance over at her to see if she was serious. She was.

"Now?" I asked her.

"Yes, now. That's what this whole night was all about, wasn't it?"

"Well, yeah," I admitted, feeling the three-grand bulge in my jacket pocket. "I guess."

"You guess," she mumbled darkly, her head dropping halfway to her chest. She scrunched her eyebrows down the way someone does when they've reached their limit. Knowing better than to fight her along with the Domino Boys, I pulled into the tennis court parking lot down from the Narrows. Fishing the ring out of my pocket, I turned to her, noticing myself in the rear-view mirror. My eyes were panic-narrow, darting and blood shot. My hair was strand-smeared with sweat. I didn't look real good. She didn't look much better. Taking her hand, I said;

"Sweetheart..."

"Don't you `sweetheart' me..."

"Awww, now look – I really don't have time for this kind of bullshit. Do you want a goddamned proposal or not?!"

"Yes, goddamnit! I want you to fucking propose to me!"

"Christ!" I growled, the edge in my throat deep and rasping. "You're making me fucking crazy. Goddamned bitch – will you marry me or what?!"

"I'll marry you!" she screamed back.

"Fine!"

"Fine!"

At that point we both got quiet, then we looked at each other and laughed. She shrieked to the point of silliness, tears awash in each of her spring green eyes. I half-laughed, half-barked, choking myself so badly I couldn't talk. Finally when we were both calmer, I asked;

"Did I just propose...I mean `marriage'?" She smiled at me and nodded shyly. "And, did you...like...accept?" The smile became a grin; the nodding moved up from shy.

"Well, then," I said, pulling the ring from my pocket, smiling myself, "I guess this is yours."

She grabbed it and slid it on quickly, as if I was going to change my mind. While she admired it in the headlights of the passing cars, blinking through the sweat running down her forehead, I told her;

"I'm sorry things worked out this way. I had a much smoother number rehearsed for the restaurant – honest."

She smiled at me again, this time in that unguarded way women smile during those special moments when they think there's some hope they'll someday actually be able to communicate with the man in their life. I smiled back in that way men do when they try to convince those women that they're right. I would have thought we were both too old to actually be in love, but maybe that's what it was. Not wanting to worry about it at that moment, though, I told her;

"We're going to have to get going."

She looked at her ring one more time, then nodded, her lips drawn straight and tight. "This plan of yours...?"

"What about it?"

"Try to make it a good one," she told me, quietly, actually looking more beautiful than ever as she did it. "I want to live long enough to tell our kids about the night Daddy proposed."

As I pulled my Skylark back out into the traffic flow, I told her;

"I'll keep them in mind while I work out the details."

***

I glanced over at the convenience store's phone booth, one of the last left in the city, Sally hidden behind the shadows of its door glass' reflection and the gloom. Looking out the window I saw that the rain had slowed to a drizzle again. Handing the place's bony young counterman a twenty I said, "Pack of Camels." As he slid them over toward me, I added, "keep the change."

He stared at me for a moment, narrow-eyed, off-balance. He knew I wasn't a powder merchant, or a polit, or anyone else who should be passing it out. He pocketed his tip, though, then slipped into a bored stance – one that would allow him to stay uninvolved if he didn't like the answer – as he asked;

"What's the deal, man?"

I glanced out the window again, telling him, "Just my way of saying thanks for letting me tie up your pay phone."

"Yeah, right." Then, after a second, he broached the obvious, "like everybody don't have cell phones dese days. You got heat on yo' ass, man?"

"Don't worry. Nothing's going to happen to your store."

That brought a high-pitched, reedy laugh from deep within his skeletal frame. Pulling a fat joint from his front shirt pocket, he fired it, laughing as he muttered, "Shit – I don't cares what happens to dis place no way."

I smiled, understanding crap jobs and crap employers and how much loyalty anyone owes them. He appreciated my smile and returned it. As I took another look out the window, he asked;

"Hey, you covered, man? You cool?"

I smiled back at him. "Cool enough...but thanks."

"Anytime, man."

The phone rang. No one doubted it was the call we were waiting for. Sally let it go twice, then picked it up. I'd made contact with the Dominos – with Mailbox, really. I'd made him a proposition. Now I'd find out what he thought of it. Sally talked into the receiver for a moment, then waved me over. The counterman offered me a hit. The service was a long time back, but a guy always knows the smell of the good stuff. I didn't even hesitate. At that point, who cared?

I exhaled, gave my benefactor a wink and a nod, then turned and crossed the store. The counterman's eyes shifted for a moment toward a spot under his counter. Taking the phone, I asked;

"So...is it is or is it was?"

A voice without access to merriment chalked its way through the phone. "Yo' kilt Picnic." I admitted to "kilting" Picnic.

"Das cold business. Yo must hump a big picture o'ch yoself. Why da Dominos care 'bout yo?"

"Picnic's dead, Mailbox. You're in charge."

"A white man gotta die. Das what da Wizard says."

"I'm ready if you are."

"Everyone agree – yo woman can witness, den she can leave."

I strained, listening to every tone in his voice. If I could've looked into his eyes, even seen him at a distance to watch the heat in the air around him...but I couldn't. All I had was his voice and a heartbeat to decide whether or not he could be trusted.

"Yo comin', o'what?"

"The Boardwalk pier?"

"Dass what we said."

"We'll be there."

Hanging up the phone, I looked down at Sally, still sitting on the tiny stool bolted to the wall. I nodded, head down, lips tight. I could see her heart clench, watched time stand still around her for a second as she gathered more courage to her out of the scant energy in the air. As she stood up, shaking out her hair and her tension, I said;

"You know, you don't have to do this, now. You can just get on a train and head in to the city."

She looked at me without speaking, which was all the answer I needed. Turning back to the counterman, I told him, "Well, here goes nothing."

He snorted, laughing as if he had just gotten a joke. I wasn't so sure what was funny, but his tone told me that it wasn't me. He opened the door for us, saying, "Kick their ass, boss."

I smiled. So did Sally. As she took my arm, we stepped down to the sidewalk, the counterman coming out behind us. As I turned, he leaned toward me in earnest.

"Man, I don't know what's landin', but I'd sure like to be there when it do. S'cool?"

I thought about it for a hard second, then shrugged one eyebrow upward, indicating his security shutters. "How long, ah...?"

Pulling a corrugated wall down with one hand, he spun three large locks around on two fingers of the other, answering, "Darnell. Just take a minute – one minute."

I looked at my watch and nodded.

***

The approach to the Coney Island fishing pier is only about twenty feet off the ground where it first branches off the boardwalk up on the beach. By the time you actually get to the pier, however, the land has dropped off to where you are about sixty feet above the water. At least at low tide, which is what it was that night.

Darnell, Sally, and I walked across the boardwalk's zig-zagged slats, heading for the pier, trying to make out through the darkness and the rain just how many figures were waiting for us. They were hunched too close together for us to tell. As the dotted jackets started to come into focus, though, the counterman said;

"Shit."

"You've got time to go back," I warned him.

"White boy bad enough to walk into that – they know everybody want see that kind fun. Your knees ain't meltin'? Neither's mine."

Sally set her shoulders straight, blocky – back high and tense. Her eyes stayed forward – so did mine. No use looking to the sides. You do that when you're looking for something. We knew where the fun was going to be. We continued forward with gang members all around us – lounging – yawning. Waiting.

We reached the end of the pier, stopping just a few feet onto the massive end fishing platform. The Domino Boys' grand wizard came forward, shaking a pipe at us – half-lead, half-glass – wrapped in colorful strips of leather with a small mammal's skull attached to its end. The mouth was open, snarling sharp teeth aimed at my face. We had to make magic on each other. He went first.

"You bad news, pink thing. I wish you die six times tonight. I wish your guts spilled, your blood in rats' bellies. I wish the dark curse of all the lives taken by Domino hand come down on your head – die pink thing. Die six times!"

"Curse you, too," I spat back. "Curse the killers in the darkness. Curse all the night things that fear the light. My pity to your mother."

Lightning split the sky then. I had had a lot more to say, but I let it hang there, knowing when I'd been handed a good moment.

"This's it," came a voice from the side. One of the elders of their tribe, one of their oldest and wisest – I made him at twenty-three – came forward from the outer rail, pointing out toward the boardwalk. All eyes followed his hand through the drizzle. A police cruiser was rolling across the zigzagging planks toward us. The car turned onto the approach walk, moving slowly down to our position.

It parked a few feet beyond the gathering bodies, a lone figure getting out from the driver's side. "I am so happy to be here," called Fisher. "You just can't imagine."

Black forms moved in on all sides of the car, checking its contents, ushering Fisher forward onto the stage the pier had become. Rubbing his hands together, he jerked for a second when a Domino security man asked for his gun belt, then he complied, dropping his service piece and cartridges into the outstretched hand.

"Mailbox is going to carve you up like a broiler, you bastard."

"Maybe, but not before I do you."

The smile dropped from Fisher's face. He sputtered, "What the fuck are you talking about?"

"He mean dat da night has changed." A large black man dressed in flowing silk came forward. I recognized his dead voice – Mailbox. "Da only fight we here to see be you and him. Two in da center. One walk away, one sleep with wet sheets."

Fisher turned to stare at me, hate seething from his eyes – his mouth a straight line, tight, shaking. He looked about at the ring of faces hemming him in, at Mailbox, at me. His finger stabbed at me;

"Just another one of your low shit punk tricks."

I shrugged my shoulders – nodding, smiling.

"Afraid of him," shouted Fisher at Mailbox. "Afraid of one miserable white guy. You nigger bastard."

Mailbox smiled wide, the insult such a pitifully small thing. "Poor little Fisher," he laughed. "Get too hot, eh Fishie? Just like Picnic. Dat's why you both lose. I keep my head, Picnic run to kill. Now Picnic dead. But da night say, white man must die. Hagee not get hot. Ask to become Domino. I says `you ever kill white man?' He says `I kill plenty man. All colors.' He make me laugh. We tell you Hagee come to duel on pier – invite you to see. You come. Now you two fight. One die. One walk away. Domino magic served."

Mailbox stepped back, finished with what he had to say. Fisher came toward me, shaking his head, looking as if he didn't believe what he had gotten himself into. Spreading his hands wide, he closed with me, sputtering for just the right words. Then he threw himself forward.

I couldn't believe I'd been taken off guard by such an old gag. We went down in a thrashing heap across the wet boards, me hitting first, Fisher crunching all his weight onto me. The crowd screamed bloody murder, all of them pushing each other out of the way, jamming forward for a better position.

We fought mostly from instinct, trying to find each other's vulnerable spots. His fists raked me in the darkness, mine him. Suddenly, though, I connected with his jaw, sending him flying backwards from me. Both of us took the moment to regain our feet. Finding mine first, I crossed to where Fisher was rising and kicked hard, booting him across the jaw, bouncing him off the crowd. They pushed him forward back to me. I sent a sidekick into his bread basket, sending him flopping backward again.

Fisher crumpled, slobbering for air. Several of the Dominos started to help him to his feet, but Mailbox's voice rang out;

"Leave him. We say we don't interfere – we means it. Dey can pick each other up iff'n dey want to. Now make it clear. Give `em room. I wanna see dead white boy eyes lookin' up at me."

Fisher used the seconds of Mailbox's speech to regain his wind. Then, coming up in a crouch, he ran forward trying to catch me in a body block, but I sidestepped him with ease. Whirling around, he ran at me again, once more missing me by a fair margin. Standing at his end of our little arena, Fisher eyed me through the darkness, then braced himself like a bull in the ring. Readying himself for another charge, he sucked in his breath, then came at me again – moving at top speed, head down. I sidestepped him once more, wondering at the stupidity of his attack, and then I understood. He hadn't been trying to hit me at all.

Plowing into the knot of Dominos at the entrance to the pier, he knocked them to both sides, clearing the way so he could make a run for the boardwalk. Having been warned by Mailbox not to interfere, the Dominos remaining in his way let him go. They knew whose job it was to stop him. So did I.

I started running after Fisher, straining to overtake the lead desperation had given him. He kept running flat out, never turning back – no glances over his shoulder – smart enough to know that someone would be after him – smart enough to hope it would only be me. I cursed him as we ran the length of the pier. I'd been caught off guard – badly. It hadn't dawned on me that Fisher would abandon the patrol car he had arrived in, run right past it in the hopes of reaching some lonely street cop on the Coney beat.

I'd closed to where I could hear the thuds of his feet hitting the boardwalk along with mine, watch the splash as each one hit. Fisher was strong – no easy opponent, but he'd been an officer, been behind a desk just a little too long. He was losing his wind, starting to drop a few inches with every forward lunge. Grateful to be the few inches taller than him that I was, I poured on more steam, pushing with everything within me to catch up to him as I listened to the war cries of the Dominos coming up behind me.

By the time we were closing on the boardwalk we were only a few yards apart. I knew he could hear me gaining on him, could feel the power draining from his legs. My hands were extended in front of me, grasping for the back of his shirt, his collar, belt, hair – anything that would have given him to me. Suddenly, though, he tricked me again, faking to the right then hard-wheeling to the left. The turn sent me off balance, slipping and falling on the soaking boardwalk.

I'd been so sure Fisher would head for the right, toward the amusement center and its lights and people, it never dawned on me that he might go to the left. There was nothing there. The boardwalk went on for what looked like miles in that direction, but with no places to hide, nowhere to run to except the old parachute ride.

Making use of his gained seconds, Fisher bent low to grab something strapped to his leg – the darkness keeping me from seeing what – and then continued on through a hole in the fence into the area of the abandoned ride. I followed him in as soon as I was on my feet, moving cautiously, eyeing the center of the massive tower of rusting girders and plating. I knew where Fisher was – the problem was knowing what kind of weapon he now had. A knife was no big problem – a gun was another matter.

I could hear no sounds from the inside, the building rain and the howls of the Domino Boys drowning out any noise Fisher might be making. Knowing how much good standing out in the rain was going to do me, though, I started forward, peering through the drizzle into the blackness of the parachute ride's base.

As I moved forward, Fisher came from the left of the gaping hole, charging, knife held high. His downward stroke caught my shirt, but not me, tearing it open from collar to bottom. I swung but missed him, ducking back too early to avoid his next swing. The knife kept me at a distance, backing up across the jaggedly broken concrete upon which the parachute ride sat. The wind outside was picking up, whipping the ride's old cables against its sides, banging out its fury.

Fisher stabbed at me from waist level, trying to get me to back up over the edge of the concrete – an easy thirty-foot drop. I took two steps toward where he wanted me, but on the third I pulled back and to the side, my hand snaking out to get his wrist. Catching his weapon hand in mine, I shoved off with all my might, forcing him backward step after step until we crashed into the far wall. Trying to keep him pinned there, I gave him his chance, saying;

"For Christ sake, Fisher – they're outside, we're in here. We could get out through the bottom of this thing. Make it to the street. Stop fighting me, you idiot."

"Fuck you, you bastard." Fisher spat in my face while we struggled. The spittle hit just below my left eye, a sticky wad that dribbled quickly under my collar. Sick of it all then, I decided it was time to play the game Fisher's way.

"Okay. You want it," I told him, shutting my eyes, pulling in on myself, "you got it."

Grinding him into the wet rust of the wall, I suddenly let go of his empty hand. It sprang forward to push against me at the same time I swung. The blow hit his arm, jarring him. I swung again, and then again, first hitting his arm, then breaking through to his side. He went over a step, his grip loosening on the knife. I shook his weapon arm as hard as I could, using both hands after a second. He slammed his free fist against my back. The knife fell away into the darkness.

Losing the knife gave him a moment of strength which he used to push free of me. Chasing him across the broken terrain on the long dead ride's inner chamber, I slipped on the wet concrete, going down badly on one knee. I tried to stand–found I couldn't. Fisher stopped scrambling, sensing there was no bluff in my pain. Crossing carefully back toward me, he said;

"I shoulda known I could take care of you. I shoulda known you're just a fuckin' bluff."

I tried to get back on top of both legs but the pain in my knee was just too crippling. Before I could straighten out, Fisher was on top of me, kicking me in the back and side.

"Take that, you faggot bastard. Take that, take that, and that – you shit – you shit bastard, you fucking shit fag bastard fuck –"

I curled in on myself, taking each booted kick as best I could – knowing Fisher was trying to send me over the edge onto the jagged steel and broken concrete waiting below – not able to do anything about it. Rain hit my face, blowing in from the gaping holes up and down the sides of the ride. Fisher continued kicking, each move paining me further, moving me closer to the edge. Then, sensing he was ready for the blow meant to finish me, I turned and blocked his foot with my hand.

The impact of it made me think he'd broken my hand, but the block had worked. Fisher went stumbling backward two steps. Two off-balance steps giving me a small handful of seconds to think of something else to do besides lie on the ground and get kicked to death. I'd felt my car keys in my pocket while I'd been battered by Fisher. Grabbing them out now, I had them moving in a swinging arc just as Fisher came at me again. I took the kick square in the gut but, managed to ram the keys into his hip joint.

Lightning split the sky as his scream erupted. Holding on with everything I had, I twisted the keys into his leg, feeling them scrape in between bone and muscle. Fisher jerked away from me, howling with liquid pain. His screams stopped when he hit the bottom.

I lay on my side, peering over the edge at Fisher's body sprawled in the ruins below. There was no doubt he was dead. Sally was at my side a moment later, making sure she wasn't a widow before she became a bride. Darnell stood behind her, smiling. Mailbox stepped into the interior of the ride as they helped me to my feet.

"So, you got him." He smiled at the irony of the situation, rain splashing off his perfect teeth. "Now you a Domino."

"Yeah," I agreed, trying not to fall over. "I'm just the luckiest boy in the world."

Fisher's patrol car, still parked on the end of the pier, exploded suddenly, all of the Dominos in sight headed away from it. Mailbox grinned at me again.

"Guess you better take yourself on outta here," he paused for the effect, then added, "...bro."

"Yes, sir. Massa."

Mailbox wheeled and stared at me, searching my face for enough defiance to allow him to break his word to me, to let him finish me off. Being my normal stupid self, I tried as hard as I could to work it up for him, but I didn't have enough left in me to do it. He laughed again, heading for the exit, calling over his shoulder;

"You takes care o'yoself, Hagee. I be lookin' to sees you again."

I let his crack go unanswered. Breathing was tough enough – thinking seemed impossible. Sally and Darnell managed to get me down to the street levels of the park before more cops could arrive, alerted by the burning car on the end of the pier. It defied the rain, sending its smoke up as an offering, a distant point of light behind our backs.

Darnell helped Sally get me into my car, but turned down our offer of a ride. "No, thanks," he told us. "I got people I gotta tell about this."

As he walked off into the rain, Sally slid the Skylark into drive and headed us for my apartment. I could tell my leg wasn't broken. I'd just hit a nerve, torn the skin, alerted some old injuries that I wasn't dead yet – enough fun to almost get me killed but, nothing permanent. Enough to keep me from driving, though.

The next day, resting at home, I caught my fiancée on the tube, reporting on the "mystery" surrounding Fisher's death. She told the city that the police had no leads, that it was a shocking crime, that Fisher was a fine officer with an outstanding record, and that his murder was just one more sign post that New York City was on its way to ruin.

I clicked the set off, petting my dog Balto's head as he lay by the couch, wondering about Sally's report. Of course, I knew, she above anyone else was going to lay it on thick to help me cover my tracks. Not that I was overly concerned. No matter who knew what, everyone who could do anything about the situation also knew Fisher was in bed with the Dominos. No, I was fairly secure that anyone with such knowledge was going to be doing all they could to keep that can of worms as securely sealed as possible.

Noticing that Balto already had his favorite squeaky toy in his mouth, I pulled it free and threw it through the hallway into the bedroom, the big lummox chasing after it instantly.

"A fine officer," I thought, watching Balto claw his way under my bed for the toy. As he pulled himself out and headed back with his prize, I said aloud;

"Well, who knows? Maybe he was – once."

Then I took Balto's toy from him and threw it away again, waiting for his return.

In 1880 Sheriff Dan Brayton took on the Dutch Bascum gang in a legendary showdown and won. Now, thirty-eight years later, the fledgling movie industry is making a film about the shootout called Code of the West. But another showdown is looming. The sole surviving member of the old Bascum gang is waiting for the real Sheriff Brayton's arrival so he can settle an old score ...

FOR COURAGE AND HONOR
Michael A. Black

I guess old Whitey heard about the job with the motion picture studio the same way I did – the newspapers, but it wasn't until after I'd already started that he showed up.

We'd been filming a couple of weeks and Mr. Creighton, the director, had a reporter come out and do a follow-up story on how we were making a moving picture called *Code of the West* about the famous Contention City Shootout that happened in 1880.

The papers played it up big, since it was an actual historical event and all, and especially since the real-live hero of the shoot-out, Sheriff Dan Brayton, was coming out that month to be sort-of an advisor to the filming of the gunfight in which he and his deputies shot it out with the Dutch Bascum Gang. A few years back a man named William Henry Cox had written a book about it called *For Courage and Honor*.

Whitey showed up the next day asking if we could use a laborer or groom. Mr. Creighton hired him on the spot when he saw how skilled Whitey was with horses, which was good for me because it elevated my job from extra to stuntman. I was about the same size and build as Arthur Weeks, the famous stage actor from New York that was playing the role of Sheriff Dan Brayton. Mr. Weeks was a real good actor, but trouble was, he didn't know much about being a cowboy. He couldn't rope or shoot, and when they set him up on top of a horse the first time he just about fainted.

When Mr. Creighton saw how I could do all those things so well, he made me what they call a stunt double, meaning that whenever they had to film a shot of Sheriff Brayton riding or jumping off his horse, they'd just have me dress up in Mr. Weeks's costume and take his place.

I saw a couple of the pictures afterwards and you could hardly tell the difference. I played some bad-guy roles too. In all, it up'd my pay to fifteen dollars a week, plus board, which was ten dollars more than I'd signed on for.

I could see right away that Whitey was an old cowboy and that he knew a lot about horses. His face was brown and creased from the sun and the wind, and first thing in the morning he moved like he had a thousand-and-one aches. But he was still up before all the rest of us each day brushing the horses so they wouldn't get any sores from wearing the saddles. And at lunch break he'd always go around and loosen the cinches some, then walk the horses off before putting them away at night. He didn't say much to the rest of us, and kind of looked down his nose at the crew members who pretended to be cowboys but didn't know much about riding and roping and such.

One day we were eating lunch and I was sitting under a big maple tree reading the copy of *For Courage and Honor* that I'd taken out of the town library. The book had actual photographs of the real Sheriff Dan Brayton and the outlaws after they'd been shot. It even had one of the actual Dutch Bascum Gang all dressed-up like dudes in suits and derby hats. Whitey was watching me, then meandered over and asked if I minded him sitting there.

"Plenty of shade to go around," I said.

He grinned and sat down next to me.

"Name's Whitey Hedlund," he said, holding out his palm.

"Tim Bishop," I said, shaking his hand.

He put his coffee cup on the ground between us and started scooping the beans off his plate. When he'd finished he set the plate on the ground and nodded over at my book.

"What you reading, Tim?" he asked.

"It's about the Contention City shoot-out," I said, closing the book and handing it to him.

"Is that right?" he said, pinching a bit of tobacco from his pouch between his thumb and forefinger. He stuck the wad inside his lower lip. "Pretty good, is it?" He wiped his fingers on his pants then paged through the book.

"Yeah," I said. "It's real good. I'm just about at the end of it. Want to read it when I'm done?"

Whitey looked at me for a moment, his lower lip bulging out from the tobacco, and shook his head. I suddenly wondered if maybe he couldn't read, because he kept lingering on the pages with the old photographs. But he closed the book, looked at the title, and then said it out loud, sounding out the words real slow.

"*For Courage and Honor.*" He paused and seemed to consider this for a moment, then handed the book back to me. "Well, now I never much trusted all that stuff they put in them books," he said, punctuating his sentence by sending a long looping stream of spit out about four feet in front of us. It was immediately swallowed by the dry earth. He grinned and said, "But maybe I will take a look-see at that one when you're done."

Whitey noticed that I knew what I was doing around a horse, and little by little we began to talk more. He asked where I was from, and how come a guy who talked like I did knew so much about being a cowboy.

"I grew up on a farm in the Midwest," I told him. "When I was seventeen I enlisted in the army and they trained all of us as cavalrymen."

"See any action?" Whitey asked me.

"Yeah, some," I told him. "I was with the American Expeditionary Force in Peking during the Boxer Rebellion. How 'bout you, Whitey? Ever in the army?"

Whitey spat out some more tobacco juice and shook his head.

"Not hardly," he said. "But I seen my share."

His grin was wicked, suggestive, and I didn't doubt that he'd been around the bend more than once.

That next day we set up for a rehearsal of the gunfight scene. Mr. Creighton had Arthur Weeks all dressed up in a bright blue shirt that buttoned up the side. The large sheriff's star on his chest had a dull white look to it, so it would show up better on the film, I guess. Weeks had on a high, Texas-style Stetson, even though the actual gunfight had taken place in Arizona.

I had a small part as one of the Bascum gang this time. We were all dressed in dark outfits with black hats, and I was supposed to get shot and fall off my horse as I was shooting while trying to run away. We did a run through with Mr. Creighton sitting in a canvas-backed chair with a big megaphone shouting as to where he wanted us to be, and how he wanted everybody to move.

We must have done it at least a dozen times before he said he was ready to film it. I went over to check my horse's cinch to make sure it was tight, because I was going to have to throw myself off and needed a good solid base. Whitey was standing there scowling at us. Mr. Creighton walked by carrying a large white hat, and Whitey shot a stream of spit off to the side.

"Tim," Mr. Creighton said. "Can you handle a gun?"

"Yes, sir," I said. "Fair to middlin'."

"Good," he said. "I need you to take this hat out and shoot a hole through the top of it." He showed me an X on the top of the Stetson. "I want one of the outlaws to take a shot at Arthur when they ride up ostensibly to get their amnesty papers. We'll stop filming at that point and substitute this hat for the one Artie's wearing now."

I nodded and took the hat.

"You got a real gun, sir?" I asked. We had plenty of prop guns around, but they just fired blanks.

"Why, no," he said. "I figured you'd have one."

"I got one in the stables," Whitey said, his voice low. He spat another long stream in the dust and motioned at me with his head. I followed him off toward the large barn at the edge of the western town the studio had built. Whitey had set up a small room for himself in the rear. He pushed open the doors and walked the length of the stables to the back. Stopping at a wooden door, he took out a set of keys and opened the padlock that hung on the hasp. Inside, the room held a small cot, a few shirts, and a spare pair of pants hanging on a rod near the window. Next to the bed was a wooden footlocker, painted dark brown and secured by another padlock. Whitey stooped and slid another key from his ring into the lock. After popping it open he lifted the lid and took out two shiny Colt revolvers. Each was fitted in a fine leather holster with its own belt.

I gave a low whistle. "Are these actual Peacemakers?"

Whitey nodded. He slipped one of the weapons out of its holster and handed it to me. I felt the weight of it in my hand, and admired its polished sheen. It was obvious that Whitey took as good care of his guns as he did of the horses, and I told him so.

"Always take care of your gun, son," he said. "Never know when you might have need for it." He stooped and grabbed a box of cartridges, then let the lid of the footlocker slam closed. "Let's go out back so we don't scare the animals none."

We went out about a hundred feet or so in back of the barn where everybody piled up their garbage till someone got the gumption to bury it. Whitey stopped and held out his hand for the Stetson. I gave it to him and he walked over to a fence post about twenty-five feet away and placed the hat on the top. Glancing around, he spotted a pile of old discarded cans and bottles, and plucked out a few and set them on the ground about three feet apart. He came back to me and handed me one of the Colts.

"You want to get the feel of it?" he asked, opening the box of cartridges and handing me six. He took out a handful himself, folded the end back into the box, and began loading his gun. I slid the six rounds into the cylinder and popped the catch closed.

"I assume as an ex-cavalryman that you can shoot?" Whitey said. He buckled on his gun belt and then pinched some fresh tobacco from his pouch.

"Pretty well," I said.

Whitey nodded over at the row of cans. I raised the pistol and sighted in on the last one on the left. Thumbing back the hammer, I squeezed off a round. It skimmed through the dirt a few inches next to my target.

"It's been a while," I said smiling.

Sighting the weapon again, more carefully this time, I squeezed the trigger. The can flew in the air. Whitey spit some juice on the ground and grinned at me wryly.

"In my day a man didn't always have the luxury of a second shot," he said.

I was about to say something when he quickly drew his pistol and shot it four times. He seemed not even to aim, but each of the three remaining cans jumped with an explosive bounce. The Stetson cascaded off the fence post and onto the ground. I walked over and picked it up. The old man had put a bullet smack-dab through the tiny X that Mr. Creighton had drawn on the hat.

"Whitey," I said, flabbergasted. "I never seen such shooting. That was real swell."

"Like I said, a man don't always get a second chance." His eyes looked cold and hard as he spun the cylinder to remove the spent brass.

When we shot the scene it worked real good. I was playing one of the outlaws and after trying to shoot the lawmen I had to jump on my horse and start to ride away. Then, after I turned around to shoot, I had to pretend that I got hit and fall off the horse while it was still galloping. I threw myself off and tumbled into the dirt, rolling with the fall. Mr. Creighton yelled, "Cut," and turned the megaphone toward me. "Are you all right, Tim?" he asked.

"I'm fine, sir," I said, getting to my feet and brushing myself off. I'd been thrown enough times to know how to take a fall. The trick was to stay relaxed and not tense up.

Mr. Creighton seemed real pleased with the way the shoot-out scene had gone. Looking around at the flat-board walls of the roughly made buildings, the purplish mountain range looming in the background, I couldn't help wondering what it had really been like on that dusty street in Contention thirty-four years ago. I glanced at Whitey who'd been leaning sullenly alongside one of the structures with his arms crossed.

Mr. Creighton came up to me with a big smile. He always wore a suit coat and one of them small-brimmed hats that seemed better suited for some city like New York or Chicago. He pushed his little gold-framed glasses up on his long nose before he spoke.

"That was great, Tim," he said. "Really great. You keep this up and maybe we can star you in a one-reeler next time."

I grinned and nodded appreciatively, trying to imagine what it would be like to see my name up on a marquee.

"Whitey," Mr. Creighton said. "Could you bring up Thunder? I want to get a few shots of Arthur in the saddle. And, Tim, I'll need you in to change shirts so we can film you riding away."

I nodded and went over to the truck where the equipment man had an extra blue shirt with a star on it. Whitey returned with the big gray stallion that we'd used for Sheriff Brayton's horse. Thunder was pretty fast but a little bit skittish sometimes. Usually he had to warm up for a bit before he'd settle down. Whitey stopped and lashed the horse to the hitching rail.

"How soon you want to ride him?" he asked.

"I just want to get a few shots of Arthur in the saddle. Close-ups," Mr. Creighton said. "Then we'll film Tim from the back as he takes off and rides out of town."

Whitey nodded and started to adjust the cinch.

"Do I really have to get on this damn animal again?" Arthur Weeks said. He was supposed to be from New York but had more of a Bostonian accent.

"We just need some close-ups," Mr. Creighton said with a forced smile. It had been a long day and his nose was red as a beet from the hot sun. The assistant director told him he'd better put on a hat with a bigger brim before he blistered. "I guess I'd better," he said. He moved over to the equipment truck and both cameramen slipped out of their black shawls. Whitey had been patting Thunder's nose and rubbing the horse's long snout, whistling softly.

"Oh, dammit, let's get this over with," Weeks said, stepping up to the left side of the horse and jamming his foot into the stirrup. "This side, right, old man?" Weeks said. Whitey nodded, but as the actor grabbed the pommel and began to pull himself up, the whole saddle slid to the side and Weeks fell onto his butt. A couple of us chuckled, and two equipment men rushed forward to help him up. He brushed them away with angry arms and stepped over toward Whitey. Without warning Weeks drew back his fist and smacked the old cowboy squarely on the jaw. Whitey, who was a couple of decades older than the actor and a hell of a lot smaller, crumpled into the dust.

"You damn old coot!" Weeks yelled. "You caused that, didn't you? You did something to that saddle."

Whitey rolled over and started to get on his hands and knees. Weeks strode forward, drawing back his leg so he could deliver a kick. That's when I stepped in and smashed a hook into Weeks's stomach. He stopped in his tracks and bent over. Then, with tiny little steps, he edged over toward the hitching rail, but stayed all hunched over. His breath came and went in short rasps. I watched him for a few seconds more, then went over and helped Whitey to his feet. The old cowboy dabbed at the stream of crimson flowing down his leathery chin and smirked.

Between carefully measured breaths, Weeks looked over at us and raised his arm and pointed at me.

"I'll have your job for this, Bishop," he muttered. "His too."

"I don't think that's something you want to do, mister," I said evenly. Then, added with a trace of malice creeping into my voice, "Cause that would give me a reason to finish this fight."

"Damn fool," said Whitey. "Don't even know when a horse has puffed himself up. He's a good one to play old back-shootin' Brayton all right."

I looked at him quizzically. "Huh?"

"Never mind," Whitey said. "Here comes the boss."

"What's going on here?" Mr. Creighton asked, his forehead wrinkling up with worry. He'd smeared a white paste of some kind over his nose, and it made it look half-a-foot long as it jutted out from under his spectacles. Weeks was still all bent over and Creighton went over to him.

"Douglas," Weeks said slowly. He was the only one of us who called Mr. Creighton by his first name. "I want you to fire those two. They conspired together to make me look ridiculous and either they go or I do."

Mr. Creighton managed to help him get straightened up, and Weeks walked off the set towards his brand-new automobile. He got in the passenger seat and his driver started the car and took off, leaving a cloud of dust blowing back at us. "It wasn't Tim's fault," Whitey said. "The damn fool tried to get on the horse too quick. Before I'd had a chance to adjust the cinch. The horse was all puffed-up after being saddled and when he relaxed a little the cinch was too dern loose."

Mr. Creighton looked at me. I nodded.

"Some of them horses are almost as temperamental as movie stars," I said.

"I'm sorry, Tim," Mr. Creighton said with a sigh. "But he is the star. The studio can't complete the picture without him."

"Seems like you can't complete it either without Tim here doing all that sidewinder's riding and shooting for him either," Whitey said. He looked in the direction of the dust cloud and spit out a long, looping stream.

"I'll try and talk to him tomorrow," Mr. Creighton said finally. "Maybe he'll cool off by then."

I could see that Mr. Creighton wasn't too happy with the incident. He was a real good boss and I told him so. But I didn't expect that Weeks would change his mind, knowing what kind of a man he was. As Mr. Creighton told us that it was a wrap for today, I could see those dreams of my name on a marquee fading quickly.

"And don't forget," Mr. Creighton shouted through the megaphone, "Everybody's welcome at the luncheon tomorrow at the train station in town. The real Sheriff Dan Brayton will be arriving on the noon train."

"You hear that, Whitey?" I asked sullenly. "The real-live hero I been helping to play is arriving tomorrow, and we're out of a job."

Whitey spit in the dirt again and withdrew his pouch for another pinch. He held it toward me but I shook my head. He shrugged and placed a fresh wad inside his mouth.

"Come on," he said, with his distended lip. "I got me something back at the stable."

We rode back, and Whitey insisted on us wiping down all the horses and walking them off before he put them away. Then he led me to that small room in the back and popped open all the padlocks again. He rummaged around in the foot locker some and came up with a bottle. The label had been stripped off, but I could see the fine amber fluid through the clear glass. He grabbed a couple of tin cups from inside a mess kit and handed me one. I held it toward him as he pulled the cork out of the bottle and filled my cup. He splashed some into his own cup and held it out in a salute. The whiskey felt like fire going down my throat.

"Whooeee," I said. My eyes commenced to watering.

"Been saving it for a while," he said with a grin. He tipped the bottle toward me again, then refilled his own cup. "Sorry about you getting fired."

"Yeah, well, maybe I just wasn't cut out to be a movie star," I said.

"Here's to good friends," Whitey said, raising his cup again. "And honor."

The whiskey went down smoother this time. And I only had to blink a couple of times.

"So, Whitey," I said. "What did you mean about old Weeks being a good one to play Sheriff Brayton?"

Whitey ran his tongue over his teeth and grinned humorlessly.

"You been reading that book," he said, "but do you want to know what really happened that day in Contention City?"

"Sure," I said.

He held out the bottle and filled our cups again, then he settled back against the wall and got a distant look in his eyes.

"Sheriff Dan Brayton was probably the most *dishonorable* man that ever lived," he said. "He never faced down a man in his life that he didn't have covered every which way to Sunday. And most of them that he killed was shot in the back. How do you think he got that fancy job as assistant to the territorial governor after the Contention City shoot-out?"

I sipped my whiskey and listened to him ramble. His speech seemed pretty much unaffected by the booze, and he reached out several times to refill my cup, then his own.

"Dutch Bascum was an outlaw, sure enough," he said. "Rode with Quantrill after the War Between the States, then the James Boys and the Youngers when they robbed all them banks. But things was different in them days. Dutch started his own gang once all of them sorta fell to the wayside. But by then the West was changin'." He reached out with the bottle again. The fire had all but disappeared as I swallowed. "Too many lawmen, too many posses, too many railroad detectives... Lots of them outlaws got tracked down and killed. At that time a lot of the territories were trying for Statehood, so they didn't want folks back in Washington hearing tales of how wild things was. Offered up amnesty to a lot of them boys, if they'd turn themselves in and promise to be good citizens." He smiled and tilted the cup to his lips. "Dutch Bascum and his boys were on the way to Contention to get their amnesty papers. It'd been all set up. But that back-shooting Brayton dry-gulched 'em as they rode into town." His eyes looked moist and he stared at the dusty floor.

"But I thought that the Bascum gang shot it out with Brayton because they were against the amnesty program?" I said.

Whitey just snorted derisively. "Brayton let the first member of the gang ride in and get his papers," he said. "But it was just a ruse to draw in the others. After that first rider left, and the others came in…"

"How do you know all this?" I asked.

He looked at me.

"Cause I was there," he said.

My jaw fell open. He kept on talking.

"When that first man rode back and told the others it was okay, they went in and good old back-shooting Brayton cut 'em all down. Every last one of 'em." He had a vacant look on his face, his eyes bleary and not focused.

"Damn," I said. "What about the book?"

Whitey smirked and filled my cup with the last of the whiskey. "Oh, yeah. I been meaning to ask you if I could borrow it."

I woke up the next morning in a tool shed out behind Miss Dolly's Palace. It was a local establishment a few miles out of town where a lot of nice young girls made their living by having men buy them drinks. The girls did other things too. I vaguely remembered Whitey dragging me there, not that I was doing much complaining, but that was all I remembered. I blinked my eyes a couple of times from the bright sunlight that was shining in my face and started to make out two large figures standing above me framed by the doorway.

"You ain't gonna get sick, are you, cowboy?" a harsh-sounding feminine voice said. "I gotta enough problems without having to clean up another mess out here."

I blinked some more and saw that it was Miss Dolly herself talking to me. She shifted slightly, and her bright red hair shielded my eyes from the glare of the sun.

"What?" I managed to say. "How did I get out here?"

"Bruno drug ya," Miss Dolly said. She cocked her thumb at the big rough-looking ex-pug standing beside her. He glanced down at me with a smug-looking smile. "Your friend convinced us to let you stay in here. Normally I don't allow no over-nighters, but you boys was so well behaved, and that old guy could charm the rattles off a snake."

"Where's he at?" I asked.

"Him?" Dolly said. "He left a long time ago. Said he had something important to do." She flipped a sealed envelope onto my lap. "Here, he asked me to see that you got this. Gave me two whole dollars to make sure it was delivered. So here it is. Now pick yourself up and scram."

"Yes ma'am," I said. "Ah... what time is it, anyway?"

"It's eleven-fifteen," Miss Dolly said over her shoulder. "The old guy made me promise not to wake ya before noon, but I figure this is close enough." She let out a phlegmy laugh.

"Let's go, bud," Bruno said, reaching a hand out for my arm. I didn't argue. He had a hickory club dangling from his belt.

On the way back to the stables I stopped a couple of times and thought I was going to puke. Finally, I did and felt a little bit better. The blood was still pounding in my temples and my tongue felt like something that had swelled up and died. I slowed my walk and took the envelope out of my jacket pocket. It had my name written on the front. I peeled it open and started to read it as I walked.

Dear Tim,

I ain't much good at writing letters, but you'll understand why I wrote this one after today and I do what I set out to. I just got one favor to ask you. I got a son somewhere in the area of Missoula, Montana, and I'd be obliged if you'd look him up and give him this picture of me. I didn't give him much, except my name–Elwood Dodge Hedlund, so he would be a junior and about your age. Tell him his pa was a–

The rest of the line was scratched out, then after it he'd written: *Just tell him his pa was sorry for the way everything turned out and that at the end I done what I had to do.* The final line of the letter just thanked me.

I unfolded the next piece of paper and saw that it had been wrapped around a torn-out page from my library book.

It was the one with the picture of the Dutch Bascum Gang, all dressed up in their derbies and suits. I blinked my eyes studying the faces closely, and damned if one of them didn't look a lot like old Whitey, except younger and with dark hair. At the bottom of the page, in Whitey's handwriting, was scrawled: *I spent too long running. Now it's time to set things straight. It's For Courage and Honor._*

___I licked my lips and shaded my eyes as I looked obliquely up at the sun. It was pretty close to being straight overhead. That meant it was almost noon. Whitey had told them not to wake me before then, but why? The answer came to me in a flash. The train. The real Sheriff Dan Brayton was set to arrive on the train at noon. I knew he planned to do something stupid and that it was up to me to try and stop him. I started running as best I could in my boots, not thinking anymore about the aches and pains in my head. Only about getting to the town in time.

When I got to the edge of the studio ranch, I was wheezing and felt like I had to throw up some more. But I knew I couldn't stop. Had to keep going, forcing my feet to move. Then I heard a distant train whistle and knew I'd never make it in time. I was near the barn and I heard Thunder's familiar whinny. I forced my stumbling legs into the stable and moved down to his stall. Glancing toward the little room in back, I saw the door standing open, Whitey's padlock gone. Inside, the foot locker lid was propped open as well, the small room stripped of its meager contents. I took a moment to look for the Peacemakers. Both were gone.

I tossed a blanket on Thunder and looked around for a saddle. The first one I found was an old McClellan, which I figured would be good because it was so light. I strapped it on the big horse, keeping him as calm as I could, and led him out through the doors. His snout must have picked up on my scent 'cause he reared his head high and took off at a quick gallop as soon as I was up in the saddle. In the distance I could hear the echo of the train's whistle again.

I stayed low in the saddle and rode the big horse hard. It was prit-near three miles into town, and we seemed to cover it in no time flat. But as I neared the outskirts I saw the long column of black smoke belching up from the locomotive as it was slowing to a stop. I kicked Thunder's sides harder as we started along a parallel course with the tracks. Up ahead, about half a mile, was the caboose. The front-end of the train was already in the station. A huge crowd of all the movie people and a good portion of the townsfolk were up there milling about. I could see the bright red and yellow uniforms of a dress-band, and began to catch the vestiges of their slightly off-key marching-music as I rode closer.

Thunder's chest was heaving as I drew into the tail end of the crowd. I reined him to a rough stop and scanned things. Mr. Creighton was there on a stage right next to the train. The mayor and all the important studio people were up there too. I looked frantically for Whitey, wiping at my eyes with my fingers trying to clear the dust from them. Mr. Creighton was leaning on a podium, and I heard him say something about a real living legend. He took off his hat and held it out and everybody started clapping. I jumped off Thunder and lashed the reins to a near-by banister, then trotted over toward the fringes of the crowd, my head bobbling in every direction.

Up on the stage I saw an old guy dressed in a business suit with one of those string ties. He was wearing a low-cut white Stetson and dark spectacles. Next to him was a real pretty girl in a blue dress who looked younger than me. The old man's hand was on her arm, and he looked a bit unsteady on his feet as they walked to the front of the platform. He waved to the sea of applause as Mr. Creighton loudly said, "Ladies and gentlemen, Sheriff Dan Brayton."

The applause grew louder and the band's music swelled up to a finishing crescendo. I tried to push my way toward the front. Sheriff Dan, sandwiched between the girl and Mr. Creighton, had a broad smile stretched across his face. I pushed up closer, still looking for Whitey, but unable to find him. The people were crammed together so tight that I couldn't get up close enough to the front to warn them. I scanned the crowd frantically. Still no sign of Whitey.

I moved my way toward the back of the crowd and ran along-side the train to where the people had thinned out by the baggage cars. The locomotive expelled a blast of steam. Glancing both ways, I stepped up onto the metal rungs of one of the rear cars and went across the coupling to the other side. Jumping down to the ground, I caught some movement out of the corner of my eye. Someone had gone between the train cars just as I had, only farther up the line. I ran down there.

Then suddenly I saw Whitey climbing up to go through the open door on this side of a passenger car a little ways ahead. His face looked grim and intense, and he had the big Colt pistol strapped to his hip. He shot a quick glance my way, then shut the door behind him. The car was right about where the stage and Sheriff Brayton must have been. I started to call out to him, but it was too late. He had already disappeared through the opening.

I ran down to the car that he'd gone through and pulled myself up the metal rungs. The door was locked. Through the opening between the cars I could see the platform on the other side. He was already on it. Maybe I could still stop him, but I doubted it. I went through between the cars, crawling over the couplings to the other side. I crawled about ten feet ducking through the underpinnings of the wooden stage and came out near the back of the platform.

"Whitey, no!" I called out but the fading applause drowned me out.

Mr. Creighton was speaking again, and Sheriff Dan and his pretty girl stepped up to the podium ready to say something. I was rushing up to the edge of the platform when I heard the crack of a pistol above me. The noise from the crowd subsided immediately, leaving a sudden stillness, then Whitey's voice.

"Why don't you tell these folks how many men you shot in the back, you dirty low-down scum-sucking sidewinder," he said. He held the shiny Colt Peacemaker high in the air. In his other hand he had the second gun in a leather holster, the attached gun belt wrapped around it like a snake.

A murmur of sounds swept over the crowd, followed by another hush.

Whitey threw the holstered gun down on the stage at Sheriff Dan's feet.

"Pick it up, back-shooter," he snarled, holstering his own weapon. "We got some unfinished business from about thirty-four years ago to settle."

Sheriff Dan's head had rotated toward Whitey. The girl was already staring at him with a look of terror on her face.

"Leave my father alone!" she cried.

Sheriff Dan patted her arm softly, then smiled, gently pushing her away.

"We know each other, friend?" he said. Then he sniffed the air. "Smells like you been drinking some, partner."

"What I been doing ain't no concern of yours," Whitey said. "Now pick up that gun and let's settle this."

"Well, who are ya?" Sheriff Dan said.

People had drawn away from the edge of the platform now, and I was able to creep up almost behind Whitey. I was still way too far to try to intervene, though.

"Name's Elwood D. Hedlund," he said. "That name mean anything to you?"

Sheriff Dan considered this for a moment, then shook his head, his lips pulling into a thin line. The opaque lenses of the dark glasses masked the intensity of his face.

"Can't say that it does, partner," Sheriff Dan said slowly.

"I was the one you let ride in to get them amnesty papers," Whitey said, his lips curling with hate as he spoke. "Just so you could set-up Dutch and the rest of the boys. I ran that day, and for a long time after thinkin' you were a trackin' me. Then one day I realized that I had to put things right. When I read that newspaper article about you comin' here, I knew it was a sign."

The girl looked ashen, and she drew toward the old man again and whispered, "Daddy, please." But he just patted her on the arm, lightly pushed her away, and stood there impassively, his face betraying nothing.

"Dammit, Brayton," said Whitey. "I don't care if you don't remember me, but either you pick up that gun and we settle this, or I'll shoot you where you stand."

"Whitey, don't," I yelled.

"Stay outta it, Tim," Whitey said glancing back over his shoulder nervously. "I swore me a blood oath a long time ago that I was gonna get this done." Then turning back to Brayton, "What's it gonna be?"

Sheriff Dan started to smile, then chuckled softly.

"I don't have much use for shootin' irons no more, mister," he said. His hand reached up and removed the dark spectacles. "You see, it doesn't really pay to handle a gun when you can't see what you're aiming at." A murky film covered each eye, obscuring even the color of the iris. His lips stretched into the wide confident smile again. "So I guess you're gonna have to do what you came to do without any assistance from me."

Whitey's jaw seemed to drop, his chin jutting out. Sheriff Dan began a deep resonant laugh. After a few moments more Whitey moved forward and picked up the holstered Peacemaker from in front of the old lawman's feet. He stuck the gun under his arm, and said in a quiet voice, "I guess I'll be going now." I watched as he stepped slowly down from the platform, his whole body looking crooked, broken, deflated.

Someone in the crowd yelled to call the police, but Sheriff Dan raised his hand and shook his head and said that wouldn't be necessary. A round of applause went up behind us. Mr. Creighton smiled and said something about brave heroes and great showmanship, and the people cheered even louder. Maybe they figured it was all part of the show, I thought as I fell into step with Whitey.

"Where's your horse?" I said.

"Over yonder," he muttered. He was silent for a few more steps, his face somehow seeming pale under the leather-like skin. "All these years I spent hating him, and he just turned into a damn old man. An old blind man." He held the holstered Peacemaker with slack fingers.

We walked alongside the gravel mound of the railroad tracks, our boots making small cyclones of dust in the sandy earth.

Sometimes retirement comes sooner than expected

LAST DAY ON THE JOB
Ron Fortier

When Detective Joe Gagne woke up bright and early Wednesday morning, his stomach was on fire. Rolling over in bed he belched, and the sour taste of bile reached the back of his throat. Opening his eyes, he mentally cursed his out of shape body and wondered for the millionth time how he'd come to this sorry end. Okay, so he wasn't eighteen any more, but hells-bells, fifty-five wasn't supposed to be ancient either. Today was his follow-up doctor's visit after having taken a series of hospital tests – lower and up G.I. series – to find out what was eating at his insides.

Got to be the mother of all ulcers.

He reached over to the bureau near his bed and grabbed the bottle of antacids. Two were in his mouth and quickly chewed by the time he sat up and planted his feet on the cold, hardwood floor. Damn it, he hated winters in Maine, even though he had lived in the state all his life except for a three year stint in the army. The house had been built after the Second World War and was slowly dying around him, the furnace being just the latest thing to go; some days it worked, others it didn't. He'd lost count how many times he'd had to call the oil people and get them to fix the damn thing. They kept telling him he needed a new one, but he wasn't about to shell out any more money on the place, not when he was going to put it on the market come summer.

Joe Gagne, after twenty-eight years on the Portland PD, was going to retire and move to some place where it was always warm.

In the bathroom he emptied his bladder, brushed his teeth and took his pills; a baby aspirin for his ticker, a multi-vitamin and something his doctor had given him for high blood pressure. His face stubble was only two days old so he let it go. He hated shaving and no one at the station gave a shit one way or another. Being a cop wasn't about being clean, it was about getting dirty. The play on words made him chuckle. There was another kind of dirty and that's why he was smiling. *Oh, yeah.*

Back in the bedroom he dressed quickly and then headed down stairs to the kitchen. It was a small house but as he was all alone, it was plenty. He rarely thought about his wife anymore, the divorce was so long ago he couldn't remember what it had been like being married.

That's what time does to you, he thought as he poured himself a glass of orange juice. *It fogs your brain up so you can't remember too good.*

He sat down at the kitchen table to pull on his winter boots, then took his heavy, lined coat from the closet by the back door. Two minutes later, scarf draped around his neck and woolen cap on his head, Joe braced the winter morning. The snowflakes were big and fluffy and as he slogged to his parked Toyota pick-up truck, he estimated the accumulation on the ground was over an inch and rising. The beat up gray truck had four-wheel drive, but downtown the slick roads would still be tricky to navigate. A thin veneer of wet snow was always more dangerous than a good foot of packed powder.

As he turned the key and gave the cold engine a little gas wake-me-up, he noted the dash clock indicated twenty-minutes of eight. Good. He'd be able to stop at Hal's luncheonette on Marble and get an egg sandwich and a cup of decent coffee before reporting to headquarters on Congress St. His appointment with Doctor Walters wasn't until 10 a.m. He backed out of his driveway slowly and started up the street.

Gagne hadn't gone two blocks when he spotted a familiar black Acura parked on a side street surrounded by a couple of teenage boys. He snapped his head around, found the next intersection and turned a hard right. Suddenly the day was as sour as his stomach. At the next four-way he turned right again which brought him back to the side-street where he'd seen Beaujoux Gunda's black, fancy car.

His worn brakes made a screeching noise at the stop sign and four boys huddled by the driver's side all looked around, recognized Gagne and took off like the scared rabbits they should be. Meanwhile, Gunda's thin black face smiled wide as Gagne parked his truck in front of him and climbed out, leaving the engine running.

Hurrying across the slippery road, the fat detective waved his arms. "For Pete's sake, do you have to do this out in the open!"

Beaujoux, still smiling got his tall, lanky frame out of the Acura. He too kept the motor running. "Aw, whatcha you gonna do, detective, bust my hump for selling drug to the little children?"

Gunda was second generation Somalian, over six feet four inches tall and skinny as light-pole. He was decked out in a pea green Boston Celtic's tee-shirt, jogging pants and high-top sneakers. *Oh, yeah a real*

sports fan! Dump asshole didn't even know how to dress for the cold.
Still, Gunda ran this section of the neighborhood for Wild Wally and
Gagne had to play along or lose his meal-ticket.

"Aw, be reasonable, will yah ," Gagne said, as snow continued to
rain on both of them and the world beyond. "It's just that out here in the
open, a block away from a school! It could cause trouble!"

"A brother's got to make a living, Joe," Beaujoux said, the silly
grin still on his face. "You know that better than anyone, don't you? You
and me are just two guys making a few bucks. Ain't that the way it is."

"But you're one corner away from Monjoi High School."

"Those rich boys need their candy. You're not going to give me a
hard time, are you, Joe?"

The arrangement Gagne had with Beaujoux' boss was simple
enough. He looked the other way and collected a nice fat paycheck. But
selling to kids, that was a new wrinkle. It wasn't that Gagne had moral
qualms. But schools, especially in the heart of the city, were heavily
patrolled. If Beaujoux was caught, there would be hell to pay.

"Can't you at least hold off until dark?"

Beaujoux started dancing up and down, slapping his arms. "Come
on, eh Joe, give it a rest before I start thinking you don't want your cut
anymore. It's cold out here!"

Gagne wanted nothing more than to smack the man in the face.
He wanted to punch him silly but he couldn't. Too many years on the
pad had invalidated whatever claim he had to any decency or righteous
anger. He was a cop on the take and if he didn't play along, he was
nothing. A big fat zero.

"Well, you want your damn money or not. I haven't got all day
… detective!"

Joe's stomach was still burning and his anger only aggravated his
condition. With a sigh, he forced himself to calm down and held out his
hand, palm up. "Alright, alright. Give it to me."

"That's better. Now that's the Joe we all love."

"Whatever. Just give to me and get out of here before a patrol
car comes along."

Laughing, the tall black man dug his hands into his pant pockets
and pulled out a roll of greenbacks. He looked at it hesitantly and then
handed it to the detective. " From your pal, Wild Wally. Don't spend it
all in one place. Hahahaha."

Gagne unrolled the wad and counted six hundred dollars in tens and twenties. "Right. Tell Wally, I said thanks. But please, get out of here now. Please."

Wallace Fuchay, better known in the neighborhood as Wild Wally for his long, heavy dreadlocks, was the big cheese where drugs were concerned on the waterfront docks. Fuchay had been a two-bit punk back in Africa and was run out of his homeland by Muslim Extremists who wanted to close down his business. Fearing for his life, he fled to the states and had ended up as yet another refugee on the Pine Tree's front steps. Once safely dug in, he quickly adapted to western crime and was soon the head man once again. Only this time in the sweet land of milk and honey.

Gagne had been Wild Wally's pocket since the day the African arrived in Portland. He'd gotten rich in the process. Still, being Wally's flunky rankled him more and more as he got older. *Whatever happened to the simple days of being able to take a bribe without selling your soul in the bargain?*

Gagne pocketed the dough. "Thanks."

The laughing black man nodded, his feet still moving up and down in the slush. "My pleasure, detective."

"Now, please, Beaujoux, go before someone sees us talking!"

No sooner had the words been uttered then Gagne saw a black and white in the distance turning the corner. Beaujoux purposely took his time sliding back into the warm car, threw the shift into drive and as the overweight cop moved out of the way, pulled away from the curb.

Sliding his hand into his coat pocket, as if to keep warm, Gagne made sure his new found cash was completely out of sight as the patrol car neared. He stayed in the middle of the road a few minutes longer, assuring they would slow down and stop. When they did, he casually walked up to the driver's window, recognizing Sgt. Morrison behind the wheel. His partner was a rookie named Slatter.

"Joe," the gray haired veteran greeted as he rolled down his window. "Wasn't that Beaujoux in that car?"

"It was." Gagne played it safe. "I was driving by and saw him just parked here."

"You think he was setting up shop for the kids?"

"I didn't give him a chance, Sarge. Told him to scram and if I saw him hanging around here again, I'd pull him in."

"Low life scumbag." Morrison had no love for street pushers. "Think he'll try it again?"

"Not sure, but you guys might want to circle back around here a few times during the day, just to make sure."

"We'll do. Hey, you feeling okay, Joe? You look a little sick."

Gagne shrugged. "Think I got me an ulcer. Got a doctor's appointment later today to find out."

"Well, you'd best get out of the cold, or you'll add pneumonia to that."

"Amen to that. Catch you later." Gagne waved and watch them drive off. *That was a little too close for comfort.* He got back into his car and let the heat soothe his nerves. He brushed snow off his shoulders, grabbed the wheel and headed for downtown.

His stomach felt awful.

"Stomach cancer!" Gagne repeated, suddenly hoping against all the odds in the universe that he had not heard Doctor Fisher correctly.

He'd been going through the morning on rote-mode, it being like any other typical, snowy Wednesday with its usual assortments of petty annoyances. One of which he'd assumed would be this follow up visit wherein he be told to he had another ulcer and blah ... blah ... blah.

But when Fisher pulled up the X-ray images on his computer monitor, his expression had been anything by jovial. "Joe, you've got advanced stomach cancer."

Just like that, wham! A two-by-four to the back of the head would not have startled him any more than those words uttered so calmly.

"But I thought it was an ulcer."

"I'm sorry, Joe. You really should have come to see me months ago."

Gagne had no rebuttal for that one. Fisher was right.

"Joe, considering your family history," the doctor continued, "this shouldn't be a surprise."

Gagne's father had died of cancer, as had three of his grandparents. It was all in his records. Fisher had cautioned him over and over again about regular check-ups. But he'd been too stubborn to listen to any of it. The truth was, Joe had always feared that one day the Big C would come knocking and as long as he stayed away from doctors and hospitals, his luck would hold out.

Now that luck had run out. "You say advanced. What exactly does that mean?"

Fisher took a breath and pointed at the monitor. "These show multiple tumors through your intestines and we expect they'll continue to spread. At this stage, rapidly."

It was a death sentence, plain and simple.

"How long do I have?"

"Well, if we can start a program of …"

"Doc, cut the bullshit!" Joe was in no mood for word-waltzes. "You and I both know there isn't anything you can do if I'm that far gone."

"With drugs we can alleviate any pain …"

Gagne stood up and moved to the edge of the Fisher's desk. "How long?"

"Six weeks…maybe eight."

And there it was. The hard answer no one really wants to know. *I've got six weeks to live.* For a second he felt nauseous and that the room was closing in on him. Fisher was still yapping away, but he couldn't hear him. He had to get away. Just far, far away.

"Okay, then." Gagne took his hat off the armrest and headed for the door. "Thanks, Doc. See yah around."

"Wait, Joe! Don't go …" Fisher was talking to an empty room.

***

Gagne drove around aimlessly, his mind trying to focus on the treacherous roads. When he almost drove into an oncoming city plow, saved only by the blaring horn of the irate driver, Gagne pulled off the street into an empty mini-mall parking lot. He sat there, sweat beading his forehead, the truck idling while snow continued to fall from dark, gray clouds.

His mind was locked in an internal dialogue loop. *I have cancer. I'm going to die in six weeks. I'm going to die. I've got cancer.* Around and around the same thoughts went, like a crazy mental carousel unable to stop.

BRRRING! He jolted, the ringing a noise surprise that instantly ended his reverie. He shoved his hand into his pants pocket and tugged after his cell phone. It gave another chirp before he was able to get it free, open and to his ear.

"What?"

"Joe." It was Dan Merito, a firefighter and buddy. "It's me, Dan."

"Yeah, what do you want?"

"Just to remind you, it's your turn to bring beer tonight."

"Huh? What beer?"

"Hey, are you alright?"

"I'm fine. Why?"

"Well, unless my calendar is out of whack, it's Wednesday, right?"

"Ah … Wednesday. Right."

"Come on, Joe. You forgot the game tonight?"

Game? What …? Poker! Every Wednesday night with the gang.
"Right, the game. I'm sorry, Dan. My mind was just somewhere else for a second."

"Okay, then. I just wanted to remind you it's your turn …"

"Bring the beer. I got it. Thanks."

"See you at seven."

"Yes, seven."

After the line went dead, Joe snapped the phone shut and stared at it. His windshield wipers keep beating back and forth, valiantly fending of any accumulation of the white stuff. Sitting there watching the snow fall, Joe had an epiphany of sorts. The world was just going to keep going, now, tomorrow and six weeks from now without the slightest notice of his expiration. The world didn't care about a fat, corrupt cop from Portland, Me. Neither did the most of the people in it.

He put the phone back in his pocket and with a poignant clarity of thought, understood his two remaining options. He could wait for the cancer to cripple him and die wired to all kinds of tubes in a hospital room somewhere, or … Or he could tell the world where to shove it and go out on his terms.

Gagne sat up straighter, gripped the steering wheel and put the Toyota back in drive. He had things to do!

***

Gagne drove home, rushed into his house and once inside made for the cellar. Located behind the furnace was a black, old fashion safe. Under the naked light bulb swinging overhead, he looked around at the clutter and junk that had amassed over the years until he found an old canvas gym bag buried under a pile of magazines. He took it to the safe, carefully dropped down on one knee and began twirling the dial to the digits of his social security number. When it clicked open, he pulled the heavy door wide open and gazed upon the rows and rows of green bills he had illegally collected over the years. The last time he'd counted it all the sum was just a little over three hundred thousand dollars. It would have paid for his retirement to some nice little tropical island.

Yeah, right. Couda, wouda, shoulda, he mused and began stuffing the money into the beat up bag.

It was just after noon when he emerged carrying the satchel. He started to lock the door behind him when he realized he most likely would never be coming back. With a laugh, he pocketed the key and hurried to his truck. Joe Gagne had things to do.

***

He had passed St. Michael's Catholic Church a thousand times and never given it a second look. Gagne had been raised a Methodist, although neither of his parents worshipped on any regular basis. His ex-wife, Mary, had been a Catholic but only went to church on Easter and Christmas. Her attempts to drag him along had never worked. After all the things Gagne had seen on the job, what little faith he had was all wrapped up in his .45 Glock automatic and the sawed-off shotgun he kept under the passenger cab seat. Hell was here on Earth, and if there was a heaven, he was sure there wouldn't be any welcome mat laid out when he came knocking.

So why was he now stopping along Broad Street in front of St. Michael's was as much as source of bewilderment to Gagne as it would have been to anyone else. The snow was getting heavier as the day wore on and he guessed they'd already gotten a good three inches as his boots sank into it as he walked up the cleared path to the giant front doors.

There were two men in winter clothing, hats pulled down over their ears, working away with shovels, trying to keep the five cement steps clean. One was a youngster, maybe in his late teens, the other an old codger with a thick, neatly trimmed beard.

"Hey, Pops! You got a minute?" Gagne stopped at the base of the steps.

"Ain't your Pop," the old man snarled, tossing another clump off snow onto the banking to the left of the building. "What da yah want?"

"Is the head priest around?"

"You mean the pastor?"

"Yeah. Is he around?"

"Nope. He's up at Maine Medical visiting sick folks."

"I see." Gagne wasn't disappointed. The idea of confronting a man of the cloth hadn't appealed to him at all. "Could you do me a favor then?"

"What would that be?"

Gagne took the cleared steps and stopping at the last one, so that the old janitor was still looking down at him, and handed him the brown satchel. "Would you see that he gets this? It's for the church."

The old man looked at the bag, at Gagne's face and shrugged. He took a step and reached for the handle.

"Careful, it's heavy."

At that the janitor dropped his shovel and took the bag with two hands. He hefted it and nodded. "Damn straight it's heavy. Whatcha got in here?"

Gagne sighed. "A life time of mistakes" Then he turned and walked away.

***

The Dockside Café was a seedy bar located in the middle of the harbor district that had changed hands dozens of times in the past two decades. Gagne remembered as a kid growing up that it was run by Greeks. After the sixties, a group of Vietnamese showed up and took over the joint, added some fresh paint and tried to make it respectable. They failed. It remained a hangout for prostitutes, addicts and other assorted lowlifes. Decent folks took one look at the black painted windows and stayed away.

With the snow banks to either side of the street reaching a height of six feet, the bar was nearly lost behind that wall of dirty, gray snow. A small path had been kept clear to the sidewalk but not much else. Gagne, clutching his sawed-off shotgun under his winter jacket, moved carefully, not wanting to slip and fall on the slick path. He pulled the front door open and had to blink his eyes. The inside of the place was as dark as a mountain cave. A few bar lights offered only the dimmest of lighting. He stomped his boots on the mat and surveyed the gloomy interior, seeing what he'd expected. A few crack whores were over at a corner table talking and nursing highballs. Some drunk was asleep on another table and sitting behind the long wooden bar, Big Al Jonseaux was drinking a beer while watching the weather channel on a small TV mounted to the wall behind him.

At Gagne's stomping, he turned, recognized the fat detective and went back to watching the TV. "Hey, Joe, it's a shitty ass storm out there."

"You got that straight," Gagne concurred as he trudged to the bar, his hands bringing out the shotgun. "And it's gonna get much worse."

"So, what can I get you?"

"Nothing, Al." Gagne brought the twin barrels up to the man's head. "I'm good."

He pulled one of the two triggers and noise sounded like a canon in the confines of the small enclosure. Most of Al's head vaporized and the TV screen blew up, blood washing over it as well.

Gagne turned and pointed his smoking weapon at the now frightened women. "Get the hell out of here! NOW!"

Forgetting them, he hurried around the bar and into the small passageway that led to the back room just in time to make out Beaujoux Gunda emerging from it. There were no lights in the hallway, thus the tall Somalian was backlit by light in Wild Wally's office. Likewise, Beaujoux couldn't quite make out the fat detective. He was waving an automatic around in his right hand.

"Al! What's happening out there?"

Gagne raised his weapon and fired his second shell. The booming noise in the narrow corridor was massive. Still, through the numbness he heard Beaujoux's cat-like scream as the buckshot ripped his groin apart. He staggered back, dropped his gun, grabbed his crotch and fell to the floor.

Gagne shook his head to stop the ringing in his ears. Blood was everywhere. He hurried now, stepping over the still groaning Beaujoux. He knew he had only seconds to reach the office and he was right.

As he came through the door, a huge black man reared up in front of him, gun in hand. Gagne swung the empty shotgun around like a baseball bat and hit the thug in the head. The man reeled backwards into a heavy metal desk. Behind it, Gagne could see Wild Wally scrambling to open a drawer where he obviously kept his piece. The room was without windows and the only light source was a desk lamp. As Wally's henchmen collapsed senseless against it, he knocked over the lamp and it toppled off the desk. Suddenly the room was bathed in a mixture of dancing light arcs and invading black shadows. Wally was in the darkness. Everything was surreal and time seemed caught in molasses as Gagne dropped the useless shotgun and clawed for the .45 Glock he carried in his hip holster. The black blur that was Wild Wally was frantically digging at the drawer now extended from its slot, his dreadlocks waving in the air behind his head. Even in the blackness, his size was impressive. He was a big, powerful man, muscles upon muscles.

Panting for breath, Gagne fell across the steel desk and pushed his gun-arm forward to within inches of Wild Wally's face, one side aglow from the lamp on the floor. The African's face was a mask of seething hate, his white eyes widened with the acknowledgement that he had lost one time too many. His hand fell away from the drawer and both of them felt time return to normal.

"You're crazy!" Wally yelled, spittle flying from his mouth.

"You got it," Joe Gagne agreed and shot him in the face. The bullet hit between the gangster's eyes and exploded out the back of his skull, spraying the walls with blood and gore. Wild Wally's eyes sunk as his entire body seemed to deflate in front of Gagne and slide out of the swivel chair and out of sight on the floor.

Gagne gulped air, pushed off the desk and turning, tried to regain his balance. His heart was racing like a jack-hammer and he put his empty hand over his chest forcing himself to calm down. *Can't go having a heart attack now! Now with a whole six weeks of living left to do!* The morbid humor made him chuckle aloud and he shook his head. Maybe Wild Wally was right after all. He was crazy.

He exited the room of carnage and made his way back to the bar. Passing over Beaujoux, he noted the man was no longer making noises and assumed he was dead. Just another dead drug dealer. Gagne had no illusions about his actions. Killing a few bad guys wasn't going make amends for all the years of being a dirty cop. Still, he did feel good about it. If had to die, then why not take a few scumbags along for the ride?

As he entered the bar, he moved to the shelf and looked at all the bottles lined there. He was thirsty. Shooting people was taxing work. He could feel his adrenalin high bottoming out. What he needed was a good, stiff belt. He picked up a bottle of whiskey, walked around the bar, avoiding looking down at Big Al's headless remains. He set his gun down, unscrewed the bottle cap and took a good, long drink.

BLAM! The bullet hit him square in the back and the bottle flew out of his hand as whiskey spit out of his mouth. There was a jolt of searing pain and he clutched the bar's edge afraid he'd fall. The pain subsided and he grabbed his own gun and turned to see who shot him.

Standing twenty feet away from him was one of the prostitutes he had seen upon entering the place. She was white, skinny and a mess, her makeup looking as if a child had applied it. Tears tracked down her hollow cheeks as she sobbed, a .38 caliber revolver in her trembling hands.

Gagne couldn't believe it. He'd been shot by a crack whore. He pointed his gun at her as a searing lance of pain hit his chest. It felt like something was loose inside.

"You frigging piece of ... *cough ... cough ...*" He spit up blood.

She stood looking at him, frightened out of her mind. Yet she had managed to shoot him. For a second it was all confusing. Shoot her. Don't shoot her. And the hurting in his chest. Had the bullet hit his lungs?

"You stupid bitch," he finally said, suddenly very tired. He pointed to the front door with his gun. "Get out of here before I change my mind." The girl, not more than eighteen, looked at him, then the door, as if he were speaking a foreign language. Gagne really didn't have time for this bullshit. "GO!"

Running on wobbly legs she bolted out the door, leaving it open behind her. He took a few unsteady steps and followed her outside. The cold air and snow on his face felt good, but the pain was still there. He doubted he had much time left. In the distance he could hear the wail of sirens.

He took a few steps and then fell sideways into the snow bank, letting it ease him down onto the covered sidewalk where he sat, as if just taking a rest. Across the street he could see people beginning to gather, wondering what all the commotion was about. He wondered if his shoot-out ending would make the six o'clock news.

BRINGGG! His cell was ringing. Through a haze of agony, Gagne managed to dig it out of his pocket and flip it open. A voice was speaking and he held it tight to his ear. He was starting to feel cold all over and it wasn't the weather.

"Yeah ..."

"Joe! Thank God I got you! It's Doctor Fisher."

"Who...Doc..."

"Doctor Fisher, Joe. Can you hear me?"

"Yeah, yeah. What do you want, doc...I'm kinda busy ..."

"They made a mistake in radiology, Joe. You don't have cancer."

"What...say again?"

"It was a mistake, Joe. I'm so sorry about this. They have a new clerk down there and she mislabeled your files, mixed up your X-rays with another patient. Joe, it's just an ulcer. You're not going to die after all!" Detective Joe Gagne heard the words as if they were coming from very far away. His hand dropped to his side and Doctor Fisher's voice faded ... although he was still chattering away. *So how about that for a joke, huh Joe? Now that's funny!*

He fell onto his side, grateful the awful pain had left. So had all sensation. As the black void swallowed him, he looked up at the gray skies and wondered when the snow would stop.

Good cops go to heaven, bad cops go to hell.
When a really bad NYC cop makes a deal with the Devil, even Hell's
Detective can get a little...

DYSMAYED
A Case of Hell's Detective
Patrick Thomas

I'll be the first to admit that sneaking off from work to watch a movie is not exactly typical tough guy behavior. But when the job is working for Hell and the movie is a double feature of Bogie, I don't really care.

There's an old theatre down in the Village in New York, the city so good they named it twice. It's a tiny place, but on Tuesdays and Wednesdays it shows the classics, mostly in black and white. Today's double feature was The Big Sleep and The Maltese Falcon. Film making just don't get any better than that.

I like my movie watching to be quiet, without participation from the audience, but even I make exceptions occasionally. There was one guy, almost a kid, who seemed to think he was at The Rocky Horror Picture Show and was shouting at the screen. Not so much shouting as cheering and commiserating with Bogie. Instead of annoying me, I found it endearing that someone still cared enough about Bogie after all these years to get so worked up.

What I did find annoying was a couple of real life toughs raining on the kid's parade by yanking him out of his seat in an attempt to drag him out of the theatre before the first movie was done. Or at least they tried. Seems someone got up and blocked their exit, namely me.

"What's the problem? He lose his ticket stub?" I asked.

The older of the two had started to go to pot around the middle and was thinning a bit up on top. He attempted to make up for it by growing a thick bushy mustache, the kind that works on a cowboy in a cigarette ad but not on too many other people. Portly was no cowboy.

"Who do you think you are? Sam Marlow?" said Portly.

An instant dislike for the man came over me. Anyone who couldn't keep Sam Spade and Philip Marlow straight was barely worthy of air, forgetting the mocking he was giving my wardrobe. I'm a forgotten god from down around Babylon and Sumeria way. My old mode of dress really doesn't go over well these days so a while back I adopted Bogie as my fashion template, which means I tend to lean towards a suit and tie with a trench coat and fedora. Sadly, these days it looked almost as out of place as my old togs.

"You should be so lucky. I just don't think you shall interrupt a man when he's watching Bogie. It ain't right," I said. A few moviegoers where watching us out of the corners of their eyes, trying hard to pretend as if they weren't.

"But what you think don't matter." Portly flashed his detective bag. The name on the ID next to it read Frank May. Now most of the people in the theater were pretending not to watch us. Not one stood to help or leave. "This is police business. You'd best back off."

"I don't often do what's best for me," I said, slapping the badge to the ground, grabbing Portly by his collar and lifting him off the ground. Considering his girth, May was more than a little dismayed.

Instead of threatening, cajoling or even trying to fight me, May whispered one word. "Brimstone."

The mook standing next to him was wearing a trench coat of his own, but underneath it was an NYPD uniform. The thinner partner didn't look like he would be much of a threat, at least not to me. That is until he hit me broadside and knocked me to the floor of the movie house. I was a fool and damn sloppy for not noticing it before, but Officer Brimstone wasn't human. He belonged on my beat, not May's. Brimstone's face transformed into a giant maw filled with darkness and teeth. If I was human I might have wet myself. I'm not, so I put my hand in front of his face and let fly some fire. One of the gifts I still have from my sun god days.

The masque demon reacted in pain and started to attack, that is until he got a good look at me. And his borrowed face went white.

"Chief," he said, genuflecting on one knee in front of me. I wasn't exactly considered a demon lord, but my position was considered on a par with them. Most lords would consider a half kneel an insult and skin the kneeler for it. I didn't have the time or the inclination. The rank and file was encouraged to show me respect, just not of the extreme variety. It didn't happen often enough for my taste, but it made things easier when it did.

"Explain this to me," I said.

"I'd like that too," said a familiar voice. I turned to find Officers Lee and O'Malley of the NYPD looking back at me. I smiled before catching myself. Luckily, the masque demon still had his eyes drilling a hole in the floor and didn't notice. That or maybe he was hoping to strike oil.

"Gentlemen, it's a pleasure to see you again." And it was. I had chased a demon that was possessing people and turning them into zombies. Said demon used the pilfered corpses to rack up an impressive body count, far over the quota Hell allowed for that kind of thing. I had to bring him back to the Pit and Lee and O'Malley had proved very helpful. They also watched my back, something that doesn't happen in Hell. Well, it does but mostly because everyone's looking for a chance to stab something into it.

"It's good to see you again Chief, but we're confused as to what's going on," said O'Malley. "And what exactly what are you doing here, May?"

"This isn't exactly your precinct," added Lee.

May had a look on his face that indicated he'd been caught with his hand, both feet and head in the cookie jar. "This man just assaulted an NYPD detective. We're going to arrest him and take him in." The two officers and I shared a chuckle. Even Brimstone snickered. May was confused.

"And why the hell are you calling him Chief? He sure as Hell ain't our Chief," said May.

"Hell is probably as good an answer as you are going to get on that," said Lee. I'm well known in certain circles as the Chief of Hell's secret police, but most people aren't even sure that there is a Hell and Nick likes it that way.

"I'll ask the questions here," I said. I looked down at the masque demon. "Are you here officially or otherwise?" At any given time there were dozens, if not hundreds, of demons lurking on Earth. Most of them had very strict parameters to stay within, but we also had a pretty high escape rate. With a place as big as the Pit it was understandable. Too much real estate and not enough demon power to guard all of the borders. Luckily it wasn't my job to keep everybody in, but occasionally I got to bring one back. My gut told me this was official; otherwise the masque demon wouldn't have backed down. The shifter would have made a break for it.

"It's official," said Brimstone. Nodding his chin towards me he added, "He's under contract."

Crap. Nick gets a kick out of buying souls, offering mortals something in exchange for the only thing they have that is truly beyond value. There are always a lot of promises and something they think is worth the trade, although things don't always turn out the way the idiot soul seller expects. The question on my mind was why did May rate his own personal demon cop as a partner.

"What's the nature of the contract?" I asked.

"Hey!" barked May, stepping forward. I treated him like a bad dog and hit him in the chest with the palm of my hand. The cop flew backwards into the wall of the theatre.

"You'll speak when spoken to, not before," I said. I turned back to Brimstone. "Now explain."

"The usual terms for payment. In exchange the detective gets to be super cop long enough to earn his pension out. There's also the matter of a major motion picture to be made about him, plus a couple of books," said the masque demon.

A real idiot. He sells out his soul and his badge for some fleeting fame. May wasn't even bright enough to make sure it would be a hit movie. It might be some crap that goes right to DVD.

I turned my attention bad to May. "What is your interest in the movie watcher?"

May smiled, still trying to get a grasp on what is happening. "Just an informant. Had a few questions to ask about a current case."

I looked over at the Bogie fan who had been quietly cowering, too afraid to run away.

"Just exactly what kind of information does he have that you need?" I asked.

"It's NYPD business, which makes it none of yours," said May, going the tough guy route. "You keep this up and I'm going to take you downtown for questioning."

"You keep this up and I'm going to take you to my downtown. Take a look at your partner here and you'll have an idea of where that might be," I said. May started to look nervous. Small beads of sweat were starting to form on his forehead. I knew it was a mistake as soon as I said it. It was an empty threat, the type you should never make because if someone figures out you're bluffing you lose a lot of standing. A demon just can't drag a mortal or a mortal soul down to Hell without just cause. Not even forgotten gods who happened to work there. There are all sorts of just causes varying from evil deeds, someone else selling your soul, to making a deal that you renege on or fail to fulfill, but I had none of that.

I was lucky that May wasn't bright enough to call me on it and the masque wasn't dumb enough to try. Him I could drag anywhere I want.

"Hey, I have a deal with your boss. Why are you messing with this?" asked May. Lee and O'Malley's eyes went wide on that one. They just figured out something about their fellow cop.

"What about your deal involves this guy?" I asked.

May sort of shrugged and gave me a smile, the type a real S.O.B. gets when he knows he's gotten away with something and he's not stupid enough to brag about it, but not smart enough to keep it all to himself. "He saw something he shouldn't have. Maybe I'm just seeing to it that he doesn't get a chance to tell nobody anything he shouldn't. It's all part of the deal."

I may work in Hell and I'm definitely a mean S.O.B. myself, but the difference between me and most of the demon ilk is that I have some standards. Bring all the evil people you want to Hell for punishment as far as I'm concerned. Evil deserves the Pit and the Pit deserves the people. But when it comes to those who are innocent, they don't deserve what Hell can bring their way. The Bogie fan was a bit on the geeky side, but I didn't get the impression that he was deserving of the Pit or its keepers' none too kind intentions. The question was how was to handle this without pissing off the Devil.

I smiled. "That's fine then. Why don't we let Lee and O'Malley take him in for this questioning?" May got a look on his face as he sized up his two fellow cops and stole a glance at his demon partner. I could see him working out the details in his mind on where to hide the bodies after he got Fanboy away from them. "And just so you know, both Lee and O'Malley are under my protection. Anything happens to either one of them, whether or not you had anything to do with it, I am coming after both of you. Deal or no deal." And there I was actually in my rights. In my role as Chief of Hell's PD I'm allowed to extend my protection as I see fit. Anyone who goes against my expressed orders gives me every right to take said scumbag down, whether human or demon. I could tell that the masque demon was thinking along the same lines as May and was trying to figure out a way to get around that. Maybe getting another masque demon or two to fill in for Lee and O'Malley for a while until my interest waned.

I kneed the demon in his jaw. A masque's face is pliable, so I knocked his jaw clear to the other side. Brimstone took his hands and pulled it back into place.

"Both of them are personal friends of mine. I would know if they weren't them. Comprende?"

Both May and the demon nodded. Several folks snuck out the back of the theater, real life violence being too much for them.

"I am afraid I just can't let them take my prisoner. The investigation is at too delicate of a stage to let anything get out of my control. I am sure you know how it is," said May.

Actually I did which is why I wasn't about to let it happen. "Fine. I'll take custody of the prisoner until you can prove to me that he's in danger. Barring that, he's under my protection too."

May practically snarled before getting his face under control. "But he tells what he knows, and the deal's broken and your boss loses his pay."

"Not my problem," I lied. The Devil gives me a lot more leeway then others, mainly because I wasn't gunning for his job, but that didn't mean I had free rein. If Nick wanted this poor sap given to May I would have to hand him over or quit. Quitting meant a one-way ticket to oblivion, to the unknown place where the forgotten gods go when their time is done. I had postponed my trip by taking this job. I had no desire to hop on that train. Unfortunately for me, it might be that or hand over this kid. I'd have to quit and I hated that, but what use is living for a few extra centuries if every day you get up hating yourself?

Problem was, I couldn't keep him safe. On Earth my power is limited. Not as limited as the keepers of the damned, but not enough to hold off the Devil himself. Same reason I couldn't hide the guy in Hell. The Devil can know everything that is happening in Hell. In fact, he tries to make it known that he knows everything that is happening all of the time. It's a load of lies from the lord of lies. He can know anything that is happening, but it has to be something to which he is paying attention. That means I might be able to hide the kid in the Pit, but the moment the Devil starts consciously looking for him, the jig is up. Not to mention that as an embodied human, every demon that saw him would try to kill him just for the sport of it. He didn't look terribly imposing in his physique. I doubt if he would last past the first encounter.

"Now the two of you get the blazes out of here," I said to May and the masque demon. "Don't think about waiting around outside. I'll know you're there and I'll fry you up just a little. Not enough to give you serious damage, just serious pain."

"What about these two? They heard..." said May.

I held up my hand. "They're friends of mine and smart enough to know when to keep their mouth shut. Besides they can't do you any harm. You didn't say enough for them to know anything and the little they did hear would only be hearsay in a New York City court. And lest you forget, they are under my protection. If I have to repeat myself again I am going to be pissed. Now get out of my sight."

May and the demon did as I instructed.

"What just happened here?" asked O'Malley.

"Something from my jurisdiction that's spilt into yours. Sorry it had to pour onto the two of you." And I truly was. I don't have many friends, but given better circumstances I'd count these two in that number.

"I can't say I'm crazy about it, but we appreciate you having our backs," said Lee.

"You had mine when it counted. I'm only returning the favor," I said.

"Rumor has it May's being looked at for popping three crack dealers," said O'Malley.

"Another rumor has it that it was because they were holding out on some bribe money," said Lee. "Nothing can stick."

"Probably part of his deal," I said. "And that won't change as long as it's in effect."

"That might explain why a video record of the murder scene from an ATM went conveniently missing from the bank's security room," said O'Malley.

Fanboy started to open his mouth I put my hand over his choppers to make sure he didn't succeed. "Not a word. Go sit over there and watch the movie," I said pointing several rows away. One of the moviegoers had given up on surreptitious watching and was outright staring. One glare from me was enough to turn his attention back to Bogie.

"Okay," said Fanboy obeying. His life was in danger and I could see him still watching the movie out of the corner of his eye.

When he was out of earshot I turned back to New York's true finest. "If you hear him confirm anything of that sort it will put you on May's hit list. And his demon pal may come after you."

"So this is something above your pay grade?" said O'Malley, no malice to the question.

I nodded. "My boss makes his deals and so long as he stays within the rules he answers to no one but himself. That includes me."

"So you're just going to hand the kid over to May?" said Lee.

I didn't even want to admit that out loud so I just shook my head.

"Won't you get in some serious trouble for that?" asked O'Malley.

"The kind of trouble you don't come back from," I said.

"You want us to help you hide the kid?" asked Lee.

They knew what that involved and still made the offer. My opinion of them jumped another notch. "No, but it is appreciated. I have an idea how to keep him safe, but I don't want either of you to know anything about it. It's safer all around that way. You two probably should get going as well," I said.

"You'll call us if you need help?" said O'Malley

"What he said," said Lee.

"I will." But it was better if I didn't need to. Then I came up with something. "You have an address for May?" They did, gave it to me and left.

A short trip to the lobby netted me two tubs of popcorn the kind of crap that was pre-popped and cold. Luckily I was able to use my control over fire to heat it up a little bit before the butter went on. I went back into the flickering dark, sat down next to the kid and gave him a tub.

The kid thanked me for the stale but warm snack. "What happens next?"

"We finish watching the movies. Then I take you to a safe house."

I waited until the credits rolled on the Maltese Falcon. Of course I was right about May and the masque demon not leaving well enough alone. The masque tried twice to sneak into the theatre in another human form. The first one was male, the second female. Brimstone made the same mistake with both. One, the guy was too good looking, with muscles too far above that of the average New Yorker, especially one that would show up on a Tuesday to a Bogie double feature. The shifter made the same mistake when he formed his dame shape. Impossibly beautiful and in proportions that didn't exist outside of strip joints and cartoon fantasies. The masque are mid-level demons and, fortunately for me, most only have a partial grasp on the humans thought process. Most demons tend to want to fulfill fantasies first, and nightmares later, not realizing that – to quote what I just seen – they are just the stuff that dreams are made of. Most mortals know nothing unbelievable is just going to drop in their laps but they are sometimes willing to convince themselves otherwise. Most need more than a little motivation to sway their common sense and it helps if it's larger than life because even a mook knows that when something is too good to be true it's time to start looking for the catch. The trick sometimes is to give them something better to look at.

Getting rid of the demon was simple. I just stood up, walked up to him and stared him down. Each time he cut and ran.

If I left the building with Fanboy, I'd be almost guaranteeing that May or his buddy or both would follow me. A transport by hellhole was too risky – something might pick up the scent or the use of magic. Camping out in the theatre wasn't a good idea either.

And on the matter of safe houses, what place is truly safe from the Devil? Unlike the demons beneath him, holy ground is no deterrent. Of the very few mages who might have the power, few had the cahones to face down the Devil. The magk Hex would, but I wasn't about to ask him for a favor. That left few options, most of whom would want far more than I could afford to pay in exchange for safeguarding the kid.

There was one option that wouldn't cost me a thing, people who would do it just because the kid needed help. That is, they would if they could get past the fact that it was me delivering him to their doorstep. I wasn't exactly rainbow colored.

I had untraceable cell phones that I used sometimes on earth. Believe it or not, I dialed the number of a bar.

Unsurprisingly, one of the bartenders picked up. "Hello, Murphy. This is the gentleman in the fedora who works in the real underworld." At this point in time I didn't want to invoke either my name or that of my office. The Devil was going to know what I was doing soon enough, but keeping the window for him being in the dark open as long as I could was high on my list. "You remember me? Good. I need to speak to your boss, please." I heard the wise cracking bartender call for his leprechaun boss, who eventually got on the line. "Hello Mr. Moran. You know who this is?" He answered affirmatively. "I prefer not to use my name at this juncture." I explained to him in brief what was going on. "I would very much for you to take custody of the young man."

Of course, the leprechaun asked me what my game was. Paddy Moran had no real reason to trust me. I couldn't blame him for that. I worked for the Devil after all and Nick and Moran weren't exactly friends. In fact, Moran almost killed him once. Normally the Devil is eternal, unable to be killed, destroyed, or truly hurt. Moran's bar is called Bullfinches' Pub, named after his late Mrs. The place is unusual in many aspects, not the least of which is rainbows lead the troubled to the place and magic doesn't work there without the leprechaun's say so. The Devil made the mistake of pushing too many buttons when Moran's was piss drunk on the anniversary of his wife's death. Moran snapped and came within inches of utterly destroying the Devil. The only thing that stopped

Moran was his adopted kids. They knew that Moran held all life sacred and killing anyone in anger, even the Devil himself, would eat him up inside.

In the current situation that history was a plus because I knew that Moran wouldn't have any qualms about the risks involved.

Moran asked me a simple, but very valid question. He wanted to know why he should trust me.

"Because I give you my word." For most in Hell that wasn't a whole lot of guarantee unless you had it signed in their blood with an ironclad contract, and even then you had to watch your back for loopholes. I'm old school from back when a god's word was his bond. I don't like to give it for that reason. I sighed. I was going to have to involve Hex, at least peripherally. "If you need someone who cans vouch for at least that aspect of me, why don't you call your magí and get his opinion. Then perhaps you can send that messenger of yours to pick up the kid and get him to you with out anyone being the wiser." I told him where we were. "You call, I'll wait."

It didn't take long, just a few minutes until a tall man in a gray trench coat and red high top sneakers with wings appeared in front of me suddenly and without warning. I was prepared for it and it still took me off guard. Luckily, working in Hell involving a lot of playing it cool in situations where it was practically impossible, so my startle didn't show.

"Hello, Hermes," I said, lighting up another cigarette. An usher had talked to me about the no-smoking law. He didn't try it a second time.

The Greek god lifted the front of his hat, a baseball cap with Bulfinche's Pub's shot o' gold logo on it.

"Hello, Negral."

I had my issues with the divinities that weren't halfway to oblivion. The Greco-Roman pantheon tops that list. That lot all had much better publicists after their worship had faltered. A god needs belief or at least the awareness of humanity to get on. Worship is stronger, but comes with more pitfalls. Hermes is one of the smartest of his family. You see the guy everywhere, from flowers to a stone-carved relief in Penn Station. What that all boils down to is he's one of the few gods with no shortage of power in the modern age. And these days it's not about the worship, it's about surviving and being able to use your powers without drawing on outside sources. It's about avoiding oblivion.

Even though he's thousands of years old I consider Hermes a snot nose kid. I'm quite a bit older. But once you get past his trickster aspect, he's not all bad.

"I understand you have a package for me," said Hermes.

I nodded. "Moran brought you up to speed?"

"Yes. So why are you doing this? Nick's not going to be happy when he finds out and I was under the impression you didn't want to split off from your pimp."

I held back a chuckle at his use of the word pimp. I would have used something a lot harsher. Not that the Devil hasn't been good to me in his own way. It just sticks in my craw that I need to be dependent on him for my continued existence.

"It's a distinct possibility. But this May character interrupted a Bogie film fest and roughed up the only guy who was a bigger fan than me.

The messenger god's brow furrowed. "So because the guy interrupted a sixty plus year old movie, you're going to risk ticking off Nick just to stick it to him?"

"Pretty much."

Hermes smiled. "I could think of worse reasons. You understand that we are not going to give him back to you?"

Moran hadn't mentioned it, but I pretty much figured. They weren't going to take the risk that I'd change my mind on the matter. I respected Hermes for actually telling me the truth. Not that I could stop him from taking Fanboy at this point. Hermes could grab him and have him in Tokyo before I managed to take a single step. But if I couldn't stop him, then neither could May or the masque demon. I simply nodded my answer and made introductions.

"Thank you for helping me," said the Fanboy.

I nodded. I wish I could've used a line like I was just doing my job, but the fact is I was doing anything but. "You just listen to what these folks tell you. They're smart, they're sneaky and they will keep you safe. And if you ever see me coming toward you again, run."

Fanboy was confused. "But why?"

"It's too long a story. Just trust me on that."

Hermes grabbed a hold of the guy under his armpits and suddenly neither of them was there. It was time for me to do the same. I had to go get a hold of May's contract and see what I could do about digging myself out of the crater I was in.

I briefly contemplated going back into the Pit and trying to find it that way. My office gets files on all the new arrivals but I don't get cc'ed on contracts. I could try Hell's law firm but I'd angered one of the senior partners by the name of Dewey a while back and didn't want to get caught there in need of something. It wouldn't be pretty. I could ask the Devil himself, but I didn't want to go that route just yet. I knew Nick would find out sooner or later, but later would be better all around. Even in Hell it's easier to ask forgiveness than permission, although neither is usually granted.

That left me one option. In any transaction involving a soul, it's one of the rules of the first Hoard-Host Treaty that mortals be given a copy of any documents dealing with their own choices about where their souls will spend the rest of eternity.

That meant May had a copy of the contract somewhere. The dirty detective didn't strike me as terribly bright, but he wasn't stupid either. He probably had a sub genius level of street smarts, not to mention a mean ability to work the system to his favor. The paperwork wasn't just going to be lying on his kitchen table marked as *Contract with the Devil*.

May would have a hiding place for it. It could be a normal type hidey-hole, but I doubted it. It wouldn't be a safe deposit box because May wouldn't want his ill-gotten gains or his contract to be found with something as simple as a search warrant. And May was the type to not want things too far out of his control. He likely didn't trust anyone which meant that it was probably somewhere in his apartment.

The question was where? One of the easiest and yet hardest things to do is to put yourself inside of the head of a perp. Even in Hell it's difficult. There are degrees of evil and different kinds of crazy. Human and demon psychology overlap in some areas, but differ in others. I was used to dealing with people in the rigid framework of the Pit where deviousness was its own reward, mainly so you weren't punished.

It was similar on Earth, but not the same. May was already pretty high up on the food chain. In New York City very few people mess with a cop. Even less with a detective. May was used to getting a wide berth, but only as long as his illicit activities stayed unknown.

As a cop he'd undoubtedly made hundreds of searches for everything from murder weapons to drugs. He would avoid the obvious hiding places like the toilet tank or the underside of the couch or dresser. I had enough control over my fire power to burn away the entire apartment one layer at a time, gradually eating away at everything until I found what I was looking for. The problem with that was if I was wrong and the document wasn't here, May would know that I was looking for it just by the charred remains of his furniture.

The same risk of tipping him off went for more mundane means like tossing the place, cutting into his furniture and so forth. Didn't stop me from going through all those drawers and checking underneath them just in case I was wrong. I looked carefully at all the furniture looking for any signs of re-upholstery. Most of his stuff was new and made out of leather. I couldn't find any signs of reworking it. I ended up checking the whole place from the freezer to the mattress and box spring. Nada.

I ripped apart that place as inconspicuously as I could including the inside of his televisions and toaster, under the floorboards and searching the walls for any hidden compartments. Luckily his library consisted of five books, none of which looked read and had nothing hidden in between any of the pages.

Something was bothering me. May had a telescope situated out one of his windows. He didn't strike me as the stargazing type and a quick peek out didn't reveal any easily accessible windows or a fetching dame that might catch his spying eye. A look through the eyepiece revealed a view of a brick wall. However, the outer circumference of the view seemed smaller than it should. Spinning the telescope around, I unscrewed the end. Bingo. Inside was a rolled up document. I took it out and put the lens back on.

As I started to unroll it, I heard footsteps in the hall. Two sets.

I didn't need another confrontation with May and his pet demon until I knew what was in the contract.

Technically, stealing his contract was against the rules in Hell, but technically the rule applied only to demons. Despite my time in the Pit, I didn't qualify. It was splitting hairs, but it was enough of a loophole for me.

I couldn't get out the door without them seeing me so I made my way out the window. May's apartment was on the sixth floor. It wasn't much of a ledge, maybe four inches wide. It wasn't a building from the days they made things last. From the looks of it was probably put up in the late sixty's or early seventy's. I stepped onto it, letting my fingers grab in between the crevices of the bricks and held on with my toes and fingers after slipping the paper inside my coat.

May came into the apartment, but I heard him shouting long before he had opened the door.

"Your boss should be able to take care of this. That's part of the deal. The Devil said I'm supposed to be untouchable!" yelled May.

"Untouchable by mortal authorities. The Chief doesn't qualify," said

Brimstone

"Yeah well if that witness turns stoolie, my goose is cooked. Busting him is how I found out about all this. He hacked your system and he gave me everything just to avoid being busted for some pot. And one of his pothead buddies told me he hacked a copy of the bank's video surveillance of me capping those dealer scumbags before you destroyed it. If he has that and gives it over, they'll have me in Ricker's so fast my head will spin. Ricker's ain't a good place for any kind of cop. And it kind of screws up your plans, although not our deal, cause I've kept my mouth shut. But that guy will cave if a cop even looks at him funny."

"What do you want me to do about it?" said the masque.

"Like you did with the other guys. Take care of it," said May.

The shifter laughed. "I don't think you understand. Negral is of the same ranking as a demon lord. I'd have to get real lucky or real powerful to take him out." It was my turn to chuckle. I work hard to develop and maintain my reputation. I could be hurt, possibly even killed the same as in any other denizen of the Pit, but as a non-native, non-damned resident, whether or not its magic would be refuse to let me croak is the matter of some debate. As the only way to settle it for sure is for me to die, I'm comfortable letting that question go unanswered.

"So then take out the witness," roared May. "After all, isn't that your job?"

I could practically hear the shifter bristle. Almost to a one, demons hate mortals. Some because they are reminded of what they lost when they were thrown out of Paradise for the Pit. Others were just trained and taught that way and when hate is all you know, it's hard to learn anything better. Being bossed around by a human couldn't be sitting well with the masque.

"I would, but he's dropped off the face of the Earth," said the demon.

"Could he be in Hell?" said May.

"Doubtful."

"Can't you check?" asked May. Brimstone didn't want to do that. It would mean that he had lost control of the situation topside and put him at risk of being recalled. No demon wants to leave a cushy assignment on Earth to go back to the Pit, especially since failure meant punishment. So he did what all good little demons do, he lied.

"I'll put out some feelers and check, but unless you can find him there's nothing I can do."

I chuckled silently until I heard a throat clearing below me. I looked down at the Devil and almost fell off the wall. Looks like my window of opportunity had just slammed shut. Hopefully neither my fingers nor any other part of my anatomy got caught.

Nick indicated with a nod of his head that he would like to converse with me. Six stories is a long way down, even for me. Yeah, I'd survive the fall, but I'd be hurting for days. I shimmied my way over to a drainage pipe and climbed down.

When I jumped onto the sidewalk, I tipped my hat. "Evening."

The Devil's expression didn't change. "Explain."

"Why? You already know," I said, not sure if he did. May had mentioned the Devil, which likely means he's only clued in since that point.

"I want to hear your side of it," he said.

I shrugged. "May pissed me off. I don't let that slide."

"You are aware of my agreement with the detective?" asked the Devil.

"I am now."

"But you weren't at the start?" I nodded. "Would it have changed things?"

I was not above lying to the Devil, but to fool the master, it has to be believable. I wasn't going to be able to sell that one, so I told the truth. "Not by much."

"It's bad form for those of Hell to be working against my interest," he said.

I managed to keep a straight face. Those of Hell did nothing but. They rebelled against the benevolent control of the Creator, which is how they ended up in the Pit in the first place. Lucifer's reign in Hell was nothing like the Creator's in Heaven, but the Devil had a system, much of which involved keeping the damned and their keepers too busy to foment rebellion. I was one of the few who wouldn't take Nick's job if it came to me with his head on a silver platter. I'd already staged a coup of my pantheon's afterlife back when we still had worshippers. Ended up running things and married to the former and present ruler. It was more trouble than it was worth and ended poorly. For me at least. My ex made out pretty well, if you call ruling eons dead shades doing well. Ruling is akin to juggling dozens of spiked spheres, never knowing when someone would throw a new one at your face or balls. The Devil was far better at it than I ever was. As far as Hell goes, he can have it, except for the little bit of manna I take to stay around.

"It's bad form for the future damned to think they can lord it over the Satan's delegated authorities too," I said.

The Devil gave me a single chuckle. "As much as you are useful, Negral, don't ever get the idea that you aren't replaceable."

"True, you could replace me, but you'd never find someone with my charm and good looks," I said. We stared at each other, but I didn't turn away. I was scared of the Devil. Any sane being would be, but I don't roll over for nobody. It's a character flaw, one I share with the noir PI's I emulate. I didn't want to die, but I wasn't going to be anyone's bitch, not even the Devil's.

"So if I told you to turn the witness over to May…"

I kept silent at the unfinished question. I broke the eye lock to light up a coffin nail. We both knew what that would do to our working relationship. If we were in the Pit right now, I'd be getting ready to run or fight, probably both. Fighting the Devil head on in his home territory would be suicide. Still I had planned for just such a contingency. I doubted I'd beat him, but maybe I'd hurt him enough to get out of the Pit.

Fortunately we were in the mortal realm. The Devil could just drag me back to Hell. It was within his rights. I was his employee. Unless of course I quit. I was very careful in how my contract read. If I quit he couldn't take me there against my will and I could quit in any number of ways, not all of them verbal. I had several clauses in my contract to that effect. Of course, my days of staying around in existence would be numbered.

Best way for this to go down was to avoid it ending in a showdown.

"Why bother to offer May anything? From his behavior, I'd say his soul was already yours for the taking," I said.

"It would seem that way. May had spent most of his years pretty much making a gift of his soul to me, but then something changed," said the Devil. "He started to reform. Care to guess why?"

May didn't strike me as the type to have found religion. "A dame."

"Yes, the bad detective fell in love. Worse, it was with a good woman. He felt he was not worthy of her and in truth, he was not. Frank May decided to reform and was going to turn state's evidence in a case which would have screwed up deals I had going for a half a hundred good souls, so I made him an offer. At first he refused, so I sweetened the pot. If this deal goes bad or May reforms, I will be very upset," said the Devil.

"If you would be so kind as to let me read a copy of his contract, I'd be happy to see what could be done to have May break his contract without actually reforming," I said. "The kid is forgotten and you get his soul."

The Devil's laugh sounded so normal it sent chills down my spine. "I'm afraid that would be bad form on my part and I wouldn't want to take away your fun. After all, how would you improve your detective skills?"

I shrugged. "I suppose. I'll be on my way then."

"Very well," said the Devil. "Oh, one thing." Nick reached inside my coat pocket and took out the rolled documents I had stashed there. "That isn't May's contract, but it is something equally damning."

The Devil unrolled an 8x10 photo of May and some dame. May's face was practically transformed, so I was guessing the broad in question was his ladylove.

"Don't screw up," said the Devil, walking away from me.

Good advice, but just like most advice from the lord of the damned, just a little too late to do any good.

***

When in doubt in an investigation, it's best to fall back on the basics. So that's what I did, doing my best to follow May from a distance without being noticed or caught. In this Brimstone had an advantage over me. The only forms I could change into involved fire or sunlight, neither one of which would be terribly hard to spot, especially on the streets of New York at night.

May stopped into the station did some paperwork, made some phone calls and then left. He didn't go home, instead going to a strip joint down by the west side piers along 11th Avenue. The days of the area being seedy were long gone, it now being home to cruise ships and the like. Fortunately it was a big enough club that I was able to hide in the crowd. It helped that I had ditched the fedora and the trench coat. Now I was just one more stiff in a suit. I sat in the back trying to deduce what type of meat was in the mini buffet that was put out for the patrons. Scantily clad dames wandered about the place, wanting to talk, listen or wiggle in exchange for some greenbacks. It's sad in a way, both for them and their customers, but at least everyone should have known what they were getting out of the deal. Though there were certainly some men who thought the women really liked them and some women who believed one of the men might really take them away from all this.

May ignored most of the broads, even though he had a front row seat for the show. His demon partner was nowhere to be seen, with them having parted ways back at the station house. Some of the dames had proportions that succubi would envy, but May was more interested in his bourbon. That is until one particular broad made her way to the stage. The DJ claimed her name was Rosie Cheeks. If that was her real name, her parents set her up for this kind of work at birth. At the mention of the name May looked up, his bourbon forgotten.

The stripper came out and I could see why the men, particularly May, were paying such rapt attention. The dame was the same one from the photograph in the telescope. At least that's what I thought at first. As I watched Rosie gyrate to the beat heavy music, I realized that the resemblance was close, but no cigar. Besides, the stripper calling herself *The Intern* had done that bit earlier.

On closer examination Rosie's face looked just like the dame in the picture but the rest of her was enhanced – smaller waist, curvier hips, larger top. Every part of the anatomy was practically perfect. The dame must have one gifted surgeon and one hell of a body to start with. Doing the dance Rosie seemed to only have eyes for May, which was probably a good thing. From the look on May's face he was likely to hurt anybody who tried to make time with the stripper. After her routine, which involved a few long silk scarves that were thrown around like ribbons and briefly doubled for clothing, Rosie stepped down from the stage. May put a stack of bills on the counter and his lap dance began. It lasted a good half hour, but there was enough money there to justify the use of the stripper's time.

I watched and something seemed off about the whole thing. It took me about halfway into his semi private show to figure it out. As at one point in the dance May's face was in the Rosie valley and the twin peaks surrounding his face actually seemed to grow in size. As I didn't see any sort of pneumatic pump attached to Rosie, I figured it out. Rosie was really the masque demon.

I laughed. And I came up with a pretty good way to shake things up. I left the place noting that only half of the bills were gone, so I figured I had at least twenty or thirty more minutes before May's private dancer would leave him wanting more. I made my way out of the strip club and started walking along the streets looking up. I suppose I looked like a tourist but I didn't care. I wasn't looking high up, more a medium kind of height. I was searching for a church, preferably a Roman Catholic one. I didn't find one so I grabbed a cab and had it take me to St. Patrick's Cathedral. It was the middle of the night and the doors were locked. Fortunately that didn't mean much to me. I simply heated up the deadbolt on the door to the point where it bent as I pushed the door through. I touched the metal and moved it back into place. Just because Nick's got a mad on for any religion that actually preached something that might take a soul away from him there is no reason for me to do serious damage. I found a holy water cistern and filled up the bar glass I had lifted from the strip club.

While the Devil himself has certain immunities to religious icons, or at least heavy resistance, the rest of the keepers of the damn weren't so fortunate. Not being one of them myself, I could handle holy water with no more difficulty than the regular variety.

My glass full, I grabbed another cab and made it back to the strip joint before the private show was over. Rosie was still riding on May and there were a couple bills left on the stage. I searched around the room, attempting to figure out which of the other dancers didn't much care for the improbably proportioned Rosie. There were several candidates, but I noticed one in particular scowl in her direction several times. As soon as she was done with her current customer I lifted my finger and motioned her over.

"Would you like a lap dance, sugar?" said the woman in what was quite possibly the worst southern accent north of the Mason-Dixon Line.

"Not exactly. I was wondering if you'd do me a favor?" I said.

"I don't do that kind of thing. I just dance," she said. "Besides you look like a cop."

That gave me a chuckle. "It's not like that. I'm a buddy of the detective …" I figured I might as well use her assumption that I was NYPD to my advantage. "And we like to play practical jokes on each other. He's got this thing about wet girls. I was wondering if you would throw this cup of water onto Rosie there, making sure to get her face and chest."

The dancer scrunched up her face and sniffed the glass. "What's in it for me?"

I took out a folded hundred-dollar bill and held it in between my index and middle finger. "You get to take Benjamin Franklin home if you do it."

The dancer looked at me, then at May and Rosie. Then back at Ben. "Okay, I'll do it."

I held up the money instead of sticking it into her g-string. That raised her eyebrow, but she was willing to take it from me the old fashioned way, with her fingers.

"You gonna give me the money up front? Ain't you afraid I won't follow through?"

I smiled. "Cop, remember? Besides you wouldn't do that, would you? You just aren't that crazy about your coworker."

The dancer snorted and nodded. Taking the cup from my hand she put it on a tray and walked over to where they were. The dancer pretended to stumble and let the glass fall forward, dowsing Rosie in the blessed H_2O.

As far as the rest of the patrons were concerned what was in the glass may as well have been acid. The stripper literally burst into flames, her boobs disappearing in a puff of smoke. It made sense; after all they were her most prominent feature and got most of the liquid. Rosie screamed and then transformed back into his demon form. Strippers and patrons ran away like the building was on fire.

May stood up, pushing Brimstone off his lap onto the ground. The bad cop wasn't too happy. Obviously this was supposed to be some sort of fantasy fulfillment, a surrogate for his lost love. But May was the type of guy who didn't take well to either being deceived or being with a man. Don't get me wrong, back in my day many of the upper class that worshipped me had both wives and boy toys, so it doesn't faze me one way or the other. I've just learned to use people's fear and prejudices against them on my beat. It makes manipulating people that much easier. And more fun.

"You son of a bitch!" yelled May, actually drawing his piece on the demon. The few remaining dancers and patrons of the naked arts took cover behind tables or vamoosed out the doors.

Unless May had his bullets blessed by someone truly holy, they wouldn't do much more than piss the demon off.

"This wasn't part of the deal," said May.

The masque crawled over to the bar and up to the stage where there was a shower set up for one of the other dancer's routines where she soaped herself up and rinsed herself off for the crowd. He used the water to get the more blessed liquid off of him and was able to regain his male cop form.

"Don't be a fool. You haven't stopped talking about how much you've enjoyed your time with Rosie. I got a chuckle out of it having been both with you and listening to you brag about being with me. We own you, so don't try and pretend otherwise. You try and renege on your contract and we'll drag you right down to Hell," said Brimstone.

Now he was bluffing. Maybe. There had to be a fairly serious breach for that to be allowed. Without seeing the contract I couldn't say whether it was a total or partial bluff.

May told him to go screw himself. Actually it was much more colorful than that, but Bogey never used that kind of language so I try to avoid it whenever possible. At the end of it the masque left. So did May, but not before grabbing an almost full bottle of bourbon from the bar. The bad cop started work on emptying it before his feet touched sidewalk.

Through it all I managed to remain hidden or at least not noticed as I followed him out of the bar, trying my best to fade into the shadows. I needn't have bothered. Half the bottle of booze was gone before we made it a block. Good thing the place watered the booze. I could have been at the head of a marching band and he probably wouldn't have noticed me.

Despite his drunken stupor and the more than occasional stumble, May moved like a man with a mission and he had to take the Queens bound E-train to complete it. I got on the subway car one down from him. May stumbled in, almost sitting on a guy who started to give him quite a bit of grief until May flashed his badge and the guy moved down the car. We rode for quite some time and at one point I could have sworn the dishonest detective had fallen asleep. When we ended up at the last stop in Jamaica, May headed topside. I did likewise. Apparently he had slowed down on the drinking because only a quarter more of the bourbon had gone in his gullet on our ride.

Still determined, he headed off through the streets until stepping into an alleyway. I crossed the street to the opposite side and watched as the detective stood there looking up longingly at a certain window. That's all he did for a half hour until the strain of remaining upright became too much for him and he sat down on the concrete, his back against the wall. It was probably a mistake because he fell asleep. I could hear him sawing wood from where I was tucked away. May held onto the bottle like it was a glass teddy bear. Nothing much happened until about an hour after sunrise. I've got to admit it's my favorite time of day. The sun coming up, even in a city as polluted as New York, was great for me. Better than sex. I miss the old days where that happened every day with no pollution. I baked in the sunlight until May woke. Never hurt to recharge the old power cells when I had the chance.

It took the dirty cop a few moments to realize that he wasn't home. It was a few seconds longer for him to realize where he was. May jumped up, brushed himself off and straightened his hair before moving to the front of the alley to stare at the apartment building's door. May made like a statue when a broad came out the door. There was no doubt that this was the one from the photograph.

May ducked back in the alley and dumped the bottle, but not before taking one last slug. The dame went the other way. May the detective was not bad at his job, being careful to follow her at enough of a distance so she didn't realize she was being followed. Still he wasn't good enough to know that the same was happening to him. In his defense, usually the cops are not the ones being tailed. Part of me felt like the last man on a conga line.

I wasn't sure where we were going to end up, but I wasn't too shocked to end up at what they would have called a flop house in the old days. Apparently May's lady friend had devoted herself to helping others. May watched her go inside, but stood there as if debating whether to follow. No won the day and he turned to walk down the block. I still made like his tail and followed after, surprised when I saw him walk into a second apartment building. The outer vestibule door locked behind him. I was debating as to whether or not to force my way inside when another resident came out and I hustled to catch the door. I watched from the bottom of the stairs as May made his way up to the third floor. He moved slow and a little too steadily, but otherwise hid his hangover well. I crept up the steps, waiting on the second level landing. I heard a door open followed by a series of beeps indicating he was pushing buttons on an alarm panel. A longer, higher pitched beep indicated the alarm had been turned off. The door shut and I moved up, getting a quick look at which door it was. I kept moving until I was on the fourth floor landing.

May wasn't inside long, less than a half hour. When he made his exit this time I let him go solo. Fortunately I wasn't the type of cop who needed things like search warrants. However I didn't want to draw attention to myself. I could have melted the deadbolt and gotten into the apartment, but there was the alarm to worry about. I'm able to see in the infrared and ultraviolet spectrums so there was a good chance there would be enough residual heat on the key pad for me to tell which buttons May used. The problem was I had heard six beeps. Even though the Sumerians first developed many of the aspects of math that are still used today, I didn't consider myself a big numbers guy. Still, this was pretty basic and I figured the odds at significantly less than the one in a million I'd have without knowing which keys were used, but not enough that I'd bet money on me succeeding in guessing the right sequence before the time ran out and the alarm sounded.

I made my way outside the building and stood beneath one of the utility poles, basking in the sunlight long enough to build up some excess heat energy which I redirected at the transformer box. The power blew for the entire block. It was a simple matter to go back inside and jimmy the door. It was a basic apartment, not much in the way of personal touches. There was a bedroom with a bed and a dresser. A living room with a couch and a TV next to a kitchen with a serving set that could service two people if they didn't mind sharing the salad fork. I suspected I had found his former love nest. I searched the place. Behind some moldy food in the refrigerator I was surprised to find a safe bolted into the extra wide appliance. I guess it made sense. No one was going to be able to sneak out with a cooler that size. And who'd think of looking behind the vegetable rack for a tiny little safe.

There probably was some way to listen to the tumblers and figure out the combination. I could see they had been touched during May's visit but it didn't help me figure out what numbers to use any more than it did with the keypad. Instead I melted the bolt from the outside in and swung the door open.

Bingo. It was the contract. And his evidence. May wasn't so dumb after all. The Devil wasn't allowed to mess with the contract, which meant hiding the evidence with it gave it quite a measure of protection.

I took out the contract and went through the mumbo jumbo. It seemed simple language at first glance because complicated jargon would spook the marks. People thought they understood what they were signing but on closer examination it was never that simple.

It was pretty boilerplate. Reading it and leafing through the other documents painted a picture of what had happened. Fifty souls my eye. The Devil was working on some Ponzi scheme that was even worse than the recent ones that had already come to light. It threatened to entirely destroy a large portion of the banking community, bankrupting the FDIC and several small countries. May had accidentally come into possession of information that would blow the lid off of everything. If he went the reformed route and turned over the evidence it was still possible to stop what was going on. The Devil was not directly behind it, but I had little doubt that he was helping manipulate things behind the scenes. Most of the other schemes had hit the filthy rich primarily, with trickle down to everyone else. This would get Joe Paycheck. Something like that would ruin millions, maybe tens of millions of people, many of whom would despair at the loss of their savings and retirement funds. Some would undoubtedly do things that would put their souls in jeopardy, justifying their actions by blaming it on the loss of their savings. It could be a windfall of souls for the Devil.

The contact basically stated that May agreed to not turn in the evidence and fork over his immortal soul. In exchange the bad cop became not only super cop, but rich and famous as well. The only unusual aspect was he put in a clause protecting his lady friend, whose name was, I kid you not, Daisy Bhutts. Apparently she got a long, healthy life out of the deal. There was nothing in there guaranteeing their continued relationship, and I guess things had gone south. There was however a clause guaranteeing sexual services, but it was worded in such a way that they didn't have to be provided by Daisy herself, just a reasonable facsimile. That explained the masque's masquerade as Rosie Cheeks.

I had my idea of how to get the contract broken without screwing up the Devil's Ponzi scheme but to do it I had to take Lee and O'Malley up their offer of help. I took out my disposable cell phone and made a call. O'Malley answered.

"Chief, what can we do ya for?"

"I was hoping you could do me a favor and start a rumor that May had contacted the New York State Attorney General's Office and was going to turning state evidence," I said.

"On what exactly?" asked O'Malley.

"You don't know. It's just something that you heard. And I need you to do in the same general vicinity as his partner from the theatre yesterday," I said.

"Do you need us to be next to him?"

"No. His hearing is good enough that anywhere in the same room should be enough."

"Why?"

"It's still best that you don't know the whole story, but sufficed to say that I need to turn one against the other. Will you do it?" I asked.

I could hear O'Malley sigh. "Yes, we can do it. He's actually downstairs talking to the duty sergeant and waiting for May to show up."

"Thanks. I owe you one."

Now it was just a matter of waiting and seeing which way the crap hit the fan.

***

Now when I said I felt like the caboose on the tailing train, I hadn't been terribly accurate. I was actually the car in front of the caboose. The person following me was in fact so good I didn't know he was there, other than the fact that I knew he had to be. I opened up the window, and felt a breeze as if something that had been hovering nearby had quickly moved away. I put the document back in the safe and melted the metal enough that it fused together. Working the tumblers wouldn't do a bit of good now, but Hermes was supposed to be a god of thieves with no small skill set himself in that arena. Inside the safe was the proof that May had been keeping on the Ponzi scheme. I had no doubt that the Greek messenger would be in here checking what I had done, if he hadn't already figured it out from watching me through the window. Moran was a major financial player, easily worth tens of billions, but was so good that he was able to keep under the radar. Knowledge of this Ponzi scheme might allow him to divert it, maybe even stop it.

I wasn't about to give the information to the Devil's enemies. I was working for Nick after all. However, the Devil had threatened me in his own none so subtle way. I don't like threats unless I'm the one giving them. The Devil would have no problem believing that Moran and his crew were able to figure it out on his own somehow. They had that kind of luck and no small skill. It wouldn't be traced back to me. And even if it was, I had plausible deniability. However I was in debt to Moran for protecting the kid, and I wasn't about to let that debt go unpaid. Making sure Wingfoot knew that I knew he was out there, I took a beer out of the fridge popped it open and left it on the counter.

It was a subtle gesture, but I knew it would not go unnoticed. I turned to the window and tipped my hat before leaving.

Moran was a do-gooder with a soft spot on his head that matched the one on his heart for helping those in need, even the ones that didn't really deserve it. Leaving behind this information squared my debt with him as far as I was concerned.

I decided to try and pick up May's trail again, but I didn't think it would be too hard. It wasn't. I went back to the outreach center and went inside. May was already there. Apparently the bad cop had gotten up the gumption to go inside and talk to Daisy. There wasn't a whole lot of room to hide, just an open area. It wouldn't be long before I was spotted. I did my best to hunker down behind a couple of guys searching for job postings.

I was amazed by how quickly the masque demon arrived.

"Stupid flesh sack. You thought you could betray us?" shouted Brimstone in full NYPD regalia. It was enough to make the bums scatter.

"What the f..." May looked out of the corner of his eye at Daisy catching himself. "... hell are you talking about?"

"I know about you turning evidence. Did you think we wouldn't find out?"

"But I'm not," said May, telling the truth, probably for the first time in a long while.

The masque demon pulled his gun. "You're no longer protected by the contract." It wasn't exactly true. That determination was quite a bit above his pay grade. Not to mention the fact that until he was sure of it, he couldn't kill May. I figured it would just get May angry enough to pull out of the agreement on his own. I just hadn't figured on the masque being a complete idiot, especially since the Devil is usually a better judge of competency on those he personally sends into the mortal world.

"So since the contract is no longer in effect, she's no longer protected," Brimstone said with glee.

I realized my screw up instantly. Even though Daisy didn't enter into the contract of her own accord, she had been in love with May and by even unwillingly accepting Hell's protection she became part of the spoils, at least until such a time as she realized that she didn't have to be. It was a confusing state of affairs because the Host–Horde Accord allowed other people to put souls into jeopardy that they only had a marginal claim on. Conversely, it allowed the reverse, allowing the opportunity for a mortal to save another's soul. If the person was strong enough and good enough they could actually get out of Hell's claim, but they had to know what was going on. I was betting Daisy had the good part down, but not the knowledge portion.

Brimstone lifted his gun and pointed it at the center of Daisy's chest. May was horrified and I was reeling from my screw up. The same pair of humans I was hiding behind blocked me from having a clear shot, at least without frying them. A demon would cook them first and worry about the consequences later. Without knowing if they deserved it, I couldn't just take the shot. I wasn't that far gone yet. The masque demon got off two shots, faster than I could get to him. However, he wasn't faster than Detective May, who actually dove in front of his ladylove and took both slugs, one to the gut and the other to the chest. I lifted my hand

and poured out sun fire at the masque, reducing his demon form to a mass about the same consistency of burnt hamburger. Because he was in his demon form as opposed to a borrowed one, he was hard to kill, but because my power wasn't of Hell it brought him pretty close. I turned in time to see Daisy cradling her former lover in her arms.

May wasn't going to make it. He was already coughing up blood and too much damage had been done. It was only a matter of time and it there wasn't going to be much of that.

"I have always loved …," May wasn't even able to finish his last words before his eyes rolled back in his skull.

Daisy started to wail and all the folks at the outreach center moved to surround her and stare. I grabbed the lump of gristle and quickly moved toward the door.

As I exited I actually saw Hermes hovering a few stories up. Even he hadn't been fast enough to get in there. Hermes may have been faster than the speed of sound, but sound didn't move any faster traveling to him. By that time it had been too late. Our eyes met and this time he tipped his baseball cap to me before vanishing. I found a back alley and poured out my fire against the wall making a huge circle. I did the necessary mystic manipulation and opened a hellhole, stepping though back to my regular beat.

I knew it wasn't going to be pretty and delaying wasn't going to help matters.

I made it to the Devil's office, surprised he still had the same receptionist. Most of her face had grown back since the last time I was here. However she appeared to be having to staple her tongue over and over to multiple documents. I didn't ask and frankly didn't want to know.

"Is your boss in?" I asked. She nodded. "Let him know I'm here."

The former drug dealing human soul tried to tell me okay but the words came out as gibberish. Instead she nodded frantically and rolled her chair toward the door. She was ridiculously top heavy enough that her back had to be screwed to her chair so she wouldn't fall over.

She raised her hand as if to knock, then hesitated. I was guessing the stapling had something to do with a punishment of using her hands in some way. She put her wrists back on the armrests and instead banged on the door with her skull.

"Tell the Chief to come in."

More gibberish followed I ignored it walked forward and pushed her out of my way to roll across the floor, the papers on her tongue blowing in the breeze. I opened the door slowly.

"Negral, explain to me what exactly happened. And why I lost May's soul."

"Lost?"

"May is dead and his soul's been moved to arbitration." Translation-limbo. "Apparently he died in a selfless act, giving his life to save another."

No greater love has any man, not that I dared say that out loud. I'd be sent to the deepest, dankest corner of the Pit.

"That shouldn't automatically negate the contract," I said. Otherwise everyone would engineer a selfless act right before they died and the Devil wouldn't get anybody. Of course that would hardly make the act selfless, but just the attempt would complicate matters.

"I'm going get him back. I've got Dewey and the rest of the lawyers on it. I just need to know what happened," said the devil.

I gave him an abridged version, leaving out what I could.

"And you had nothing to do with the rumor that he was turning state's evidence?" the Devil asked.

"I might have had something to do with it, but the masque overstepped his bounds. If he hadn't shot at the dame, May wouldn't have tried to save her."

"You expect me to believe that?"

"Yes."

The Devil was glaring at the lump of gristle I was holding. The masque demon wasn't regenerating. That was unusual.

"You fried him with sunlight on Earth?"

"Yup."

"The fact that he's not regenerating backs your story."

"Why isn't he?" I said. On Earth I could understand but Hell takes care of its own. Death can't occur here because the demons are beyond it and the humans have already experienced it. Hell makes sure that any damage done eventually regenerates so it can be done again and again. All part of the fun of eternal damnation.

"If the masque did indeed shoot at the woman, he broke the contract with May that protected her. He went outside the rules, breaking his own covenant with Hell. If an outside power damaged him, Hell itself is not going to be able to repair the damage easily."

I had to catch myself from smiling because that meant Nick couldn't question the masque, which meant he had to accept my story for the moment. It was time put the icing on the cake.

"I thought you should know, when I came out of the mission, I saw one of Moran's goons watching me. The one with the wings on his shoes." Just in the same way you don't want to mention the Devil's name if you don't want to him to hear what's going on, you don't want to do the same thing to a god. I'm not sure if Hermes would be able to hear the conversation in Hell, but why take that chance? "You might want to take precautions just in case."

By warning the Devil, I gave him the heads up. However Moran and his crew would have already taken my doing that into account and were probably already working frantically to put an end to things.

The Devil flew into a rage and yelled at me to get out of his office. I obliged.

I wasn't sure if he bought my story, but for the moment he at least had to accept it. He's going to be too busy trying to get back May's soul and still make sure his best laid plans didn't go astray.

After all, in Hell there's always the Devil to pay. It's just more fun to watch when he actually has to work to collect it.

Two brutal cops, two drug dealers, one unknown dude. Someone is going down in

HEADBANGERS
A Hammer & Frye story
Michael Berish

"Who's the dude in the middle, pickin' his ass?"

Three black men stood under a street light – so they could clearly see the drug deal they were about to transact – next to the Safari Diner. Looking like a silver bullet, the Safari was one of those old fashioned, rat-infested, hash-house type diners whose slogan over the door should have read, "HOME OF THE FIVE SECOND RULE: If it falls on the floor, but it's back on the plate in under five seconds, it's good to go." The diner stood on the corner of Northwest Second Avenue and Eighth Street, right in the heart of *the Pit*: the black ghetto in downtown Miami. It did not occur to the dopers that if they could clearly see the buy go down, others could too, like the team of patrol officers that had just, strictly due to happenstance, turned the corner.

The cops were Hammer & Frye; two down-home, white, Florida Crackers. They were a couple of insidious fart hammers left over from the ole boys' school of over-the-top, kick-ass cops collectively known as "Headbangers;" cops who specialized in *body modifications*. Asshole buddies on and off the job; they were products of genetic pollution – picture a plague of locusts coupled with Baghdad boils. Notorious legends around the halls of the City of Miami Police Department, they were the Teflon Brothers – no matter what evil they perpetrated on the streets, nothing stuck to them. The deeds that citizens described to Internal Affairs as "police brutality," they referred to as "tune-ups." To Hammer and Frye, a "tune-up" was anything short of burning out a suspect's eyes with heated copper coins.

"I recognize Slick Willie and Khamageon, but … who's the dude in the middle?" repeated Patrolman Frank Hammer. "Numbnuts over there, the short one with his thumb up his ass, all tricked out like a downtown Christmas tree in red threads with the yellow Superfly hat. He sticks out like a turd on a wedding cake."

"Don't recognize him; must be a new player tryin' to score some scag. You're right though; it sure looks like some fast-handin' is goin' on around here," answered his partner, Patrolman Jules (Julie) Frye.

"Let's shake 'em down."

And with that, Hammer pulled the squad car over to the curb and the Teflon Brothers jumped out.

"Hands on the car, Shit-birds!" yelled Frank.

The three druggies stood motionless, gawking at the two officers, not believing any of this was happening.

"You heard *the man*!" chimed-in Frye. "Let's get those jive-asses movin' – NOW!"

Slick Willie Charles, a.k.a. Mr. Potato Head, was a part-time crackhead and infamous pusher to the youth of Miami. A notorious pimp, degenerate child molester, all around cretin and scumbag extraordinaire; Slick Willie knew the drill. He shrugged his shoulders and assumed the position.

Khamageon, whose name reminded one more of a Japanese fighter pilot than a junk connection, started to protest, thought better of it and followed suit.

Only the unknown dude in the middle said anything. "What's haps, bro?" Immediately sensing the shuckin' and jivin' routine wouldn't work with these two prairie dogs, both of whom appeared to have brain abysses, he reverted to a more subdued tone. "Listen officers, this is not what it appears to be. I have some I.D. in my …"

"Did I ask ya fer sum I.D., you stunted half-pint? Shut up and get your fuckin' hands on the car," repeated Hammer, whose short fuse was about to burn down, "before I pop your face inside out!"

Numbnuts in the red threads didn't have to be told a third time, he got his "fuckin' hands" on the car. But, he forgot to shut up. "You know, officers, this is all quite illegal."

Hammer stopped what he was doing … for the moment. "What a whiner!" he said, followed up with a question. "Can ya count ta five?"

Mystified by the question, the dude in the middle replied, "Sure."

"Would ya like ta try it without any teeth?"

Jules finished patting down Khamageon. "Nothing."

Hammer frisked Mr. Potato Head, pulling several $10.00 decks of heroin from his pockets. Beaming with a torturer's smile, and without saying a word, he slapped on a pair of cuffs and tossed Slick Willie into the cage in the back of the prowl car faster than a whore walking past a church. At the same moment, Frye snapped his bracelets on the Japanese fighter pilot, who joined his pal in the backseat.

"Hey! I ain't done nuthin'! I didn't have no brown sugar on me!" protested Khamageon.

Looking ugly and all sparked up, the cop with the short fuse leaned into the vehicle, positioned his mug within inches of the defendant's, then in a half-whisper explained the facts of life: "Ya do now!"

Khamageon started to lean forward in an effort to exit the cruiser. Hammer seized his arms and shoved him back into the seat: "You're beginin' ta frost my balls!" Leaning in even closer, "Ya like the way your arms still fit in their sockets?"

The Japanese fighter pilot got the message. So scared that he farted, he closed his eyes and tilted away as if the officer was radioactive.

"Good. I don't wanna have ta come in there after ya. 'Cause if I do, I just might lose control of myself and do sumthin'… sumthin' we both might regret." Hammer paused as if reflecting. "Well, at least you might regret it … sumthin' like me pullin' your liver outta your fuckin' ass and shovin' it up your nose! So, just sit there, happy as a monkey in a cage, so ta speak." Looking as if he needed protection from the things in his head, he continued: "Now, I gotta funny story fer ya, so get ready ta laugh.

"The way I see it, ya probably snookered tons of people and pulled all kinds a shit that nobody ever caught ya at, so's as far as I'm concerned, youse were both holdin' that smack. Just think of it as evenin' up the score in life." A sadistic grin, as if he would gleefully torch you in bed while you slept, passed over Hammer's features. "Some days you get the bear, some days the bear gets you."

Hammer turned and nodded towards Frye, "See my partner there? Ya know what the guys at the station house nicknamed him? Shakespeare." Both of the defendants looked at each other, wondering if Shakespeare was another dope dealer like themselves. "Because he's real good at what we call … *creative writing*," he explained, then winked and closed the door.

"That ain't right," said Numbnuts, "framing them up like that."

"Hey! Nobody's perfect," said Frank, turning his attention to the dude in the middle. "And ya forgot ta say, 'May I?' Smart-ass."

"May I … what?" asked Smart-ass, sensing a nasty moment coming up.

"May I … speak? Oh, I almost forgot," said Hammer as he pulled out his nightstick. "You're the Superfly bupkis who thinks he's a lawyer; who knows all about what's illegal and what ain't. Well, guess what? I'm the sugarplum fairy who's come ta put ya ta sleep," he decreed as he proceeded to thump the would-be pettifogger over the head with his baton. The blow hurled the third suspect into the phone booth as if he'd been launched from a cannon, where he staggered around like a gut-shot deer. A simultaneous "WOW!" came from both of the stunned defendants in the squad car. The cop with the short fuse big-footed the would-be attorney into the box like a psychotic child on a sugar buzz, bashing him in the ole beanbag, then he began an old-fashioned kicking about.

Not one to be left out, Frye pulled his nightstick and shoehorned his way into the melee; he wanted a piece of this action. He reached over his partner, calling out, "Watch your toes, nuts, and knees!" like a carny worker on the Tilt-a-Whirl, then landed a bone crunching whomp to the noggin. The wannabe legal eagle teetered about like a man all-at-sea on a paper boat, then slumped to the floor. Instantaneously, like bullwhackers, both cops began to batter Numbnuts like a piñata at a Cuban birthday party while Frye screamed, "You're The Man, Frank!"

During the pummeling and tumbling about, a .38 snub-nosed revolver fell loose from Superfly's ankle and rattled out the door.

"Got your fuckin' ass *real* good now! You're gonna need one hellava whiskey-dick lawyer ta get ya outta this one!" yelled Hammer with verve in his voice and a sadistic glee in his eye that was reminiscent of Captain Ahab at last spotting Moby Dick.

The beating continued until Superfly was "finally subdued." (That's the way Frye, in his Use of Force Reports, usually worded these "resistances" by offenders to justify their hospitalizations.) The Headbangers dragged the unconscious, hashed-up dope fiend out of the crowded phone booth and rolled him over. He was out; there would be no best two out of three in this knuckle buster. The drubbing was similar to a lightning strike, all over in seconds. Blood trickled out of one of the defendant's ears, his face had the consistency of pastry, and his body involuntarily shuddered like a man with St. Vitas Dance stretched out over a termite hill.

Welcome to the dark side of police work.

Patrolman Hammer was still chatting incessantly to the comatose victim, "How come ya ain't talkin' now, Smart-ass? Come on… talk! Confession is good fer the soul, they say." Then to his partner: "I think I strained my groin. Oh well, I'll fill out an Injury Report and get a couple of days off the job fer some R & R, compliments of this scumbag … Now, let's find us that I.D. he was talkin' about."

They didn't find any I.D. on him; it was across the street, in a parked white van. However, they did find, tucked under Numbnuts' red threads, was what is commonly referred to in police parlance as … a wire.

The Teflon Brothers stared at each other, then went white with horror as they saw their pensions dissolve into mush, mush like the outside of Superfly's cranium that was now resting on the sidewalk. The cop with the short fuse began to vomit on his shoes. The dude in the middle was an undercover cop working out of the Narcotics Squad and several of his fellow detectives were across the street, in that white van, taping the entire incident; that white van, the door to which was now sliding open; that white van where several men were now jumping out of and running towards them with guns in their hands.

A little ambition never hurt anybody unless they're laundering money for the Rossiter gang.

BLOOD TELLS
Vincent H. O'Neil

"It's in the blood – and blood always tells." My Uncle Marty said those words when he gave me my current job. "You take a snitch, for example. His kids can grow up far away from the rackets; go to the best schools, never so much as meet a real criminal, but the blood will tell anyway. Look 'em up wherever they land and they'll be the office rat, telling the boss who's coming in late and who's using the phones for personal calls. Blood tells."

Uncle Marty said those words ten years ago, when he made me the manager of the Quick 'n Easy Car Rental shop owned by the famous Jo Jo Rossiter. Jo Jo had been reinventing himself as a real estate tycoon at the time, but being Marty Barnett's nephew I knew the truth. I knew that Jo Jo and Uncle Marty were the founders of a criminal gang that controlled much of our city, and that they'd done this with the help of a dirty cop named Ernie 'the Evil Eye' Thorson. I also knew that the Eye scared just about everybody, cop or criminal, and that it was a good idea to do whatever he asked. Finally, I knew that the Quick 'n Easy was not just a car rental shop.

That was why Uncle Marty mentioned blood. As his sister's son I could be trusted to keep my mouth shut and do my job, which was to rent cars while laundering part of Jo Jo's wealth through the Quick 'n Easy's books. The agency had lots of cash-paying customers, which helped me to disguise the loot dropped off by Jo Jo's bag men. Phony rentals and other accounting tricks quickly changed Jo Jo's dirty proceeds into nice, clean earnings.

I had a suspicion I was not the only guy doing this for Jo Jo, as they never brought me more than five thousand dollars a month, but it was hard to be sure. The Rossiter Gang, as the newspapers used to refer to it, had shrunken considerably over the years. Uncle Marty had tried to explain this to me shortly before losing his long fight with lung cancer.

"You see, kid, Jo Jo's one of those guys who never stops learning.

A few years back he read about something in the computer world called a distributed network." He had smiled proudly, like a parent with a gifted child. "The idea is that instead of having one giant computer handle all your work, you break the jobs up across a bunch of smaller ones. They're all connected, so if one of them breaks, you just shift its load to another computer.

"Jo Jo's been trimming the organization ever since. Now he's got the jobs spread out just like that network idea, each worker handling one small piece of the whole. That way, if anything goes wrong, he can just switch the load to somebody else."

This explanation suggested that I was but one small cog in the big Jo Jo Rossiter machine, each mechanism unaware of the others around it. I suppose I could have asked if other people were performing functions similar to mine, but Uncle Marty had never encouraged questions. He always explained gangland stuff to me as if I was a child, and he'd never considered me for anything more important than running the Quick 'n Easy. Heck, he'd only introduced me to Jo Jo once, when all three of us ended up at the same wedding reception and it was unavoidable.

So maybe blood does tell after all – and Uncle Marty had found the story spun by my corpuscles to be just a little disappointing.

***

Mickey Matches knocked on the back door right on schedule. Matches was the lackey who brought Jo Jo's five thousand to me each month, and he had the imagination of a lug wrench. Always at the back door and always at the same time. He didn't seem to recognize that the Quick 'n Easy was openly connected to Jo Jo and that one day it might come under surveillance. Ernie the Evil Eye had convinced the local police to look the other way long ago, but you could never tell when the boys from the Justice Department might show up.

Matches' nickname came from his fascination with fire, an obsession which had earned him a ten-year stint in prison twenty years earlier. His time inside seemed to have cured him of his pyromania, and maybe even gained him some points for loyalty, because Matches had survived Jo Jo's personnel reductions. And even though Matches was dumber than the proverbial bag of hammers, he looked down on me as a non-combatant restricted to desk work.

"Hey, Mick." I said as I opened the back door to let him into my office. The Quick 'n Easy sat on a side road next to the municipal airport, backing onto a dry wash choked with scraggly trees. I stood there holding the door open and looking at the bent, storm-twisted trunks behind Matches' car for what seemed a long time.

Matches almost didn't come in. He was glancing over both shoulders and holding the usual green bowling bag, but the way he was carrying it was odd. Normally it hung freely at his side, but that afternoon he held it in front with both hands like an old lady holding her purse. He finally moved past me and sat down on the folding metal chair that was the only seat in the office besides my own.

"You seen anybody hangin' around here lately? You keepin' on your toes, Jackie?" His dark eyes bored into me, now that they weren't flitting around like fireflies. Matches was somewhere in his fifties, balding badly, and dressed like a guy getting ready to mow his lawn.

"Mickey, you come in here every month on the same day, at the same time, clutching the same color bag, and you want to know if *I've* been keeping on my toes?" I brought an identical bowling bag out from under my desk, the empty from last month, and slid it across the scratched enamel desktop. "If anybody's watching this place, it's because you brought 'em here."

Matches' face hardened at this, and he tossed the fresh bag at me. I didn't look inside, knowing it contained roughly five thousand dollars in small, used bills rolled up in rubber bands. The monthly exchange, with its small amount of scruffy currency and its mangy delivery man, always left me feeling vaguely insulted. Although I had never wanted to get involved in the dangerous side of Jo Jo's organization, I had hoped to someday reach a higher position with better associates. Each monthly delivery was a reminder that I had not gotten that promotion, and over time I had developed a real distaste for the bag and its carrier. I guess Matches picked up on that, because he rose abruptly, snatched up the empty, and started for the door.

"Just keep your eyes open, bean-counter." That was his favorite put-down, calling me an accountant. As I said, a bag of hammers looked like an astrophysicists' convention when compared to Matches. "Somethin's up. I can feel it."

***

The dark premonitions of a failed firebug didn't hold my attention for long, so I counted the money, locked it up, and went out front. Neither of my two assistants at the main desk greeted me, which was exactly how I liked it. I was intentionally mean to them, and as a result no one held those jobs for more than a few months.

You see, high employee turnover was the key to beating an audit of my books. When you're trying to explain bogus income, you have to be able to show the events that created it. I liked to spread Jo Jo's bowling bag money across an array of phony car rentals, inflated returns on auctioned vehicles, and extra rental fees which the customers never actually paid. Despite this scattering of the evidence, an in-depth investigation might show these transactions to be false. That's where recently departed employees and incomplete files come into the picture.

The files for the bogus deals were all missing important details, and I was in the clear as long as I could reasonably explain the shoddy paperwork. It's hard for investigators to prove a car rental never took place when they can't contact the customer, and it's easy to blame the incomplete file on a departed employee who never liked the work in the first place.

I looked past the two guys who currently hated this job, through the building's glass front windows and across the sun-baked road toward the airport. I watched a charter flight slowly lifting into the air from one of the far runways, the sun turning its tiny windows into mirrors, and almost didn't hear the banging on the back door.

Matches hadn't been gone even twenty minutes, but I knew it was him because no one else ever came in that way. Not that he came in, though. I pulled the office door shut so my two assistants couldn't see what was happening, and pushed the back door open in time to receive another bowling bag, this time a red one.

Matches looked like he'd seen a ghost. His eyes were darting around wildly, his beat-up old car was still running, and his hands were actually shaking. As soon as he got the bag into my arms he turned and jumped back behind the wheel.

"Take care of that! Somebody'll be by to get it!" he shouted, and might have said something else except he was already racing away in a cloud of dust.

I stood in the doorway for a long moment, watching the dust settle and listening to a bird chirping in the dry wash. I was smiling when I went back inside; trying to imagine what toasted wraith had materialized in Matches' diseased mind to scare him that way, and sat down at the desk with the new bag.

Matches had never come unglued like this before, and I was enjoying it immensely. Some tough guy. I was considering how I would respond the next time he called me a bean-counter when I undid the bag's zipper and saw the stacks of crisp new hundreds.

It was just quiet enough in my office to make out the distant sound of police sirens.

***

My house backs onto a deserted stretch of the airport, a storage area from a few wars ago. The chain-link perimeter fence separates my sun-burned back yard from an identical stretch of dead ground which quickly moves uphill until it reaches the derelict shells of three Quonset huts. Scraggly, wind-maimed trees cover much of that ground, and brush chokes the spaces between them.

If you walk out my kitchen door, duck through a break in the rusted chain link, and then fight your way up the incline on the other side, you'll come across an ancient electrical relay box of some kind. It stands about waist high in the middle of a clump of those dry, deformed trees, and the trunks are so close that its door only opens halfway. The box's guts were removed decades ago, and there is almost no chance of anyone stumbling across it by accident because it is, after all, on airport property.

The sirens I heard at the office that afternoon never actually approached the Quick 'n Easy, and after I had recovered from my initial panic I decided to get the cash off the premises. I thought of the relay box immediately, for the simple reason that I had considered stashing money there when I first took the job at the agency. Not that I began this work planning to rip off my employers; it's just that as the years went by and the money didn't get any bigger, I did begin to wonder about my future. I had never done anything about it, though, and until that moment with Matches it was nothing but a fantasy.

And I want to be clear that I had no intention of stealing the money when I first stashed it. Matches had placed both bags in my care, and I was hiding them only until a time when they could be safely retrieved. I just didn't want them anywhere on my property or at the office, and so the relay box seemed about right.

The only problem I faced was making the drop in daylight, but on that I had little choice. I left the office by way of the back door without telling anyone, something I did frequently, and drove to the other side of the airfield without attracting attention. Neither of my neighbors seemed to be home, so I tied the two bowling bags up in a large trash bag, forced my way up the hill, and put the whole thing inside the box. There was no way to lock the ancient container, so I covered it with some of the brush and headed back to the office.

Matches was on the news when I returned. We had two televisions set up in our waiting area, and the first thing I saw was a fire truck hosing down a large blackened area off the side of the highway. The camera shot widened to show a large number of police cars, and I even caught a glimpse of Ernie the Evil Eye off to the side. His famous headlights were covered by sunglasses, and he was in a solemn discussion with a senior firefighter who looked pretty uncomfortable. It was only a glimpse, of course, and then the shot shifted back to a local reporter who was trying hard not to smile while telling the tale of what had happened.

According to the reporter, Matches had returned to his bad old ways. He'd torched an abandoned house, but the fire had eventually consumed two other dwellings. Police had been circulating a sketch of the suspected arsonist for days when he was finally spotted, and a wild chase had ensued. Somewhere on the highway Matches had flipped his car clean over the guard rail, where it had become pinned between the embankment and the same kind of trees I had just fought in back of my house.

The car had exploded, and the resulting brush fire had taken an hour to subdue. Traffic had been backed up for miles, and by the time it was all over Matches and his car were nothing but ashes.

That's when I decided to keep the money.

***

The next two days and nights passed in a weird state of suspended animation, while I fluctuated between disbelief at what I had done and terror at what might result. I figured it would take a while for Jo Jo and Ernie to determine what had happened, and of course they had plenty of questions to ask before any of those answers might lead them to me.

For example, what was Matches doing with that second bag, the one full of hundreds? I had retrieved the stash from the relay box the night of the accident, wanting to know just how much it was. I had carried the entire trash bag inside, cringing at the noise as I pushed through the parched underbrush.

Sitting on my living room floor with the shades drawn and only one light on, I counted the bills and was astounded to see how quickly you get to one hundred thousand when you're counting in hundreds. Although I'd never seen that kind of money before, I resisted the temptation to play with the loot and got it back out to its hiding place while it was still dark. During the whole trip through the unyielding brush, and after I got back inside, I was trying to figure out what Matches was doing with that second bag.

No doubt it was a delivery of some kind, and the more I thought about it, the more likely it seemed that the bag was meant for another money laundering operation. Matches was too dumb for anything more involved than picking up and dropping off, so I felt safe in assuming my stolen money was intended for someone just like me. Somebody outside the rackets, no one dangerous, because that's the kind of person who can make your dirty money look clean.

This sounded reasonable, and it calmed me down a bit. I figured Jo Jo would have Ernie go over the wreckage of Matches' car, and that they would decide the money had not been in it. There was a chance they would think it had been completely incinerated (it had been a heck of a conflagration, a worthy sendoff for a firebug) or that Matches had thrown it from the car during the pursuit. I doubted that, though; their own natures would convince them that he had made the delivery and that the recipient had decided to keep the loot in light of subsequent events.

After all, that's almost exactly what happened. Now I had to convince them that somebody else was the culprit.

***

I'd practiced my answers and rehearsed my facial reactions for the entire two days since the crash, expecting Ernie the Evil Eye to come and see me. I'd even fooled myself into believing I wasn't spooked by the most feared cop in the local underworld, but luckily I didn't have to put that belief to the test. The Eye simply called my office and told me to ring him up from a pay phone.

Despite this modest reprieve, I was fighting a bad case of nerves as I dropped the coins into the slot. I had to keep telling myself to stick to the plan, which was to feign ignorance of any extra money. As far as the Eye was concerned, I was just a guy waiting to be told who the new bag man was.

I could have saved myself the effort, though, as Ernie was only calling to tell me there would be no further deliveries until they decided on a replacement for Matches. He hung up before I finished offering my condolences.

Although I had been ignored all my life, and had resented every minute of it, that day I was absolutely overjoyed to be considered a nobody.

***

When I got back to the agency I stayed in my office for a good hour, wondering what had just happened. I'd been ready for questions, accusations, and even threats, but Ernie's simple message had completely thrown me. He hadn't even asked if Matches had been by on the fateful day.

That made me think of something I'd long suspected about the infamous Rossiter Gang. It went all the way back to Uncle Marty's description of Jo Jo's organizational downsizing. Uncle Marty's stories usually followed one of two themes, which were the value of blood relations or the genius of Jo Jo Rossiter, and I had come to question the latter point.

Several years earlier, once I got good at managing the Quick 'n Easy, I suggested to Uncle Marty that Jo Jo might invest in a few more car agencies. I offered to run these franchises, using them to hide even more money for the group, but Jo Jo never expressed interest in the idea. Uncle Marty swore he mentioned it to him several times, and I came away believing the big man simply couldn't understand the potential in the deal. Jo Jo's lack of business savvy fit the Rossiter gang's roots in leg-breaking, and so I began to question the tales of his intelligence. Besides, how smart could Jo Jo be if he entrusted a hundred grand to a dunce like Mickey Matches?

I finally decided that Jo Jo was not the mastermind Uncle Marty always said he was – and that made me suspect that Uncle Marty had known it too. If that were true, his insistence on broadcasting Jo Jo's brilliance might have been his way of hiding the boss's dimwittedness. This in turn led to another idea: If Uncle Marty's assertion of Jo Jo's genius had actually been a ruse, perhaps his explanation of the gang's dwindling size had been a trick as well.

It was simple: Tell enough people that the gang downsized by choice, and they might never guess that it was simply dying. Keep telling that story and they might not see that the gang was nothing more than a few fossilized hit men, shifting money around like bankers and living off the interest.

This all made sense, and even suggested a rosy explanation for the Eye's failure to question me. Perhaps the gang had gone to seed so badly that they had no idea how much money Matches had been carrying in the first place. I liked that thought, but it still left one burning question: Who had been waiting for that last delivery, and did they know how much it was?

***

I got my answer late in the afternoon of the third day. She walked in and asked to see me, and one of my assistants called me out to the desk. She was average height for a woman and wore a smart blue business suit that looked comfortable even in the hot weather. Her brown hair was pulled back in a severe bun, and she wore oval-shaped glasses. She had a nice figure, but the look on her face was one I'd seen on many a dissatisfied customer over the years.

"Hello, Mister Barnett. I'm Gloria Haller." She said from across the counter, as if I should know this without being told. Her already dark expression clouded up even more when she saw I didn't recognize the name. "Mickey's daughter."

That told me why she had come to the agency, and why she looked ready to kill me. She knew about the money and was here to get it back. Despite my surprise, I recovered quickly enough to get her away from the assistants, and ushered her into my office. She came without batting an eye, and if she'd been carrying a bag I would have been fearful that it might contain a gun. She let me get seated behind the desk before starting in.

"Mister Barnett, I need the money that my father gave you."

"What money?" It was all I could manage. I had no idea where she fit in all this or what she knew, and I certainly hadn't rehearsed this little confrontation.

"Look, buster, I'm in on the game. My father would drop five thousand dollars with you once a month and then bring me a much larger amount where I work. I've been investing it for the J-Man, and up until the other day it was working fine. I know my dad was carrying roughly one hundred thousand dollars on the day he died, and I've already been visited by our friend the Eye. For some reason he thinks my dad delivered the money and that I decided to keep it after the accident.

"The only good thing is that he thinks it was a lot less cash than it actually was – twenty grand. So even though you don't deserve it, if you give me twenty grand from the money you stole I can get the Eye off my back. And you're going to do it."

I could have jumped for joy. I recognized the squeeze they were putting on her as an old game played by the mob when the smaller gangs in their territory misbehave. Let's say, for example, that a gang of independents has decided to rob a mob-protected bookie. The smaller group is betting the wiseguys won't be able to figure out who did the deed, and this is sometimes concealment enough. Unfortunately, the mob's reputation suffers if no one is punished for the offense, so they usually just go ahead and pick somebody.

In this case the Eye had picked Matches' daughter, probably thinking she would be easy to squeeze. And to think I hadn't known she even existed when I took the money. It was a godsend, and all I had to give her was the brush-off to be completely in the clear.

"Lady, I don't know what you're talking about."

"Really? Then you won't mind if I tell the DA that you've been laundering money for Jo Jo Rossiter." She had no way of knowing if my office was bugged, and she clearly didn't care anymore. "Believe me; I've got a record of every drop my dad ever made here. He never trusted you, and he wanted me to have all the information in case something like this happened."

I had the luxury of knowing the office was not bugged, as one of Jo Jo's helpers swept the place weekly, and so I spoke my mind.

"Go ahead. From this crazy story you're telling me, it sounds like you were expecting a lot more cash than this Eye person knows about. How come there's so much of a difference?" I had to be careful here. Detailed arguments like this one usually tipped your hand by divulging information only a guilty man would have, but I had to make the girl accept her fate. And I did want to know why Matches had been hauling so much loot that day.

She was steaming mad by then, and the set of her jaw told me her teeth were gritted nice and hard. Once again I was glad she didn't have a bag. She stayed that way for a good thirty seconds before answering.

"Okay. You're gonna make eighty thousand dollars just because the cops chased my father on the wrong day. I've been putting some money away for him, investing it just like for Jo Jo, and the extra was my dad's. He'd cashed in some bonds through another broker, and I was going to reinvest the proceeds."

This was too good. She was spilling her guts to a total stranger, and with no hope that I would cooperate. Blood does tell, after all. Her father was a knucklehead firebug who was obviously skimming from Jo Jo, and she was just as stupid as her old man if she believed Matches had a hundred grand of his own. Jo Jo and the Eye were going to eat her alive.

"So you're a stock broker."

"Yes." She replied testily, probably forgetting that she'd mentioned 'another broker' and wondering how I guessed this. "Now here's what I want to do ..."

"Well then why don't you get the twenty from your job? Or out of your own pocket?"

"What?"

She was just like every broker I'd ever met, a pauper promising to make their clients millionaires. I decided I'd had enough of this, and stood up with finality.

"Thanks for coming by, Miss Haller, and I wish you luck with your problem." I took her arm, and even though she shrugged it off, she did leave the office when I opened the door. I stayed behind the counter as she headed for the parking lot, looking teary-eyed and defeated. She'd scrape the twenty grand together somehow, proving she took the money in the first place, and I would be in the clear.

She wasn't even out of the parking lot when I decided to make sure of it.

***

It was raining that night when I went out the side door, crossed the blackness of my back yard, and found the break in the chain link. I was thankful for the rain and had waited until well past midnight before setting out.

The small trees and the scrub brush whipped around in the wind, making it doubly difficult to climb the slope. I was wearing a dark raincoat, but the wind was so strong that I had to use one hand to hold the hood in place while using the other to hold the flashlight. I fought my way through the seething, scratching branches until I was propped against one of the trees which surrounded the relay box, and took out the trash bag.

I reached the house with great relief, even though I knew I would have to go back with the remaining money once I took out the twenty thousand which would seal Miss Haller's fate. I already had an envelope prepared, and my plan for mailing it was pure genius.

I had checked Miss Haller's story as soon as she left, and learned she was in fact a broker with one of the city's bigger firms. I had then called up one of their secretaries and tricked her into giving me the account number for their overnight delivery service. I had picked up a blank shipping label from their carrier, and once I filled that out with their account number I could place the parcel in any of a hundred drop boxes throughout the city. In case there was any doubt, Ernie the Evil Eye would be able to determine the parcel's origin from the information on the label. Miss Haller's firm would be paying the postage, and it could not be traced to me.

Just to be safe, I'd even called up the mortuary that had handled Mickey Matches' funeral and confirmed that my naïve visitor had been in attendance at the burial. I laughed at that after hanging up the phone, figuring a good burial plot had been wasted on a firebug who had been cremated at the moment of death.

My side door goes right into my kitchen, and I took off the dripping rain jacket in the dark, having turned off all the house lights before going out. The drapes were all drawn, but I still only switched on a single lamp as I sat on the living room floor and began counting money out of the bag. It was so much better than the first night, when I had done the same thing while quaking with fear. This time I was practically cackling out loud, knowing the eighty thousand was going to be mine forever. This must have distracted me, because I didn't hear a sound until someone flipped the switch which turned on the overhead light.

My heart got a nice jolt of adrenaline when the light came on, and then a second one when I saw both Miss Haller and Ernie the Evil Eye standing in the kitchen doorway. They were dripping wet, but not too wet, which suggested they had come from a car or one of my neighbors' homes. The Eye was using one of my kitchen towels to dry what was left of his hair, and Matches' daughter was pointing a large handgun at me in a motionless grip.

"Hey there, Jack. Looks like you came into some money." Ernie announced brightly before tossing the towel behind him. He was only a little taller than the girl and not much bigger, but the eyes for which he was named bored into me like a drill. He crossed the floor in a way that did not put him in the line of fire, scooped up the bowling bag, and stuck out a hand for the money packet I was holding.

Dropping into a chair, he began slowly emptying the bag, stacking the bundles carefully on my side table.

"Wondering how we caught on?" This came from the statue holding the gun. Looking up at her, I now saw that her damsel-in-distress routine had been just an act. I wondered dumbly if she was even the Miss Haller who sold stocks and attended pyromaniacs' funerals.

"Oh I'm Matches' daughter, all right." She read my mind, but her face stayed blank. "But I'm Jo Jo's granddaughter too. On my mom's side. We moved away when my dad went to jail, but I didn't see any reason not to come home when he got out."

"You're looking at the future of the entire operation, right there in the doorway." Ernie offered, having finished the counting. "Stock broker, smart as a whip, hides more money in an afternoon than you've hidden in the last ten years."

She tossed him a friendly glance before speaking. "I knew you took the money, but my granddad – and Uncle Ernie here – just couldn't believe Marty Barnett's nephew could do such a thing. So we decided to find out. We made sure Ernie didn't even mention the missing money, and then I told you my little story. I figured you'd be tempted to set me up by sending it in yourself."

Ernie jumped in then, having put the money back in the bag. "Me, I wanted to just come by and ask. I've known you a long time, and even your Uncle Marty knew you got no heart. But Gloria talked me out of it."

The gun was still pointed at me, and I was pretty sure they were going to use it when the story ended, so I asked the obvious question.

"So how did you know for sure? Or did you just stake out my place and hope to get lucky?"

She smiled for the first time, the way a kindergarten teacher smiles at a kid who's just never going to get very far in life.

"Oh, I knew the moment you met me. I told you I was Matches' daughter, and you didn't say anything about me losing my dad. You were already trying to figure out what Mickey might have told me, or if I was the one who was supposed to receive that delivery.

"If you hadn't taken the money, you'd have said something about my dad's passing – like you did on the phone with Uncle Ernie. But you didn't. That's when I knew." The smile flashed again. "Oh, and I talked to both of your assistants a little later. They said you had two visitors that day, in quick succession, the second one right before they heard the sirens."

The Eye laughed at that. "Your assistants don't seem to like you very much, Jack. You should have listened to your Uncle Marty all those times he tried to teach you about loyalty. But you're not much like him after all, are you?"

So that's why I'm writing this. They took the money and left after telling me I was being allowed to live because I was still needed at the shop. The next day a mean old dinosaur cousin of Jo Jo's appeared, announced he was now my boss, and took over my office. The nice bonus I received each year for my laundering services is now a thing of the past even though I still do the laundry. I'm little more than a salaried employee at the car rental place I used to run, and my two former assistants still haven't stopped smirking.

And even though I've been told I can stay on as long as I want, I can't help wondering if they'll decide to fire me the old mob way once the dinosaur learns the job. Maybe Ernie will come by the office one afternoon and suggest we go for a drive. Or maybe Miss Haller will walk me up the incline behind my house one night.

Or maybe another of Jo Jo's unidentified grandkids will do it. After all, it's in the blood. And most of the time blood tells.

In the game of "Good Cop, Bad Cop" sometimes it's hard to tell which is which.

SHOULDN'T BE CHARGED
Austin S. Camacho

The second I saw Officer Al Nolton through my office window I knew something was very wrong. Walking into the headquarters building on his first morning back after a week of special training it seemed to me that he ought to be happy, but his expression was downright grim. His clenched fists and general body language told me that this was a man looking for a fight.

I set my coffee down on my desk and headed for the door. The Chief doesn't hire trouble makers to work out of the courthouse complex, and I don't take trouble makers into the Criminal Investigations Bureau. In fact, Nolton was one of my sharpest, most level-headed men. I wouldn't have sent him to training out of state if he wasn't. But here he was in full uniform, including his service weapon, wearing the face we save for staring down drunks.

I watched Nolton stalk toward the break room without looking left or right. He's a beefy dude, a couple of inches over six feet and, like me, he still wears his hair exactly the way it was cut in the Marine Corps. He was on a collision course with three of my other men gathered around the high tech gizmo we still call a coffee pot. Something told me to follow him.

All three cops getting their morning coffee looked up as if to greet Nolton, but their welcoming smiles faded fast. Carson, my senior uniform, was on the left and Decker, the new kid, was over by the sink. Bennett stood in the middle. I saw the quizzical look on his face as Nolton approached. Then I lost sight of Bennett's face, because Nolton put his right fist all over it.

I was running toward them before the other two uniforms reacted. Nolton had dropped on top of Bennett and was unloading a series of rights down into his face. Bennett's not as big as Nolton but I figure he could have handled himself okay if he hadn't been sucker punched. The other two men each grabbed one of Nolton's arms but they were hard put to control him. Decker looked at me as if asking what to do. He didn't expect his plainclothes boss to get involved physically and even if I did, he didn't think it would make much difference. I was the only guy in the room you'd call average in height and build. Maybe that's why my first thought wasn't wrestling with an enraged, trained fighter.

I snatched the mace canister off Nolton's belt and gave him a good shot in the face. He snapped back and the other two backed off to let him flap around on the floor for a while. I was surprised to see Bennett still conscious, and he still looked clueless.

"Lieutenant Rissik," he said, trying to sit up. "What the hell? Is he on drugs or something?"

Before I could offer my opinion, Nolton bellowed, "She's dead. Sheila's dead and he's to blame."

***

Fifteen minutes later we were all in my office, five boys in blue, four in police uniforms. I put Nolton in a chair on the left side of my desk facing Bennett on the right. Both had cleaned up their faces. Yesterday I'd have said Bennett was the handsomest guy in my bureau, but right then his face looked a bit like a well tenderized steak. Nolton seemed to have gotten hold of his anger, but now both men appeared to be wrestling with grief.

Carson stood behind Nolton with one of his abnormally large hands resting on Nolton's shoulder. The gray in his mustache spoke of his experience. I had Decker behind Bennett. The kid was wiry, a couple inches over six feet, with a thatch of straw on his head. I was taking the rookie on as a personal project. He was quick and dedicated, and might be senior officer material someday. I wanted him to see how really tough situations could be handled.

I stood leaning back against the front of my desk. I was in *my* uniform too: one of my dark blue suits, starched white shirt and a conservative tie, up tight to my neck where it belonged. I sipped my fresh coffee, took a moment to enjoy the aroma, and then put the cup down and turned to Nolton.

"All right, you first. What were you saying about your wife?"

Nolton clenched his eyes tight, and when they opened they locked onto Bennett. "She's dead, Lieutenant. She killed herself while I was out of town. I was only gone a week."

"I know that, Officer," I said. "I handpicked you for that forensics course at the Body Farm down in Tennessee. When did you get home?"

"I drove in last night," Nolton said. "She wasn't home, but I just figured she was out shopping or something. I was beat, so I went to bed figuring she'd wake me up when she got in. When I woke up this morning, still no Sheila. I got frantic and started really looking around. I finally found her in the garage. In the Saturn. She was so still. Her skin was..."

I said the hard part for him. "Dead behind the wheel? I take it the garage door was closed?" Nolton nodded. "And what's this all got to do with Bennett?"

Nolton returned his attention to Bennett and the rage returned. "The note." He fished in his shirt pocket and handed me a folded piece of stationery. I opened it and found small writing in a very feminine hand. I read it aloud.

"I love you both. I feel like I'm breaking in half. Al is my rock, but I can't live without Dan I can't..." It trailed off there, but it was enough. Bennett was known as Fancy Dan around the building. Off duty he dressed like a pimp and drove a red Corvette. Everybody said he was a lady's man. I asked him straight up.

"So, Officer Bennett. Were you spending time with Mrs. Nolton?"

Bennett started to answer, but then his eyes went down and to his left. His lip quivered. Crooks are much better liars than cops. It was enough to bring Nolton out of his chair.

"He was fucking her and now she's dead." His fists were clenched but Carson had a grip on his shoulder. I stepped between the two men and looked up into Nolton's eyes. Our chests almost touched but even in this state he knew better. I kept my voice low but I know he understood that I could take him down if I had to.

"Where is she now?"

"Right where I found her," he said, but for the first time today he didn't sound too confident.

"Let me make sure I got this right. You found your wife dead in her car this morning, and instead of calling it in you left her in the car and came in here to beat up her boyfriend? Sit your dumb ass down."

I paced over to the door and back, just to get a few seconds to think. When I looked up Decker was the first face I saw.

"Rookie, get me a vehicle. You're driving me over to Nolton's house. Carson, get the crime scene people and the Medical Examiner's Office on the horn and tell them they got a customer today. Then you drive Nolton home. We need to do this right and we need to close it quick."

Everyone mobilized but when Bennett rose from his chair I froze him in place with a cold stare.

"In addition to dealing with Sheila Nolton's suicide, all of a sudden I got two cases for Internal Affairs to investigate," I told him. "You can simplify this mess. First there's the matter of your own misconduct."

"I'm in the wrong, Lieutenant," Bennett said. He actually hung his head in remorse. "I won't waste anybody's time with denials. I'll answer whatever they ask and take what's coming to me. Boss, I really did care about Sheila."

"Uh-huh. And then there's the matter of Officer Nolton assaulting you. You can bring charges and that would probably end his career in law enforcement."

Bennett raised his palms toward me. "Don't worry, Lieutenant, I sure as hell don't want to cause Al any more problems. He shouldn't be charged for what he did. Another guy might have come in here and put his service weapon against my head and pulled the trigger."

***

The Fairfax County Police Department doesn't have too many spare cars in the motor pool. It took Decker more than an hour to get us a black and white. That gave me time to clear my inbox and deal with all the other live cases, the ones that didn't involve cops. Time to wonder what Carson and Nolton would be talking about, sitting in that house. And hopefully, it was enough time for the Medical Examiner's team to carry poor Mrs. Nolton away.

I was ready to go when Decker drove to the door to pick me up. I had looked up the address so I could navigate. Nolton lived right there in the City of Fairfax. It would be a short drive.

As we pulled out onto Chain Bridge Road I asked Decker, "What would you do about Nolton attacking Bennett in our own headquarters?"

He took a few seconds to think about it, and then said, "I'd try to get Bennett to drop it. Nolton shouldn't be charged for beating up a guy who slept with his wife and might have driven her to suicide. Should he?"

"No, I think you're on the right track."

"Thanks, Lieutenant," Decker said. "I want to be you someday."

"Be me?"

He had stopped at a red light but kept his eyes straight ahead. "Someday I want to be the straight arrow in charge of a bureau. I want to be the guy in the starched white shirt who never has a piece of paper on his desk except what he's writing on, who keeps his inbox empty, who demands the respect of all the men under him."

I closed my eye and sat back. How do you teach an eager young trooper not to be a suck- up?

***

It took Decker a while to find a place to park that morning. The streets are generous and wide in the Warren Woods neighborhood, but too many official vehicles crowded us out of the driveway and the rest of the cul-de-sac. When we finally hiked up to the house, Carter and Nolan were standing out front.

Nolton lived in a nice brick split level with some siding on it, built in the 50s like everything else in the neighborhood. It was an intimate little subdivision, the kind of place where neighbors know each other and look out for one another. They probably wondered why the ambulance and cop cars were there. I started toward the center of activity but Nolton intercepted me.

"Lieutenant, I just want to apologize for my behavior earlier. I think I was kind of in shock or something. I hope you can get the boys in there to wrap up fast. I got a lot of ugly details to take care of."

"The coroner's in there now," Carson said, "His quick assessment is carbon monoxide poisoning and she looks to be about three days gone."

I nodded and walked on, waving to Decker to stay close. I could smell the roses Sheila Nolton had planted along the front of the house. Who would tend them now?

"Tell me, rookie, why am I going into the garage? The coroner's got this, right?"

"Because you're kind," Decker rushed to say. "You want to reassure everyone that Mrs. Nolton's death is an obvious suicide. It might shorten the investigation and speed up any settlement."

"So you've already decided that Nolton's a victim, eh?" I asked. "Look, kid, Nolton's a good cop, and Bennett clearly did wrong, but right now everything we know we heard from them. You always want to see for yourself whenever you can. It's possible her husband was crazy with jealousy and jumped to the wrong conclusion."

When I stepped into the garage the crime scene fellow recognized me and didn't give me any grief. I pulled on a pair of gloves and just looked over his shoulder when he opened the driver's door. They'd hauled the body away, but the stench of three-day-old corpse had stayed behind. He started dusting for prints, but we both knew that if he found them from both Noltons it wouldn't mean anything. An empty CD case lay open on the passenger seat. It wasn't labeled. I leaned over the tech to poke the stereo's power button.

"What are you doing, Lieutenant?" the tech asked, bumping my arm away with his shoulder. I backed off. I knew better.

"Sorry, buddy. I was just curious."

He gave me an understanding smile, turned the key a click in the ignition and pushed the button himself. Dolly Parton's voice poured out, claiming in strained tones that she would always love me. Whitney Houston covered that tune, but Dolly did it best.

"Music to die by, eh?" the tech said, continuing his work. I shut it off and walked back out on the driveway.

"That son of a bitch," I said under my breath.

Decker looked stunned. "Lieutenant! You couldn't have seen anything that fast."

"I saw enough," I said. I looked at Nolton over in front of the door. A plainclothes detective was taking a statement from him right then, so I waved Carson over. When he was close, I looked him straight in the eye.

"Tell me straight. You ever have anything to do with Sheila Nolton?"

"You know better than that, boss." He looked more hurt than angry.

"Yeah, I suppose I do," I said. "Listen, wander down there and don't let Nolton wander off. And when we head back to headquarters, tell the tech boys to fast track the handwriting analysis on that note and process it for prints. We're going to need a warrant to seize the car, not hers but his, so we can check the GPS. Better get somebody checking the airlines too. I want to verify Nolton's actual whereabouts every minute of the day and night since he left for Tennessee."

Carson nodded and moved off, but he kept his walk casual like a pro. On the other hand, Decker's face was so transparent that I pulled him by the arm back toward the car so no one else would see it. Besides, I didn't want to stick around there. The whole situation sickened me. It took the rookie a minute to regain the power of speech.

"Okay, you think Officer Nolton came back here three days ago and killed his wife."

"Nolton is a good investigator," I said. "Maybe he found evidence of his wife's infidelity."

"And then what?" Decker asked. "He starts a fight at headquarters to throw blame on Officer Bennett?"

I spotted one of the neighbors in a window and made eye contact until he backed down. "Or maybe he just did it for fun. Maybe he just wanted to enjoy pounding his wife's lover to a pulp in a situation where he could get away with it."

It was a nice neighborhood. He gave her a good life. She shouldn't have been screwing around on him with one of his coworkers. I understood the anger, but adultery isn't a capital offense.

"I guess I see jealousy as a motive," Decker said. "But from the Body Farm in Tennessee? It's got to be close to an eight hour drive, each way. He could have done it, I guess, but what makes you think he did?"

"The CD," I said. We stopped at the car.

"Yeah, a pretty depressing choice, but how is that a clue?"

I sighed and shook my head. I wanted him to get there on his own. "Think it through, rookie. A woman goes in her garage, she shuts the garage door and gets in her car. She writes a brief note and leaves it next to her on the seat. She starts the car, starts the tear-jerker music, and sits there until she's dead, right? Does she turn the car off?"

"Of course not," Decker said. "But isn't it reasonable to assume her husband came home, found her in the garage and once he was sure she was dead, took the note and turned off the car?"

"Not likely," I said, looking down the block to watch Nolton in front of the house. Crooks are such better liars than cops. "Not three days later. The car would have run out of gas. But if nobody found her in that time, the ignition would have still been on, with the stereo playing. So..."

Decker's mouth dropped open and if he was in a cartoon I think I would have seen a light bulb appear over his head. Then he actually blushed a little.

"After three days the battery should be stone dead. But you just turned the stereo on and it played."

"Uh huh. Which means that somebody shut off the car not too long after the woman was dead. Now who might have done that?"

"Well, anybody who found her would have called the police," Decker said, pacing on the sidewalk, "unless they wanted her dead, and didn't want her discovered. That could be Nolton. But it could be Bennett too, couldn't it?"

"Easy, kid. So far all you've got is a clue that it was murder," I said with a small smile. "Only the killer would shut off the car, but it could still be anybody. So now you've got to ask yourself why. Why would somebody have a reason to turn off the car?"

Now Decker was tracking with me. "The only reason I can see is if they were worried about carbon monoxide seeping into the house the last couple of days. And that would only matter to somebody who was planning to sleep there all night before revealing that he knew she was dead."

"Very good, rookie," I said, slapping Decker's arm. "We can't prove he did it yet, but at least we can pretty much rule out suicide."

"Not proof, but a solid case," Decker said. "Assuming we don't find a third person's fingerprints inside the car, I'm afraid Officer Nolton will be a defendant soon. So I was wrong in the car on the way here."

"How's that?" I asked, opening the door to get in the car.

"Well, sir, that car's battery shouldn't be charged, but since it is, I think Officer Nolton should be."

Most men are not defined by the work they do.
But for others, their job can become the best – or maybe the worst –
part of them

THIS OLD STAR
Wayne D. Dundee

It was late in the afternoon when I cut fresh sign from the posse. The cold, rainy drizzle that had been falling on and off all day was turning to flecks of snow as the light started to fade and the air grew steadily cooler. The edge of darkness wasn't far behind, slicing quickly across the land, spurred by the bloated, low-hanging cloud cover that crowded the sky.

Spotting the flicker of a campfire up ahead in a copse of cottonwood trees was a welcome sight.

I reasoned the fire had to be that of the posse, settling in for the night, but I approached with caution all the same.

"Hello the camp!" I called out when I was within earshot.

After an uncertain pause somebody called back, "Come ahead on in … easy-like!"

I swung down out of the saddle and walked in slow, leading my horse. Nearing the circle of campfire light I took note of the half dozen men standing around its shadowy edges. All were watching me and all were poised warily, weapons close at hand. I recognized each of them as good citizens of Flatrock Crossing – the town back to the south where I also hailed from. As I moved further into the light they quickly recognized me in return.

"Jeb?"

"Jeb Stander, is that you?"

"By God, it is … It's ol' Jeb hisself!"

They converged on me then, wide grins, hand claps to the shoulder, everybody suddenly at ease and glad to see me. Only on the face of Ben Tembow did I see a hint of reservation. He was the last to step forward, the sheriff's star on his coat tossing a glint of yellowish silver in the firelight. Ben managed a grin of his own, albeit a somewhat more tentative one than the others, as he said, "I guess you're a sight for sore eyes, Jeb … but what in the world brings you clear out here on a night like this?"

I grinned back at him, back at all of them. "What? You think I was gonna just sit on my duff and leave you boys have all the fun?"

"Fun?" echoed Elmer Dunlop, the newspaper editor. "Riding all over creation, freezing our asses off on what's turning out to be a wild goose chase? You got a mighty peculiar idea of what fun is, Jeb Stander."

Ben turned on him and snapped, "You knew damn well what to expect, Elmer. The weather was already turnin' bad, and I made it clear when you said you wanted to come along that it wasn't gonna be no joy ride. You're the one who insisted it was a story you needed to cover first hand."

"Some story," Elmer grumbled. "Two days now and so far we haven't caught even whiff of Shake Whitley."

The sheriff glared at him.

I spoke up. "Young Ben's as good a tracker as any around. You know that, Elmer. Rain and mud – and now snow, it looks like we're gonna get … Those are tough odds to buck. And don't forget Shake Whitley's a damned crafty dodger to begin with, that's what's made him so successful at duckin' the law in three states for the past dozen years."

"I appreciate the words, Jeb," Ben said. "But Whitley ain't ducked us yet. Nossir. Leastways *I* ain't ready to give up … are any of the rest of you boys?"

He got a general muttering of responses signaling everybody was still with him – even Elmer Dunlop – but it was clear that the wet, cold, weary bunch wasn't exactly busting with enthusiasm over the prospect.

I stepped up in front of Ben and locked eyes with him. "Look," I said, "I heard about the trouble back in town – the jailbreak and bank robbery, and how you fellas lit out after Whitley. I didn't come taggin' along to horn in on your show. I ain't the sheriff of Flatrock Crossing no more – you are. So if you want me to step on back out of the way, just say it straight out and I'll understand. On the other hand, if you're open to the notion of me ridin' along as one more deputized citizen then I'd be honored to do so and I figure I could be of some use to you."

Emotion and firelight rippled across Ben's face. "Jeb," he said quietly, "what kind of fool would I be to turn down an offer of help from the likes of you? Of course you're welcome to ride in this posse. And havin' you would make *me* the honored one."

"Just wanted to make sure how you felt, that's all … I couldn't help thinkin' how you never sent word when you took out on this thing."

"I never sent for you because I didn't want to impose. You already shouldered more than your share of hardship and danger, bein' sheriff for all those years. I figured you didn't owe it to nobody to take on more. What's more, with you livin' in that cabin way out on Wolf Creek nowadays and me needin' to set this posse in motion as quick as possible … well, there wasn't a whole lot of time." Ben grinned again. "You taught that me that. Remember? When there's trouble, you always said, you got to make up your mind and make it quick … So that's what I done."

"Fair enough," I allowed. "And as far as settin' myself up for any hardship or danger that comes of this, that part's my decision and my own doin'."

"Fair enough right back at you." Ben turned and gestured to some of the others. "Here now. A couple of you fellas take Jeb's horse and get him staked over there with the others … That first pot of coffee ought to be cooked by now and then we need to get some grub in our bellies, too."

"So happens," I said, "that in those saddle packs, before you lead off my horse, you'll find some things to help with that. I know how it is when you light out in a hurry on a posse chase. I got extra coffee in there, a side of bacon, a couple spare blankets, and a sack of buttermilk biscuits that Miss Dolly over at the café sent along."

"Now you're talkin'," somebody said. "Hot coffee and a couple of Miss Dolly's buttermilk biscuits – that right there sounds to me like the makin' of a feast!"

"Also, if the sheriff don't object," I added, cutting a sly look over at Ben, "I brung along a couple bottles of a little something to help warm everybody's innards on a mean night like this."

That brought another whoop, even more eager than the news of Miss Dolly's biscuits.

With exaggerated reluctance, Ben said, "Well … long as it's strictly for healthful purposes like keepin' the cold from seepin' clean into our bones and such … I reckon a nip or three before we turn in ought to be allowable."

***

The events back in Flatrock Crossing that set all of this into motion started with the arrival in town of the notorious outlaw and bank robber Shake Whitley. Even though he'd been raising hell all through Missouri and Kansas and clear down into parts of Texas for over a decade, he would later admit, after Ben had him behind bars, that he "didn't figure anybody out here in this pissant corner of west Nebraska would ever recognize me." But sharp-eyed Ben Tembow did, and before Whitley had barely cut the trail dust out of his throat with a shot of redeye at the Silver Belle saloon, Ben and his deputy Billy Skipper had him under their guns and under arrest.

While waiting for the U.S. marshal out of Deadwood to arrive and haul Whitley away for trial, Ben had determined that the robber's purpose in coming to Flatrock Crossing was to hit the bank there before it transferred over the big payroll it was holding for the railroad crew building a bridge across the South Platte River west of town. Whitley claimed he had a whole gang who would be showing up soon to bust him out and help him still finish the job, but Ben took that for a bluff. Nevertheless, as a precaution, he deputized more men and posted a round-the-clock guard on the jail. Ben took the overnight watch himself. On the second night Whitley was in custody, things went wrong. Somehow the prisoner managed to pick the lock on his cell. He slipped out in the middle of the night, cold-cocked and hog-tied Ben in his bunk, then broke into the bank and blew the vault with dynamite he must have hidden somewhere close by. Went tearing out of town as the handful of citizens who'd been awakened by the explosion were still rubbing sleep out of their eyes and trying to figure out what all the commotion was about.

Ben, cracked skull and all, had formed his posse and ridden in pursuit the next morning at first light. But the rain and intermittent snow had made tracking the fugitive robber all but impossible and now, after two days of being out on the trail, the pursuers were wet and cold and weary and without any clear idea whether or not they'd gained any ground on their quarry.

***

After supper, the men were so played out that most of them wasted little time spreading their bedrolls and turning in to get some much needed rest. A light snow had begun falling steadily and moaning gusts of wind blew over the darkened landscape.

Ben and I stood apart from the rest, sipping from tin cups of coffee laced generously with some of the "extra warmth" I had provided.

"You got a plumb tuckered bunch here," I observed.

"Yeah, that's for sure. Clerks and shopkeepers, most of 'em. One stable hand. And one newspaper editor ... Not exactly trail-hardened law dogs."

"Fewer and fewer of those kind left around these days. Unfortunately, too many of the trail-hardened ones have rode to the other side of the law." I sighed. "But, with a posse, you take what you're able to pull together and be grateful."

"Yeah, reckon you'd know. You did your share of ridin' out ahead of posses that were made up of pretty much the same mix."

"I usually had you at my side, though."

Ben looked thoughtful. "I got Billy Skipper for a deputy these days. He's a good, earnest kid but is Lord-awful young. He would have added considerable to what I've got here, I guess, but I decided instead to leave him mindin' things back home. Hell, you never know ... it could turn out Whitley *does* have a handful of gang members prowlin' somewhere in the vicinity. Thought it best to leave some protection for the town, just in case."

I nodded. "Good thinkin', I'd say. I saw Billy before I headed out, by the way, and he seems to be lookin' out for things real tight. I don't figure you got any worries there."

"Good to know."

I drank some of my coffee. "Took a minute to look in on Ruth Ann, too."

"Appreciate that." A sidelong look. "She's doin' okay, right?"

"Worried about you. But that's natural enough for a gal in her position. My Clara, when she was alive and I was still sheriffin', she fretted every time I stepped out the door."

"Ruth Ann worries too much."

"Funny. She said the same thing about you ... that these days you're worryin' too much."

Ben swiveled his head and looked at me. "She meant about Sally, I take it?"

"That's what's got you so worried, ain't it?"

"How can it not? Our daughter is sick, Jeb. Bad sick. Weak heart, Doc Barnhart says. He also says he ain't good enough to make her well. Says there are doctors in Denver – specialists, he calls them – who know more than he does, know things that would help."

"Denver's a long ways away."

"In more ways than one ... in distance, and in money. Even if I got

Sally there I could never afford to pay those so-called specialists."

"Ruth Ann said Doc Barnhart thinks there might be a chance Sally's heart could mend itself, get stronger in time."

"I want better for my little girl than 'there might be a chance'."

Things hung quiet between us for a minute or so. Of in the distance a lone coyote yipped mournfully.

I cleared my throat. "I won't say something stupid like 'I understand how you feel'. No person can know the grief or misery inside another. But I *do* know what I went through watchin' my Clara fade until the cancer finally took her ... Times like that test a man, Ben. And there ain't no shame in relyin' on the hand of Providence to reach out and steady you some in order to get through it."

Ben looked at me again. "You're a strong man, Jeb. A stronger one, I fear, than I may be ... But as far as the hand of Providence, you'll pardon me if I say that I ain't seen one damn sign of it reachin' out to help us with Sally's sickness."

The camp was already stirring when I woke the next morning. This was both surprising and disconcerting to me. I'd always been a light sleeper, alert to things around me, especially out on the trail. I reckoned that my deeper-than-usual slumber was a sign of getting older and being out of condition for this kind of business. My long ride to catch up with the posse yesterday must have exhausted me more than I'd realized or wanted to admit.

But the good thing about getting up late, I found out, was that somebody else already had the coffee made and the bacon frying. So, having made this discovery, I wasted no time taking advantage of it by retrieving my cup from the night before and pouring myself some of the scalding brew out of the bubbling pot over the fire.

The storm had passed during the night, leaving two inches of fresh snow on the ground. The sky was clear now and a bright, warming sun was edging up above the eastern horizon.

I was taking my first sip of coffee when Ben walked over to me. "Appears we got ourselves a new development this mornin', Jeb."

"What's that? You cut sign of Whitley?"

Ben shook his head. "No such luck." He jabbed a thumb over his shoulder, indicating the other posse members who, I noticed for the first time, were sort of huddled together casting anxious looks our way. "Seems ol' Elmer got the boys to talkin' at some point and now they're tellin' me …"

"You just hold it right there, Ben Tembrow," Elmer, the newspaper man, interrupted. He took two or three steps in our direction. "I'm in favor of this plan, I'll own up to that much, but don't make it sound like I'm the one who somehow spearheaded the whole …"

"Save your breath, Elmer," Ben cut him off. "All that matters is that the lot of you have gassed it over you're of a same mind. That's the way you laid it out to me a minute ago, ain't it?"

"That's true enough. And it's also true that I was the spokesman when we approached you. But that still doesn't mean …"

"To hell with that part of it," I said, taking my own turn at interrupting. "Exactly what is it you're blabbering about? That's what I want to know."

Ben made a gesture. "You're the spokesman, Elmer. Go ahead. Tell Jeb what you and the others have come up with."

Elmer *harrumphed* a couple of times, then took another step forward. "Okay. Here's the thing, Jeb. Since you've shown up and agreed to ride on this chase after Shake Whitley … well, me and the other men no longer see where it's necessary – or even sensible, really – for the rest of us to stay with it. You and Ben are the professionals, the ones who know how to track and handle gunplay if it comes to that. The other fellows and I were willing to back Ben rather than have him ride out alone. But let's face it, mostly all we amount to is a show of numbers. Now that there's an alternative – namely you, Jeb – we can't help but feel there's no need for us to be here. Plus, we've got families and businesses to think of back in …"

"In case you don't remember, *I've* got a family back home, too," said Ben.

"Of course you do, Ben. Of course you do. And we're all sympathetic that you've got issues of concern there. But, not to sound uncharitable, you're the one who wears the sheriff's star, Ben. Matters like this are part of your job, part of what you signed on for."

Tom Cutler, the mercantile clerk, spoke up. "Comes to that, if you ask me, Ben has done all a body could be expected to do under these circumstances. He rode out with a busted head, for cryin' out loud, and gave it his all to lead us on chasin' down this damned Whitley. We're way past town jurisdiction by now. The U.S. marshal has already been notified and Whitley was on the run from the law long before he ever hit Flatrock Crossing. We made a stab at runnin' him down, tried out best, but the weather and everything else worked against us … I don't see no shame in the whole bunch of us turnin' back and goin' home and lettin' the U.S. marshal take over from here."

Ben shook his head. "Thanks, Tom, but for me there's a whole lot more to it than that. Yeah, maybe I'm out of my jurisdiction by now so technically Shake Whitley don't have to be my concern. But, damn it, *I'm* the one whose jail he busted out of and then went on to rob the bank of the town *I'm* supposed to protect … I ain't ready to give up on settin' that straight. Not by a damn sight, I ain't!"

"Seems to me," I said, "that's what it comes down to in a nutshell. I can understand where Ben's comin' from. And, I gotta admit, I can see the point of you other fellas, too." I turned to Ben. "What they're sayin' ain't really unfair or unreasonable. You and me are the ones who know how to track, how to shoot if and when it's called for. If there's any chance of runnin' down Whitley it's as good with just the two of us as it is with the whole bunch. Hell, with this new snow and two days already gone we might come up bust no matter what. I'll stick with it as long you want to, Ben. But let the rest of 'em go on back … and don't hold it against 'em."

***

So that's the way it went. Elmer and the others headed back to town, Ben and I stayed on.

We struck north, fanning out and riding in a switchback pattern hoping to cut some sign in the new fallen snow. When I asked Ben what made him think Whitley was headed north, he explained, "Because that's what I'd do in his position. He's too well known down to the south and east. And he can't go west, can't count on gettin' through the mountains this time of year. That leaves north, up into the Dakotas. He's got a sackful of money, things are boomin' up that way, and it's a place he's not well known. With no clear sign otherwise, it makes the most sense that's where he'd head."

I had no argument for his logic.

At noon we stopped for a meal of hot coffee, jerky, and the last of the biscuits Miss Dolly had sent with me. The day was bright and sunny, but still damned cold. And a stiff, cutting wind had kicked up. We hunkered into a pocket of boulders and pine trees to rest and take on some nourishment.

Chewing on a bite of jerky, I said, "Occurs to me you never deputized me, Ben. Reckon that's something we oughta take care of?"

Ben grinned. "Deputize *you*, Jeb? Is that really necessary? You may be retired, but you're still a lawman through and through. Always have been, always will be. Sworn in or not ain't gonna change that."

"Suppose you're right," I allowed. I fished in my pocket and came up with the tin star I had worn for all the years I'd been the sheriff of Flatrock Crossing. "Wanna see something corny? You let me keep this when I stepped down and you took over. I carry it with me every day. Sorta like a good luck piece. This old star means a lot to me, Ben. Bein' a lawman wasn't *all* I ever was as a person ... but it was a big part. Maybe the best part. I hold it mighty dear."

"Everybody knows that, Jeb. Like I said a minute ago – you're a lawman through and through."

I held the star before me and studied on it for a long minute. Then I swiveled my head and looked at Ben in a way I never had before. "So how much longer you gonna try to carry on with this?" I asked.

Ben blinked. "You heard what I told Tom and Elmer and the others. I'm a long ways from bein' ready to give up. Hell, I can't be *exactly* sure how long. As long as it takes. As long as Whitley is on the run out there ahead of me."

I shook my head slowly. "That don't wash, Ben. Just like the rest of it don't ... the jailbreak ... the bank robbery... none of it."

"What are you sayin', Jeb?"

"It's just the two of us here now. That's why I was so willin' to go along with the others turnin' back. I'm hopin' with only me and you there's a way we can talk this out, work it through somehow."

Ben's eyes narrowed. "If you got something to spit out, Jeb, quit chawin' the cud and commence to spittin'."

"Two things bothered me right from the git-go," I said. "First, I couldn't figure out why you didn't send somebody after me to ride in your posse right off. No matter what you say about not wantin' to bother me, it flat don't make sense that you wouldn't ask for my help with somebody as important as Shake Whitley ... Second, I couldn't rightly picture how anybody could pick the lock on that cell at the jail."

"Any lock can be picked, Jeb. And, in case you never heard, Shake Whitley has been in and out of a powerful lot of jail cells."

"But nobody picks a lock that solid unless they got the tools to do it. And you're too good – I know because I taught you – to put a prisoner behind bars without makin' sure he's clean of any such tools."

"So I got sloppy one time. I admit that much and I'm miserable damned sorry for it. Why do you think I'm pushin' so hard to run Whitley's ass down, to try and set things straight?"

"Maybe I could've swallowed that much. Wouldn't've went down easy, but maybe … Only then I ran across a couple more things. You know the kind of things I'm talkin' about, Ben. The kind of un-expected, quirky little things a lawbreaker almost always leaves behind to trip hisself up if somebody comes along with either the skill or the luck to spot 'em."

"You're wastin' a lot of time sayin' nothin' so far."

"When I stopped in to see Deputy Skipper," I continued unhurriedly, "he offered me a cup of coffee. Only he'd let the pot run dry settin' on the stove and a hole had burnt through the bottom. He was gonna to go down to the general store to buy a new one when I remembered we had a couple spare pots in that little cubbyhole in the back room. Leastways we did a year or so ago, when I was still sheriffin'. Seemed worth havin' a look before goin' out and buyin' a new one. Trouble was, Billy couldn't find the key to the lock on the cubbyhole … Guess you made sure of that part, didn't you? … But what you didn't think of – and I never did either, not until just then – was that I still had my extra key from the old days. So I put it to work on the lock, then leaned in to rummage for one of those spare pots … Reckon I don't need to tell you what caught my attention instead."

"You're too damned helpful for your own good, Jeb."

"I snatched out one of the pots and locked the cubbyhole back up before Deputy Skipper saw anything. I went ahead and had a cup of coffee with him but all the while my head was reelin' from what I'd seen. I chewed up a dozen, maybe a hundred different possible explanations for how the bank money could have ended up there … but it kept comin' back to only one that held up. *You* put it there, Ben."

He nodded. "Yeah. I did."

"And Whitley? The jailbreak? You staged it all?"

Ben kept nodding. His gaze was aimed somewhere away from me and there was a faraway look in his eyes. "Whitley's deep under the ice of Wolf Creek now, not too far from your cabin as a matter of fact. Got a bullet hole in his head and a couple melon-sized rocks stuffed in his shirt to keep him down."

"So you did for him, then robbed the bank yourself. Blew the safe, hustled back to the jail to hide the money, then staged the rest of it by clubbin' yourself in the head and tanglin' some rope around yourself on the bunk till somebody came runnin' to find you."

"You got it all figured. I confiscated a half dozen sticks of dynamite off some drunk construction worker who was wavin' 'em around in the Silver Belle one night a couple weeks ago. Was meanin' to get 'em back to the construction foreman out on the railroad bridge but hadn't got around to it yet. Turned out they came in real handy for the safe."

My coffee had grown cold. I flung what was left in my cup off into the snow. I said, "Got a lot of things boilin' in my gut I'd like to say to you right now, Ben. But I guess none of 'em really matter. Reckon you already told yourself most of 'em ... But you went ahead and did what you did, anyway."

Now his eyes found me and I could see torture and desperation in them. "Don't you see, Jeb? I did it for Sally – for the money to take her to Denver. I got to get her the best care possible. She's my baby girl. I can't just let her stand by and ... "

"And you can't do what you did, either. Not and get away with it."

"Once I had Whitley behind bars and he spilled to me what he was plannin'," Ben went on as if he hadn't heard me, "how he was gonna hit the bank and take the fat payroll that was waitin' there to be plucked ... That's when it came to me, all in a rush. How *I* could be the one to pluck that money and use it to get Sally the proper care to fix her poor little heart. Blame it all on Whitley. And then, after I ran out this phony chase, I figured I'd go back and resign out of shame for lettin' Whitley escape. Then me and Ruth Ann and Sally would pull up stakes and go off ... go off and head for Denver as soon as we was clear."

"There *had* to have been other ways, Ben. Damn it, I've got a little nest egg put away. It woulda been yours for the askin' if you'd only spoke up. And there are other people in town, good people who appreciate all the years of service you've given Flatrock Crossing. I'm sure enough of 'em woulda chipped in, just like me, to get Sally to Denver."

"And leave me beholdin', indebted to all those people for the rest of my life? I got too much pride for that, Jeb Stander, just like you'd have in the same position."

"Maybe. But I'd also have too much pride – in myself and for the star pinned on my shirt – to turn to murder and bank robbin'."

"To hell with you and that lousy tin star you think so highly of!"

"You're right, I do think a great deal of this old star, like I already told you. And I think a great deal of you, too, Ben ... It's for those two reasons I can't let you get away with this."

"I won't go back in irons, Jeb, if that's what you're thinkin'. I won't add humiliation and shame and prison time on top of already not being able to take care of my child. That can't happen."

"There are other ways. I pondered long and hard on the ride out here to find you ... I reasoned that a desperado like Shake Whitley has *got* to have rewards out on him."

"I'm a lawman. I can't claim rewards."

"But I'm not a lawman. Not anymore. I ain't even deputized. We do it this way ... We fish Whitley's body out of the creek where you sunk him, reclaim the bank money out of the cubbyhole and turn everything over, sayin' we caught up with Whitley and had to kill him in a shootout but still saved the money. I'll claim the rewards on Whitley and hand the pay-off over to you for Sally. Your slate is wiped clean and nobody is the wiser except you and me."

"I killed Whitley in cold blood, Jeb."

I gritted my teeth. "I can live with believin' he was overdue for killin'."

"You'd do that for me?"

"I offered it, didn't I?"

Ben passed the back of one hand across his mouth. "I don't know ... How sure can we be of those rewards? How long will it take for them to be paid?"

"It's the best offer you're gonna get, Ben. It's all I got. I'm bendin' as far as I can."

His eyes hardened. "Do you know how much of my adult life I've been in your shadow, Jeb? All the years I was your deputy and now, even a year and more since you stepped down, I can still *feel* it hoverin' over me. I can see it in folks eyes every time there's trouble in town. They watch what I do, listen to what I say, but all the while they're wishin' *you* was still there handlin' things."

"That's crazy talk, Ben. The folks in Flatrock Crossing think just fine of you."

"And now you make me the offer you just made. The big, grand gesture." Ben sneered. "You think *that* ain't gonna lay the weight of your shadow even heavier on me, Jeb?"

"It's all up to you, Ben. Like I said, it's the best offer you're gonna get."

"What makes you so sure I *need* a stinkin' offer from you? What if

I tell you to shove it and go ahead with my plan the way I already had it laid out?"

I shook my head. "I can't let you do that."

"And you think you're good enough to stop me?"

"If I have to."

We both stood up, slow. Ben brushed the coat flap back away from the gun holstered at his hip. I did the same.

"I didn't want it to come to this, Ben."

He made no reply.

We stood facing one another for what seemed like a long time. The fire crackled under the coffee pot. The pine trees creaked under gusts of wind.

And then two gunshots rang out, momentarily shattering all other sounds around us.

***

It took some doing to first find the spot on Wolf Creek where Ben had sunk Shake Whitley's body and then to get it hauled out of the icy water. I finally managed it, though. Took the frozen carcass back to my cabin where I stripped it down, thawed it out some, dried the clothes then redressed it. While I was doing that I kept Ben in a cold enough place to keep him from starting to spoil. Then I tied both bodies belly-down across the back of Ben's horse and rode with them back to Flatrock Crossing. I stopped by the jail long enough to report in to Deputy Billy Skipper and to send him to break the sad news to Ruth Ann. While he was doing that I covertly sneaked the bank money out of the cubbyhole and into my saddles bags. By then the rest of the townsfolk were converging and I was ready to tell my tale to them.

I related how Ben and I had finally cornered Shake Whitley and how he'd put up a fierce fight, mortally wounding brave Sheriff Tembrow before I got lucky with a bullet of my own that cut down the outlaw a second too late. I turned over the bank money and told everybody to never forget how lucky they'd been to have had a man like Ben Tembow packing a star for their town.

The reward for Shake Whitley was paid to me in short order and I used it to make sure Ruth Ann got Sally to those specialists in Denver. From the letters they write it sounds like Sally is doing well and the doctors are confident she will lead a long and healthy life.

The townsfolk tried to get me to go back to sheriffing, but I turned them down. Billy Skipper is growing into the job right nicely.

I keep mostly to myself these days, out at my cabin on Wolf Creek. I fish and hunt and fuss over a little garden in the warm months. When they're in bloom I take fresh flowers every couple weeks to put on my Clara's grave in the town cemetery. While I'm there I'll usually pause for a moment beside Ben Tembrow's grave. But for him I leave no flowers.

I still carry the old sheriff's star in my pocket. For luck, I tell myself. But when I take it out sometimes and ponder on it, it no longer seems to shine quite as bright as it once did.

Cops on the beach – sun, fun and guns. For somebody it's going to be ...

THE LAST CONVENTION
John L. French

Owens was the first to wake up, which was only fair; he had been the first to pass out.

Consciousness came slowly. He heard the sounds of the ocean through the open windows, then felt the morning sun on his face. When he finally did open his eyes, he realized that he was in the wrong room.

He looked up, the ceiling was wrong. In his room it was tiled, this was stucco. The cheap picture on the wall was of the Bay Bridge, it should have been Assateauge Island. The bed was far too lumpy, there was only one pillow and he had company.

Owens could feel the weight of the body next to him. He did not remember asking anyone to join him last night, but, then again, he did not remember much of anything last night. His last memory was of a karaoke bar on 4th Street. Jackson had been singing the wrong song to the music.

As Owens tried to push past the memory of Jackson's version of "Colour My World", the person next to him began to snore, in baritone.

"Oh, God! I could not have been that drunk." The thought forced him fully awake, and a wave of relief passed over him. He was fully clothed, nothing felt undone, and the baritone belonged to the forever off-key Jackson.

Owens sat up and looked around. Jackson was snoring next to him. Bryant had the chair nearest the balcony, feet resting on a coffee table. Face down on the floor was . . . Owens could not remember his name.

Checking his watch, Owens saw that it was still early. If he and the others hurried, and were not too far from their condo on 40th St., they could still get back, wash and change, and make it to the Convention Center in time for check-in.

"What's the point of renting a condo across from the convention if you're going to sleep somewhere else?" he thought as he considered getting out of bed.

It had been a good idea, Jackson's actually. The three of them had come down from Baltimore for the Fraternal Order of Police convention. Held once a year, the convention supposedly was for the exchange of new ideas in police work, to introduce and promote the latest advances in law enforcement technology and for the discussion of the problems facing cops in the 21th century. What it really was was an excuse for a weeklong party.

It was the convention that the Ocean City town officials feared the most. Sure, it brought in lots of money and filled every vacant room from the Inlet to the Delaware line, but the general idea of it was frightening. A city filled with conventioneers is one thing, but most of these conventioneers were armed, and did not fear the law because they were the law.

It was not that the FOP convention caused more trouble than any other, it was the nature of that trouble that bothered the Town Council. This year, for instance, there had been an impromptu shooting match on the beach between officers from Anne Arundel County and those from Montgomery County. Tired of arguing over which semi-automatic pistol was the more accurate, the officers, at 1:30 in the morning, decided to settle the matter on the sand. Using chemical light sticks as skeet targets, one cop would yell "Pull!", another would throw the light stick toward the ocean and a third would empty a clip in its direction. Since all of the participants had had a little too much to drink, most of the light sticks floated back to shore undamaged, to be used over and over until the cops ran out of ammunition.

The Ocean City police, seeing that their fellow officers were shooting over the water, wisely waited until all the firing had stopped. Then they stepped in and offered their comrades in arms rides back to their lodgings, making sure to get the names of the would-be marksmen to report to their respective commands. For weeks later, old men walking the beach with their metal detectors would be digging up cartridge cases, wondering why news of the obvious shootout had not made the papers or TV.

The next night, a fight almost demolished the popular nightspot Big'uns. A Maryland State Trooper had been droning on and on about the rigors of the training that the Maryland State Police gave its cadets. After letting him talk for a good twenty minutes, a civilian assigned to the Baltimore City Police Crime Lab quietly said, "Gee, that's sure a lot of work for twenty years of writing speeding tickets." The trooper punched the crime scene tech in the mouth.

Members of the BPD who witnessed this of course felt obligated to defend one of their own, however stupid and ill-timed his remarks were. The trooper's buddies joined in, as did most of the other cops present, and a good time was had by all. When the fighting was over, there was hardly an unbroken table in Big'uns, the crime lab tech had been hospitalized, and every uniformed member of the BPD and the MSP agreed that, no matter how useful they were on a crime scene, civilians had no place in a cop bar.

So that some kind of control could be kept over the visiting police, convention officials had decided that all participants would have to sign in at the various seminars and discussion groups for which they had registered. Miss too many events, and you would be denied your certificate of participation. This certificate was more than just another piece of paper to hang over your desk. Without it, an officer could not take the week in Ocean City as administrative leave. And without something official, at tax time the government just might decide that the trip had not really been business related and disallow its deduction as a work expense. At least, that's what the officers were told. Having been on the receiving end of bad government decisions too many times, most of them believed it.

So Andy Jackson got his good idea. A friend of his owned a condominium directly across from the Convention Center. With three people sharing the expense, the cost to rent it would be comparable to the cheap hotels where the cops usually stayed.

"It'll be great," Jackson told the other two. "In my nineteen years on the force, and in the last four going to these conventions, I ain't never seen a nicer set-up. We can sleep in a little and get over to the Center just as it opens. We sign in for the first session, duck out after the break and come back in the afternoon. Get us some beach time."

"Then after lunch we sign in for the p.m. sessions," Bryant picked up for Jackson. "And then we're one break away from having the day off."

"You guys do what you want, some of those classes may actually be interesting."

"Owens," Bryant chided, "You mean you're really here to go to the convention?"

"Well, yeah, most of it. That's the idea, isn't it?"

Owens felt embarrassed about wanting to go, to hear the new ideas and see the new technology. Why was it that the ones who though themselves "good cops" never wanted to be better policemen?

"Your choice, son. You tell us about the convention, and we'll tell you all about the babes on the beach and all the fun you missed."

"That's a deal, Andy."

Jackson's second idea had not been as good as his first. The three had been in a bar on Somerset St., just off the Boardwalk, when Jackson got his brainstorm.

"We're only a few blocks from the end of the Boardwalk. What say, we start at this end, walk north until we come to the other end, and have a drink in every bar we see?"

"Great idea, Andy," voted Bryant. "But wait, do we go to just the ones on the Boardwalk, or on the side streets too?"

"I think, Officer Bryant, that if we can see a bar from the Boardwalk, it counts, but we don't go any further than one block down."

"I agree, Officer Jackson. You in, Owens?"

Even as he agreed, Owens asked himself why he was going along with this crazy idea. He, of course, knew the answer.

All this week, he had been the good boy in school. He had gone to most of the sessions, picked up what literature he could for both himself and his partners and had conscientiously examined every display at the Convention Center. He had seen the fingerprint computers, the new patrol cars and the latest in non-lethal weapons. He could describe all of the restraint systems that he had been shown. He had bought himself some new handcuffs, a quick release holster and a couple of T-shirts. He had even gotten a "Crime Lab" cap for that idiot in Atlantic General Hospital. What he had not done was have a whole lot of fun. It was time to cut loose and be one of the boys.

"What harm can it do?" he thought. "There can't be that many bars between here and 28th St. We'll probably run out of money long before then anyway. We'll leave our guns back at the place, and when we finally do collapse, the Ocean City PD will see us home. They should be used to sweeping drunken cops off the street. Worse comes to worse, we sleep on the beach."

So Owens agreed.

They started at Charlie's, at S. 2nd St. on the Boardwalk. From there they worked their way north, having a drink at any place that would serve them. Most of these places were named for oddly colored animals or after vaguely vulgar body parts.

They were refused entry at an under-21 club on Division St.

Bryant would have forced entry but was told that the place did not serve alcohol. Hearing this, he demanded to know why the doorman was wasting the group's time, and had to be pulled back to the Boardwalk by the other two. At Talbot St. the trio became a quartet, joined by an officer from the Maryland Transportation Authority Police, the agency that patrols the toll roads and tunnels of Maryland.

("Monroe, that's the name of the guy on the floor," thought Owens as he recalled what he could of the evening.) Any discussion over whether a MdTAP officer was a "real cop" was forestalled when it came out that Monroe not only made more money than the other three, but was willing to spend some of it by buying the next few rounds.

The odyssey moved north. Owens had been wrong about the number of bars. Drinking was big business in Ocean City, surpassed only by miniature golf, T-shirt shops and the beach. Every block had its nightspot, and every side street one or two more. By 4th St. there was talk of surrender.

"We can't give up," Monroe slurred. "I thought you Baltimore boys were tough."

"Tough as you, Tunnelman, tough as you, but," Bryant checked his wallet, hoping that more money had somehow miraculously appeared, "I got enough for one more round then I'm out of ammo."

"Got a question for you guys."

"You always got a question, Owens. Where's Jackson?"

"That's not the question, smart man."

"Who cares, where's Jackson? He said he was going to the can, but he's not back yet."

Monroe pointed to the stage. "I think that's him."

Bryant groaned. "I knew when we saw 'Karaoke' we should've passed on this place."

"But I got a question."

"What is your damn problem, Owens?"

"Bryant, where's your car?"

The three Baltimore cops had driven down from 40th St. and had left their car on the metered lot across from Trimper's Amusements. At fifty cents an hour it was the cheapest they could find without waiting for an open off-street spot.

"It's parked, isn't it?"

"Sure is, and it's twelve blocks away and going to stay there. How are we getting home?"

" What's the problem, it's a nice night for a walk."

"I think your buddy's trying to say is that you can walk it, but you can't drive it. You may not have noticed, but we've all had a little bit to drink."

"Maybe you and Owens have had too much, but I'm as sober as a judge."

"Which one, some of them drink their lunch."

"I would too if I had to listen to lawyers all day. OK, Officer Bryant, assume the position. You know the drill."

"Certainly, Officer Monroe, do your worst."

As the manager of the bar tried to get Andy Jackson off the stage, Monroe gave Bryant the standard field sobriety tests.

When asked to walk a straight line, Bryant refused, saying that the line Monroe had pointed out would not stay straight.

When he tried to extend his arms and turn in a circle, Bryant had to use what was left of his money to pay for the drinks he knocked over when he fell on the table of a couple close to him.

Bryant did manage the one legged stand, but then stood there like a stork until Owens forced his leg back to the floor.

Monroe wanted to give him the horizontal gaze test, but could not focus his own eyes on Bryant's pupils. He turned to Owens for help, but found the younger officer asleep, head on the table.

"Rookie," he said to Bryant and the other shook his head in agreement.

"Let's face it, city boy, we're drunk and out of money. It's time to go home."

"Can't go home, got to sleep on the beach."

"No, you don't gotta. You drag Jackson off the stage. I'll wake Sleeping Beauty. You guys can crash at my place. I'm down on 17th St."

Monroe shook Owens awake. "Come on, kid, it's time to go. You're staying with me tonight. Tomorrow I'll take you to your car."

"So that's how I got here," thought Owens as the evening came back. "Nice of Monroe to take the floor. I could never fall asleep like that."

Owens shook Jackson, trying to wake the older cop. All he accomplished was to change the volume of the snoring for the worse. He shouted and shook some more, but Jackson's eyes stayed shut.

"Hell with it," Owens said out loud, "I'll try Monroe, maybe he can wake this beast."

As Owens slid out of bed, Jackson suddenly sat upright. "Signal 13, Officer needs assistance. " Whatever dream he was having had put

Jackson back on Baltimore's streets. His shout had done what Owens could not. Jackson woke up and looked around.

"Where are we, kid? Oh yeah, the tunnel cop's place. I remember him looking for his key for about ten minutes. Dimbulb had put it in his shoe so he wouldn't lose it."

"You remember the karaoke bar?"

"The what?"

"Never mind. We're running late. We got just enough time to get back to our place, wash and change if we're going to check in."

"What about Bryant's car?"

"Leave it. We'll catch a bus later today and pick it up, but right now we got to get moving. You wake Bryant and I'll peel Monroe off the floor."

Jackson jumped out of bed. "I'll get Monroe, I'm closer than you are. You take Bryant. He looks like he wakes up ugly."

Owens had only to touch Bryant and the latter was on his feet. As soon as he stood up, Bryant hit his shin on the coffee table and collapsed on the sofa again.

"Great, at least now I have an excuse for feeling this bad." He put one hand on his head while the other rubbed his leg. "I'm never doing anything that stupid again in my life. Whose dumb idea was that anyway?"

"Andy's."

"Owens, you're the serious one. Why the hell didn't you stop us?"

"Because it seemed like a good idea at the time?"

"Guys." Jackson interrupted the two. "We got a problem."

"What kind of problem?"

"Well, kid, Monroe here ain't gonna wake up."

"That's not a problem. We'll put him on the bed, lock the door, hang out the 'Do Not Disturb' sign and walk back to our place." Owens turned to Bryant to see if the man was up to the walk. Bryant nodded and Owens turned back to Jackson.

"It's only 20 blocks. Maybe we'll be lucky and catch an early bus. If it gets too late, we'll go straight to the convention. I've seen worse than us there."

"Yeah," Bryant added, "We'll tell them we're modeling the latest in undercover clothes."

"You guys don't get it. He ain't gonna wake up because he ain't asleep. This guy is dead."

Bryant and Owens just stared at the other cop. Finally, Owens asked the stupid question.

"You sure?"

"Let's see, Sherlock. His skin is cool, he's not breathing and there's no pulse. Sounds like dead to me."

"How did he die?"

"I don't know, Owens. Maybe he just went 'Ack!' and fell over."

"You'd better check."

"What do I look like, the flipping Medical Examiner? You're the one who bought the 'L.A. County Coroner' T-shirt. You check."

"The kid's right, Andy. You'd better check." Bryant pointed to the middle of the room. There on a table was a 9mm pistol. Without moving, each of the three men searched the room with his eyes. Jackson finally pointed past the other two.

"There, by the balcony door."

It was what they had been looking for and hoping not to find, a shell casing from the weapon on the table.

"You'd better check, Andy," Bryant repeated.

Jackson knelt over the body. He carefully looked it over.

"Nothing on this side. Maybe he was playing with the gun earlier, shooting seagulls from the balcony. He probably died of heart failure, or from too much booze."

"Turn him over, Andy."

"Hey, Bryant, who died and made you chief?" When he saw the odd looks on the faces of his friends, he looked down at Monroe. "Sorry, poor choice of words."

Putting one hand on his right shoulder and the other on his arm, Jackson gently levered that side of Monroe off the floor. He stared awhile at his chest and then just at gently lowered him to the floor.

"Well?" Owens asked impatiently.

"Did anyone notice if Monroe had a hole in his chest last night?"

"Damn!" Bryant had been standing next to the couch. Now he broke and stormed toward the balcony. He was about to slam his palm against its glass door when he suddenly stopped it short. He stepped away and lowered his hand as if afraid of contact with the smooth surface of the glass.

"Owens, what in the hell are you doing?" The younger cop had moved as well, around the bed to the telephone on a table on Jackson's side. He had picked up the receiver and been about to dial when Jackson's question stopped him.

"Calling it in, of course."

Bryant walked away from the balcony. "Andy's right. 911 is not a good idea right now."

"Guys, a man's dead, shot to death. We're cops. It's our duty to report it."

"And who . . . " Bryant stopped, He had started to shout, and the last thing he wanted was for anyone outside the room to hear and remember an argument, however belated.

"And who," he continued in a softer tone, "do you think shot him?"

Owen's hand held on to the receiver as he thought the question over. "We're on the fifth floor."

"Right."

"Andy, has the door been tampered with?"

"Looks OK to me, kid."

"We're in trouble."

"One of us is, kid, One of us is."

"No, Andy," Bryant corrected. "All of us are, if we're connected to it."

"How do you figure that, Bryant? Only one of us shot him."

"Did you do it, Jackson? You, Owens?" Both men quickly denied it.

"Neither did I, but one of us had to."

"Bryant, there are other possibilities."

"Like what, Owens?"

"Let me think." Owens sat on the bed, his head in one hand. "What about if someone was in here, robbing the place when we came in? We scared him, he shot Monroe and ran out the door."

"Or," Jackson said enthusiastically, joining in as if playing some game, "Maybe Monroe had a roommate, who wasn't all that happy about us bunking down here. They argued, then fought, and she or he picked up the gun and ended the argument."

Bryant shook his head. "And maybe the Blue Fairy flew through the window and shot him with her wand gun, leaving that thing on the table as a decoy. Do you guys see any ransacking? Any sign of a burglar? Any sign of a roommate? And don't you think one of us might have noticed a violent quarrel and have done something about? A drunk cop is still a cop, and the training would have kicked in."

"I don't know about either of you," Owens said from the bed, "But I don't remember anything past 4th St. and Jackson singing."

"I was singing?"

"You two get it now? None of us remembers much of anything from last night. Last thing I can recall is Monroe taking off his shoes looking for his room key. After that the kid was waking me up."

"Unless one of us is lying."

"What was that, Owens?"

Jackson quickly got between the two as Bryant started toward Owens. Holding him back, Jackson turned toward the bed.

"You'd better explain yourself, kid, and make it good. Otherwise, I'm letting him go."

"It's like this. I know that I can't remember any about last night. I also know that if I did remember shooting Monroe, I sure as hell wouldn't admit it. Better one third of the blame then all of it. So I got to figure that if one of you did it and remembered, you'd keep quiet too."

Jackson nodded. "Kid's got a point. None of us is stupid enough to admit it if he did remember. The question is – what do we do now?"

Owens looked at the telephone, then at Bryant. "Not much choice. Call now or later. The later we call the worse it looks."

"There's always a choice." Bryant sat at the table near the gun. He looked at the polished surface of the tabletop and returned to the couch.

"There are always choices," he repeated. "We could call it in. As long as we each stick to 'I was drunk and don't remember' none of us will get charged. We just met the guy last night. No motive except for what had to be a drunken argument or stupid accident. They'd holler for a while, won't prove anything, and let us go."

"Then why don't we call it in?"

"Andy, you got what, nineteen years? We call this in and you won't see twenty. Our careers are down the toilet. You know the Commissioner. We'll be charged and fired before our kids go back to school."

"Maybe not. All they can prove is that we were drunk. That applies to most of the cops down here."

"We were drunk and a cop died. Does the phrase 'conduct unbecoming' mean anything to you, Andy?"

"So what are our choices." Owens had gotten up from the bed and was now pacing between it and the balcony.

Bryant held up a hand and began to tick off options.

"One, we call it in. One of us gives himself up. Any volunteers? No, I didn't think so.

"Next, two of us could decide that the third one did it and put together a story that the OCPD would believe. How about it, Owens, Jackson? Ready to sell out the other, or me?"

Owens stopped pacing. Jackson just stood there. Neither man moved or spoke. Neither looked at the other. All eyes were on Bryant.

"That just leaves us with something Owens said earlier. We leave him here and get on with our lives."

They all liked that. Each convinced of his own innocence, they would readily let a killer walk to insure their own safety. Especially when the killer was a cop and a friend, and the victim a near stranger.

Jackson broke the silence. "We could do it. Wipe the place down. Leave him on the floor. Put out the 'Do Not Disturb' sign and we were never here."

Bryant stood up. "Let's get to it. Wipe off everything that'll hold a print."

"It won't work," Owens came over from the balcony. "Try thinking like a cop instead of a suspect and you'll see why."

He stood in front of Bryant, half turned to Jackson and made a show of holding up his hand. He ticked off his own points.

"By now the story of our 'every bar on the boards' is making the rounds. Everybody has heard it or will hear it. A lot of people saw the four of us together. When Monroe is found, somebody's going to drop the dime to the OCPD.

"Next, your car is still at the inlet. By now it's got a ticket or two for that meter that hasn't been fed since last night. That puts us on foot and a long way from home.

"We got no one but ourselves to say we were back at the condo like we'll have to tell the detectives. The OCPD won't find anyone to back us up. Think, what are the chances that no one saw or heard three drunken cops coming home?"

"No one heard the shot that killed Monroe, did they? If they had, the ocean cops would have been here and gone by now."

"Andy," Bryant said from the couch, "This town is full of cops shooting guns off at two-thirty in the morning. People have stopped paying attention."

Owens interrupted, anxious to make his final points. "Besides no one seeing us come home last night, someone is bound to see us coming in today. By the time we get back, the beach goers will be heading out. One of them will see us.

"Finally," he pointed to the body on the floor. "That is a dead cop.

What makes you think they won't pull out all the stops? The OCPD will bring in the State Troopers. Those guys will dust and vacuum better than the maids at the Ritz. When they're done, Internal Investigation will send our Crime Lab down to find what the State boys missed."

Owens out his hand down by his side. "OK, let's do it. If you think we got in here without being seen, can get back without being seen, and didn't leave DNA or a single hair, fiber or print for the Lab to find, let's go." He walked over and collapsed next to Bryant on the couch.

"Nothing else for it then?" Bryant surrendered.

From over near where Monroe was lying, Jackson offered a slim hope.

"We could solve it ourselves."

The "What?" came in unison.

"Look, we're cops, not accountants. We're trained to investigate scenes, question suspects and solve crimes. We each tell what we remember from last night. The other two will pick the stories apart. We keep at it until we're all sure who done it."

"What good would that do? It's the other cops we have to convince, not ourselves."

"It's like this, kid. Once we're agreed on who done it, that guy stays behind, calls the cops and takes the heat. The other two walk out of here clean. Agreed?"

"Agreed." Bryant was quick with his assent. Owens was more reluctant.

"And if we make a mistake?"

"One in three chance, kid, one in three."

"We'd all have to agree?"

"One for all, all for one."

"I'm in."

"Good, Bryant, you start."

"Let Owens go first, he claims to remember the least."

The sound of the door being unlocked was as loud as a gunshot. Jackson rushed over to the door in time to stop the maid from coming in.

"Listen, hon," he said, blocking her view of the room with his body. "Can you come back later? We had a rough night, and it's not over yet."

"You don't want the room cleaned now? You should have hung the sign on the door."

"Hon, that would have been a very good idea. Wish we'd thought of it." He reached into his pocket and handed her a bill, not bothering to check its denomination. "Come back later, please."

The maid left. Too late Jackson hung the sign on the outside doorknob. He slowly walked over to the table. Sitting down, he took out his handkerchief and carefully wiped off the 9mm pistol. Then he just as carefully placed his thumb on a smooth surface near the safety, leaving an excellent print.

"It doesn't matter now who pulled the trigger. The maid can put me in here. You guys might as well go."

"Andy . . ."

"Look, kid, why trash three careers? I'll tell them what I know. I don't remember how I got here or what happened when I did. I'll keep you two out of it. They'll draw their own conclusions and charge me with manslaughter.

"The FOP lawyer is pretty good. He'll be able to drag this out long enough for me to make my pension. Then I'll retire, and we'll make a deal. If I got to go away, it won't be for long."

Jackson picked the gun up, studied it for a while and returned it to the table.

"Whatever happens, I know that my good friends will take care of my family for me. Right?"

"Yeah, Andy, we'll look after everything, won't we, Owens?"

"Andy . . ." Owens was stuck on the name.

"You two go, and make sure you get your stories straight."

Being careful not to look at the body lying on the floor, Bryant and Jackson left. Jackson sat alone, staring at the pistol on the table.

As the door closed behind them, Owens paused and stood in front of it.

"What are you waiting for? We should be gone from this place five minutes ago."

"The gunshot."

"It's the cop's way out. Do you really want to be here if he does it?"

"Let's go."

They snuck down the back stairs. No one noticed them leaving.

Neither man spoke until they were halfway back to 40th St.

"Bryant."

"What?"

"Back there, you said that no one would have paid attention to a gun going off at two-thirty in the morning."

"So?"

"So, how did you know what time the gun went off?"

Bryant stopped turned toward Owens. "I didn't. I picked a time out of the air to make a point. Why? Does that make me guilty?"

"I . . . I don't know. One of us did it, it might have been you. 'One in three chance,' Andy said. It doesn't really matter now. One of us did it, none of us meant it, Andy's going to pay for it."

"Yeah, listen, let's get moving before we attract attention."

They walked further down the street.

"How's this sound, Owens? When we left the karaoke bar, Andy went with Monroe. We saw them to the door, then decided to go home. We woke up this morning and we too tired and hung-over to go to the morning session."

"Sounds good to me. We'll get cleaned up and sign in this afternoon. If we don't hear anything by this evening, we call 911 and report Andy missing."

They continued to polish their story all the way home, each wondering if the other would hold up, and neither sure how he would feel if Andy picked up the gun for the last time.

An hour later, the maid passed by the room again. The "Do Not Disturb" sign was still on the door. Try as she would, she'd never understand cops. This morning, as she was just starting her shift, the big one had given her twenty dollars to come and clean the room at eight. Then when she came, he gave her another twenty to go away. A good day's tips, and she hadn't done anything.

As she passed the room, she heard the sound of a man's laughter. Inside, Jackson and the formerly dead Monroe were enjoying another laugh.

"What I want to know is what made you think of such a thing?"

"You know, Monroe, when I woke up this morning, and saw you on the floor, I thought to myself that the only way I'd sleep like that was if I was dead. Then I started thinking that maybe you were dead."

"And you woke me up when you checked."

"Sorry, I was still half asleep, and still a little bagged. But after being glad that you were alive, I started thinking about what those two would do if you really were dead, and things took off from there. I thought that kid would never wake up. Those fake snores were loud enough."

" But good enough to fool him. I tell you, Andy, I never thought I could lie still that long. I don't believe that they never checked me out for themselves."

"I don't believe that neither of those dimbulbs ever checked the gun or the casing. Your gun still had all its rounds and the casing's from a .380. Where'd you get it anyway?"

"Picked up some at the show, the shooting demonstration. My kid collects them. Go figure."

"I can't wait to see their faces when the two of us walk in on them tonight." Andy Jackson had another laugh, then another sip of beer. "I tell you Monroe, with my twenty coming up, this is my last convention. I'll miss coming down here with guys like you, but at least I went out in style."

*Raymond Maddox was just one of many cops who got burned by the
LAPD Rampart scandal. Now he's patiently waiting for some other
cops to get released from prison. But is he waiting for his share of
millions of dollars of drug money that's been buried in the desert for all
these years ... or is he waiting for something else?*

RHYTHM AND BLUES
Art Monterastelli

Raymond Maddox, aided by several shots of Tequila, was slipping
into a warm and fuzzy sleep. The unexpected whimper of his dogs
broke the spell. Raymond's dogs didn't normally whimper. Technically
speaking, he was supposed to be some kind of dog trainer; but that was
a stretch of his landlord's imagination. Raymond himself never claimed
any such skill. He merely said he was *good* with animals. The landlord
was looking for someone to look after the four-acre desert compound
about five miles north of Joshua Tree. It had originally been a high desert
pumping station and there was pending litigation over the oil and mineral
rights. For his part, until the lawsuit was settled, the landlord liked the
idea of having a former badass LAPD detective living on the property.

Hushed voices broke the silence that followed the first whimper.
Raymond reached quietly for the back-up revolver he kept by the side
of his bed. There was an LAPD-issue nine-millimeter in his safe. But a
revolver never jammed and therefore made a better sleeping companion.

Raymond didn't bother with a shirt or a pair of shoes. He stood
near the trailer's side door. In the darkness the small window beside the
door and the larger one at the front of the trailer afforded him a limited
view of one side of the property. It looked pretty clear. Which meant
whoever was out there was hiding in an obvious blind spot.

There was a row of empty fuel barrels about twenty feet from
the front of the trailer. Raymond took a deep breath, opened the trailer
door, and dove forward in the direction of the fuel barrels. He hit the
ground hard and rolled the last seven or eight feet, tearing the hell out of
his elbows and the side of one arm. The desert night appeared clear and
cloudless. Raymond didn't hear a sound, until whoever was concealed
in the shadows behind him stepped forward and jabbed him in the neck
with a cattle prod. Raymond's entire body convulsed violently from the

jolt of electricity. In less than two seconds the convulsion ended and he lay unconscious on the desert floor.

***

"Raymond Maddox."

The voice belonged to a six-foot-five black man in an expensive Italian suit and a gray cashmere pullover. He wore the kind of watch a conservative banker might wear. No bling. This was the first thing that impressed Raymond as he struggled to consciousness. He was wrapped in a thin blanket and laid out on his own bed. A younger, smaller black man stood behind the larger man with a gun in his hand. Raymond's own gun was tucked neatly in the younger man's waistband.

"You've got a nasty reputation for a white boy, Raymond. Which usually shakes out as good press and no backbone. But the people I talked to, even brothers on the force, say you're the exception. Regular stand-up homeboy."

Although he wasn't much of a contemporary music fan, Raymond recognized the voice and face immediately. Stanley Hammer was the Teflon-King of Rap and Hip Hop. He had built a small empire on the ashes of Suge Knight's infamous Death Row Records. While Suge was in prison Stanley brazenly signed away his biggest acts; then he tweaked everybody's comfort level by parodying Suge and calling his new company 'Death*star* Records.' The gang war everybody anticipated never materialized.

"Why's a big shot record czar like Stanley Hammer interested in someone like me? Hell, it must've taken you five hours to drive out here."

"Three-hours-fifteen. Couple of my boys know the area."

Raymond tried to prop himself up on the bed, but his right elbow slipped out from under him like a mound of jelly; the cattle prod had done nerve damage.

"That's right," Raymond said, with a grimace. "I remember hearing about a spot just north of here. Supposed to be a lot of bodies buried out there."

Hammer shrugged nonchalantly.

"I don't want to ruin your evening, but if you harmed my dogs I'm gonna bury you and every one of your homeboys in one of those same unmarked graves."

"You got me confused with the other guy. I am a legitimate businessman. Besides, you're dogs are fine, we used a special sedative. They're sleeping it off in the empty horse corral next door. Truth be told, I got more compassion for dogs than I do people."

Hammer gestured to the younger man behind him. A fat envelope appeared. Hammer took the envelope and dropped it in Raymond's lap.

"I've got a handful of LAPD's finest who do a little security work for me."

"You giving 'em recording deals?"

"That was Suge's scene. These guys are supposed to make sure the book-keeping is in order, as it applies to a popular product we supply outside our regular business. Last six months, two, possibly four, of these cops skimmed off a cool million. Tried to blame their own shady accounting practices on Mexican gangbangers."

Raymond finally managed to raise himself on the bed. He grabbed the fat envelope with his good hand, felt the familiar brick of cash inside.

"There's twenty-five thousand dollars there. You get twenty-five more after you've had a chance to conduct a little covert investigation. I'd take care of it myself but certain *personalities* are about to re-enter my life and I can't afford to get caught up in some crazy ex-con's revenge fantasy. If you know what I'm talking about."

Raymond knew exactly what he was talking about. David Trax, a rogue LAPD cop who had been convicted of multiple bank robberies, was finishing up a twelve year prison sentence that very week. Raymond and his now deceased partner, Nicky Fernandez, had been added to the Trax investigation in the eleventh hour, payback for playing ball with the brass and letting a potentially controversial case of their own die a slow death. But instead of simply riding the glory train of somebody else's victory, Raymond and his partner had been determined to dig even deeper into the Trax case – both equally obsessed with flushing out any accomplices who were still working in the department. It was a gutsy longball play that came up tragically short. Fernandez was killed assassination style in the parking lot of a well-known cop bar in the Miracle Mile. The murder sent shivers through the entire department. Even though it happened around 8 p.m. in a lot adjacent to an establishment that contained at least a dozen police officers, not a single credible witness came forward. When Raymond returned from special assignment to his Rampart unit, none of his fellow officers were willing to risk more than a polite hello. It was only a matter of time before one of the numerous task forces assigned to

Rampart turned its attention to Raymond.

"Stanley, you've got the wrong guy. I don't carry a shovel in my trunk."

Stanley Hammer's eyes danced with some unknown humor as he opened the trailer door and prepared to climb out. "I've done my homework, Raymond. You've got child support and one particular loan you've had a bitch of a time repaying." Stanley paused in the doorway. "Whatever else you think, *take the money.* You're the only smart cop who ever came after me. And look what they ended up doing to you."

There was a telescope on top of a tripod twenty feet from the front end of the trailer. Stanley was crouched over it, dialing in some constellation near the southeastern horizon, when Raymond climbed out of the trailer on still rubbery legs. Two of Stanley's men were walking up from the horse corral next door. For a moment Raymond thought he could hear one of the Rottweilers snoring.

"You know what this constellation is over here, right above the horizon?" The big man innocently asked, his eye glued to the lens.

"Actually, that's two constellations. Sagittarius and Scorpio."

"My man, Raymond. *Star*gazer."

"You see that bright star, looks like it's caught in the Scorpion's neck?" Raymond asked, clearly testing Stanley's own 'stargazer' bonafides.

"Uh huh."

"Know the name of it?"

Stanley hesitated for just a second. It was impossible to read his mind. There was something else beneath that horizon that dwarfed everything else they had talked about; dwarfed the twenty-five thousand and the two sleeping Rottweilers. But in this particular poker game, the first man to show his hand would lose.

"That big red star over there?" Stanley grinned. "That there's *Antares.*"

Stanley joined his two bodyguards and walked towards one of the two tricked-out Cadillac DeVilles parked outside the cyclone fence.

"Leon and Weezil will drive you into town. They got all the information you need." He hesitated again, a frown covering the pearly white teeth. "I'd prefer if you use them as your *escorts* and leave the muscle to somebody else."

"Neither one of us is in the muscle business. Isn't that right?"

"My man, Raymond."

It was two-fifteen in the morning. Raymond sat in the backseat of the second Cadillac DeVille, which was parked in an alley behind an after-hours club in Korea-town. Leon was slumped behind the driver's wheel, mumbling into an ever-present cell phone. Weezil had his side window open as he methodically scanned the alley. Raymond was going through the personnel jackets of the four detectives Stanley Hammer wanted him to check out. The files looked like they had been lifted straight from the LAPD records room. The department had a new tough talking Chief, a white man who had run departments in Boston and Philadelphia, but who had already become a victim of his own overly optimistic spin. It wasn't his fault; LAPD was a culture almost impossible for an outsider to understand. What some people viewed as corruption was tolerated as *networking* by the rank and file, the kind of networking that allowed a detective to borrow files or evidence from a separate division without going through cumbersome red tape or the usual chain of custody. Raymond himself, a supreme pragmatist, had ended up making a *separate piece* with the culture, a decision that allowed him to side step the myriad controversies and outright scandals that plagued the department and, for a long time, continue doing what he did best: *make cases.*

"Who would've pegged Stanley for a stargazer?"

The two thugs in the front seat barely reacted, so Raymond, eyes glued to the police files in front of him, repeated the question.

"Who would've pegged *Stanley* for a stargazer?"

Leon continued mumbling into his cell phone, his other ear closed to the world at large. After a moment, Weezil looked over his shoulder.

"What you talkin' about?"

"Stanley. The telescope. The constellations in the desert."

"Muthafucker don't share no shit 'bout no telescope." Weezil turned completely around in his seat and eyeballed Raymond for the first time.

"I's supposed to keep *my eye* on you."

"Is that right?"

"That's right." Weezil grinned. There was something physically off-kilter about him. The puffy eyelids rolled back in what had been a lazy countenance. A live wire suddenly lit Weezil up as he groped for a *look* that would intimidate Raymond. Sometime in the last half hour Weezil had evidently added cocaine to whatever he had been smoking.

"I's also suppose to remind you that David Trax's getting' out of prison tomorrow morning. Case you forgot."

"I thought it was Friday?"

"They bumped it up, in case a lot of reporters and stuff was waitin' to talk to him. Prison doesn't like no paparazzi."

Weezil's face beamed as he nodded to the back of the club.

"Deats and Alba used to run with Trax, isn't that right?"

"That's right," Raymond said.

"And Bettis, the one used to be Trax's partner; he's the one who's dead?"

"Uh huh."

"How come when cops kill each other the cases are usually unsolved?"

"Luck of the Irish."

"What's that?"

"Bettis isn't officially dead," Raymond said. "His body has never been found and he's technically still listed as a *missing person.*"

Weezil howled. "Bullshit! All that fucking *money* is what's missing. You cops make the best bank robbers! You know that shit is true."

Absolutely true, Raymond thought.

Raymond followed Weezil and Leon through the back of the K-town club. A narrow hallway discreetly connected the club to what had once been a fancy Korean restaurant next door. There were sliding paper doors and paper walls, but there wasn't a diner in sight. The private rooms in back appeared to be filled with people either getting high or getting laid. Leon installed himself beside the pay phone at one end of the hall as Weezil and Raymond entered one of the private dining booths.

From the sulfurous smell of burnt matches and the look on their faces, Deats and Alba had been getting high. The Black and Hispanic partners were practically jumping out of their skin as Raymond and Weezil squeezed into the seats across the table from them. There were two bottles of Crystal on the table that hadn't even been opened.

"Yo, mutherfucker. Raymond. Are you currently working for any law enforcement agency in the Los Angeles vicinity?" Deats immediately asked.

"No, I am not."

"You wearin' a wire?"

"No."

There was a long strange pause. Deats was trying to psyche him out by screwing his eyes into a single-eyed stare. An effect that could sometimes be intimidating was rendered comical. Alba was so twisted on crystal-meth that it was impossible to get any kind of read off him. Raymond figured they'd have their guard up, but he hadn't counted on them being this wasted. The risk level continued to go up.

"I say we just waste his ass and bury him in the desert."

"Keep your mouth shut, Albie."

Deats did his best to stare Raymond down. Alba buttoned his lip, but couldn't sit still. He was driving everybody crazy with his version of St. Vitus' dance, when he bolted straight up in his chair and climbed over the entire length of the table.

"I gotta shit."

"What's he so anxious about?" Raymond asked.

"*You,*" Deats replied, "You and this whole masquerade."

"Masquerade?"

"It ain't what you think it is, Raymond. We're not ripping Stanley off. We're *blackmailing him* for a better deal."

Raymond had to think about this.

"Maybe I can help you negotiate."

"You going outta your way to fuck with me; or you suddenly get stupid?" And then: "Stanley's just playing with you, Raymond; he's playing with all of us. Can't you see how this is goin' down?"

"No, Donnie, I honestly can't."

"David Trax is getting out of prison early tomorrow morning. He's already pissed off 'cause his man Bettis stopped comin' around about six months ago. Since everyone believes Bettis has been holding the man's money – two-point-three *million* of his money – well, you can understand how pissed off he might be."

"I didn't know everybody thought Bettis was holding *all* the money. I always thought there were other people involved."

"Other people like *what?*" Deats asked.

"Like cops."

The air in the paper-walled room evaporated. Even Weezil tugged mindlessly at his collar, feeling the pressure. Deats flashed his trademark mean little smile, the smile anyone who had worked Rampart would recognize as his *prelude to violence* – torturing low level street dealers was one of Deats' specialties.

"You're mistaken about that, Raymond. Most everyone believes Bettis was the only one holding Trax's money. The whole two-point-three."

"Okay."

"Okay *what*? You got something figured out?"

Raymond took a deep breath and decided to tell the truth. He was afraid Deats, in his manic hyper-alert state, would pick up any bullshit.

"I think you're blackmailing Stanley because you want a bigger cut of the *collections* you're making for him. Or maybe you and Alba took Bettis down, and now you want your payday *before* Trax gets out of prison and decides to kill everybody."

A look of pure menace filled Deats' face. His sense of humor evaporated in the stale air. Without warning he swung both of his guns up on the table top. He pointed them right at Raymond's stomach, his fingers twitching on the triggers.

"We didn't touch Bettis," Deats whispered hoarsely. "Somebody is setting us up. Somebody who knows Trax'll come at us like he's buying a cup of coffee."

Raymond stared at the two guns that were pointed at him. He knew that Deats would have no problem, high or straight, pulling the triggers.

"Just so I have my facts straight. Stanley mentioned that there might be two other Rampart detectives who were involved in this."

"That's Stanley's *redundancy thing,* okay? There were two other guys, but me and Alba took care of them a ways back; made all the accounting shit easier. Right now only two dudes who mean anything are Trax and Bettis. And since my man Bettis is presently dead or missing, well, you can see how tight this whole thing is."

Raymond, who had known Deats for almost fifteen years, could see that it was very tight indeed. Deats was a mean, street smart narcotics cop. He wasn't particularly honest but he was usually smart enough to keep his mouth shut, and he didn't waste time on idle boasting. Raymond knew that if he had 'taken care of' the other two cops that they were simply no longer among the living.

"Seems like everyone's running a little scared. I think we ..."

"Everybody but *you*, Raymond."

Deats, fear, paranoia, and crystal meth accelerating the general rot of his mind, pushed both guns a little closer to Raymond's stomach.

"What about me, Donnie?"

Donnie Deats flashed a beautifully malicious grin; the crazed dope-fiend/corrupt cop grin for the new millennium. He simply wasn't listening to a word Raymond said. He was listening instead to a well-edited tape of how *he read the situation,* a tape that played on an end-less loop through his over-cooked brain.

"I heard this rumor *you* killed Bettis, Raymond. I heard you killed him and then you buried his body out in the desert."

Raymond kept both hands on the table, his eyes focused on Deats: a crooked hair-trigger cop in a hair-trigger situation. There was however one point where Deats was right on the money. Stanley Hammer was definitely setting somebody up.

"Why would I kill Bettis? Why would I risk a murder rap?"

"I got a whole bunch of reasons, Raymond. First, you want a shot at the money you missed out on, being all holier than thou. Second, Bettis or Trax is the one who killed your partner. I happen to know you were a lot closer to that little Mexican than I happen to be to my own little Spic. It doesn't even matter. Anybody who ever wore a badge, especially in Rampart, is gonna try and avenge his partner. It's just what you do."

"Donnie –"

"And three, I never believed your *standup dude* routine. You crawled through the same sewage as the rest of us. Besides, 'standup guys *do time.*' And you, Raymond, you never done a nickel's worth. Only busted cop who didn't."

"There were never any charges against me, Donnie. They didn't have anything on me. And yet they still made sure I lost everything." Raymond avoided mentioning his daughter or ex-wife.

Deats' giblet eyes danced quietly between the fluid joy of screwing with everyone's head and the sudden irrevocable finality of pulling the trigger.

"So cry me a white-boy river."

"You really think I killed Bettis to avenge my partner's death?"

"I think you mighta' done that, yeah. And to stick it to Trax. Get him all insane just when they're getting ready to release him."

"What purpose would that serve?"

"*The money, the two-point-three million dollars that's still missing.* That is a lot of rhythm, Raymond. Seems to me either you or Stanley, maybe the two of you together, got some kind of plan to take Trax off."

Raymond glanced at Weezil, who was suddenly paying attention to everything Deats said. Underneath the table, Weezil secretly cradled his own gun.

"Donnie, if I'm that smart, what the hell have I been doing living in a thirty-foot trailer in the middle of the desert for two years?"

"Waiting."

Alba picked the perfect time to return from the bathroom. First he bumped into Leon, who was still standing by the pay phone in the hallway. Then, when he finally stepped back into the paper-walled dining booth, he saw Weezil reaching for a gun under the table. Alba took his own gun out and pistol-whipped Weezil across the side of his head, knocking him off the bench he shared with Raymond. Weezil started yelling the moment he hit the floor. He rolled around like a crazy person, dabbing at the blood that trickled down his right ear. Alba started kicking him in the ribs and stomach. Raymond slid across the bench and tried to help Weezil to his feet. Deats started laughing manically. When Alba continued to kick the shit out of Weezil, Deats turned his revolver in that direction and pulled the trigger. The explosion brought the activities of the entire building to a halt. Alba twisted towards Deats in utter disbelief, the tip of his left index finger neatly blown off.

In the next instant Leon busted into the room waving a Magnum 44.

"You stupid fucks, this was supposed to be a *conversation!*"

***

It was six-thirty in the morning. Raymond, Leon, Deats, a traumatized Weezil, and a hastily bandaged Alba sat at a corner table in a truck stop outside of San Bernardino. There was fear and confusion in everybody's eyes. Raymond and Deats were the only ones who appeared to be focused, each of them silently yet methodically working their own private agenda. No one else had a clue.

At six-forty-five Leon's cell phone rang.

It was Stanley Hammer. He told Leon he was on his way out there. Then he asked Leon to hand the phone to Donnie Deats. Deats listened silently, even suspiciously, for a couple of minutes before nodding his head and saying, "I'll tell him."

Deats hung up the phone and looked across the table at Raymond.

"Stanley says we should meet at that place Bettis used to have."

"Bettis?" Alba exclaimed.

"Stanley says Raymond knows exactly where it is. Said he has a telescope trained on the place." The next part Deats himself did not quite understand. "Something about the star in the Scorpion's throat?"

"Antares." Raymond said.

"That's right."

"Donnie." Alba complained, cradling his blood-stained hand, picking at the gauze at the end of one finger with his teeth. "My hand is fucking killing me. And I ain't too keen on walking into an ambush."

"Might not be our ambush."

At approximately eight-fifteen that morning a single Cadillac DeVille pulled off the Twentynine Palms Highway and headed north on Highway 247. Fifteen minutes later the car turned onto a dirt road that went a good two miles along a high desert plateau. A burnt-out pickup truck and a brand new limo with blacked-out windows were parked outside of an officially condemned ranch style house. There were a couple of utility buildings on the other side of the gravel drive. There was a half finished swimming pool on one side of the house and a small cluster of prickly Joshua trees behind the pool.

Deats, Raymond, and Alba were crowded into the backseat of the DeVille. Leon and Weezil were up front. At some point during the drive both Weezil and Alba had been crying. Raymond ignored their plaintive sobs and focused on his own perilous situation. Stanley had done a brilliant job of eliminating whatever options he once thought he had.

"Stop the car right here." Deats said, the only one in the car holding a gun.

Leon pulled over thirty feet from the limo with the blacked-out windows.

"What the hell we gonna do now?" Alba demanded.

"Now we wait."

There was an odd ping on the roof of the DeVille. Everybody inside the car reacted, but nobody said a word. A moment later there were several more pings, each one sounding less odd than the one before it.

"What the hell is that?" Weezil asked.

"It's rain, you moron."

Weezil twisted around to face the front windshield. Giant raindrops splattered the glass right in front of him. A child's pure awe filled his drug-ravaged face.

"I didn't know it rained in the desert."

Two hours later the rain came down in buckets. Everyone in the Cadillac was pretty much in the same place. The windows were cracked open, the glass steamed up, and everyone but Raymond was smoking American Spirit cigarettes. They were Alba's smokes. He bought them because he thought it was important to *try* and do something patriotic.

"I still don't like this, Donnie. I can't see shit with the windows steamed up." Alba began rubbing his own side window like a mad window-washer. "I can't see shit. Man, we don't even know if Stanley is in that limo!"

Almost on cue a second limo rumbled down the dirt road and pulled up behind the first. Everybody in the DeVille craned their necks for a better view. A tall, fairly young bodybuilder with long blond hair climbed out of the driver's door and hurried to the other side of the vehicle. He opened the back door and stood at attention in the rain. A moment later David Trax unfolded his long body and stepped out of the limo.

"Oh, Christ," Alba whispered. "I'm not up for this shit."

Stanley Hammer climbed out of the first limo and greeted Trax with a big smile and what appeared to be a warm hug; they looked like long lost brothers. Then Stanley nodded to the condemned house and the two men quickly disappeared inside it.

"All right," Deats said. "Everybody out. Single file until we reach the front door. Anyone tries to take off, they get a bullet in the head."

Inside the derelict ranch house every single wall had been gutted and stripped. Eighty percent of the floorboards had been ripped up and stacked haphazardly in what had once been the dining room. There were several piles of dirt marking the spots where holes had been dug beneath the missing boards. There was a huge row of painter's plastic, duct tape, and several shovels in what had been the master bedroom. Raymond recognized the plastic and all the shovels. The holes were new.

Everyone made their way through the bedroom's sliding glass doors and out onto the slab of concrete that was supposed to be the patio. The unfinished swimming pool was an even bigger eyesore. The fourth retaining wall was a mountain of dirt that rolled down and flooded nearly half of the pool's bottom. The other half was filled with a green liquid that had attracted the interest of several varmints; carcasses of the local road-kill floated on the gooey green surface in various stages of decay. Everyone stood around the half-finished pool, hating the steady rain, waiting for somebody else to make the first move.

"My man, Raymond," Stanley finally said. "Stargazer."

"Star-what?" Trax asked. "Who the hell is Raymond?"

"Raymond Maddox. Formerly *Detective* Raymond. Him and Nicky

Fernandez, his partner, were the ones kept working your case *after* you'd gone to prison."

Trax squinted his eyes, pretending he didn't recognize anyone.

"You remember Nicky Hernandez, don't you?"

"You told me this was gonna be all business."

"It is. We just got some *old* business to take care. You see, I got a pretty good idea where your old partner, Richard Bettis, is actually located. But no matter how hard I try, I can't seem to find the *money*."

This only added more fuel to Trax's fire.

"That's why we brought Raymond along. See, he lives just about a mile up the road. Without anyone knowing it, he's been nice enough to keep an eye on this place for the last couple of years. Isn't that right, Raymond?"

"I don't like this, Stanley." Trax said.

"This part doesn't even concern you. You were in prison when Nicky Fernandez was murdered. And that's the *only* part of this thing that concerns Raymond. You see, he thinks you paid Donnie Deats to kill his partner. Wants some kind of revenge."

"What the hell you talking about? I didn't kill Hernandez!" Deats exclaimed. "And hell, even if I did, it was a long time ago. What's it got to do with this?"

"Donnie," Alba whispered.

"Shut up, Albie."

"I need to talk to you."

Deats slowly turned towards his own partner, a burst of breaking information flashing across his face. Alba was holding his bloody hand, looking for some sympathy.

"That's right, Albie," Stanley said. "Time to get clean; tell Donnie how much money Trax paid you. How you kept it all from him."

Deats glanced briefly at Trax, who didn't even bother to shrug. Without a word Deats raised his trusty revolver and fired two quick shots into Alba's head and chest. Alba's body hit the green sludge at the bottom of the pool with an unexpected thud.

"I believe there's some kind of construction platform underneath the slime." Stanley said. "What do you say, Raymond, should we dig it up, see what's under there?"

Deats and Trax were both lost. But Stanley was in championship form. Despite the high cost to everyone, Raymond had to admire his skill and bravado.

"It's your show, Stanley."

Stanley smiled. His skinny sidekick came out of the house with a couple of shovels. Leon and Weezil climbed into the pool with him. It took more than ten minutes to wedge a double-sided platform out of the sludge. A piece of somebody's *arm* seemed to be rotting into the wood. Weezil turned away and started to puke.

"Well, well, well. I hate to break this to you, Mr. Trax, first day out of prison and all, but I believe that arm belongs to your old partner." Stanley looked back down into the pool. "Hey, why don't you guys see if you can find some kind of identification tag? I'm sure the face is pretty much eaten away by now."

The guys in the pool did as they were instructed. But Trax was suddenly tired of the games. He gestured to his blond driver, who handed him a fully automatic machine-pistol. Once the bullets started flying it was nearly impossible to know who was shooting at whom. Raymond had enough sense to dive behind a pile of concrete blocks and wait for the smoke to clear. Deats wasn't so lucky. He actually looked surprised when Trax started shooting in his direction. Wily veteran cop to the end, Deats put at least one bullet into Trax and four or five into his slow moving bodyguard. Trax, meanwhile, pumped fifteen shots into Deats.

When the smoke finally cleared...

Trax was crawling away from the pool, trying to reload his machine-pistol. The two holes in his arm were oozing blood. Raymond climbed out from behind the pile of concrete blocks in time to watch Stanley pull a pair of surgical gloves over his huge over-sized hands. Stanley winked at Raymond. Everyone else appeared to be either dead or dying.

"What the hell's going on?" Raymond finally demanded.

Stanley flashed his big pearly white smile and pulled Raymond's almost forgotten revolver out of his jacket pocket. "Insurance policy," he said. Then he jerked his head towards Trax. Raymond obediently followed him.

"Hey, David. Raymond here was wondering if you could give him some kind of *closure* before I kill him. A simple thing like you admitting you hired Alba to kill Nicky Hernandez, his old partner, would really go a long way."

"Fuck you."

"C'mon, David, play the game and maybe I'll patch you up when we're done. We still haven't found the money."

Trax coughed up some blood and looked directly at Raymond.

"What's the big deal? I paid one spic to kill another spic."

Although Trax was dying, Raymond wanted to kill him even more.

"See how easy that was? Now, Raymond, tell Mr. Trax where you buried his two-point-three million dollars. Fair is fair."

"You can both rot in hell."

Trax emitted a litany of obscenities and for a moment it almost looked like he was going to climb to his feet and strangle Raymond. But he ended up collapsing down on a single elbow. He'd simply lost too much blood.

Stanley stared at Raymond with new found respect. He pointed Raymond's own revolver at him. "You really want to go out like this?" He asked.

"I'm already gone."

Stanley considered his own alternatives for a moment. Then he turned the revolver on David Trax and squeezed off three fast rounds.

"Raymond, I enjoy your company, but business is business. You don't tell me where the money is I'm gonna kill you and bring in a new crew to tear this place up."

"How do you know it's even here?"

"Because I've had my boys watching you for the last two years. They were here when you lured Bettis to the edge of the pool and killed him. They were probably taking a crystal meth break when you actually hid the money."

"That's what you get for hiring retards."

"Raymond, don't you have a twelve year old daughter stashed away somewhere? Wouldn't you like to see her grow up?"

Raymond stared at his own revolver, which, unfortunately, was pointed at him.

"You wouldn't have gone through all that trouble with the surgical gloves if you were just going to kill me. You're gonna keep my gun as collateral."

"That wasn't the question."

"You see those three Joshua trees over there? There's a fat old *yucca* right behind them. There are two metal suitcases inside the yucca."

"Raymond, I do admire your style."

"You still gonna kill me?"

"Kill you? I'm thinking of making you a business partner."

Luc Rudd thought he knew what it meant to wear
a badge in America's heartland.
Then she drove into his small town.

THE BIG TIME
James Grady

Luc Rudd wore a black leather jacket over the badge on his shirt and the Glock on his hip that April morning as he stepped out of his house in Shelby, Montana and scanned for snipers.

Sage dust scented the wind. Sixty miles to his left, white-tipped Rocky Mountains saw-toothed the sun-lit prairie. Forty miles of empty stretched between his eyes and the indigo shimmer of the Canadian border.

Nobody shot him.

Luc drove his Jeep past the cemetery, down the hill past the indoor swimming pool. Homes flowed past his passenger window.

On the curb stood old widow Kavendish in her pink bathrobe. He saw her spot him, then pull her trash cans back closer to regulation placement. She watched him pass. Didn't wave to his nod. He took the two-lane truck route along railroad tracks behind Shelby's four block Main Street.

Saw a man, a *stranger*, standing on a corner arguing with Wade Dunn, a local thug who Luc was sure ran meth labs in abandoned farm sheds and gully stashed trailers. The stranger wore blue lens sunglasses.

Wade recognized Luc, muttered to the stranger.

Mister Blue Lenses stepped away from a tan Ford, Nevada tags.

Luc memorized that plate number. His Jeep rumbled across the railroad tracks just before warning bells dinged and white crossbars lowered for a freight train. He parked at a sea-green cement blockhouse:

TOOLE COUNTY EMERGENCY SERVICES
SHERIFF RESCUE AMBULANCE HOMELAND DEFENSE

Luc entered that green fort, followed hallway tiles mopped with pine disinfectant, took a left through the glass door he had a hard time believing was bulletproof, stopped at the reception/dispatch desk.

"Do me a favor, Jenny?"

She quit lettering her daughter's school BAKE SALE sign. He walked past the bullpen's four deserted desks to the Sheriff's glass office.

Sheriff Earl Cockrell beckoned him in: "Congratulations!"

"Thanks," Luc told that grizzly bear wedged into the big chair.

Luc glanced back at the bullpen: Still empty. Jenny working.

"Don't worry, Andy's fine with you being the new Undersheriff," said Earl. "But now you gotta finally decide."

"Not this again."

"You're a born badge, Luc. Me, too. I'm a peace officer. I do what I gotta do to keep the peace for my folks. But I worry that your badge is pinned so tight you'll only ever be lawman."

"So why did you back me to the Commissioners instead of Andy?"

"You're a vet, got more schooling. 'Feds like that. And maybe you hanging alone in your house listening to satellite radio gives you more outside world savvy than a homeboy like Andy. But you gotta feel the music at the Tap Room and the Thriftway and at the high school basketball games."

"That doesn't add up to you picking me."

"Remember those six drunk wind farm workers 'tried to bust up the Oasis? You stood back and maced 'em. Andy worked his blackjack."

Luc frowned. "You think Andy is ... a bit brutal?"

"You're both trigger pullers. Andy likes it more, you hesitate less. That makes you better for the job. 'Course, it fucks you up as a man."

Entering the office, Andy shouted: "There's our winner!"

Andy shook Luc's hand. "Gonna be a pleasure working for you."

"Working together." Luc didn't contest Andy's steel grip.

"You're both my boys and I'm still Boss," said Earl. "Jake's in Cruiser 2. You two go pick up number 3 from its service. Luc, black leather's cool, but until the swear-in, you ain't ranked to wear civvies."

"My uniform jacket is at the cleaners. Wino Pete's up-chuck."

Jenny brought a pink memo slip to Luc: "That car came back registered in Vegas to Calvin Nazar."

Andy said: "Cal Nazar is back in town?"

"You know him?" asked Luc.

"Hell yeah. Lived here 'till he was – what Earl, about 7th grade?"

"Good riddance," said the Sheriff. "Why do we care about him?"

"I don't know," said Luc. "Yet."

As Andy drove the two of them to get Cruiser 3 from the County Shop, Luc said: "Look, if there's any problem between us..."

"Naw, I'm cool with what's what. 'Though I'd like to figure how to rise up out of here while I still got a chance to make the big time."

"The time we make is the big time."

"Yeah, but Luc, we're in the middle of fucking nowhere," Andy said, then added, "Will them new motion sensors really seal the border?"

"The Feds are gonna get flooded by radar hits from hungry deer and lost horny teenagers, but *yeah,* they'll probably know when something's crossing over. When are you in midnight rotation?"

"Tonight, tomorrow, then up north squad goes back on," said Andy.

The sheriff's department kept deputies in the even smaller two hamlets of this 1,958 square mile county. Since 9-11, local badges worked with Homeland Security's Border Patrol and Immigration, Customs and Enforcement agents patrolling the desolate border with Canada.

Andy left Luc at the county garage.

Jenny radioed Luc as he drove Cruiser 3 out of that shop: "Tourist called in. Cows on the west highway."

Luc found three Black Angus steers grazing along the two-lane highway nine miles from town by the wind farm. He flipped on the cruiser's red & blue party lights, parked, got the towrope from the trunk.

He hobbled two steers, squatted to tie the third. A trucker driving by blew his horn. The steer bolted, knocked Luc down to the rocky prairie. He sprawled on his back staring up into a deep blue bowl of forever. Had to laugh. 'Took him 15 minutes to lash those mooing beasts to a fence post.

Could have shot them. Left them for the crows.

Luc stood at the barbed wire fence near the black cattle. Red & blue lights spun on his white cruiser. Beyond the fence rose 285 feet tall ivory towers topped by 124 feet long, 3-blade white propellers, one tower after another, an army of giant robots arrayed by a Spanish company in this golden sea of Montana to spin electricity out of thin air and send it far away.

This is the time I'm making.

Driving to town, he radioed Jenny: "Call Maggie Clarke, tell her she won't collect some sucker's car insurance for hitting her cows. 'She doesn't keep them fenced, we'll seize them, fine her. Tell her to bring us our rope.

"And Jenny, run that Nevada plates guy."

Luc hung the radio mike, cruised past the truck stop café –

Spotted blue lens Cal Nazar.

With a woman, the two of them standing by the tan Ford. *Arguing.*

Dark hair floating in the wind, leather jacket like a black mirror. She wore no sunglasses on her pale face and drew her mouth as a ruby slash.

Never seen her before.

Police radio squawk of Jenny's voice blinked him back as the arguing couple slid into his mirrors: "Calvin Victor Nazar, no wants or warrants, but he's off paper after five years California prison."

"Why did they lock him up?"

"Possession with intent, heroin, plus a fugitive charge, a gun charge."

"Thanks. On patrol."

But he swung the cruiser into the parking lot of a farm supply store, backed in between two chemical-fumed pickup trucks to hide his vehicle.

The tan Ford drove past Luc's windshield. He followed. The Ford surged past the shuttered elementary school, past the old high school nobody used even though it had officially been cleared of asbestos. Turned left.

Luc gunned the cruiser through that left turn, saw the Ford gliding past the Methodist church. Hit siren & lights, stopped the Ford by the O'Hare Manor motel apartments.

He called in the stop. *You never know.*

Walked to the driver's window, right hand by his side, eyes on the two shapes in the front seat. Cal wisely held the Ford's steering wheel as Luc reached the lowered glass. Blue lens sunglasses hid Cal's eyes.

"Morning officer." Strong voice. No scent of alcohol. "What's up?"

Luc glanced at the woman cupped by the passenger's seat.

Her hands were empty on her blue jeaned lap, lean thighs, mirror black leather jacket. Dark hair cascaded to her shoulders. High cheekbones and eyes like slate. Her lips stayed as straight as the horizon and were painted the color of blood.

"Everybody OK?" asked Luc.

Cal said: "You tell me."

"Sir, you were speeding through a school zone."

"Those are boarded-up schools."

"Their zone law is still on the books. License and registration, please."

Cal fetched nothing from the Ford's glove compartment except the registration slip he handed Luc with a Nevada driver's license. Luc walked back to the cruiser, radioed Jenny who wondered why the hell he was doing that again. Blue lenses rode the Ford's rear view mirror the whole time.

"Any problems, officer?" said Cal when, just like a regular cop, Luc returned to the open window and gave him back his documents.

"No sir." Luc bet that Cal knew a routine traffic stop would not have picked up his ex-con status. "But I need to write you a ticket."

"Everybody needs something."

Luc filled out the citation, his eyes as full of Cal as they could be.

The woman haunted the edge of his vision.

"What are you doing in Shelby – *sir*?"

Cal reflected the lawman's image in his blue lenses. "Just chillin'."

Luc passed the pink ticket to Cal: "Have a nice day."

"They say it's a free country, Officer. I'll have it like I want."

Luc got in the cruiser. The Ford stayed parked as he drove away.

Why bring a woman like that all the way out here to fight with her?

Luc went back to the office. Couldn't stay inside. He let Jake come in to catch up on paperwork and post as React with Earl, sent Andy home for a nap before his midnight border patrol, took Cruiser 3 out looking for –

Black hair woman driver blue Honda.

Without thought, with *zero* probable cause, Luc flipped on his siren & lights and pulled the Honda over on a street where houses held wrinkled souls waiting for whoever came first, the ambulance or the undertaker.

She was alone in the car. Told the cop standing outside her open window: "Must be a smaller town than I remember."

"It's the size we got." Luc smelled soft powder on her cheeks, musty perfume. Music came from the Honda's sound system: upbeat Appalachian violins & Motown drums, rock guitars and a *been-there* man singing: "… *bitter melodies, turning your orbit around.*"

Luc said: "I didn't figure you for a Wilco fan."

Those slate eyes blinked. "And how did you figure me?"

"Maybe pop stars off some TV game show. Maybe gangsta rap."

"Gangsta rap?" She turned off the CD. "Why did you stop me?"

He stood there.

"Gotta have a reason," she said.

"There was a stop sign you rolled through."

"There's always a stop sign."

"License and registration, please."

Her short nailed hands pulled a wallet from her purse, fished out a California driver's license and found a rental car agreement in the glove compartment, passed them to him. He asked her to wait. *Please.*

The routine run from Jenny came back with no wants or warrants, valid license and confirmed name: Valerie Nazar.

He returned her documents. "I'm only giving you a warning ticket, Mrs. Nazar, so please remember to be careful. Lot of kids in our town."

"Gotta take care of the kids," she said while he *slowly* wrote.

"I'm surprised you and your husband drove here in two cars."

"Cal's my brother."

The wind blew the pink ticket in his hand.

"You in town for a family reunion?" he said.

"Sure. Why not."

She stared at him. He stared at her.

"Can I have my ticket?" she said and he gave it to her.

She started her engine. "Your turn to have a nice day."

He walked to the cruiser. Heard her drive away. Refused to look back.

Sat in his vehicle. Jenny radioed about trashcans blowing down a street. *Make this time.* He used his personal cell phone to make the call.

"ICE, Agent Burrows," said the woman who answered in her office at the border, then read her caller I.D. "What do you want, Luc?"

"Can't a friend call a friend?"

"We stopped being like that a year ago."

Luc pictured her naked on her elbows and knees; pictured their relief after *the talk* freed them from two years of only lust; pictured their smiles when she told him she'd be marrying a local banker.

"Inez, can you work a fast background outside of ICE logs?"

"An FBI agent in New York went down hard for that kind of shit."

"This is only to help me. Fellow cop. Any other way, I lose control."

"And then the universe will explode. Yeah, I'll do it – *one time.*"

Luc told her data about Valerie Nazar.

"Okay, Luc, I never got this call or made the one you'll get."

Luc drove back to the green fort. Signed on to his Department's internal website, clicked to WAP – the Watch & Alert Page. Earl had posted names and address of three more ailing senior citizens to the "drop by & check" list. Jake reported the corpse of a burnt-alive cat in an alley – the third torched cat in five months. Luc and his fellow badges knew the horror odds of that, knew all they could do was hunt and hope. In the "Observe & Report" window, Luc typed "Calvin Nazar" plus the Ford's data, Wade.

Entered nothing about a blue Honda. Nothing about any *Valerie*.

He found Earl in his glass office, phoning voters.

Before Luc could speak, Earl said: "The *Promoter* wants a photo of you getting the new badge. You'll do it, because I'm in the picture, too."

"Whatever. Right now, I want to roust Wade Dunn."

Earl frowned. "Is he going to kill anybody tonight?"

"How the hell should I know?"

"Then *whatever* will wait until tomorrow. Go home. Better yet, go celebrate. Find some woman to get real with. My Bev's got some names. And remember, you 'n' Jake and his clan are coming to Sunday dinner."

"I just –"

"Yeah, you *just*. Take that damn limit off your life. Now go home."

Luc was driving over railroad tracks when his cell phone buzzed.

"I saw her photo, Luc," said Inez in the phone he pressed to his ear.

He felt naked in front of a million merciless eyes.

"It's not what you're thinking," he said.

"Who's thinking? Thinking puts me into too many conflicts. You asked, I did: Valerie Nazar, 33, five-nine, 137 lbs. on her license. Gypsy for a while, then leveraged her way into owning a shack with a lawn way outside of San Fran. Listed occupation as pharmaceutical rep, one of those hot babes with roller suitcases full of samples and flirts for doctors, plus get this: part time librarian. Wonder who she conned there."

"She's a grifter?"

"You tell me. She's on prison visitor logs for Calvin Nazar, a brother. She'd posted her smidgen of home equity for his bail. When he skipped, she lost that place. Rents *not much* now. A passport she's never used shows birthplace as your turf. And that's all you get from me like this."

Luc closed his phone with a snap.

Driving up the long hill home, he spotted Mrs. Kavendish picking wind-blown litter off her wintered lawn in the reddening evening light, pulled over and parked, climbed out with the tug of an unexpected smile.

"How are you?" he asked the old lady wearing a windbreaker.

"I'm fine." She frowned at the cop. "What do you want?"

"Can anybody ever pull anything over on you?"

Joking! Like she was one of his squad back in A-stan!

"They can try," she said.

"Can I ask you about what happened before I moved here?"

"Well, there used to be some dinosaurs …" She shrugged. "Ask."

"Did you ever know a Nazar family?"

"A small man who married a big woman, made her feel grateful for it, then made her pay, a real mean s.o.b."

"What about kids?"

She nodded her gray head. "I worked in the library then. Big sister would bring in her snotty little brother. Try to keep him out of trouble. Mom was too busy trying to keep from getting ground down to dust."

Her face softened. "What are you doing, Deputy?"

He shrugged. "Getting by."

She gave him a *me-too* nod. "Ain't that the truth?"

Luc parked at his rented house. Entered, saw the bedroom and bathroom doors still open to *empty*, living room furniture abandoned by some previous refugee. A bookcase crammed with paperbacks held three photos – his younger ghost with five other uniformed men in a dusty landscape of low rocky hills, his sister and her two kids in Ohio, Sheriff Earl presenting him with a deputy's badge.

I could be all gone in an hour.

He set his holstered Glock on the bed table. The refrigerator fed him leftovers as he jumped stations on satellite radio. *So what.* Music is intel. He washed dishes. Showered. Put on black jeans, a clean blue shirt. *No reason to go out.* Darkness pressed against his windows. *Celebrate.* He clipped the Glock onto his belt, stuck the badge in his pocket, grabbed his black leather jacket. *I own this fucking night.*

Earl had said *the music in the Tap Room.* Jukebox guitars escaped through that bar's back door as Luc stepped inside its aroma of beer, the glow of cyber-souled poker machines. Twinkling booze bottles guarded the bar mirror. At the rear of the bar, owner Gary laughed from his bones with a married couple he'd known since local high school in the 1960's.

Gary's shock flashed to a grin as Luc walked in: "Whoa! Now here's a good man. He's even got handcuffs!"

The married couple chuckled as the jukebox played Roy Orbison.

Only one other customer. Sitting alone at the bar near the front door's escape. Long dark hair. Black jacket. Vampire lips.

She caught his reflection in the mirror. Muttered: "Give me a break."

A phantom wind stood him next to her barstool.

"So much for thinking I was just paranoid." She sipped from her glass of ice and liquid amber.

"I didn't know you were here. I'm not on duty."

"Really. Then why did you walk in here tonight?"

"Like your brother said, it's a free country."

"Yeah, you'll do swell listening to him."

Gary came over: "You black leather jackets look like the midnight twins. Luc, first time drinking here, you're having the good Scotch."

He put two full glasses on the bar. "Yours is on the house, Val."

Then he grinned, walked back to the married couple.

Still standing beside her, Luc said: "You know Gary?"

"I used to babysit his daughter."

"Oh."

"'*Oh*'? Suddenly you've got nothing to say?"

"Not if you don't want to listen."

"What the hell, the devil I know. You're the first guy who's come in here who Gary didn't shoo away before I had to do it myself."

Luc claimed the stool beside her. At the end of the bar, Gary smiled as he lifted a dollar off his friends' stack of bills.

"My name is …"

"I know who you are," she said. "I read your tickets. I'm not talking about what I don't want to talk about."

Luc and Val watched each other in the bar mirror.

He said: "I don't want to talk about anything not worth talking about."

The mirror's slate eyes blinked. "Who do you owe?"

"Besides a bunch of guys who did their job so I didn't die?"

"You were a Marine, right?" Her reflection shrugged. "You've got that serious but off the hook, *always faithful* kind of vibe."

"Afghanistan. Brown hills, rocks, tough people, extreme weather, remote. 'Place where law means no more than the man making it work."

"Sounds like here. And you're the man."

He sipped a burn of smoky Scotch. "I'm figuring that out.

"Earl Cockrell," added Luc. "The sheriff. He's who I owe."

"Because he gave you your powerful and glamorous job?"

"Because one day on the highway, I walked up to a wrecked tanker, didn't smell the spilled gas until the blast left me sprawled in a ring of fire. Earl ran through the flames, saved me, so … There it is."

"That's a good story." She sipped her Scotch.

"Who do you owe?" he asked the lipsticked face trapped in the glass.

"That's a good question." Her black hair smelled of warm. Clean. "What would you give for one clear moment?"

"What would I get?"

She grinned from somewhere deep inside her, saw a smile lift his lips.

But her grin crumbled. "Maybe you'd see the whole truth of who you have to be."

She caught his eyes in the mirror looking at the bar's front door.

"He's not coming here," she said. "He knows I was gonna stop in."

"What's he doing?"

"My brother's one of those things we're not going to talk about."

"What are you doing here? In town?"

She shrugged. "Reading gravestones."

Luc dropped his gaze from the mirror. Let his forefinger touch the drink glass smeared by her lipstick.

"Evidence, right?" she said. "My uniform. Proof I was here."

He stared at her until she turned from the mirror.

"You can be anywhere you want," he told her face to face.

"You've been listening to the wrong songs."

"Maybe. But I'm still right about you."

Her eyes softened for a heartbeat. The jukebox played Springsteen.

"Damn," she said.

"Luc," she said.

Then from her came: "One of us has to walk out that door."

He stared until her eyes shimmered like water but she never moved.

Standing tore bones from his chest. He dropped crumpled money from his black jeans on the bar. As he walked toward the back door, he saw Gary pass *lost bet* bills to the married couple.

Luc drove dark streets to his empty bed.

Got up the next morning and moved through time propelled by the prow of some giant throbbing warship pressing against his spine.

Walked into his coffee and cinnamon buns scented cop shop home.

Andy glanced up from keyboarding his border shift report: "Whoa! You look like you're the one who worked a night tour."

Sheriff Earl walked out of his glass box, coffee mug in his paw.

"Luc," said Earl, "Andy says the Homeland folks could use you up at the border today to work with them for their sensors turn-on."

"The Feds don't need me. I'm going to roust Wade Dunn."

Earl frowned. "Why?"

"Because I'm a peace officer and he's disturbing mine."

Andy said: "Wade's no genius, but he's mean as a badger and more'n a little nuts. If he's been cooking meth, he could go off some kind of bad."

Earl said: "You want to go that way, Luc, you ain't going alone."

"Hell," said Andy, swinging his uniform jacket off the back of his chair, "I'm on for the double anyway. Dibs on being *good cop*."

Luc said: "I don't –"

"My people play it safe, make it home," said Earl. "Take him."

Luc logged on to WAP, saw that Deputy Brenda had observed the Ford parked outside Cabin 4 at the dumpy Big Sky Motel during her night patrol. Cruiser 2 was still checked out to Andy, so he drove, Luc rode shotgun. They reached the railroad crossing as warning bells dinged and white crossbars lowered. A yellow school bus stopped beyond the white crossbars on the other side of the tracks.

"What do you figure on getting from Wade?" asked Andy.

"Whatever wrong he's doing with Cal Nazar."

A clattering past freight train shook the cruiser and its deputies.

"Cal's outta state bad ass, Wade's local. They're solo shitheads."

"So what."

The freight train's caboose rolled past and the white cross bars rose.

Wade lived beyond the east edge of town, out past the railroad roundhouse at the end of an empty gravel road in a double-wide trailer.

"That's his pickup," said Luc as the trailer loomed in their windshield.

That low metal castle reverberated with barking dogs.

Officers of the law parked, got out of their cruiser.

Luc yelled: "Sheriff's deputies, Wade! Chain your dogs! Open up!"

The dogs raged.

Luc banged on the trailer door. Dogs inside slammed that metal so hard they punched out a dent. Luc tried the doorknob – *locked.*

"Sounds like two of 'em, big and nasty," said Andy. "He's gone."

"Post up here," said Luc. "Don't let anybody rabbit out that door."

Gravel crunched under Luc's shoes as he walked around the trailer. Junked cars rusted behind the trailer; all its windows had closed slat shades.

"What are you doing back there?" yelled Andy.

A battered pickup on cinderblocks still clung to its rectangular side mirrors. Took Luc three slams with his black leather jacket elbow to knock a mirror free – the glass cracked, showed Luc his cut in half reflection.

Luc wiggled the mirror below a window's angled-down slats. Caught reflections from inside the trailer: Fake wood paneled walls. A chair –

"Fuck!"

"What! Luc, what's –"

But by then Luc had run back around the trailer, ran past where Andy stood guarding the door. Luc yelled: "Draw your weapon!"

"What's going on?" But his Glock filled Andy's hand.

Luc popped open the cruiser's trunk.

Andy twisted this way and that, herky-jerky in front of the trailer, clutching his pistol in the two handed combat grip: "Who do I shoot?"

A crowbar from the cruiser filled Luc's hand: "Lean against the door! Hold it shut! Watch your gun barrel!"

Andy pushed his shoulder against the trailer door as Luc drove the crowbar's blade into the door crack. Dogs slammed into that metal slab. The locked tore free. A dog slam rocked Andy but he kept the door closed.

Luc added his shoulder to the door, drew his Glock: "Watch your weapon! Know your target! Jump back on three! One! ... Two! ..."

Three!

They flew back, eyes and guns on the trailer as its door burst open.

A German shepherd charged them.

Luc then Andy fired, three blasts each.

The shepherd spun tail over muzzle *whump,* sprawled at their feet.

The trailer doorway filled with a snarling Rottweiler.

Luc fired once, Andy blasted two.

The Rottweiler fell dead.

Inside the trailer:

Male sprawled in chair – *Gun on floor! Gun on floor!* Male – *Wade,* head hanging backwards over the chair, gaping mouth. Red mush neck. Hands dangling above splotches on the green carpet. Chewed fingers.

"Holy shit!" whispered Andy as he stalked into the trailer with Luc.

That metal box reeked of dog shit. Gunsmoke. Sour meat. Stale beer bottles by two padlocked metal boxes of dog food. No one hid in the dank bathroom or the bedroom where a plasma TV reflected a rumpled bed. Clothes and naked women magazines lay everywhere.

Back in the living room, Andy and Luc holstered their guns.

Andy said: "I never shot a dog before."

The crime scene crackled in Luc's eyes.

"Locked door." Andy nodded toward the carpet. "That revolver's a .357 Magnum, drop a grizzly. Wade damn near blew his head off."

Luc whispered: "Why would he kill himself?"

"He's Wade! Maybe this criminal mastermind lifestyle just wasn't working for him. Maybe you spooked him.

"Hell," continued Andy, "could have been weeks before anybody sent us out here to check. The dogs would have tore him down to scattered bones. As it is, we're lucky they left us enough evidence to close the book."

"The wound," said Luc. "The bullet tore out his spine at shoulder level. He had to stick a six inch barrel of a heavy gun in his mouth, angle it down to make that shot. That's not how you blow out your brains."

"So if there's no gunshot residue on his hand –"

"GSR is easy. Sit him by the window. Ram the gun in his mouth. Nobody believes they're gonna die, he'd buy that as someone making a point but BOOM! Open the window, wrap his hand around the .357, BOOM! Nothing out there for the slug to hit. Fix the gun. Close up the trailer. Count on the dogs, on us calling it suicide. We got no crime scene team. This happened last night. Drive away lights off, nobody knows."

Luc drew his weapon, switched the four rounds gone ammo mag' with a full mag' from his belt pouch, re-holstered the Glock.

"Preserve the crime scene. Give me the cruiser's keys."

"What are you doing?"

"Chasing a killer."

"What 'killer'? No probable cause, no evidence. Get some, then –"

"*Then* will be too late. Give me the keys."

"No."

"Andy, I'm going."

"Not alone," said Andy. "That's not how Earl's team rolls."

"This isn't just about the job."

Andy switched his rounds-gone mag' for a full stack, smacked it home in the butt of his gun. Said: "OK."

Their cruiser swirled a dust cloud on the gravel road. Luc told Andy where to drive, no siren & lights. Radioed Jenny to scramble everyone to the trailer, claimed to be in 'hot pursuit' of a suspect. Ran down Cal Nazar's rap sheet for Andy.

"If he's there, will he be alone?"

"Don't know." Luc's heart thundered in his chest. "Hope so."

The Big Sky Motel meant peeling white paint cabins jumbled together two blocks off the highway in a neighborhood of old trees and sagging houses. Tourists seldom found the motel. Wind farm workers leased some cabins. A tan Ford with Nevada plates crouched outside Cabin 4.

"Drive on by," said Luc. "Don't stop close enough for him to hear."

Blue Honda! End of the cabins, parked in the alley!

Andy nudged the cruiser to the curb half a block from the Ford.

"Turn off your handset," Luc said. "Radio chatter could let them – could let *him* know we're coming."

Andy blinked. "Good idea. No radio. We stage it first."

They eased out of their cruiser. Scanned the block. All the other cabins looked empty. They saw no flutters of curtains in the neighborhood windows. Heard wind skittering over the potholed road, no barking dogs.

Luc smelled the street, the hint of spring from scraggly lawns, rotten *yuck* in a trashcan as they eased past the alley and an *empty* blue Honda.

Ten steps from Cabin 4, Andy drew his Glock, then Luc.

Angry male shouts came from inside that cabin at 5 steps: *"... so damn sick of little mother I could kill you!"*

Luc whispered: "Probable cause."

Kicked in the cabin door, leapt inside.

Cal and Val stood stunned in the tiny cabin.

Wearing blue sunglasses, Cal glowered by the bed that held a suitcase.

Val trembled on Luc's left.

Luc locked Cal in the Glock's sight: *"Don't move!"*

Behind Luc ... *The cabin door closed?*

Steel kissed his skull.

He heard Andy say: "Don't *you* move, Luc."

"Wha-*What?*" said Luc – but he kept his Glock zeroed on Cal.

Who yelled: "Get him off me!"

Andy pressed his gun against Luc's head.

Visions flashed in Luc, a kaleidoscope of ideas and answers. Nausea. Lightning shocked his skin. The world spun – froze.

Luc said: "Andy, you squeeze your trigger, your partner dies."

"Your Glock's double trigger safety –"

"Won't stop me," said Luc. "Nothing will."

Cal said: "Maybe, maybe not. Let me show you something."

His right hand floated down to the open suitcase on the bed ...

... magically filled with a black revolver.

That pointed at Val.

Who said: "Cal! What are you doing?"

"You think you're so right, so smart, don't know *what's what* but you chase me, gonna butt in and stop it, *save me*, well, you get your wish.

"Cop," said Cal, "give up your gun or watch her die."

"She's your sister!"

"Not my choice, not over my $200,000 packed-to-go future. And just like you told Andy, if you shoot me, I'll still squeeze a bullet into her."

Andy pushed his gun barrel against Luc's skull.

Luc said: "The border."

"All you had to do was go work there today like I set up!"

"Before the sensors went on, you and Cal and dead Wade –"

Cal frowned: "Wade's dead?"

"He freaked out last night!" said Andy. "I staged a suicide, woulda managed that, but Luc here …"

"A three-way," said Luc. "Cal has the heroin connections, meth man Wade knew ambitious dealers across the border, and Andy, you back-roaded them and the dope across the line last night."

"Went to Vegas for fun, ran into a friend, parlayed my future."

Luc said: "It'll kill Earl, one of *us*, one of *his* going crooked."

Andy said: "*Yeah!* 'Wrong story comes out, Earl goes down. But you can fix this with us. Or join the dead."

"Get her out of here," said Luc.

"Not a chance," said Andy. "She dealt herself in."

The revolver locked on Val didn't tremble.

Tears rolled down her pale face.

"Now is when, cop," said her brother. "One…Two…"

"OK!" yelled Luc. "But I'm not dropping my weapon."

Cal said: "You're in no position to deal."

"From where I stand," said Luc, "we've got the same hand."

"Listen to him," said Andy. "He's saving her, figuring a way to protect Earl, staying alive."

"Deal is, I give my gun to her."

Andy said: "Why?"

"Gives her a chance," said Luc.

"What the hell," said Cal. "Keep it in the family."

"I'm not so sure," said Andy.

"Sis is loyal, no matter what – plus this lets her off the hook."

Luc flicked his eyes to hers, flicked them back to his aim locked on her brother. "You can do this."

He coaxed her toward him, slowly, *oh so slowly*, one step at a time.

"You're getting outta here with your life and dollars, Luc," said Andy.

As instructed, Val cupped her hand around Luc's double-fist grip of the Glock, wrapping her own right hand grip around the weapon, replacing his finger for hers, carefully not putting pressure on the double-trigger.

Her skin felt like lava coming in, going away felt like fading sunlight. The Glock Val held drifted between the three men as she backed up.

"Way to go, Sis! I'm so proud of you! He totally bought our bluff!"

"Our bluff," she whispered. The gun shook in her outstretched hand.

"Let her go now," Luc told the room. "She doesn't need to be here for the rest of this."

Her brother said: "I never figured you for a softie."

"Cal," said Andy, "you pack up your sis, get ready to get gone."

"OK," said Cal drifting the bore of his revolver off Luc…

BOOM-BOOM!

Orange flashes of gunfire burned Luc's eyes.

Andy crashed to the cabin's worn gray carpet. A dark stain flowered on his uniform chest. Crimson flowed over his badge.

"Don't you fucking move, cop!" Cal's smoking revolver zeroed Luc.

"No no no no!" Val trembled, the gun in her hand swinging wildly.

"Sis 'had to do it I had to!" Cal aimed *dead center* at Luc's chest. "Andy killed Wade! Probably ripped Wade's cut. And when that set-up went to shit, when this cop rolled here, Andy was staging you and me as shot while resisting arrest, blaming us for killing this cop here, too."

"No," said Val. The Glock weighed her hand. "No."

"We're in this together," said Cal. "Not my idea. You put yourself here. That's your fault, that's on you. So you gotta make it right. We gotta be totally together so I can trust you.

"You gotta shoot the cop," he said. "That's our only choice."

Val trembled, the gun drifting in front of her.

"This is the blood we've got to share," said her brother.

Luc told her: "Do it.

"Makes sense," he told her. "It'll buy you more time. And you –"

Luc charged Cal, heard the revolver BOOM!

White hot flash tore through his left side. BOOM! fire ripped a line on his cheek "NO!" screamed Val & *I'm falling* scramble on the floor, Cal backtracking toward the bed aiming the revolver –

Three shots cracked over Luc.

Cal flopped dead onto the bed. The suitcase fell over and dumped bundles of money onto the pale sheets.

Luc sprawled on the carpet.

Saw dead Andy crumpled on the motel floor.

Val dropped Luc's smoking gun.

Stepped toward where he struggled to sit, blood flowing from his chest and back, wetting his cheek, his ears ringing, she reached toward him –

Perfect clarity.

"Don't touch me!" yelled Luc. "*Oh Jesus it hurts* don't touch me! Don't get blood on you!"

She crumpled to her knees.

"Listen to me! You were never here! You're not here! What happened … You don't know. 'Came to town, tried to keep your brother from some scheme, 'didn't know what, you stayed – where, *where?*"

Words fell out of her with no thought: "The O'Hare Manor."

"Listen." Luc fought growing weakness. "Listen.

"You saved my life. You saved your life. He would have killed us both. Even if he didn't shoot you, the law would've hunted you down. Now you'll still be smeared with this blood, 'n' that's wrong, not you, you."

Val's hand fluttered – stopped before it touched him.

"You just held the gun," said Luc. "He pulled his own trigger."

Couldn't stop himself, laughed: "Me, I'm just a peace officer.

"The bathroom window," he told her. "Crawl out, close it. Drive away, alleys, invisible – cemetery! You got people up there?"

She nodded.

"Here." He dropped his black spring bladed knife in her hand. "Cemetery, nobody should be there, nobody see, stab your tire, flat. You been there all morning. Walk out for help, let them find you, tell you. You weren't here, aren't here, go! Run!"

Still she knelt staring at him.

"If you don't get free," he said, waving his bloody hand at the corpses, "then this is them winning. You deserve more."

Her slate eyes ran rivers.

"Go, so I can use the radio." He smiled. "*Semper fi.*"

And she vanished.

Luc crawled to his gun. Radioed lies as sirens screamed closer and the blood scented cabin swirled him to blackness.

They kept him in the hospital for five days, though the *through & through* bullet only nicked his lung. The doctors promised the flesh and bone tunnel it tore would heal enough for "occupational functionality." They hedged on how long he'd feel pain from the parts of him that had been blown away. Offered to "minimize" the scar on his cheek.

He shook his head.

On his third day in the hospital, Earl and Brenda wheelchaired him to the cemetery where more than 400 cops came to Andy's funeral: Civvies clad FBI and ICE agents like Inez wore black arm bands. Uniformed police wore black tape across their badges. Cops came from all of Montana's 56 counties. State troopers from Oregon and New Jersey. The New York City police color guard. A Baltimore crime scene tech and a historian from D.C. who made sure Andy's named got carved in the marble of America's National Law Enforcement Officers Memorial. Montana Highway Patrolmen fired a 21-gun salute over the flag-draped coffin. The honor guard folded the flag and presented its red, white, & blue triangle to the martyred cop's heroic partner.

Earl ran the investigation that no one wanted to escape from the drama Luc broadcast into the radio before he passed out and then confirmed from his hospital bed: Wade Dunn hooked up with his childhood friend Cal Nazar in some drug deal that ended in Cal double-crossing the local thug, killing him with a faked suicide that Andy and Luc spotted then *hot pursuit* followed utilizing Luc and Brenda's logged reports, showed up as Cal was fleeing his motel with a suitcase full of presumably dirty money. Bullets flew. One cop died, his partner killed the bad guy, righteous blood, close the book.

"The sister's a curious one," Earl told Luc the morning he came to the hospital for Luc's discharge, the two of them sitting alone in Luc's flower filled room with its railed bed and ceiling-hung TV and chrome bright glare.

"Really," said Luc.

Earl wore his usual brown suit, white shirt, bolo tie and cowboy boots, but now they hung on the bear rather than fighting to keep him wrapped.

"No record of her being anything other than a sap for trying to save her brother from himself," said Luc. "Cal was running from her, too."

"Yeah. She was surprised when I told her what Cal told you."

"*Yelled* at us," corrected Luc. "He steps out of the motel. Sees us, yells: 'How'd my fucking sister rat me out?' Jumps back inside, then...."

From down the hall came a heart monitor's steady *beep beep beep*.

Luc said: "She say anything different?"

Earl glanced at the wall clock where the circling black second hand swept away one moment after another. "Most everything about her is *different*. How do you figure her?"

"I don't. Wrote her a ticket, talked to her in a bar. That's all I got."

"She kept asking how you were, where you came from, what were you saying. She's carrying a lot of guilt that you had to shoot her brother."

"Where is she?"

"Gone since yesterday. There's a fight over whether the state or the county gets the $200,000 from the crime scene, but she'll never see a cent of it. Boxing her brother came out of our budget. She said he'd hurt people here, so burying him in our cemetery was wrong. I borrowed the hearse from old man Burns, drove the coffin behind her to Great Falls, the crematorium out by the airport. She just put him on the conveyer belt, fed him to the flames. Mailed the urn to Cal's *last known* where the FBI says nobody lives. I figure there's a trashcan gonna swallow them ashes."

"What did she do after the burning?"

"Thanked me. Drove off."

"So?"

"So there's something I can't read in her. Still, I've been talking down at the Chat & Chew, the Senior Center. Now folks count her as a victim, too, so nobody's thinking they've got a score to settle with her – or that the Sheriff's department screwed up and went soft on a killer's kin."

The sheriff nodded. "Your town's gotta believe the right story."

beep beep beep

Earl said: "What happened, that's the job. I can take this."

"I know," said Luc.

A nurse bustled into the room, gave Luc discharge forms to sign, helped him into a black hooded sweatshirt gift from the Texas Rangers.

Earl walked him outside where the wind was warm and dry. "There's your Jeep, but you sure you want to drive home?"

"Yeah, it'll feel good to steer myself. But I'm not going home."

Earl frowned.

"It's personal," said Luc. "I need to say good-bye to Andy. Spend some alone time doing that. In his house. Anybody been there?"

"We had to get his spare uniform shirt for the burying, but other than that, no. It's unlocked – just like yours." Earl shrugged. "You needed clothes, your toothbrush, plus folks wanted to fill up your frig and freezer. You won't be cooking for weeks. Mrs. Kavendish honchoed that."

"Really," said Luc. "I'll be damned."

"Everybody is."

The sheriff gave Luc the keys to the Jeep and walked to the cruiser to show Luc he respected him being a man who could go it alone.

The triangle folded American flag waited on Luc's passenger seat. He knew Earl had put it there because for Luc it would surely be a treasure.

Andy had inherited his parents' house on north side of town. Flower arrangements lay scattered on Andy's front porch.

Took Luc 23 minutes to find the cash stuffed in a gym bag in Andy's bedroom closet. Luc dumped rubber-banded wads of money onto Andy's bed, counted fifty and hundred dollar bills to just shy of $400,000 – Wade's cut, too, shares equal to Cal's $200,000.

He saw himself mailing it to Val.

Saw the look on Earl's face if he brought it to the green fort.

Saw movie places like Paris or New York or even some town where there were beautiful trees, maybe a real ocean and the wind didn't blow all the time. No bitter snow or angry sun and his sister's kids could visit from college their family could afford and maybe he could get a dog.

Saw his own scarred face in Andy's bedroom mirror.

Luc climbed on and off a metal folding chair to pull the batteries from the house's smoke detectors, left the plastic detectors dangling open like slack jawed clowns. He built a pyramid of cash in Andy's bathtub. Found a disposable lighter in a kitchen drawer.

The pyre burned orange and blue shimmers. Singed scraps of wealth swirled out of the tub and he had to swat them back to the flames. He used Andy's winter gloves to scoop the black ashes into the toilet for multiple flushes. Washed the tub until it was clean enough for a bachelor's home. Put everything back, including the smoke detector batteries and chair. Only then spotted the gray smoke stain on the ceiling above the tub, a ghostly wonderment for whatever law closed out Andy's life.

What the hell, we all leave behind a mystery.

He dumped bouquets from the front lawn on the kitchen counter so the dead flowers stench smothered the legacy of fire. Stole what he needed.

His Jeep kicked up a dust trail on a gravel road north from town. Ten minutes of bumpy driving put him on a vast checkerboard of brown and yellow farmlands near the border. He saw a loping coyote. Parked. Luc stood on his Jeep and used a rope stolen from Andy's house to lash the American flag high up on a random telephone pole. No one else saw the wind flap that red, white & blue cloth.

This is where I am.

He drove home. Took the viaduct over the railroad tracks to avoid the green fort. Saw Mrs. Kavendish's house. Didn't look at the cemetery.

Parked in front of his house was a dented orange coupe.

She stood on his front concrete stoop, her black leather jacket zipped to her chin, her dark hair whipping this way and that. No lipstick.

He climbed out of his Jeep.

Glanced at the dented orange rattletrap.

"Buying it was cheaper than renting," she said. "Or a plane ticket."

"I figured you'd go someplace else," said Luc.

"I've been there," she said. "Maybe I can try it here."

"Somebody called this the middle of fucking nowhere." Luc shrugged. "Could be a place to start."

"Start to *whatever*," she said, "nothing's easy, but maybe here I can be some kind of true."

Took Luc his whole life to answer.

"If that's all you want," he said, "leave now."

The wind whipped her hair as she stood on the slab of concrete outside his front door. She clawed loose strands off her face. Thrust her hands in the side pockets of her black leather jacket and walked across the scruffy lawn. Came to one step away from him or the road.

Pulled her closed right fist from her black leather jacket pocket.

"I had to give you back this," she said as not needing directions, he let her fill his left palm with his closed black knife.

"And I had to take this," she said, and her heart side hand came out of her jacket pocket filled with nothing until she closed it around his gun hand to lead him into the house.

ROLL CALL

MICHAEL BERISH has worked as a patrol officer, detective, and as a supervisor with the City of Miami Police Department for twenty-two years; thirteen of which were spent as an undercover detective in the *REAL* Miami Vice. He has worked everything from Narcotics & Vice, Gambling, Prostitution and Pornography, to the Dignitary Protection of President Jose Napoleon Duarte (of El Salvador) and Pope John Paul II. He is the author of *Reflections from the Pit* which was named as the Best Fiction Novel published in 2007 in the 2008 Public Safety Writers Association's annual writing competition.

MICHAEL A. BLACK has been a police officer in the south suburbs of Chicago for the past thirty-one years. He is also the author of over forty short stories and fourteen books, twelve of which are novels. His most recent books are *Hostile Takeovers*, second in a police procedural series, and *I Am Not a Psychic* with television star Richard Belzer. Please visit his website at www.MichaelABlack.com.

AUSTIN S. CAMACHO is the author of five detective novels in the Hannibal Jones series – *Blood and Bone, Collateral Damage, The Troubleshooter, Damaged Goods and Russian Roulette*, plus two thrillers, *The Payback Assignment* and *The Orion Assignment*. Camacho is active in several writers' organizations and teaches writing at Anne Arundel Community College. After a career as a military reporter on the American Forces Network, Camacho is now a public affairs specialist for the Defense Department. Camacho lives in Springfield, Virginia with his lovely wife Denise and Princess the Wonder Cat.

JAMES CHAMBERS is the author of numerous tales of crime, horror, dark fantasy, and science fiction, which have been published in more than 20 anthologies and magazines, including *Bare Bone*, the award-winning *Bad-Ass Faeries 2: Just Plain Bad, Breach the Hull, Cthulhu Sex, The Dead Walk, The Domino Lady: Sex as a Weapon, Hardboiled Cthulhu, Allen K's Inhuman, Sick: An Anthology of Illness*, and the collection *The Midnight Hour: Saint Lawn Hill and Other Tales*. Dark Regions Press has published a collection of his short stories, *Resurrection House*. He lives in New York and can be found online at www.jameschambersonline.com.

VER CURTIS is a Loudoun County, Virginia resident and professional comic artist, currently working for Moonstone Comics on their "Domino

Lady" prestige edition and the upcoming "Air Fighters" comic series. He is a completely self-taught artist, having never had a formal art class. His first published work was at the age of 13 and he hasn't stopped since, with his original art appearing in literally hundreds of books and magazines in both the US and United Kingdom. He also serves as Art Director for the pulp-genre publisher, Wild Cat Books. Ver and his lovely wife Linda have lived Virginia for nearly 15 years. When he's not busy painting, drawing, airbrushing, photographing, or sculpting, he's running his own computer company, Tech Support. View his work at www.art-nocturne.com and www.myspace.com/artnocturnestudios.

O'NEIL DE NOUX has published five novels, six short story collections and over 200 short stories in multiple genres: mystery, fantasy, horror, western, science fiction, historical fiction, literary, children's fiction, mainstream fiction, religious, humor, romance and erotica. His stories have appeared in the U.S., the U.K., Canada, Denmark, France, Germany, Greece, Italy, Japan, Portugal, Sweden and Ukraine. De Noux has won two recent writing awards – the 2009 Derringer Award for Best Novelette ("Too Wise," *Ellery Queen Mystery Magazine*, November 2008) and the 2007 Shamus Award for Best Short Story ("The Heart Has Reasons," *Alfred Hitchcock Mystery Magazine*, September 2006).

WAYNE DUNDEE is the author of the Joe Hannibal private eye series --six novels, seventeen short stories to date. He is the founder and original editor of Hardboiled Magazine. His work has been translated into several languages and has been nominated for an Edgar, an Anthony, and several Shamus awards. He lives in west central Nebraska where he is currently working on more Hannibal adventures as well as Westerns and other stories. You can check out his web site at www.waynedundee.com

RON FORTIER has been writing comic books and science fiction novels for the past thirty years. He was the initial writer for Now Comics Green Hornet series and currently runs Airship 27 Productions with artist partner Rob Davis, producing new pulp fiction novels and anthologies starring 1930s pulp heroes. You can visit him atwww.airship27.com.

JOHN L. FRENCH is a crime scene supervisor with the Baltimore Police Department Crime Laboratory. In 1992 he began writing crime fiction, basing his stories on his experiences on the streets of what some have called one of the most dangerous cities in the country. His short stories have appeared in Hardboiled, Alfred Hitchcock's Mystery Magazine and in numerous anthologies. His books include *The Devil of Harbor City*, *Souls on Fire* and *Past Sins*.

JAMES GRADY was born and raised in Shelby, Montana, the setting for his story. He broke into publishing at 24 with *Six Days of the Condor*, his first novel that became the title-shortened 1975 Robert Redford movie. Since then, Grady's been a U.S. Senate aide, a national investigative reporter, and a movie and TV series writer, while his dozen+ novels and as many short stories have won him France's career *Grand Prix du Roman Noir* (2001), Italy's Raymond Chandler Medal (2004), and an Edgar nomination from the Mystery Writers of America. He lives inside Washington, D.C.'s Beltway with his wife, ex-private eye/now cyber journalist Bonnie Goldstein. Visit his website at www.jamesgrady.net.

C. J. HENDERSON is the creator of both the Jack Hagee hardboiled PI series and the Teddy London supernatural detective series. Author of some 70 novels and books, as well as several hundred short stories and comics, along with thousands of non-fiction articles, he is one of the most prolific writers genre fiction has ever known. His latest series, supernatural thriller tales of Brooklyn Museum curate Piers Knight will premier in early 2010 from Tor/Forge. For a chance to read more of CJ's stories, comment on the one in this volume, or simply to chat, feel free to drop in at www. cjhenderson.com.

GARY LOVISI is a Mystery Writers of America Edgar Nominated author for his Sherlock Holmes pastiche, "The Adventure of the Missing Detective." He is an avid Sherlockian as well as book collector. His latest books are *Sherlock Holmes and The Crosby Murders* (Linford Press, UK, 2009), *Dames, Dolls & Delinquents*, a collector's guide to sexy pulp fiction paperbacks (Krause, 2009) and the edited crime anthology, *Deadly Dames* (Boldventure Press 2009). His hard crime novels include *Hellbent on Homicide* and *Blood in Brooklyn* (Do Not Press, UK). Lovisi is the founder of Gryphon Books, editor of *Paperback Parade* and *Hardboiled* magazines, and sponsors an annual book collector show in New York City. To find out more about him, his work, or Gryphon Books, visit his web site at www. gryphonbooks.com..

ART MONTERASTELLI is currently developing "The Man Who Kept the Secrets," the Sidney Korshak story, as an HBO mini-series. He co-wrote the screenplay for last year's RAMBO, wrote and co-produced the Paramount thriller "The Hunted," and also Executive Produced the award-winning documentary "No Subtitles Necessary." His fiction has appeared in *The Pacific Review* and *Unusual Suspects - The Vintage Anthology of Crime Stories*.

VINCENT H. O'NEIL brings a piece of his life to everything he writes. A West Point graduate, he's been a paratrooper, a bank risk manager, an advertisement copywriter, and an anti-money laundering consultant. His award-winning "Exile" murder mystery series (*Murder in Exile, Reduced Circumstances,* and *Exile Trust*) features amateur sleuth Frank Cole, a background-checker trying to make ends meet in the small town of Exile, Florida. Visit his website at www.vincenthoneil.com.

QUINTIN PETERSON is an award winning writer who became a police officer in 1981, but after eighteen years of police work returned to writing part-time. Now, with twenty-eight years of police service under his belt, he's penned two successful crime novels, *SIN* and *The Wages of SIN*, several short stories, and contributed to Akashic Books' critically acclaimed crime fiction anthology, *D.C. Noir*, edited by George Pelecanos. His assignments with the Metropolitan Police Department, DC included Media Liaison Officer and Motion Picture and Television Liaison Officer. For 23 years he has acted as script consultant and technical advisor for major motion picture and television companies. www.google.com/profiles/quintinpeterson.

PATRICK THOMAS is the author of over a hundred short stories and eighteen books including eight books in the popular fantasy humor series *Murphy's Lore, Fairy with a Gun, Dead To Rites* and the *Mystic Investigators* series. He has co-edited two anthologies including *New Blood*. Patrick writes the syndicated satirical advice column *Dear Cthulhu* which has been collected in *Dear Cthulhu: Have a Dark Day*. Ten of his books are part of the props department of the TV series CSI, two of which are on Greg's desk in the Bullpen. Drop by his website at www.patthomas.net.

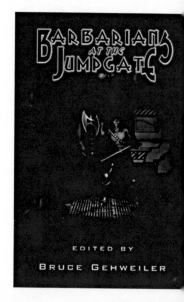

CPSIA information can be obtained at www.ICGtesting.com
Printed in the USA
BVOW040848040413

317304BV00001B/25/P